To Jeff and
Kathy ~
Enjoy the
adventure
Jill C. B

TORY ROOF

Jill C. Baker

SUDBURY
Publishing
Group

Published worldwide by Sudbury Publishing Group.

This book is a work of fiction. All characters, organizations, locations, and events portrayed in this novel are either products of the author's imagination or are used fictitiously.

Editor, Interior Design, and Production: Jonathan W. Baker
Cover Design: Jill C. Baker

ISBN 978-1-949283-00-6 (paperback)
ISBN 978-1-949283-01-3 (e-book)

Manufactured in the United States of America

10 9 8 7 6 5 4 3 2

First Edition

Acknowledgments

Many people have inspired me and encouraged me to write: parents, teachers, family, friends, colleagues, and creative collaborators. I especially thank these authors who generously shared their personal experience, insight, and resources: Daniel Blum, Connie Johnson Hambley, Jeff Miller, Satin Russell and Ric Wasley. I learned a tremendous amount from developmental editor, Karen Aroian, who reviewed an early draft of *Tory Roof.* I deeply appreciate the enthusiasm, vigilance and constructive feedback offered by my beta readers, Dagny Goldberg Baker and Gail Gamble. To my husband, Jon, I say thank you for giving me the time and space to write, for tolerating my endless musings, and for providing the professional expertise in making my content presentable. Lastly, I am sincerely indebted to Michael Gordon for his friendship, representation, guidance, and industry connections. For *Tory Roof* especially, I pay respect to the patriots and unsung heroes who paved the way.

TIMELINE

1733 — Molasses Act

1754 — French and Indian War begins

1764 — Sugar Act

1764 — Currency Act

1765 — February: Stamp Act bill passed in Parliament

1765 — March: First Quartering Act issued

1765 — July: Sons of Liberty founded in MA

1765 — August: Raid on Hutchinson House, Boston

1765 — September: Sons of Liberty founded in NYC

1765 — November: Stamp Act goes into effect

1766 — March: Stamp Act repealed; Declaratory Act issued

1766 — August: Gage's Army loots and burns Western part of Massachusetts

1766 — August: Liberty Boys rally 3,000 in New York City; Isaac Sears wounded

1770 — Boston Massacre

1773 — Tea Act, then Boston Tea Party

1775 — April: Paul Revere, William Dawes, Samuel Prescott ride (Battle of Lexington and Concord)

1775 — War of Independence begins

"Time is but the stream I go a-fishing in."

- Henry David Thoreau

1

ENCOUNTERS

She could feel the weight of his body protecting hers in the chilled autumn air, hard ground pressing under her back, her cheek raw from the rough wool of his jacket. A volley of musket fire exploded, followed by a cloud of smoke. The sound of fife and drums kept getting fainter as the mismatched band of countrymen marched further down the road. When the air finally cleared, she could smell the heady scent of Concord grapes lifting off a tangle at the edge of the field. She didn't want him to move.

With the buzz of her alarm, Sarah Sutherland realized her recurring dream ended where the town reenactment maneuvers began. She was aroused, anxious, and irritated that she'd miss the Colonial Muster, because she had to show a house.

In her four years as a real estate agent, she had never shown an antique home, let alone a property of this stature. The Covington estate was a local landmark, entrenched in American history, and preserved with considerable accuracy.

Upon the death of the last Covington, Sarah approached the executors about representing them and was delighted when her firm landed the account. Jingling her keys, she waited in her doorway, planning to drive with her prospective buyers to the location. She rehearsed her pitch as she stared out the window. "The Covington estate is one of the oldest in town…built in 1714 by a gentleman farmer, who came from England. Been in the same family for at least twelve generations," she recounted. A horn beeped, and she saw the Randolphs scuttling up her walkway.

"Sorry we're late, Sarah," Mrs. Randolph apologized, mumbling something about traffic.

"No problem," Sarah said, closing the door behind. "I'll lead, and you follow."

The Randolphs were a middle-aged couple looking to live in a vintage home. They were moving north and had heard of the Covington estate. Sarah wasn't exactly sure what they did for a living, but she knew they were affiliated with a college. She was encouraged in thinking their intellectual capacity would make them ideal buyers for a house steeped in history.

Sarah remembered the first time she saw the house…the rush of stale air that filled her lungs, the hint of smoke that lingered from long ago, and the musty odor of heavy English furniture. Wide-pine floorboards set the stage for a massive stone fireplace and beehive oven. Some of the rooms were wallpapered in delicate floral prints; others were stucco white. The style was both rustic and elegant, depending upon which corner you turned. And, there were many.

What began as a modest house sprung out like an octopus, providing space for sons and daughters, spouses and children, in-laws and parents, and in the far reaches, kitchen help, and farmhands. The property boasted a large barn, shed and smokehouse…a root cellar, stone walls, and gnarled apple orchard…all earmarks of a quaint New England past.

As Sarah turned down the winding road to Baker's Cove, she noticed that autumn was taking hold, and with it, a glorious blaze of color. Massive oaks were laden with crowns of yellow. Maples shuddered in shades of rust. Poison ivy, once deadly green, was suspended in points of vermillion as it wound like rope along a fence. Fields were harvested and baled round; she remembered growing up where bales were square.

Signaling left, she praised her shocks as she turned onto the rutted drive. A chevron of geese was forming behind the chimney of the Covington house. "That Tory roof," she thought, as she stared at the peak centered above the front door. "So distinctive. So symbolic." It immediately conjured up images of rally cries and Redcoats.

Joining the Randolphs at the side entrance, she leaned into the master key that dangled from her key ring, forcing it to fit the lock box. The door resisted. When the lock finally gave way, a mudroom with a stone floor greeted them. Pegs for drying herbs poked out from the wall beams. A spray of sage hung head-down, tied with a twist of string. A single stalk of yarrow, yellow buttons now burnt to brown, dangled from a spider web.

"Spiders can go months without eating," she thought, at the same time wondering why this random fact had popped into her head. There was something about this place that electrified her senses and opened her mind.

"What's this?" Mrs. Randolph called out. Her name was Ann, but Sarah felt more professional remaining formal. That's not to say Ann Randolph wasn't friendly, but Sarah detected something distant in her.

"Oh, that's an access door leading into a crawl space above the main room. I don't think it serves much purpose, but you can open it if you want."

Mr. Randolph, David, eyed the cleaning supplies lined up along the wall near a small writing desk. He reached for the broom and pushed the handle against the ceiling panel. Propping a stepladder under the opening, he climbed up, peered in, and craned his neck. "That's just what it is," he confirmed, letting the door slam down with a bang. A small poof of dust materialized and dispersed.

Mrs. Randolph charged ahead and went out the back door into the garden. David quickly followed his wife, making Sarah wonder if his attentiveness was due to admiration or fear of admonition. He certainly seemed to be a docile soul. He had already apologetically explained that he and his wife would sometimes be absentee buyers while they settled matters at home—home being in North Carolina, Sarah learned.

As she leaned on the kitchen counter, watching her clients weave in and out among the cold weather cabbage and dry cornhusks, she contemplated whether they might make an offer.

Sarah's thoughts drifted to a time when she and her husband, Carter, were looking for a house of their own, figuring out finances, and planning a family. She let out an audible sigh. "We were so happy when he first landed that teaching job at the local high school," she reminisced, recalling, outloud, how her husband had anticipated spending endless hours in a well-equipped science lab. Of course, the advent of two children quickly changed that.

Sarah's nostalgic smile began to uncurl when she was interrupted by a feeling that started at the base of her spine, crawled up her back and rippled across her shoulders—a distinct sensation that someone was standing behind her. She turned around, but no one was there. She dismissed it as a draft and continued waiting for the Randolphs.

When the Randolphs returned, Sarah led them up the narrow stairway to the second floor sleeping chambers, comfortably warm and smelling sweet from a tin of rose petal sachet. The last of the Covingtons had given great attention to the décor. The low ceiling of the master bedroom was met by a shallow rope bed, complete with a linsey-woolsey blanket and a beige and navy patchwork spread. She recognized the simple Shoo Fly pattern from her quilting class and admired the carefully cut triangles that played tricks on her eyes. She thought it interesting that the family had not selected a more sophisticated design—appliqué flowers centered on pristine white—since *broderie perse* was preferred by wealthier Colonial families. But, in that choice, Sarah saw a political stance—a disregard for European convention and a show of New World practicality. She liked that.

A bow-back Windsor rocker rested in the corner, scuffed at the rungs and worn where hands once gripped the arms. The shiny black finish revealed a hint of green milk paint at the edge of the seat where tired knees once bent over it and rubbed against the surface. On the spindly chair sat a much-loved doll with no face, stuffing making a quick escape at the elbows. A round silvered mirror with an ivory handle and matching comb were laid out on top of a bun-foot bureau, perhaps souvenirs from the first whaling days of Nantucket.

The Randolphs skeptically eyed the commode tucked next to the bed, but Sarah assured them that modern bathrooms had been added and that plumbing was up to code. They continued their cursory tour and returned to the first floor, enchanted by the setting.

Downstairs in the dining room, the brass chandelier glowed; candles now replaced with small flame-shaped bulbs. How grand this room must have been hosting long-skirted women and powder-wigged men. A clavichord stood near an ornate Oriental screen. "Wonder if it still works," Sarah mused, pressing a key only to jump back as a clarion note rang out.

Sarah was comfortable here and didn't want to leave, but the Randolphs were ready to go. She handed them her business card and offered to meet again.

Sarah lingered a moment longer and watched them drive away. She locked up the house and, then, walked to her car, preoccupied. She slid into the driver's seat and headed towards the highway, knowing a TV set and hungry kids would be waiting for her.

Coming home was a jolt. The television sounded more raucous than usual and the children's video games, more annoying, in contrast to the peacefulness of the Tory house. Sarah made hamburgers and a salad, but they didn't hold a candle to the plump game birds she imagined turning on a spit in that stone fireplace.

Jared, 11, and Abby, 9, were clamoring for attention, as was Carter. Their day, his day, what about her day?

Meal cleanup was tedious. There was homework to check. Laundry to do. Bills to pay. Just as she was tucking the kids in for the night, the phone rang.

"Mr. Randolph," her husband said, handing her the earpiece. He could hear his wife's side of the conversation. "Is everything all right?" He saw her nod. Nod again. She talked in a tired, but accommodating, voice.

"Tough day at the office?" Carter asked after she hung up.

"Just the usual," she sighed. "Good prospect. Lost sunglasses. Have to go back to the Covington estate tomorrow."

Carter was a calm, rock-solid sort of man—a good husband for someone like Sarah, who tended to be more volatile. Whereas Sarah was outgoing and empathetic, Carter had the unique ability to remain detached. He loved academia and the arts—and played the part well, sporting a neatly trimmed beard that matched his dark hair, which perpetually suggested he had no time for a haircut and that his patience for vanity ended at his ear lobes.

Carter alternated between two tweed jackets adorned with obligatory elbow patches, which he wore when the weather was cold. In warmer seasons, he relied on a handful of muted-tone cotton sweaters that generously bagged over his lean form. His students thought he was cool in an effortless sort of way.

Sarah could never tell whether Carter's distraction was part of his absent-minded-professor persona or a natural proclivity to ignore the non-critical. She knew he cared for her deeply, but he could be dismissive when something was on his mind. Usually he would rally with a stern look or an exasperated "Carter!" at which point he would give her his undivided attention.

Recently he had traded his wire rim glasses for square tortoise shell frames, which Sarah thought made him look like an intellectual cover model. When she enthusiastically mentioned that she liked his new, distinguished style, Carter pooh-poohed it. "I needed a new prescription and these frames were on sale," was all he had to say in his practical, man-of-few-words manner.

But, despite their personality differences, Carter knew his wife better than most men know their spouse and his cerebral nature led to a quiet understanding of give-and-take. He respected her space and, in turn, expected the same from her. When Sarah surprised him by saying she wanted to pursue a real estate license, he supported her fully, although it was a far cry from her original interest in social work. When they had children, he became an equal parental partner and bestowed in them his own trusting, almost naïve, optimistic outlook on the world.

That night, Carter could see the toll Sarah's profession was taking. Standing behind her, he massaged her shoulders until she relaxed and crumpled against him. Exhausted, she peeled herself away and headed for the couch, sinking into the soft cushions, and curling up with a magazine. She leafed through the sections: Letters to the Editor, feature story, Fashion, Food…not seriously reading but scanning the headlines and glancing at the quotes. A sepia-toned perfume ad caught her eye. In it, a man's strong arms encircled the slim waist of a woman, reminding Sarah of that sensation in the house—the presence she thought she detected, the awareness she momentarily felt—but she flipped the page, closed the magazine, and went to bed.

The next morning, after Carter had taken the kids to school and gone to work, Sarah retraced her steps to the old homestead. She watched the fields go by, the rock walls, red ivy, and zigzagged fence. She turned left and bounced along the rutted driveway.

The door key turned more easily this time, as if she and the house had come to terms. Walking into the mudroom and through the kitchen, she made her way up the stairs to the bedrooms and back down again. No sunglasses.

"What a waste of time," she groused. Then she remembered the access door in the ceiling. "Could have fallen out when he was up there," she thought.

She slid the ladder under the opening and, using the broom handle as Mr. Randolph had done, she propped the access door open. It gave way with a groan. Climbing to the top of the ladder, she looked around. There was hardly space for her shoulders to turn. Nothing up there. But, from her vantage point, she was able to see the missing sunglasses sitting on the corner of the desk below. She also noticed, on the floor near the foot of the ladder, a small white triangle.

Inching down, she bent over to retrieve it. The tiny tuft of paper had flourishes of brown ink around the edges and resembled the dog-ear of a book. Eager to get back to her office, she grabbed the sunglasses, along with the shred of paper, and slipped them into the pocket of her light wool camel hair coat.

Sarah's day was uneventful as she checked her email and online listings. She returned a few calls and left a message for Mr. Randolph. Thumbing through the local paper, she noticed her Tory house proudly displayed mid-page. The copy read, "Recapture the days of yore with this vintage home listed on the Historic Register." The ad featured a close-up of the 1714 sign decorated with a border that resembled the edging on her scrap of paper.

That evening, the Randolphs called again, wanting to know about renovations—what had been done before and what might be allowed within historic guidelines. "Let's meet in the morning at the Historical Society," Sarah suggested, "and then we can go back to the house for a closer look."

While the Randolphs riffled through reference materials, Sarah pondered the design that had been replicated in two difference places. On a hunch, she approached the receptionist and asked about it. Sarah quickly learned that the decoration was adapted from a border found in Colonial printing and was frequently used in promotional materials. While that didn't quite explain what the little piece of paper was doing on the floor of the house, Sarah figured it had surfaced during cleaning.

After poring over documents, photocopying blueprints of the home's expansive east wing, and printing images from electronic files, she and the Randolphs left the town building and drove toward Baker's Cove. Walking together from their cars, the Randolphs excitedly talked about adding modern amenities that would not affect the footprint of the home. Sarah took this conversation as a positive sign.

As the trio approached the house in the mid-day light, it was easy to see that the east wing was almost as large as the main house. They entered quietly, respecting the silence of their surroundings, and walked down the east wing corridor. Sarah poked her head into one of the rooms, spotlessly swept and basking in the sun. Were it not for a spider web in the doorframe, the room was move-in ready.

There she saw an old trunk with a gold leaf 'TC' painted on the lid. "Thomas Covington," she thought, "or maybe his son Thomas II. Could even be his grandson, Terrence."

After a leisurely tour, Sarah and her clients went their separate ways. That evening, she noticed a rosy glow on her left cheekbone, under her eye. "Strange," she thought, "Maybe a spider bit me." But, the sensation didn't hurt. It felt more like a kiss.

Several days went by without hearing from the Randolphs, but Sarah vowed not to be pushy. She busied herself at office, frequently the last to leave. One quiet evening, engrossed in her work, she failed to notice the clouds billowing across the horizon. Looking up and sensing an impending storm, she quickly shut down her computer, put on her coat, flipped the window sign from 'Open' to 'Closed', and then hurried out, locking the office door behind herself.

Rain was beating down in pellets by the time she reached her car. She took the short cut through Baker's Cove, hoping to lessen her commute, but suddenly her wheels caught a puddle and she hydroplaned across the yellow line. Slowly pulling over, adrenalin pumping, she phoned Carter to say she would be late.

"I'm glad you called," he replied. "Don't come through the meadow. The road is flooded."

"Well, what do you expect me to do?" she said, feeling the tension rise in her voice. "The main drag's no better."

"Just wait it out," he suggested in his typical, even-tempered manner.

"But I'm stuck in the middle of nowhere!" she said, frustrated by his seeming inability to grasp her predicament.

"You're near that old house you were showing, right? Why don't you hang out there 'til this thing blows over? I'm sure no one will care."

Sarah didn't like the idea of being on someone else's property, but she agreed. This time, in a sea of mud, her car wouldn't make it up the drive, so she left it at the bottom near the road and sprinted the distance to the house, trying to avoid the rivulets cascading down the hill. Flicking rain from her shoulders, she pushed her key into the lock box to open the side door, which yielded more easily than before.

The house sat solemnly bathed in gray. Flipping on the lights, she saw two sconces come to life and realized they had been wired for electricity. Their reflection danced in the windowpane—a rectangle of glass so rippled it resembled a fun house mirror. As she chained the door closed, she was immediately struck by the warmth of the room. She walked to the thermostat to see if someone had left the heat on and let her hand trail in front of the fireplace.

"That's ridiculous!" she told herself. "I'm in a deserted house." She decided the warmth was just a stark contrast to the cold front blowing in. Stepping out of her wet shoes, she peeled off her soaking coat and damp blazer, and wrapping her arms around herself, went to the kitchen. She noticed tea bags in a lidded jar and took one.

As water heated in the heavy kettle, she thought about the small piece of paper in her coat pocket. Maybe it had fallen from the crawlspace, she reasoned. After all, paper was once used for insulation. "Wouldn't it be fun to find an old newspaper up there or something even better?" she allowed. She has heard rumors about a Revolutionary War map hidden in the walls. The boiling kettle started to sing and broke her train of thought.

How good the hot tea felt coursing through her chest, and how appropriate to be savoring the same substance that had separated the Colonists and the British in this very place. She was fascinated with history and there she stood, smack in the middle of it. As she looked around the room, all her senses were on high alert.

Rain drove against the roof with the beat of a fife and drum corps. Wind buffeted the shutters, clapping them like cannon. As the old house creaked, she could almost hear the low moans of

Colonial women as they birthed their children and grieved for the ones they lost.

The tea was bitter—she had let it steep too long—but the bitterness seemed right, taking her back to the days of hardship and sacrifice. As dampness surrounded her, she could smell the history of the house. The fireplace was center to all, and its smoky residue permeated everything else. Unconsciously, her hand caressed the counter top, and she could almost feel it respond. As she glanced down at her cup where steam rose in a small cloud, her thoughts lifted with it, up to the window, and out to the dark silhouette of the barn.

Staring at the imposing structure, she replayed a scene that came to her often, ever since she slipped out of childhood and into womanhood. There she was, radiant in her youth, running around a barn like this—flushed and laughing, golden hair flying in the sunshine—startling chickens that went squawking and scattering in her path. Close behind was a tall, handsome young man, a bit older than she was, long fair hair swept back in a black twill ribbon.

Chased into the barn, he would capture her, pinning her against the wall. She was breathless and willing as he closed in for a kiss, lips soft and new. Muscular arms trapped her securely, but she didn't struggle to break free. His muslin shirt was open at the neck and his skin glistened, tan from working in the fields. He wore trim woolen britches, a honey-hued leather vest, cream-colored stockings, and black hand-tooled shoes. He was strong but gentle at the same time.

The couple giggled, nuzzled, and flirted—stopping only to pull away, look at each other intently, and resume their romp. Sarah could never tell whether this was a vestigial memory, fantasy, or part of a dream.

Suddenly there was a knock at the side door, and Sarah snapped to attention.

"Town police. Is everything all right?" she heard as a bright beam of light swept along the crack at the floor.

She hurried to the door and pulled it open as far as the chain would allow. A rain-soaked officer was outside, holding up his badge. Seeing the blue strobe of his cruiser flashing behind him, she released the chain and he stepped inside, shaking off water like a wet dog.

"What can I do for you, officer?" she asked, unnerved by the intrusion.

"Noticed your car at the bottom of the drive, ma'am," he said. "And then I saw the light in the roof…," he continued, motioning upward. "I knew this house was empty, so I figured I'd better check." Embarrassed, she explained the situation, pulling a soggy business card from her blazer. "No harm done, ma'am, but don't forget to turn off the light. These old timbers can be a real fire hazard." She nodded, thanked him, and closed the door.

"What light?" Sarah wondered as she headed for the stairs. "I wasn't even up there…unless I left it on the other day…but I didn't see it coming in…."

The third-floor landing offered a sweeping view across the fields, over the rock walls, to the hills now dark and obscured by rain. No wonder this had been such an ideal lookout for early settlers. Although a Tory roof usually signified allegiance to the King, Sarah knew that wasn't the case here. Somewhere in the Covington line there had been a change of heart. While the family remained outwardly loyal for years, word is that grandson, Terrence, secretly sided with the Colonists and helped fuel the Revolution.

Sarah looked around the eave and saw a bright lantern hanging from the rafters. Reaching to turn it off, she heard a whisper. "Wait," the voice said.

She spun around, heart racing. Again, no one was there. Frozen in place, daring not to move, she became aware of the smell of lavender and lemon. Herbal. Pleasing. Maybe with a hint of sweet grass. The scent seemed to soothe her nerves.

Trying to compose herself, Sarah took a deep breath. Slowly her anxiety lessened, changing from fear to calm—a state of relaxation so pronounced that she felt sedated. She blinked a few times, attempting to focus, but she was surrounded by the oddest sensation. She wasn't exactly dizzy but felt weightless, as if swaying in a hammock on a summer's day. She wondered if there had been something more potent than tea in her cup.

"What the hell is happening to me?" Sarah asked outloud, trying to bring rational thinking to an irrational situation. She had no answer.

Using a straight-back chair for balance, she anchored herself before easing onto on a small cot wedged under the eave. She lay back, covering her eyes with her hand to block any light that might seep through her heavy eyelids. She felt warm breath on her neck and the softness of hair falling over her face. There was pressure against her, but not in a threatening way. It was far more seductive. Caught somewhere between sleep and wakefulness, she tried to assess the situation. "Did I hit my head? Am I getting sick?" she questioned, but her thoughts moved as if in molasses. No, this was something distinctly different. Something she had never experienced before. Something she liked.

Sarah kept her eyes closed, giving in to the feeling. She was overcome with a sense of falling, a fast spiraling descent, then a prolonged landing in which she hovered, but never quite touched ground. "Going down the rabbit hole?" a cluster of brain cells taunted. Trying to stay lucid, she struggled to find a scientific explanation: "Maybe I was hyperventilating…maybe I'm hungry…." But no longer able to reason, she stopped resisting.

Sarah had no idea how long she drifted there, eyes at half-mast, brain on low battery, but a movement near the window jolted her. Unsteadily, she stood up and pulled the thin curtains aside. Nothing was there. The smell of lavender had vanished. The rain had slowed. As soon as her head started to clear, she reached for the light, but not before spotting a small tip of paper laying at her feet. She grabbed it, turned off the lantern, and went downstairs.

Fumbling in her coat pocket, she lined up the two shreds. The match was perfect as if piecing together a puzzle. Suddenly aware of the lateness, she pocketed both and rushed to leave.

The kids were asleep by the time she got home. Carter was in his favorite chair reading. Gotye's *Somebody That I Used to Know* was playing in the background. "You OK?" he asked, rising to help her with her wet gear.

"I'm fine," she said, hanging her coat on a hook. "Probably good that I waited out the storm."

"There's some tea left if you want...it should still be warm," he offered.

"I actually had some at the house," she replied.

Sarah wanted to share her experience, but something held her back. Maybe it was the thought that Carter would laugh or worse yet, grill her—or maybe it was the intrigue of savoring the unknown. Either way, the experience went to bed with her.

The Randolphs were on vacation, so final decisions about the house would not be made for a while. They had put down a deposit to take it off the market, and a week before their expected return, Sarah received a call from Ann.

"Mrs. Randolph, how have you been?" Sarah inquired, anxious to learn about their plans.

"Fine, honey—we've been thinking about the house and we want to take it to the next step," Ann replied.

"Super," Sarah said, trying to temper her excitement.

"We'd like to send our inspector out next week and were hoping you could meet him. We do want to build a greenhouse off the back, so we'll need some measurements, too."

"No problem. Just tell me when the inspector can come, and I'll be there, tape measure in hand," Sarah offered. She thought it odd that they didn't insist on being there in person, but she let it slide.

"You're a peach. I'll email you the date and time," Mrs. Randolph confirmed. "We're just so busy down here...." Her sentence trailed off.

The following week, after receiving Ann's email, Sarah bundled up in a thick wool sweater, suede boots, and a long forest-green, corduroy skirt. She grabbed her saddlebag pocketbook, cell phone, and tote on the way out the door. Someone from Stuart's Inspection agency was to arrive at 9 a.m. so she made sure to be there earlier. She waited, but no inspector came. Soon she received a text: "En route. Please wait. Flat tire. Sorry. – Stu."

Once again, Sarah was alone in the house. She walked up to the master bedroom and lifted the small ivory-handled mirror from the bureau. She checked her hair and made sure her cheeks were properly blushed. Her pale hazel eyes stared back, wide and innocent. As she stood there, she became aware of the fresh herbal scent that had greeted her before. "What a great air freshener," she thought. "I'll have to ask the cleaning crew what it is."

Mirror in hand, she paused for one last look. That's when she noticed in the reflection, a shadow that resembled the form of a man. She impulsively turned around to touch it, but it vanished beneath her fingertips. "Gotta get more sleep," she chided herself. She returned the mirror to its resting place and walked out.

When Stuart knocked, Sarah was within reach of the doorknob. He stepped in and smiled. "Oh, I know something about this house already," he claimed with a wink.

Skeptical, Sarah asked, 'What do you mean?"

"Aside from the pretty lady standing in the doorway, this house has a lot of personality."

Sarah brushed off the compliment, surprised that a housing inspector would be so forthright. She said nothing and just smiled in return. "Yup, seen it before," he went on, "but not often. Most homes just sit there—but this one has life, energy."

"Really?" Sarah replied, trying to appear nonchalant.

"This baby's a keeper," he muttered as he glanced around. "Just look at it!" he said, whacking a beam with his hand. Sarah encouraged him to move along.

"Where do you want to begin?" she asked.

"Let's begin at the beginning," Stuart chuckled, laughing at his own wit as they headed toward the cellar. Stepping aside to give him space, Sarah couldn't help but notice how his hairline crept over his skull and settled somewhere on the back of his head. His work shirt was faded but neatly ironed. Stu was just a tad paunchy, but otherwise physically fit. His nails were surprisingly clean for someone who worked in the trades.

The inspection was routine: floors, walls, a search for water damage, bugs. "I can line you up with a termite guy, if you want," he said as he headed into the keeping room. "Can't be too careful with these antiques." Then Stuart paused and looked at her intently. "Did anyone ever find that old map?"

"What map?" she asked, feigning naiveté, hoping to gain more information.

"Oh, there's supposed to be an old Colonial map hidden somewhere on this property."

"Fascinating!" Sarah exclaimed as if she had never heard the story.

Stuart continued to prod and poke, stopping occasionally to jot a note in a spiral pad which he returned by feel to his left shirt pocket.

"You seem to know a lot about this house," Sarah commented.

"Not enough," Stuart said, shining a flashlight along the ceiling. "These old homesteads always hold one more secret. Won't speak to just anyone, you know." She let him do the talking…and he did a lot of it.

"Heck, once I was in a house they said was haunted. Ten different families lived there and never a spook. Then—poof!—in moves this new family and the ghosts come out of the woodwork!"

"Was the family scared?" Sarah asked, now intrigued.

"Sure, at first, but then they got used to it. One ghost ended up being like a big brother," he laughed.

"Well, I don't really believe in ghosts," Sarah stated, "though I guess I believe in the *possibility*. I'm generally pretty opened minded."

"That's what they said," Stuart noted.

"*They,* who?" Sarah asked, puzzled.

"The Randolphs. They said you were open to new ideas and were helping them with some renovations."

"I almost forgot!" Sarah said, smacking her palm against her forehead as she remembered the greenhouse. She guided him to the proposed site and asked about the viability of the location. He assessed the ground and took some measurements of the supporting wall, producing a running narrative even though she was out of earshot. "Strange guy," she thought, now eager for him to leave.

As Sarah returned to the kitchen, Stuart walked around the outside of the house, gazing up at the roofline and making additional notes. He stepped inside for one last look, starting at the top floor and working his way down, clicking off a few photos with his cellphone and talking into it. "That about does it for the main house. I'll check the outbuildings before I leave," he said, heading for the door, suggesting her company wasn't needed or, perhaps, wasn't wanted. "I left the light on, on the third floor, as you had it."

Sarah thanked him and watched as he made his way to the barn, shed, and smokehouse. Following his form with her eyes, she imagined he was a farmhand helping the Covingtons bring a pig to slaughter. She could almost hear the squeals and could practically smell the sugary fruitwood burning in the smoking pits.

After he drove away, Sarah hurried up the stairs to the alcove under the eave. Through a small window, Sarah scanned the panorama dotted with farms and orange trees. "So glad…so glad you're here," she heard in her mind.

Again, she felt light-headed and buoyant. Her pulse quickened. Her breathing became shallow. As the pressure against her chest increased, she backed against a wall to steady herself. She couldn't move. She didn't want to. She was the girl in her daydream, trapped by unseen arms. The force was magnetic, drawing her in. She was slipping yet strangely supported. Her head was spinning, her feet defying gravity.

"I've waited…waited so long," the deep voice continued. She wanted to speak but couldn't.

"What's happening to me?" her logical brain demanded as her silent-self retorted: "I don't know, but I'm not sure I care."

Sarah could hear her own blood rushing in her ears. Every cell felt charged. Not daring to open her eyes, she yielded to the pull, and was suspended, as if being lifted and carefully carried to safety.

Drifting. Drowsy. The scent of lavender and lemon was upon her. She could hear the accelerated breathing of a man…a man who was enveloping her, pleasing her, forcing nothing but tracing her curves as if mapping a familiar road.

It wasn't until much later that she found herself laying on the small cot under the Tory roof, not quite sure what had happened. She rubbed her eyes and tried to estimate the lapse of time. She shut off the light and walked slowly downstairs as if coming out of a deep sleep. She felt simultaneously rested and energized. That's when she knew she would tell no one.

With the house inspection results filed, the transaction was underway. She sent the greenhouse specs to the Randolphs and assured them an in-depth report would follow. Although she tried to focus on daily tasks, thoughts of the Tory house kept intruding. Determined to get some answers, she planned to return on Saturday. "Someone else is looking at the old Covington estate," she told her husband in a small white lie. She knew Carter was only half-listening, but she felt a need to justify her actions. "They want to be in line in case the sale falls through."

Carter glanced up from the eggs he was scrambling. "No problem," he said. "The kids will be playing at friends. They both got calls while you were in the shower. I can take them."

"Thank you mucho; you're the best," she said, giving him a quick kiss on the cheek. She could hear Jared and Abby squabbling over a television show in the next room and knew that at 11 and 9, their age difference was akin to the Great Divide. "'Bye, guys!" she yelled to them, but neither answered.

"See you later," Carter nodded. "When do you think you'll be back?"

Knowing she had lost track of time before, she built in a cushion. "A couple hours…but don't worry if I'm longer," she covered. "I have to show them another property, too."

"OK. If I'm not here, I'll be playing golf," Carter said. "The kids are good 'til 4 and they'll get dropped off."

As Sarah headed toward the car, she told herself: "I really didn't lie…. I *am* showing houses to another family…just not this house and not today…." It was so unlike her to stretch the truth that she immediately felt guilty. "But guilty of what?" she rationalized. "Nothing really happened. No one was there!"

Morning light filtered into the house, kicking off a crystal decanter and sending small prisms of color against the walls "What a great place," she sighed. "The Randolphs are so lucky to have found it."

This time she was brazen as she walked through the rooms. "OK, whoever you are—show yourself!" she demanded. There was no response. She stomped up the stairs and announced, "I want to see you! I want to see you now!" The house was silent.

Exasperated and feeling foolish, she padded down to the basement to check the electrical panel, thinking that might explain the unpredictable third floor light. She returned to the ground level with no reasonable explanation.

A perfectly natural voice called from the dining room, "Did you want me?"

Sarah stared wide-eyed, holding her breath. There, at the table, sat a commanding young man in a crisp red coat adorned with shiny brass buttons. He was slowly smoking a long-stemmed white clay pipe, leaning back to prolong each inhale. His fair hair was caught in a black ribbon, his britches defined his trim form, and his smile was the most winning she had ever seen. She stood mute. There was nothing unreal about him—other than his being out of place, out of time…and maybe, out of this world.

He was intently studying a folded piece of paper. "Come here and look at this," he motioned. More intrigued than afraid, she edged closer.

"You'll never see it from there, Sarah," he laughed.

"My God, he knows my name!" she thought as she moved tentatively behind him.

"See, here's the plan...for when the time is right. We'll rendezvous at the house, take the weapons that are in the basement and meet the others at the gristmill. Then we'll march to Concord and engage."

Sarah hadn't seen weapons in the basement when she checked the fuse box...but then again, she hadn't been wearing a cotton apron, long skirt, and full-sleeved blouse as she suddenly was now.

Sarah was speechless, which prompted him to add, "Don't worry. They still think I'm a Tory, so we're safe as long as I'm undercover." Sarah blankly nodded as if she understood.

She noticed the tips of the page were missing and made a mental leap to the scraps of paper she had found. As she reached toward one of the corners, he looked up at her with a mischievous grin. "Oh, I was just teasing you," he said, flashing a broad smile. "I just wanted to pique your interest." She stared back, dumbfounded.

"You *are* interested, aren't you?" he asked, coy and inviting.

She knew she had to answer, but she waited until the last possible moment. "Uh, I guess so," she stammered.

"Of course, you are!" he exclaimed. "When I knew you before, we were inseparable. We'd make mad, passionate love in every room of the house," he bragged.

The thought was deliciously naughty, but her responsible brain overrode it.

"Before?" was all she could manage to say.

"Yes—though that was long ago," he said and gently added. "You returned to the cycle, but I didn't."

Sarah's mind was racing. "Before? After? Cycle? What is this?"

The attractive man pushed back the chair and stretched his six-foot frame like a lean cat. Sarah dared to admire it from a distance.

"What do you want with me?" she tentatively asked.

"I want to continue the life we had. I want you by my side when we fight for what is ours."

"Fight?" Sarah whispered.

"Yes, fight for the liberties we deserve as free people. Freedom from oppression under British rule."

Sarah started to shake her head. "You must have me confused with someone else," she said, backing away. "I don't even know how I got here."

"You belong here," the stranger said as he stood up and moved closer. "Don't run off now. It's taken me forever to find you."

Sarah forced herself to stand her ground and, in an ultimate test of proof, extended her hand to his forearm, fully expecting her fingers to pass through an apparition. To her surprise, her hand was met with cloth. Rough, hand-carded wool, dyed brilliant red, smoothed and folded many times over. She gazed up at him, amazed and intensely attracted. "Do I know you?" she whispered.

"Oh, you know me better than you know yourself. We're soul mates…kindred spirits…but we didn't have enough time together." He took her by the shoulders. "You *must* remember, Sarah! Can't you remember who we were?" he implored.

Sarah had no tangible recollection, but she felt so right standing there. "This is all happening too fast," she told herself, as he leaned over, lips hovering near hers.

Sarah stepped back. "I can't…. I'm married…. I have a husband…and kids…." she said out loud, not entirely convinced of her own words.

"Yes, and I'm that husband! Terrence Covington. I was your husband long before he was," the handsome man challenged.

"What do you mean…*before*?" she started to ask.

"Stop talking, woman," he grinned and pulled her toward him, planting a kiss squarely on her mouth. She was stunned, paralyzed. But, before she could protest, he came back for more.

When she recovered, she was standing alone in the room except for the subtle scent of lavender and lemon. She glanced down and noticed her skirt and apron were gone, replaced by a business-black pants suit. Someone was knocking at the door. Trying to look official, she hurried to see who it was.

"I was just curious," a stranger said, peering in. "I know this house in on hold, but I've never repped one like it. When I saw your car in the drive, I thought you wouldn't mind—agent to agent—if I took a little tour," the over-dressed woman said as she elbowed her way in.

"Be my guest," Sarah said, figuring she had no choice.

"Kind of old and musty," the other agent huffed. "Not my cup of tea!" she remarked as she took off toward the stairwell and headed upstairs. Sarah could hear the floorboards squeak in the alcove under the Tory roof. After a quick glance around, the woman stormed down. "Someone should fix that light. Doesn't even work," she complained.

"Oh, really," Sarah answered, amused. Clearly, the house 'liked' that woman about as much as she did.

"Well, thanks for your time," the woman said as she ran her hand along a chair rail.

"Damn, splinter!" she swore, abruptly pulling her hand back. "Probably won't be long until this property is back on the market. I can't imagine people living here." And, with that, she left.

Sarah sat down on the settle, bewildered.

"Guess you either like these old homesteads or not," said an estranged voice. Sarah looked up and saw the compelling man standing in the hallway.

"I've gotta go," she said, forcing herself to walk toward the door.

"Come back soon," he said not moving.

Sarah hurried to her car, clearly rattled. After buckling her seatbelt, she nervously glanced at the building in her rear-view mirror. She saw nothing unusual. Just a vintage house basking in the glow of an autumn afternoon.

That Monday she went to the library, making a beeline to the cordoned-off genealogy section. Molly Rifkin, the librarian, had been there for years and was a wealth of knowledge. "Do you have anything on the Covingtons?" Sarah asked.

Molly adjusted her bifocals and toddled to a tall bookcase, dragging a sliding ladder with her and pointing upward. "Maybe you can reach it for me, dear. My hip's just not what it used to be," said the elderly librarian. "That thick brown volume with the leather tie."

"Oh, sure," Sarah offered, steadying the ladder. She climbed to the top and retrieved the heavy book, handing it over.

Carefully, Molly brought it to a table. As if performing a sacred rite, she slowly opened the volume to a chapter marked with a strip of ribbon. "There you go, dear," Molly said and headed back to her desk.

Sarah slid into a chair and pulled closer to the table. She noticed the frontispiece of the book bore the same Colonial design as the pieces of paper she had found. Immediately she looked around, fully expecting to see someone standing there, but all she saw was Molly staring at a computer screen.

Sarah flipped through the pages, hungry for information. "Terrence was the rebellious grandson of Thomas Covington and son of Thomas II. He was raised on the family farm as a staunch Royalist but had a penchant for politics at an early age. Although his parents wanted to send him back to England for proper schooling, he adamantly refused, far more intrigued by the promise of a new land."

Sarah couldn't read fast enough. "Terrence maintained the air of a loyal English gentleman, but those who knew him better said he was the first in the Covington line to question the King and acts of Parliament."

"Posing as a Stamp Agent for the Admiralty Court, he'd slip away to the Long Room of the Green Dragon Tavern in Boston and meet secretly with a group of activists, who later became the Sons of Liberty. Some say he was among the men who ransacked the Hutchinson House in 1765, but that has yet to be proven. Records do show that he confronted General Gage's army in the western part of the state and later went to New York City to support the Liberty Boys."

"A well-to-do, strapping young man, Terrence was the fancy of many young woman, but he deflected their advances in favor of his true love, Sarah Hawthorne." Sarah was spellbound. Her mother came from the Hawthorne line!

"Terrence wooed Sarah until she was old enough to wed. She blossomed around him and, according to local accounts, was often heard singing in the garden behind their house. By revealing his dual identity early in their relationship, he embroiled her in a role she never expected, posing as the devout Loyalist wife, while surreptitiously aiding her young revolutionary husband."

"Sarah delighted in the masquerade as much as Terrence and was often with him during his most daring escapades. When Sarah became pregnant, friends weren't surprised. She and Terrence seemed truly in love. Her pregnancy was uneventful until the baby was born a few weeks earlier than expected. Several days later, Sarah died. However, the infant survived."

"After that, a heartbroken Terrence stayed close to home, raising his son and tending his land. Once the son had grown and taken a wife of his own, Terrence climbed into the Tory roof and shot himself. The note he left said, 'Please forgive my selfish ways, but I cannot go on. All these years, I have longed for Sarah and missed her so. I am joining her now, because I can bear it no more.'"

Sarah stared at the page, entranced. The chapter concluded: "Today you can find Terrence Covington buried next to his young bride in the Southbridge Cemetery near the old town church."

Sarah issued an audible "Wow," then walked slowly toward the ladder to put the book away.

"Are you OK, dear?" Molly asked. "You look as if you've seen a ghost."

Sarah nodded, but thought more accurately, "I feel as if I *am* a ghost."

Sarah drove to work in a daze but, not being able to concentrate, left the office early to pick up her kids.

Jared was a handsome boy now in fifth grade. He had a lopsided smile, warm brown eyes, and a constant shock of dark hair falling into his face over his right eye. He resembled his father in many ways, elusive and introspective, but capable to breaking into a string of bad puns and self-deprecating humor that would surely serve him well later in life. Sarah had encouraged him to make friends at school, but she knew it wasn't easy. He wasn't exactly a loner, but it took time for people to win his trust. She had pushed him into scouting in hopes that he would find new buddies and gain confidence in camping. That tactic seemed to be working. In recent weeks, he spent increasing amounts of time with friends, shooting her disarming looks as if to say, "I know what's going on." In fact, she often got the feeling he could strip away what others were trying to hide. Not unlike herself.

Abigail was a third-grader, who enjoyed nail paint and pigtails, microscopes and mechanical toys. She was part princess, part tomboy. Other than fussing over her strawberry-blond hair, she had her father's "I don't care" attitude when it came to clothes and grooming. Even at this young age, Abby had mastered the art of getting attention by wearing mismatched socks and sweaters inside-out that would cause people to stop and comment. Sarah suspected Abby's rebellion was related to her own career pursuits, being away more often that she should and now, distracted by the lure of the house. But, Abby never expressed resentment. Instead, the young girl busied herself with school projects and crafts, becoming precociously independent and bluntly opinionated. Sarah could see in Abby a curiosity not unlike her husband's. This was a child, who marveled at caterpillars and computers with equal awe.

Both children dove into the middle seat of the minivan, bursting with details of the day—a stark contrast to the times they sat sullen and tight-lipped. Sarah welcomed their unbridled conversation. Jared was going on a field trip and needed a permission slip signed. Abby had been selected to be a flower in the school play.

Sarah looked at their glowing faces. Life was good and full, and she reprimanded herself for mucking around in the past. Carter wasn't home yet, but she knew she could count on him to be there for dinner. As a high school science teacher, his hours were predictable, and he was the epitome of reliability. She often felt he was an anchor in life's storms.

Sarah spent extra time that night making her family's favorite meal—cucumber salad seasoned with sweet vinegar, chicken parmesan, garlic bread, and spaghetti. She even set the table with a checkered tablecloth and bright red napkins. The only thing missing was an empty bottle of Chianti plugged with the stump of a candle dripping wax dramatically down the side.

Dinner preparation took time, but she didn't care. It helped keep her mind off the Covingtons and assuage the guilt she was feeling about her clandestine encounter. But, try as she might to forget the intriguing family from long ago, she knew she would have to visit the Covington plot in the Southbridge cemetery.

That weekend, she took Abby for a morning walk. They strolled through the center of town, past the war memorial, and over the brook to the little cemetery behind the church.

Although a killing frost had wiped out much of the tender foliage, clumps of asters clung to life in protected corners of the graveyard. Bees, slowed to a catatonic state, affixed themselves to the curled purple flowers, feeding on the last available nectar and soaking up the weak rays of sun.

Fascinated by inscriptions, Abby led the way, unaware of the somber atmosphere cemeteries were supposed to hold. "Look, Mom! Here's one with angels and a lamb," Abby announced, as she slalomed around the gravestones. It says, 'Little did I know I'd die so young, but I breathed the Lord's life and my heart has sung'." Abby read slowly, looking at her mother for an explanation.

Sarah bent down and explained that it was a child's grave. Abby's demeanor darkened until a squirrel caught her eye. She followed it to a small mound. "This way!" Abby called as she conquered the little hill. "Cov-ing-ton," she sounded out. "I think the whole family is here."

Sarah felt an instant chill as she walked toward her daughter. The tallest stone was that of Thomas Covington, family patriarch, born 1690. To the right were his wife, Elizabeth, and their son,

Thomas II, born 1712. Also interred was Hester, wife of Thomas II, and their three boys, Thomas III, Theodore, and Terrence, born between 1735 and 1742. When Sarah saw the last marker for Terrence, she uttered an irrepressible "Oh!"

"What's the matter?" Abby asked.

Sarah explained, "I just read about this person."

"What did you read?" Abby bent down to pick up a handful of acorns as she waited for an answer.

"I read that Terrence Covington lived in the house I am trying to sell," Sarah replied, not telling all.

Next to Terrence's grave was a pure white stone etched with the profile of a woman. Abby's attention shifted to the carved marker. "This one's pretty. The lady looks like you when you wear your hair up," she observed. Sarah stood still, her eyes darting between the two headstones.

The inscription on Terrence's stone referred to his wife. "Too young to leave a son behind, always in my heart and mind. I will lie near you to finally rest, but only after I fill my quest."

"What's a quest?" Abby asked.

"It's like a search…a long search," Sarah answered, not paying complete attention. She was too busy reading the information on the white stone: "Sarah Hawthorne Covington: 1747-1766."

Abby reached up to touch the cold marble.

"She was only 19 when she died," Sarah said, a note of sadness creeping into her words. She remembered how full of life she had been at that age.

"That's way old," Abby decided, seeing the world from a child's perspective.

"Well, just wait until you're 19, my dear. It all goes by very fast," Sarah cautioned as she guided Abby toward the gate. "We'll come back another time, maybe in the spring," she promised.

"What happens when you die?" Abby asked, deep in thought as they left the cemetery.

"No one knows for sure," Sarah said, "but we like to think it's something pretty and peaceful." She hugged Abby and they walked home, hand in hand.

Sarah wasn't certain Abby had grasped the connection between life and death, but it felt good talking about the natural progression of things. "You can ask Daddy more about it," she had suggested, figuring Carter would provide a scientific spin.

Abby fed her fish as Sarah prepared lunch. "Could there be such a thing as reincarnation?" Sarah wondered as she set out jars of peanut butter and jelly. "Maybe there's a portal—like a black hole—that would allow us to move between realms. What if it were possible to manipulate time to make a spiritual connection?" Sarah couldn't shake these bizarre thoughts.

"Want some soup, Jared?" she called to her son, now plunked comfortably in front of the TV. "Abby?"

They both yelled back almost in unison. "Sure. Alphabet soup. Not that weird pea stuff."

Sarah laughed. "Don't worry. No green pea," she said, smiling as she went to the pantry.

Life in the present certainly had its moments.

That afternoon, just before the Randolphs were to arrive, the weather turned raw and windy. From the doorway, Sarah watched the fallen leaves spin across the driveway. "This is how it all began," she thought, getting a distinct sense of déjà vu. The Randolphs' car pulled in and Mrs. Randolph rolled down the window to wave.

"Hi, Mrs. Randolph," Sarah called as she threw on a coat and reached for her tote. "I'll be right there!" Sarah could hear Mrs. Randolph call back, "*Ann*, please!" This time the Randolphs would be driving. Sarah slid into the back seat with the idea of relaxing.

The Randolphs appeared healthy and rested. Their skin was coppered from the sun and both exuded a sense of the good life. David looked as if he had just stepped off the links at Pebble Beach, wearing a pale pink shirt, tan pants, and a navy blazer—far less substantial than New England temperatures required at this time of year. Sarah noticed a thick gold chain on his left wrist and a matching ring on his left pinky finger.

Ann's style was casually sophisticated and hinted of Old Hollywood as if you might meet her in a post-war cabaret where she would plant an air kiss on both cheeks before dashing off to someone more interesting. She always smelled of expensive shampoo and spa treatments. Sarah imagined Ann with long red nails, a thin cigarette holder, and crimped hair, saying things like "Over there, darling," or "Pour me the Dom Perignon, please."

"What a great escape," Ann sighed. "The sun. The sand. The palm trees. Splendid." Her eyes rolled back as if she were lolling on a beach.

Mr. Randolph goaded her on, "Sure, so strenuous, she almost didn't have time to think about the greenhouse," he teased.

"Nope, got my plans right here!" Ann said, patting a large flat envelope at the side of her seat.

"Have you been keeping an eye on the house for us?" Mr. Randolph asked over his shoulder. "I'm sorry we haven't moved faster, but we've been up against some deadlines at school…."

Ann completed the sentence for him, "…and we had to take our vacation days before we lost it."

"No problem," Sarah answered. "I swung by a couple times."

Mr. Randolph glanced at his wife. "And was everything in order?" he asked, quickly adding, "I heard you've had some serious weather up here."

"Oh, just fine," Sarah answered. "No damage. But I ended up there one night on the way home. I hope you don't mind; it was kind of an emergency. The road through the meadow was flooded and it was pouring so hard I couldn't see, so I waited it out. The house was amazingly warm and—no leaks!" she caught herself. Mrs. Randolph turned and smiled, seemingly unbothered by her impromptu visit.

When they got to the house this time, the door was open. "Oh, no!" Sarah said, rushing in. "Look at this!" Wet leaves were blown across the floor and there were stains where water had dried. "I'll get a cleaning crew in here tomorrow," she apologized. "I'm sure I locked this, but I know there have been other real estate agents interested in the property."

Mr. Randolph seemed concerned. "I hope nothing was taken," he said immediately, on second thought adding, "Do you think another buyer could interfere with the sale?"

"Oh, no, just looky-loos," Sarah assured. "I guess until that 'Sale Pending' sign comes down and a 'Sold' sign goes up, it's not a done deal."

As the Randolphs headed upstairs to make sure everything was intact, Sarah stayed on the ground floor. She settled into a rocking chair and called the cleaning crew on her cell. "Good, good," she said as they promised to come over the next day and tidy up.

"So good," a deep voice responded.

Sarah turned around and saw Terrence—or at least the appearance of Terrence—standing in the doorway. Tall, lanky, and terribly handsome. The Randolphs were gone, and there she sat, enveloped in a long, lace-trimmed cotton dress. "You scared me," she said, trying to regain her composure.

"Never let me scare you," he said with a tenderness she did not expect. She felt her defenses lessen.

"I, uh, just don't know you very well," Sarah replied, her words halting.

"But you do," he insisted, taking her hands. "You're my Sarah from long ago."

None of this made sense and, yet, it seemed perfectly natural. She studied him closely. His face was clean-shaven, his jaw, square. His fingers were strong from working the earth, but they were tapered and refined by heritage. His hair rivaled the hay baled along the road.

She looked up into his eyes—piercing blue eyes—trying to size them up, delve into them. They held her fast, dismantling her modern liberation, dissolving her professional reserve, relegating her present-day husband and family to another age. She stood there, vulnerable and unguarded, a woman with a fiery heart, who lived centuries ago.

"I want to know what's going on," she demanded, hearing her own voice take on the quality of a stranger.

"And I would tell you if I could, but I don't know how you came to be here and why now," Terrence confided. "I promise I won't hurt you."

While Sarah couldn't explain it either, she knew she was slipping into the life of someone else. Someone different, but remarkably familiar.

Terrence steered her down a hallway, to a rope bed. They sat for a while, talking. He traced the contours of her face and unbuttoned her blouse. She could feel the warmth of his hands on her neck and collarbone, moving down, flat against her skin. She reached under the folds of his shirt and explored the smoothness of his chest. She had traveled this turf before. White noise buzzed in her ears. Her surroundings fell away. Gentleness gave way to passion, and their intimacy left her breathless.

They lay there, spent—her hair ending where his began. Sarah looked up at the beamed ceiling and then around the room. Her lace-edged dress was crumpled on the floor, a pile of petticoats next to it. Terrence pressed his lips against her shoulder. "You'd better leave through the back door," he whispered. She numbly agreed, not knowing why.

Sarah became aware of a clavichord playing in the background and heard distant voices of children being scolded. She pulled away to say something, but he covered her mouth with his hand. "Shhh. They don't know we're here. They're too busy preparing the harvest feast."

They, who? And what feast? Her mind was galloping, trying to make sense of it all. "An early Thanksgiving," she thought, attempting to remember when the day became a national holiday. But, rational thinking had no place here nor did rigid timelines. "How can this be?" she wondered as she slid off the bed, tiptoeing as not to break the spell.

"I have to go now, too," he said, eyes turning into a blustery ocean. "They're expecting me, but I'm not sure they're ready for you."

Sarah shook her head in agreement as if she understood, but she understood nothing. It was all too strange, too bizarre, and too enticing to ignore.

She reached for her clothes, but the carefully hand-stitched garments were now replaced by denim. She slipped on her jeans and pushed her toes into her boots. As she opened the door to the back hallway, she could smell turkey, warm bread, and sweet spices. When she stepped outside, the harvest feast was gone, replaced by a gust of cold wind.

"There you are, Sarah," said Mrs. Randolph, rounding the house and jolting Sarah back to reality. "We should be going. Our greenhouse plans look like they'll work, and we have a great idea for an office." Preoccupied with their individual thoughts, no one said much as Mr. Randolph drove through the leaves that whipped across the road. Bare branches scraped the sky and tore into the clouds.

"Must have been tough traveling through these parts in the olden days," he said, finally breaking the silence. "Those folks had a lot of endurance."

"You don't know the half of it," Sarah thought to herself. That night she dreamed about Terrence and the old house.

2

HOLIDAYS

In the upcoming weeks, with the holidays approaching, Sarah was busy. Jared had a geography project for school. Her husband had term papers to correct. Abby had a recital. There was shopping to finish and bell ringers to hear…and a full calendar of social and civic events to attend. Each year Sarah was the one who put signs around town for her company's charity drive, so she would have to work that into her schedule. This was a happy time of year and she was determined to enjoy it.

Sarah was able to set the past aside until a greeting card arrived from the Randolphs. "I hate to ask, but could you go to the house again?" a handwritten note read. "We've lined up a termite inspector and hoped you could let him in. Will send you a calendar invite with the details. Thanks so much. Ann."

Sarah was getting tired of the Randolphs taking her for granted, but she wanted to close the deal, so she agreed. Besides, returning to the old house was intriguing. Carter was heading off to a teachers' conference on the selected Saturday, and the kids would be visiting Grandma, so Sarah was a free woman.

Wolfing down a breakfast of toast and eggs and, topping it off with strong coffee, she pulled a fleece jacket out of the closet, and headed toward Baker's Cove. Wreaths decorated the doors of the small houses on the outskirts of town. She saw one family bringing in a Christmas tree. Another couple juggling bags of colorful presents. An older gentleman, stooping to pat a neighbor's dog. Norman Rockwell reincarnated.

Sarah got out of the car, removed her leather gloves as she walked up to the Covington house, and slid her key into the lock box at the side door. This time the house was cold. She shuddered as she put on a light. There was no sign of Terrence and, in some ways, she felt relieved.

Sarah strolled slowly into the dining room and saw black cloth draped over the windows. She caught a blur out of her left eye that floated between the rooms, hovered, then sped away. Something was wrong here. There was no manifestation of human form, no holiday fare, no sense of celebration.

Sarah sat down in a small sewing room and heard someone crying. Peering around the corner, she saw Terrence sitting next to his mother, Hester Covington, trying to console her, but it appeared that his mother was consoling him. His father had apparently died.

Sarah leaned forward, attempting to hear the conversation, but could only catch a few phrases: "He would have been proud of you had he known," the woman said as she cupped Terrence's hand.

"Even if I'm supporting the other side?" he asked in a way that was almost child-like.

"Especially so," she smiled and slowly nodded, showing the strain of the past few days. "He always wanted you to be your own man," she reminded her son.

Terrence ran his hands over his face: forehead, eyes, nose, chin, and with a deep breath, stood up. "Excuse me, Mother," he said. "I need to get some air." With that, he walked toward the mudroom and reached for a scarf.

Glancing over his shoulder and seeing Sarah, he nonchalantly asked, "Want to walk with me?" Sarah nodded and grabbed her wrap—a felt wool cape that tied at the neck. Where this had come from boggled her mind, but she hurried to catch up with him.

He held her hand as they walked up the hill to the small orchard behind the house. The sky was dull gray, and their breath made small puffs as they moved along. The smell of fermented apples rose from the ground. They stopped and looked back at the homestead. "Now this is officially mine," Terrence said, more with fatigue than emotion. "But I don't want to live here alone, and I won't be able to care for it myself."

"You have your brothers and their families," Sarah consoled.

"They're not always around and, besides, they have lives of their own."

It took a minute for Sarah to realize that she was standing outside the house, but still in full Colonial garb. Perhaps this was possible because she was physically touching Terrence. Sarah could see the concern in his eyes. "I'll help you," she offered, "What do you need me to do?"

Terrence looked down at her and simply said, "Just be a loving Tory wife." And that's how he proposed.

Sarah felt her breath catch. "Did I just hear you right?" she double-checked as a rogue bit of modern mindset jabbed at the recesses of her brain. "Sure, buddy...subservient wife." But here she was no longer that person and she was honored to be asked.

"You certainly did hear me right," he said, wrapping his arms around her as she said yes. The warmth felt good and the embrace, safe. This was not a moment of passion but of comfort and commitment. Terrence reminded Sarah that it would be difficult leading a double life and there would be times he'd be away. "I'll have to do things you won't like," Terrence warned, "and sometimes I'll ask you to do them with me."

"I trust you and I believe in you," Sarah said, stepping up on her toes to kiss him. His nose was cold as it grazed her cheek.

"Let's go back in," he said. "We have to sort out my Father's things and help Mother pack for her sister's. I don't want her to be alone."

They quietly returned to the house, trying not to disturb Terrence's mother, who had fallen asleep in a chair. "Think about what you want to do to make this place our own," he said. Sarah tried to envision the house decorated with her favorite things: a patchwork pillow on their bed, her grandmother's blue and white platter in the breakfront, a primitive painting of a cat hanging on the kitchen wall. Maybe someday they'd have children, so they would need room for a cradle.

When she looked up, Terrence was watching her intently. "Daydreaming?" he asked, a small smile playing across his face.

"Oh, yes," she said, "and what a nice dream it was."

Just then, the mood was shattered by gunshots. Terrence grabbed his musket and ran out the back door, leaving it wide open, cold air and darkness rushing in. Sarah reached for a shawl and quickly followed. They could hear a commotion in the distance and voices that rose and fell like a tide. "Down with the King. We'll not pay your taxes." "It's not our war debt!" "You don't own our property!" Terrence looked at Sarah and said, "I have to go."

"I know. Be careful," she said, pulling her shawl tighter and turning to go back inside. This time, even without touching Terrence, her historic persona remained intact.

Tidying up the kitchen, Sarah was lost in thought until she heard his mother call out. Sarah dried her hands and hurried to the older woman.

"What is it, Mrs. Covington?"

"Oh, I just had a scare, my dear." She looked pale. "I thought I saw Thomas standing behind the drapes."

Sarah walked over and moved the curtains. "Nothing is there, ma'am," she said politely, letting the fabric fall back in place.

"I thought not but…" Mrs. Covington sighed, "…sometimes when I'm in this house alone, I see things that I shouldn't."

"You do?" Sarah asked, hoping to confirm that this was not an ordinary house.

"Oh, yes, I see my husband as he was 30 years ago…. I see the children we buried."

Sarah leaned closer to listen.

"Don't get me wrong, dear," Mrs. Covington continued, "it isn't frightening. It's like a story book." She looked up and smiled, crow's feet crinkling at the sides of her eyes.

"I understand," Sarah said, patting the frail woman's arm. "Sometimes I think I can feel the past, too." And, with that, Sarah was back in the keeping room in current attire, responding to a knock on the door. She looked over at Mrs. Covington, but no one was there.

The termite inspector had arrived in a bright yellow van with an inflatable bug affixed to the top. He was an upbeat young man, who whistled subconsciously as he checked the floorboards, rafters, and joists. Sarah watched with amusement as he reached under his gray hoodie and produced what seemed to be an endless array of tools. In between whistling and pounding, he made small talk with Sarah and ended up sharing his mother's recipe for cornbread. After he completed his work in the main house, Sarah showed him the outbuildings.

As they entered the smokehouse, Sarah could swear she saw ham hocks hanging from the heavy metal hooks. "Can't you just see those pork butts?" she asked, picking up on the residual scent of molasses and smoke. "Only in my mind," he deadpanned. A char still clung to the ceiling above the central fire pit, and a hint of salt and pickling spices lingered. An hour later, ham hocks gone, she bid him good-bye, returned to the main house to lock it up, and was back in her car with the heat blasting.

On Monday, Sarah called the Town Clerk's office about re-staking the property lines and was given the names of several surveyors. Sarah decided on a local company and set up an appointment for Wednesday. That morning, thrilled to not go into the office, she drove directly to the old house. The day was bright and unseasonably warm, so she waited outside. She could hear the surveyors' truck approaching long before she saw the green and gold seal on the side. A young surveyor and his helper got out, both armed with tripods.

As they gathered their gear, they explained to Sarah that the property consisted of two parts—the primary land grant and a division added in 1765 as part of a dowry. Apparently, with the pairing of the Covington grandson and his bride, the family had gained a sizeable tract of land from the Hawthornes. Sarah had guessed as much and left the young men to do their work.

Sarah walked across the lawn to the house with Terrence's marriage proposal echoing in her head. She imagined a grand Colonial wedding and a day of celebration. Although Terrence and Sarah were living a simple life, they came from families of means, so she knew their commitment ceremony would have been well-appointed.

When Sarah entered the house, she was immediately greeted by her younger sisters from long ago—Silence and Tilda—two giggling girls dressed in layers of ruffles. They wore high-laced shoes and had bows sitting pertly in their hair. "Sarah, quick!" Silence said as she grabbed Sarah under the arm.

"Close your eyes," Tilda added, taking her other arm. Together they escorted Sarah to a back room.

"There! You can open your eyes now!" they squealed. "We just finished the hem…and added a few things."

Sarah opened her eyes in disbelief. What had begun as a plain dress was now an embroidered masterpiece adorned with metallic thread and pink rosettes. "It's beautiful," she said, reaching to touch the rich russet cloth. She planted a kiss on the cheek of each young charge and followed that with a hug. "Thank you so much. I hope I'll do it justice."

"You will, you will, no need to worry," they said in unison, telling her that a bath had been drawn and that they would help braid her hair.

Sarah took a moment to collect her thoughts, realizing that she was bidding farewell to life as a carefree girl and embarking on the responsibilities of a wife and confidant. She worried about the dangers that could befall her husband-to-be and wondered if she could adequately carry on his ruse. She stepped out of the drab housedress and stockings she was wearing and removed her modest cap, letting her golden-red tresses spill down her back.

"This will be fun," Tilda exclaimed, jarring Sarah out of her serious mood.

"Mother and Father will be here soon," Silence added as she guided Sarah into the deep tub filled with water warmed on the hearth.

"And Terrence?" Sarah asked them, eager to see her groom.

"You know you can't see him until later," Tilda chided, wagging an invisible finger with her voice. Sarah nodded, letting herself be swept up in the moment.

In the hours that followed, there was a flurry of activity. Bathed, dried, and hair done in plaits that wrapped around her head, Sarah slipped into her dress, carefully lifting the skirt as not to trip or dirty the edges. She could see her reflection in the windowpane and gasped at the fashionable sight of herself. A fitted white cap, decorated with intricate stitching waited on a nightstand for the wedding procession.

There was a knock at the door and someone brought in flowers for her to carry. The blooms had been carefully dried from the summer garden and were tied with a dark green velvet ribbon. They still smelled of sunshine and open fields. Someone else handed her a cup of tea, warm and soothing. She could hear chairs being arranged and the muffled voices of her parents as they talked to the pastor. Then the room fell silent.

"Please be seated," the pastor instructed in a resonant tone, followed by the shuffling of shoes. A clavichord rang out, signaling the wedding party to assemble. Selected guests filed forward to line up under an exquisite brocade canopy adorned with paper maché fruits and bittersweet branches. Her favorite aunts, uncles and cousins sat in chairs toward the front; family friends, a few rows back.

After a considerable pause, someone knocked on the door and whispered, "Are you ready?"

Sarah held her breath as she heard the bridal music begin. Then, as if rehearsed a dozen times, she stepped out, took her father's arm and, in small, deliberate steps, walked toward Terrence, who was flanked by his brothers and mother.

Terrence was impeccably groomed in a finely tailored burgundy vest and waistcoat of pale gray imported wool. His black britches were fit to end precisely above cream-colored stockings that matched his shirt. The high sheen of his black shoes was reflected in the square silver buckles that adorned them. A paisley neck scarf, tied in a way that accentuated his rugged good looks, offset his hair—a sheaf of flax pulled back with a forest-green ribbon paired to Sarah's bouquet. He stood at his full height with his left arm gallantly tucked behind his back.

"How could he be mine?" she thought, studying his handsome face, broad shoulders, and confident stance, trying to quiet the heart that pounded out of control.

"How could she be mine," he marveled, finding it difficult to square his jaw when he really wanted to grin foolishly, twirl her off her feet, whisk her away, and not emerge for a fortnight.

The nuptials were genteel and included passages from the Bible, several hymns, and blessings from their guests. When it came to the vows, Sarah repeated the words flawlessly, her nervousness belied only by a slight tremble in the bouquet that she held. Terrence reached out to steady her hand as he said his vows in turn.

The pastor sanctioned their union with a sweeping motion after which a soft murmur of "oohs" and "ahs" rippled across the room. Their kiss lasted but a moment before the music began to play. The guests applauded and followed the couple as they walked to the grand dining room where three trestle tables were set end-to-end. "Hear! Hear!" the toasts began as cider and wine were poured and platters of food, served: quail, venison, turkey, duck…roasted potatoes, corn relish, lima beans…bowls of cooked apple slices drizzled with honey and dotted with cranberries, winter squash casserole, Indian pudding, and loaves of gloriously golden bread.

Silence and Tilda could hardly contain their excitement as they chattered like magpies at a children's table. Ever gracious,

Terrence led Sarah around the room to be introduced to relatives she had never met. Hugs and good wishes surrounded them.

Dessert was no less impressive than the first course: a bounty of nuts and sweetmeats, blocks of maple sugar candy and a rich wedding cake set high atop a pedestal platter. The cake was brimming with mace and molasses, currants and raisins, finely shaved almonds and delicate threads of citron. As Sarah cut into it, she could detect a generous helping of brandy that only added to the festivities. The scent of cinnamon and cloves permeated the room as guests readily passed their plates to receive a slice.

After tea and liqueur were consumed, the men adjourned for a smoke, while a group of women cleared the tables. Vats of steaming water for dishwashing had been drawn from the fireplace kettles and leftovers were put into crocks before placing them in the cool root cellar.

Long after darkness fell and only when the last guest was gone, did Terrence lift Sarah into his arms and carry her across the threshold to their room. There was no need to rush this time. They stood in front of a blazing fire, enveloped in the flickering light. They alternated in removing a singular garment from each other—slowing undoing buttons, unlacing stays—prolonging the moment until they were both standing there bare and honest. They tenderly explored each other until their need was too great. Once their desire had been quenched, they lay entwined, drifting between conversation and exhaustion. Finally, sleep won.

When a flock of Canada geese roused Sarah, all she could think about was the story of Romeo and Juliet, not wanting to hear the meadowlark, not wanting the night to end. Now man and wife, they rolled over blissfully until sun streamed through the window.

Terrence stepped out to the washroom where a bowl, pitcher, and chamber pot were stored, and Sarah followed. Returning, they sat on the edge of the bed, grinning in the sunlight and holding hands. "Good morning Mrs. Covington," Terrence said, pouring himself into her eyes. "Good morning, Mr. Covington," Sarah replied with a teasing grin.

Startled by a knock, Sarah pulled on a house gown and turned the knob, surprised to see the surveyors standing there. "Ms. Sutherland?" they queried as she blinked several times. "Are you OK? We called from outside, but you didn't answer."

"Oh, I'm fine," Sarah managed to say. "I just got engrossed reading," she bluffed, pointing to a book on the nightstand. By this time, her house gown had been replaced by jeans and a sweater, her slippers transformed into trail boots.

"Will you be billing us, or should I pay now?" Sarah asked, trying to recover her composure. The surveyors were happy to bill, and Sarah provided them with the Randolphs' address.

"Thank you again," Sarah reiterated as she ushered them out, adding "Happy Holidays" for good measure. She glanced over her shoulder hoping Terrence would still be there, but the room was untouched—and unoccupied.

In an all-too-familiar ritual, she climbed into her car and tried to separate her realities. Her emotions ricocheted between joy and guilt. Hands on the wheel, she studied her ring finger encircled by Carter's matching band. Secretly she hoped she would see the family heirloom Terrence had given her, but that belonged to another age. Or did it? The lines of demarcation were starting to blur.

Sarah told herself she had done nothing wrong—that these incidents were some sort of fantasy, daydream, or illusion—a self-preserving escape from a mundane life. But, how could they feel so authentic? Was she losing touch?

Her Colonial wedding day had seemingly been compressed into a mere few hours, so she headed to the office. That night, thoughts of Terrence coalesced in her mind as she struggled to sleep. They re-emerged with the frost in the morning.

Quiet times were the toughest. She'd stare out the kitchen window imagining him working in the woods behind the house, sleeves rolled up, veins popping, thigh muscles straining to move a boulder. She could almost see him stop to sharpen his favorite blade on the whetstone he kept in his pocket, pushing back his blond hair that had escaped the tie.

Unable to shake her preoccupation with Terrence, she wondered if she were psychologically unstable and in need of medication, but much like someone with bipolar disorder, who loves their highs, she didn't want to 'get better.' She rationalized that her intimate indulgences truly belonged to someone else and were hurting no one. But, in her heart of hearts, she knew at the very least, she was cheating her family by being away from them—physically and mentally. She vowed to do better.

That evening after dinner, Sarah busied herself making posters for her company's annual charity drive, purposely talking to Carter about school and the new lab equipment he had ordered. Carter seemed pleased that she was taking an interest. As she stacked her posters against a wall, she attentively listened to Abby rehearse her lines for the school play. While Abby began a second run-through, Sarah stitched additional petals onto the flower costume that would encircle her daughter's pretty face. At nine o'clock, taking advantage of holiday hours, she went to a hobby store with Jared to purchase supplies for his classroom project—a diorama of Fort Ticonderoga—prying out of him an admission that he liked a certain girl in study hall. She relished the normalcy of it all.

On Saturday morning, armed with Holiday Happiness signs and collection boxes, she made her rounds through town, chatting with the manager at the market, catching up with a client at the cleaners, and encountering a neighbor at the medical building.

The neighbor was quite a talker and it took several tries to break free. When she finally did, Sarah turned hastily to leave, accidentally clipping a woman, who was carrying coffee. "I'm so sorry," Sarah apologized. "I didn't see you around my signs."

"Not a problem," the woman replied, calmly ignoring the coffee that trickled down her blouse.

"I'll get some paper towels!" Sarah said, urgently looking for a Ladies' Room.

"Not necessary," the woman answered, nodding toward the directory. "I work here."

Sarah's eyes went to the directory on the wall. "Barrows," the woman said, extending her free hand before turning to leave. "Dr. Sam Barrows."

Sarah noticed that Samantha Barrows was at the top of the roster. Dr. Barrows was a psychiatrist with a long line of credentials after her name.

"Would you believe it?" Sarah joked to herself as she headed for the car. "Here I'm convinced I'm crazy, and I collide with someone who can tell me if I am." In the curve of the window glass, she caught her off-kilter reflection. "I suppose I really *do* need some help," she admitted, as she looked at the distorted image of her face. "Maybe I'd better nip this in the bud before it gets out of hand. The sooner I know what's going on, the sooner I can get back to my regular life." With that, she retraced her steps to the medical building, rode the elevator to the top floor and knocked on the door. "Is Dr. Barrows in?" she asked.

"She's with a patient," the receptionist replied. "May I help you?"

Using the coffee mishap as an excuse, Sarah offered to pay for the doctor's dry cleaning, eventually mustering the courage to make an appointment. January 14th at 2:00. Once back in the car, she felt a tremendous sense of relief.

That evening Sarah sat with her family in the pews of a small white chapel. The pristine room was decorated with fragrant evergreen garlands and generous red bows. The original candles in the vintage fixtures had been replaced with tiny LEDs that emitted a soft glow. Sarah flashed on the past, but quickly set it aside.

The bells began clear and true. Like small voices, they rang out, harked and boomed, then whispered sweet and low. "I love hearing the bell ringers," Sarah said, snuggling into her husband's arm. "The tone is so pure and peaceful." Carter reached over to cover her hand with his, an expression of contentment crossing his face. Even the kids were getting along as they leaned forward together, trying to follow each strike. Sarah scanned the audience. Some people she knew. Some she didn't. Their faces were serene, washed in the tranquility of the season and the sanctity of the small church.

As the musical director paused to explain the next arrangement, Sarah shifted her focus. Each bell ringer was dressed in a full-sleeved white shirt and red vest, a gold silk ascot tied high at the neck. Upon seeing this costume, Sarah was reminded of Terrence in his fitted red coat, crisp white shirt, and ruffled neck sock. "Funny that they were called Lobsterbacks," she mused, recalling the slang name given to British Loyalists. "They were far more elegant than any crustaceans I know," she thought, humoring herself.

One of the bell ringers in the back row looked a lot like Terrence. "So young," she observed. "So hopeful"—which made her wonder if Terrence saw *her* in the same light. Come to think of it, she had never noticed whether her hair was more auburn, her skin softer, or her breasts firmer when she was within the walls of the house. Maybe it was this 'selflessness' that made the experience so surreal. She convinced herself that Terrence must surely see her as she did him—vital and of similar age. "Could you imagine if that weren't the case?" she thought, horrified. "I'd be twenty years his senior...or we'd both be more than 250 years old!" Sarah stifled a snicker.

A week before Christmas, she went into town to pick up the charity drive donations and take them to the volunteers at Grange Hall. Sarah always welcomed this diversion from the commercial overload of Christmas. She loved folding baby blankets, pairing hats and mittens, flattening bright wrapping paper until it sat smooth over puzzles and coloring books. "Sarah, would you be able to deliver some of these things for us?" She looked up into the kind eyes of Reverend Smythe, who coordinated the effort. "There's a new family down near Baker's Cove and they haven't found work yet." Sarah nodded to confirm. The proximity to the Covington estate was not lost on her.

This was one of those early winter days when the smell of snow was in the air. Thick clouds piled up on the horizon, creating a bank against the yellow sky. As she rode, Sarah watched slow curls of smoke rise from chimneys to greet the firmament, but she couldn't tell where the smoke ended, and the clouds began.

She pulled in front of the humble house, unloaded a basket filled with food and presents and carried it to the door. The occupants protested initially, but soon a circle of boisterous children had gathered around their parents, diving into the bounty of gifts, squealing with delight. Sarah smiled as she walked back to her car.

Continuing to the Tory house, she parked just beyond it and cut across the lawn, slipping into the unlocked back door. From that perspective, she could see into the sitting room. Terrence was drinking something robust—posset? wassail?—standing close to a stunning woman. Raising his glass, he was laughing heartily, his other hand resting lightly on the woman's shoulder.

Sarah felt a pang of jealousy. She realized she was merely a spectator and had no right to feel anything, but there she was, peering at a lavish holiday party to which she had not been invited. Terrence was every bit as dashing as when she first saw him, flashing his smile readily as he bantered around conversation with the guests.

As Sarah watched, her heart sank, realizing he was preoccupied. Turning to leave, she backed up and sent a stack of cookware crashing to the floor. She could see that heads turned in her direction as she tried unsuccessfully to set the pots straight.

"Sarah, are you all right?" Terrence called from the other room.

Not knowing what to do, she answered, "I'm fine, just clumsy," as she gathered up her long skirts and made her way toward the sitting room carrying a mincemeat pie.

Long skirts? Pie? Her transition had come on extremely fast.

Terrence watched with admiration as she served the guests, sharing pleasantries and making small talk. Sarah could hear snippets of conversation, mostly from a British point of view.

"Let them pay the Sugar Tax or choose to forego sugar," one hefty gentleman chortled. "It's the least they can do to offset our debt."

"And let them house us while they're at it," another fellow laughed, patting the royal crest on his lapel. "We earn it for taking care of them."

"Hear! Hear!" Terrence toasted as they all raised their glasses high.

"Sarah," Terrence called, waving her over and nodding toward the woman at his side. "Isn't it wonderful that Lilah and Thomas are expecting their first child?" Sarah felt relieved that Terrence had been talking to his sister-in law. She felt even better when he added, "And hopefully someday soon we'll do the same."

Aware that her cheeks had reddened, Sarah lowered her eyes to avoid Terrence's playful stare. He just smiled and downed his drink, following her as she served the last of the pastries.

Sarah tried to gauge the passage of time as the party ran its course. "I must be going," she finally heard one of the guests say, and she saw Terrence hand Mrs. Brigit her cape.

Mrs. Brigit gave Sarah a compassionate look and in cultured English said, "Now don't worry too much, my dear, when he's off in Boston. Someone has to check on those Admiralty Courts to make sure they're collecting our duties."

Sarah feigned a smile, but worried about Terrence nonetheless. After bidding Mrs. Brigit goodnight, he took Sarah aside and assured her that upon completing his required rounds in the city, he'd be staying in a safe house provided by friends.

"What's going on?" Sarah asked, carefully moving a tower of Queen's Ware plates recently arrived from Staffordshire.

"I've gotten word that Boston merchants and lawyers are actively resisting the Stamp Act. I want to make sure we channel that energy into productive protest."

"Then I won't see you for a while?" she asked.

"I'm afraid not," Terrence said, hugging her tightly and whispering something into her ear. She blushed and returned to the kitchen where her long skirts vanished as quickly as they had appeared. She closed the door behind herself and headed into the encroaching dusk.

Sarah could hardly discern her car, but wound her way toward the vague shape and climbed in. She felt buoyant after this brief encounter and made her New Year's resolution then and there. Whatever this was, right or wrong, real or not, she would enjoy it. No guilt. No soul searching. No analysis. She would celebrate the holidays with her family, get caught up in the spirit of the season, and then put her head on straight.

When she arrived home, her children were abuzz with Christmas Eve excitement. Carter had brought in some large poinsettias and a bottle of champagne. She placed the bright red plants in a basket near the fireplace and the bubbly stuff in the fridge. The next morning was resplendent with gifts and magic that lasted throughout the following week. New Year's Eve arrived without fanfare and, as usual, she and Carter were happy to stay home, stream a movie, and be off the roads.

By January 13th, Sarah had convinced herself that she really didn't need professional help. "What if word got out?" she worried. "I'd be the laughing stock of the town. My career would be over, my kids would be taunted at school, and my husband would have to explain his crazy wife to his colleagues. I'll cancel the appointment first thing in the morning," she decided.

"Wake up! Sarah, wake up!" her husband's voice shouted through a fog.

Trying to see in the dark bedroom, she sat up. "What's the matter?" she asked, squinting.

"You tell me," Carter demanded.

"What do you mean?" she asked.

"You were crying and thrashing around...punching your pillow. You must have been having a nightmare."

"I don't even remember dreaming," she said, rubbing her eyes.

"Well, you were calling out something about the house—having to go back to the house…."

She sat there trying to clear her head. "Must have had work on my mind."

"Well that wasn't all. You were asking for someone named Terrence."

She looked up, startled, afraid she might have said too much in her sleep.

"You're not seeing someone on the sly, are you?" her husband teased, trying to relax her, then more seriously added, "Or is there someone named Terrence bothering you at work?"

Sarah was suddenly awake and not quite sure what to do. Carter has always been there for her and they shared a mutual trust.

"Want to hear a weird story?" she asked.

"Sure," he said with a bit of hesitation. "I'll put on some herbal tea." She shuffled down the stairs to the kitchen after him.

"I'm not quite sure how to begin, but something *has* been on my mind," Sarah started. "It's about the old Covington estate I'm selling."

Carter set down two steaming mugs, and she instinctively wrapped her hands around one of them as much for something to grip as for warmth. "Go on," he prompted.

"Well, I've been over to the house a few times and each time I've gone, I've uh…."

She took a sip of her tea. "I've uh…."

"You've what?" he asked, leaning forward.

"I've felt something there. A person, a presence. Like I wasn't alone. There, I've said it."

"You mean, like a ghost?" he asked, eyebrows lifting.

"Well, sort of, but much more tangible. At first, it was just a feeling. Then it got more intense." She noticed he was looking at her quizzically.

"Don't laugh. Please don't laugh," she begged.

"I'm not laughing," Carter said, eying her with concern.

She continued. "I went back another time, and it happened again. But it was in the past."

"What was?"

"Terrence Covington," she blurted out. "Grandson of the first owner, Thomas Covington."

"Are you telling me you've seen the ghost of Terrence Covington?" Carter pressed, both bewildered and amused.

"Well, it was more than that," she added, compelled to come clean.

"More?" he asked. "What more do you need than seeing a ghost? Isn't that a once-in-a-lifetime experience?"

Sarah took a deep breath. "I don't know how to say this, and I can't believe I am, but he was very real, only set back in time. I wasn't afraid of him. Just the opposite. I was drawn to him. He was commanding, fascinating, and (she paused to choose her words carefully) — he seemed to know me. It was as if I belonged there." Her shoulders slumped as she waited for Carter's reaction.

Carter seemed uncomfortable. "I want to believe you, I really do, but you have to admit, this sounds pretty far-fetched." He paused to think. "I'm just worried about you. Maybe you're getting sick. Do you have any other symptoms? Pain? Hallucinations?"

"I'm not sick, and this is not a hallucination!" Sarah insisted. "I feel fine."

"It doesn't sound fine. Do you know what triggers it?" Carter probed.

"Nope. Haven't a clue."

Carter slid over and put his hand on hers. "Maybe there's something else going on in the house, something environmental like black mold, fumes from cleaning fluid, or a carbon monoxide leak. You know...something that's compromising your judgment."

Sarah looked hopeful at the thought of a scientific explanation.

"Were you drowsy or dizzy?" Carter asked, trying to determine the cause.

"A little," Sarah admitted, not revealing anything more.

Carter continued in his husbandly role. "Well, you might want to have a hazmat crew check it out."

"That's a thought," she allowed but didn't seem too convinced. A stilted silence followed.

Carter tried another approach. "On the other hand, maybe you *did* see something unusual. There's a lot in science we can't explain. Maybe you were just picking up vibes from the setting and imagined what life was like back then."

"This was more than *imagining* something. I was there, in the past. Transported," Sarah protested, adamant. "You know, I'm as grounded as they come. But I saw something and felt something so amazing, so all-consuming, that I can't seem to let it go." Sarah was clearly getting upset.

"Have you told anyone else?" he asked.

"No, I'm not that stupid," she said, snorting out a little laugh that bordered on tears. He seemed relieved.

"I'm not suggesting you are." The tension between them was palpable.

Sarah swirled the tea around in her cup, buying some time to compose herself. "I just wonder if there's something mentally wrong with me."

"I doubt it," Carter said, "But if you feel that way, you could talk to someone other than me…you know, a professional."

"Funny you should say that," Sarah replied. "A few weeks ago, I ran into a shrink when I was distributing signs for the holiday drive. I forced myself to make an appointment. It's for tomorrow, but I was going to cancel."

"Why cancel? Just take a personal day. It might put your mind to ease. You could even catch some of those post-holiday sales while you're in town." Carter, she knew, was trying to allay her fears.

"Do you think I'm crazy?" she asked.

"Absolutely not," he answered, dead serious. "But this way, *you'll* know you're not."

He stood up, guiding her in front of him. "Let's go back to sleep," he said, pointing to the stairs.

"You're probably right," she relented, as they climbed into bed. "I always get too wrapped up in everything."

"I *do* know that," he said, giving her a quick kiss. "I really wouldn't worry. There's usually a logical explanation for these things." Sarah smiled, curled up, and drifted off to sleep. He, on the other hand, lay wide-eyed, staring at the ceiling.

The next morning was cold and clear. The sun shone brightly, and Sarah woke up early, only to find the other side of the bed empty. Walking downstairs, she saw Carter silhouetted in front of his computer. "You're up and at 'em."

"Got a test to prepare," he mumbled. "What time is your appointment?" he asked.

"Two o'clock." She hesitated. "You still think I should go?"

"Why not? What's the doctor's name?"

"Sam Barrows," she replied.

"Barrows… Barrows…," he said, rolling the name around on his tongue. "That isn't by any chance a *Samantha* Barrows is it?"

"It is," she said, surprised. "You know her?"

"I know *of* her. I caught her on a webinar. I remember because she had gone to the Soviet Union to lead a panel on extrasensory perception. It was captivating. She was very good, well-spoken. I think you'll like her." His comments made Sarah feel better and she was happy that he was so supportive. She kissed him good-bye and grabbed her gloves.

Sarah parked in the town lot and walked to her favorite clothing store. She loved having time to herself, rummaging through bins of markdowns and trying on end-of-season shoes. She stepped into a nearby coffee shop for lunch before heading over to the medical building.

The waiting room was quiet and not too crowded. "Fill this out, please," the receptionist requested as she handed Sarah a form. The questions were routine. Name, address, insurance company, health history—but she stopped at "Nature of illness." "What do I write?" Sarah thought to herself. "Obsessed with handsome apparition?" She decided to write down "troubling experience" and leave it at that.

Dr. Barrows had dark eyes and a firm handshake. She was an attractive older woman, about 5' 6", with her hair cut into an angled bob. She looked more authoritative than when Sarah first met her, but she greeted Sarah warmly. "What brings you here?" the doctor asked, gesturing to one of two chairs.

"So much for the couch," Sarah thought, relying on sarcasm to quell her nerves.

Words came more easily than expected…maybe because they had spilled out the night before. "Why does this bother you?" Dr. Barrows asked when Sarah was done.

"Well, I don't think it's real—but it feels real and it feels wrong," Sarah answered.

"Why is it wrong?" the doctor probed.

"Well, it's very sensual and seductive…secretive…like I shouldn't be there," Sarah explained, trying to find the right words.

"And where are you exactly when this happens?"

"In the house," Sarah said in a near whisper. "Or near the house."

"Is it wrong to be in the house?" Dr. Barrows asked.

"No, not in a legal sense. I'm a real estate agent; I have keys," Sarah explained. "What's wrong is that I'm in a strange place with a strange man…and I'm a happily married woman. I don't know if this place is in my mind or in some other…dimension. I'm just trying to make sense of it." Sarah said, getting agitated.

"Several things could be going on here," the doctor assured in a modulated voice. "There could be a physical cause: a tumor, a disease, a neural abnormality. There might be a chemical on the premises that's causing a toxic reaction." Sarah thought back to what Carter had said.

The doctor continued. "From a psychological standpoint, you might be creating a place in history as a means of self-actualizing—to reaffirm your existence, establish your value, confirm your worth. Or you could have in fact seen something unusual." Sarah sat back, listening. "But more likely, you're just grappling with an emotional need," the doctor soothed. Sarah was trying to be open-minded.

"As humans, we thrive on emotions," the doctor continued. "We crave mystery, adventure, love, excitement… all the attributes of a good book, right?" Sarah offered a weak smile in agreement.

"Well, sometimes we enhance our personal experiences when daily life is a little…dull."

"You think I'm making this up?" Sarah challenged, "…because I, uh, need to fill some sort of void?"

"Not necessarily, not even consciously, but it's a possibility," Dr. Barrows allowed. "I'd really like to learn more about what happens when you have one of these episodes."

"I'm more interested in learning *why*," Sarah retorted.

"Well, I think you may be wrestling with some unresolved issues. How's your relationship with your husband?"

Sarah stalled. "We're both busy with work and the kids. Don't talk as much as we used to…." Dr. Barrows made a few notes.

"And intimacy?"

"Not as often as before."

"Well, sometimes our needs are more easily expressed in a story than in a conversation. We create that story and repeat it so many times that it becomes real to us."

Sarah didn't like where this was going and felt herself recoil ever so slightly.

"But on the flip side," the doctor backpedaled, sensing Sarah's shift in attitude, "I do have a feeling, by the way you describe things, that you are extremely sensitive to your surroundings, aware of details, and in tune with other people…so maybe there *is* a basis for this experience."

"You mean, like having a sixth sense?" Sarah quipped.

"I don't usually call it that, but yes," the doctor acknowledged, slightly annoyed at the colloquial term. "I'm convinced that human beings possess many untapped abilities. You may have recently tapped into some of yours." The doctor was stern as she said this.

Sarah stared at her fingernails, not wanting to look the doctor in the eye.

Dr. Barrows elaborated. "People are extraordinarily capable of being receptive to each other, to animals, and to the forces of nature —but we tend to ignore it, suppress it. We become afraid. We don't practice these skills, so we lose them." Sarah sat patiently, arms braced, chin in hand.

"Not everything is crystal clear in this big universe," the doctor reminded. "We don't always have scientific proof. Look at faith and religion."

Sarah thought about that as Dr. Barrows continued. "This is probably just a phase that will pass as other interests demand your attention and as you renew your connection to your husband. But first, you should get a full physical."

"OK," Sarah agreed. "I'll set up an appointment with our family doctor."

"Good," Dr. Barrows confirmed, and then clearing her throat, she asked, "Do you want to go back to the house to try to learn more?"

"That's like asking an addict if he wants a fix." Sarah replied. "Of course, I do."

"Then you should do it, but with a safety net," Dr. Barrows suggested. "Let someone know you're going. Take a phone and a notepad. Pay attention to the things that lead up to your experience. Try to keep a mental diary of what you're seeing, hearing, smelling, tasting, touching…then afterward, write it down, send it to me, and we'll review it together."

Sarah agreed, still not sure what this exercise would prove. Outwardly, the advice seemed reasonable, but inwardly, she doubted the doctor's premise. "I don't think my life is so dull that I have to make this stuff up," Sarah told herself. "I didn't go looking for it." She thanked the doctor, got into her car, and headed home, although she hardly remembered the trip.

"Then she's not worried about a medical condition?" Carter asked, getting right to the point.

"Not really, but she wants me to get a check-up," Sarah answered. "Mostly I think she's trying to help me find a rational explanation. She suggested I go back to the house and, basically, take notes."

"Do you think that's wise?" Carter asked, letting his concern for Sarah mingle with his own insecurity in her 'seeing' another man.

Sarah shrugged. "She's the professional…."

"Well, doctors don't always know everything. It could be dangerous." Sarah thought it strange that Carter—a man who lived by facts and figures—would be wary of something so elusive.

"Well, I don't *have* to go," Sarah started to say, "but I think I should give it a try."

Carter removed his glasses, closed his eyes, and pressed the bridge of his nose, as if in pain. Once his glasses were back on, he looked at her directly. "I don't like the idea, but I guess you have to do what you have to do," he said, constructing an invisible wall between them. Sarah hated it when he sulked but getting to the bottom of this was important to her. And, yes, she wanted to see Terrence again.

3

NEW YEAR

"Are you sure you don't want to come with me?" Sarah asked, extending her invitation as an olive branch.

Carter shook his head no. "It probably won't work, if I'm there," he said, standing up to say good-bye.

"I don't know why I'm so nervous this time," she muttered as she searched for a yellow pad.

"Got your cell?" Carter asked. "That way, if Terrence isn't so interesting, you can call me instead." His attempt at humor fell flat.

"Very funny," she uttered. Clearly, Carter didn't understand how encompassing the experience was—as if she could pull away and punch in some numbers.

He kissed her quickly. "Just be careful," he said, returning to his seat.

"Thanks. Wish me luck," she called over her shoulder as she headed out the door. With a familiar purr, the car was up and running, and her concerns dropped by the wayside like the fence posts she passed.

The house was exactly as she had left it. Her key eased into the side lock and the distinctive smell of the fireplace welcomed her. She shed her coat and put down her pocketbook. Quietly, she walked into the kitchen. Nothing. She peered into the dining room where she had first seen Terrence. Nothing again. She almost felt indemnified as she walked from room to room, finding absolutely nothing out of the ordinary.

She had never called him by name before; he had always materialized on his own accord, but this time, she initiated the encounter... or hope of one. "Terrence," she said in a barely audible whisper. "Terrence, it's Sarah."

She turned around, and he was standing behind her. "Sarah, I was worried about you," he said. "I knew you'd come back, but it's been so long." He looked troubled as he said this.

"I'm sorry...but I have family...and work obligations," she answered, retaining some present-day recollection. She was not sure how realistic she should be, but he was surprisingly aware.

"I know, my love, that you also live in another age. I know you're torn between the two. I can see that in your eyes and the way you hold back your emotions." He paused. "I know you can't always be here when I need you."

Sarah felt as if she had somehow betrayed him. "You're right," she admitted. "I just don't understand it all—how I happen to be here...how I see you...how you see me...."

Terrence smiled. "First, I see you in all your youth and beauty as the day we met. Whether you see yourself that way is something I don't know. If you have aged in your other existence, so be it... but when you're here with me, you're ageless."

He walked slowly toward her as he spoke. The scent of lavender and lemon floated around him like an aura. "I'll make a mental note," she thought, "I'll write this down," but soon his lips were upon hers and his hips pressed against her hips. Recording the event seemed preposterous. Breaking away seemed impossible. She tasted a slight saltiness around his mouth and wanted more.

Pulling back, he looked at her with those vivid blue eyes. "Must you know all the Whys and Wherefores?" he asked. "Can't we just let this happen as we did before?"

"I'm trying to be rational here," she answered, attempting to gain perspective but finding it difficult to concentrate. "I want to be fair to my family," she started to say.

"But I *am* your family, Sarah," he challenged, "and besides, I need your help."

"With what?"

"In just a few minutes, Lord Bennington is coming to call. He expects me to rally with him tomorrow night on the town green to show my loyalty to the Crown. I have always taken his side and he knows the Covingtons to be staunch Royalists," Terrence explained. "You may have noticed our house is chalked with an X. That means it is to be spared by the British if violence breaks out." Sarah had wondered about the faint mark near the front door.

"What he doesn't know is that my sentiments changed a long time ago and they are getting harder to hide. The fire of freedom is in me and I am ready to take a stand. I cannot honor a king, who makes slaves of his subjects through unfair taxes and trade restrictions. I cannot respect laws that are lawless in this new land and I refuse to work for someone else's profit!" Sarah could hear rage rising in his voice.

"I know, Terrence," she said, trying to calm him. "I have heard of this anger. You confided in me when I first met you, but I didn't want to know too much. Now I do," she continued.

"Then I will tell you," Terrence said, not taking his gaze off her. "I've secretly befriended two rebel groups: the strategists call themselves 'the Sons of Liberty' and the fighters call themselves 'Minutemen.' The Sons are thinkers, philosophers, writers, derelicts, and dissidents...and the Minutemen are local farmers and merchants, who will fight at a moment's notice. These brave men are planning to ambush Bennington's military contingent tomorrow night, not to do serious harm, but to stage a show of force. In fact, the root cellar in this very house is stocked with every musket and bayonet we could find...every bullet and powder horn we could acquire."

Sarah was speechless. She felt as if she had dropped into a page from a history book. Terrence continued. "Yet, everything you and

I do in Bennington's presence must suggest our allegiance to the King. By no means is Bennington to go downstairs, though it is often his practice to stroll the premises as we talk. I need you to greet him, put on a fine show, sit him down, serve him tea, and smile your sweetest smile. Can you do that?"

Sarah shook her head yes, not quite believing what she had agreed to do. "But will he see me?" she asked in earnest.

"Of course, he will," Terrence answered. "You're with me now... in the sanctity of the house."

Sarah had just hung a kettle on a hook in the hearth when there was a knock at the door. She hurried to open it, wiping her hands on an apron, which somehow adorned her. She looked down and noticed her skirt was long, her shoes stocky, her blouse buttoned at her throat. It was as if she were wearing someone else's wardrobe.

"Lord Bennington," she heard herself say. "Do come in. May I take your wrap?" Her words sounded otherworldly.

Removing his hat, he entered, nodding good day. "And where is that man of yours?" he bellowed, displaying his own prominence.

"He's tending to the back fence. We had a rail come down and one of the lambs got out this morning. Took us two hours to find her," Sarah said, making conversation. "Terrence will be right back; he knows you're coming. Would you care for some tea while you wait?"

She was sure to flash a winning smile, though for the life of her, she had no idea where the explanation originated. Did they have lambs? She wasn't even sure they had a fence.

"Don't mind if I do, good lady," he answered, authoritatively sitting in the largest chair. Like Terrence, he was as real as could be, with a white powdered wig, ruddy complexion, and portly posture that challenged his waistcoat.

"And Lady Bennington...is she well?" Sarah heard herself ask as she poured the tea.

"Quite fine, quite fine, thank you. You should join her sometime after church. She and the ladies are quilting a coverlet for our daughter's dowry."

"That would be lovely," Sarah replied, assured she would somehow be gifted with the fine stitching skills that endowed the women of the day.

Just then Terrence entered, wind-blown and covered with slivers of straw. He quickly strode over to shake his visitor's hand. "Lord Bennington, it's wonderful to see you. Please pardon my tardiness, but Sarah must have told you we had a lamb escape."

"She most certainly did and delightfully, too. You've got quite a fine woman here, young lad!" Lord Bennington beamed, slapping Terrence on the shoulder.

"Yes, I do," said Terrence. "I am truly blessed." He glanced at Sarah in a way that went through her like a warm flood.

"Please excuse me, gentlemen. I've got bread baking," Sarah said, fluffing a pillow as she left the room. Through the doorway, they could see her maneuvering a long bread peel into the opening of the large beehive oven. Terrence threw another log on the fire as Lord Bennington lit his pipe. Sarah could hardly believe what she was watching.

Pulling the steaming loaves from the hot chamber, without a clue how they got there, she set them on a rack to cool. She could overhear the men talking. Lord Bennington was loud and pompous as he spoke of "those pesky Colonists...all full of themselves...probably couldn't scare a crow out of a corn field." Terrence responded in kind, laughing appropriately and offering equally derogatory remarks.

Both men paused to thank Sarah as she poured tea and served the warm bread with summer jam. Then they resumed their boisterous talk, amending their tea with brandy and their conversation with bravado. She heard Lord Bennington lay out plans for the Loyalist rally, praising the King's troops for their performance on the frontier, hinting at the build-up to come in Western Massachusetts and New York State. But, just as the fire started to sputter and darkness began to fall, Bennington finished his tea, stood up, put on his hat, and prepared to leave. He stopped at the door, suddenly remembering. "So, Covington, have you finished that root cellar yet?" he asked. "Last time I was here, you were going to build some shelving and show me your handiwork."

As Terrence struggled to compose a response, Sarah stepped out of the kitchen, towel in hand. "Well, he's been working very hard on it," she piped in. "I'm surprised you couldn't hear all the banging in town. Quite a racket! But he won't let me or anyone else see it until it's done. He claims it's a surprise."

"Well, so be it," Bennington said, calling a final good-bye. Terrence stood there a moment, looking at Sarah, who had stepped back to the kitchen table. Once Bennington was out of sight, Terrence joined her, reaching his arms around her shoulders from behind. "Bloody good actors, aren't we?" he said, finding the sweet spot on her neck that made her squirm.

"You were wonderful, as usual," he whispered, leading her away from the table.

"And you are a wonderful liar," she said as she followed him. "But I worry about you. Suppose you get wounded or worse yet, killed."

"I won't let that happen," he said. "It's just a standoff, and besides, I'll be with the British. It's my friends, who are in greater danger."

Sarah knew she could not change this mind, nor would she try. "Do you need anything, then? I mean, can I do anything to help you prepare?" Sarah asked.

"I just need you, my love, as I always do. You give me strength and purpose," he said. "Please stay longer."

"I don't even know what time it is," Sarah sighed. "Does time stop here?" she asked.

"I haven't figured that out yet," Terrence replied. "But I do know that when you're in this house, you defy time."

"Terrence, I've talked to a professional about you," she warned, calling up a smattering of modern recollection.

"You mean some sort of doctor chap?"

"Well actually it's a doctor lady...I mean, she's a female doctor," Sarah replied.

"Fancy that!" he said, rubbing his chin. "And do tell, what does she say? That you're crazy as a loon?" he teased. Sarah was surprised he was so direct.

"Uh, not yet," she hedged.

"And you know what, she won't! Because you're gifted. You can move through time," he stated, expressing his own philosophy. "Sarah, time is like water. You can try to contain it, direct it, control it, but eventually it goes exactly where it wants. If you're lucky, you can go with it."

His organic explanation was comforting, almost as comforting as the arms he wrapped around her. "Look at me," he said, turning her face upward.

She knew she was about to be lost in his gaze. "Was it hypnotism?" she wondered, trying to recall exactly what she was seeing, feeling, hearing... intending to record the details for Dr. Barrows...but her head was swimming and her heart was beating like a timpani drum.

"I love you. I have always loved you and I always will," Terrence said as he looked at her so deeply, she felt a surge inside. "What does it matter if we can't define ourselves by a clock or calendar? We must live for now—whatever that means—and for however long it lasts."

His fingers loosened her apron ties and lifted her billowing skirts. His hands were hot as they ran up the back of her thighs. "I can't keep letting this happen," she thought, drawing on a wisp of conscience, but she leaned into him and eagerly reached for him. "Don't stop," he said. "Everything else is a world away." And it was.

There was no tracking of time. No internet. No TV news. But she knew time had passed and finally told him she had to go. "Wish me luck tomorrow," he said, as he followed her to the door. "You're sure you can't stay longer?"

Despite the ache to do so, she shook her head no. "I can't. I have to go home." But neither of them moved. He was standing extremely close, towering over her, warm and tangible, protecting her, but also pushing her to try something daring. The lure of adventure was too great to resist and the thought of leaving him, too painful.

"What if you didn't go? What would happen?" he asked. "I really want you here when we confront Bennington tomorrow."

Sarah was uncertain. Was "tomorrow" the 24-hour reality she knew or was it a matter of minutes in this incredible time warp?

"I…I'm not sure," she stammered. "My husband knows I'm here…he's with the kids. He's aware that you exist…or seem to exist," she said, drawing from some short-term memory.

"Then he believes you?" Terrence asked, incredulous.

"Hard to say. He probably thinks you're a figment of my imagination that will soon disappear."

"I certainly hope not," Terrence declared, then more solemnly added, "So you can stay, right?"

"I guess, but only until after the confrontation."

"That sounds fair to me," said Terrence. "I'll milk Madeline, while you make supper. You do remember how to cook my favorite stew?" he asked, patting her on the backside.

"I think so," she said, not even sure what it was. But something steered her to the right ingredients. She walked purposefully down to the root cellar to gather turnips, onions, carrots, and cabbage. She found a chunk of salted meat and corn kernels preserved from the previous summer. There she saw arms and ammunition lined against the foundation…muskets, bayonets, powder horns, and kegs of gun power. Some of the weapons were simple in design, intended mainly to be functional. Others were monogrammed and edged in filigree.

"How can I be here?" she tried to reason, moving around the ominous stash. "More importantly, *why* am I here?"

Upstairs, she went about paring vegetables as if she had done it a thousand times. The thought of microwave cooking was light years away. She found the herbs she needed hanging from pegs between the rooms. Soon the kitchen smelled of bay leaf, savory and thyme, and in a candle's glow, it was all that anyone could want in a home.

Terrence opened the back door with one hand and in his other, clutched a bouquet of milkweed pods. "For you, my lady," he playfully postured, dipping into a low bow. She curtsied and accepted them, putting them into a pewter pitcher. She felt girlish and silly, but why not? She could be anything she wanted in this house.

As she set the table with pewter knives, forks, and molded spoons, she noticed the London mark stamped on the handles. Terrence affectionately watched her move deftly around the chairs, being the picture of domesticity. Sitting with him at the rough-hewn table surface, she felt as if they were part of a museum display. Each preoccupied with their own thoughts, they hardly spoke, but shared a kind of communication that didn't require words.

After supper, she cleared the plates as Terrence took out his favorite volume of verse. The book was worn; his father had it sent from England. "*Come live with me and be my Love,*" he read from Christopher Marlowe, ending with, "*And I will make thee beds of roses....*" Sarah was transfixed. No one had ever read poetry to her, not even her real-world husband. Then and there, she realized that seeing this exceptional man would not be an easy habit to break.

Sarah was exhausted by the time Terrence extinguished the candles and rolled back the bed covers. As she lay there, she replayed the day's events, but the more she wanted to remember, the less she could stay awake. That night they slept soundly between two layers of down ticking, soothed by the rise and fall of each other's breath.

"Sarah! Sarah! Where are you?" She could hear a far-off cry and pounding at the door.

"Terrence?" she said half-aloud. The bed was empty.

She wrapped herself in the patchwork bedspread, went downstairs, slid the chain, and opened the door. She stopped dead in her tracks. Instead of Terrence, it was Carter.

"Are you all right?" he asked, pushing his way past her.

Rubbing her forehead and then her eyes, she muttered, "I must have fallen asleep. I feel like I have a hangover." She tottered onto the edge of the couch.

"You had me scared half-to-death!" Carter yelled. She had never seen him so angry.

"You couldn't have called? That simple little courtesy...." His voice trailed off as he turned his back, shaking his head. "I couldn't leave the kids and come here looking for you—and I couldn't very well bring them with me, not knowing what I'd find. First, I just figured you were running late. So, I waited. And waited. I wanted to give you the time you needed."

"I'm so sorry," Sarah mumbled. "But I seem to lose track of time when I'm here."

"Apparently," Carter shot back.

Sarah sat quietly, trying to digest the onslaught. "What was I supposed to do?" he argued. "Call the cops and tell them my wife is at some deserted house, because she's hung up on a ghost?"

Sarah knew how ludicrous it appeared.

"Well, I was trying to notice all the details and take mental notes—just like Dr. Barrows wanted."

"And that took twenty-one hours?" Carter snapped.

"Twenty-one hours?" Sarah asked in disbelief.

"It's almost 8 a.m. Sunday morning," he announced, gesturing to the sun outside. "You started over here at 11:00 yesterday morning...remember?"

Sarah had a vague recollection of the timeframe, but it had gone so fast. Then she recalled Terrence asking her to stay.

"Your phone was turned off, you know," her husband fumed, just as she was about to ask why *he* hadn't called her.

"I don't remember doing that."

"Seems like you don't remember a lot these days," Carter jabbed. "Like your family."

Sarah was hurt. "I had a reason to stay longer," she started to explain, but quickly realized it would sound all wrong.

"A damn good one I hope," said Carter, pacing.

"He asked me to stay," she began.

"He—who? Lover boy?"

She deflected Carter's caustic remark, but it stung. "There was going to be a standoff with the British. He wanted me to help see him through it."

"Sarah, get a grip." Carter said, eyes drilling into her.

"I know this sounds crazy, but that's what happened," Sarah insisted as Carter stood tapping his foot, arms folded across his chest. "There was this British officer…Bennington…and I had to pretend to be a Tory wife. The Loyalists are marching on the town green tomorrow night…or is that today? Only they're going to be confronted by Colonists."

"Sarah, what on earth are you talking about?" Carter exploded. "Do you even know what year it is?"

"All I know is that I'm smack dab in 1766, with the American Revolution coming," she protested, "or at least I was."

Carter seethed through gritted teeth. "I encouraged you to see Dr. Barrows, because I thought it would help. I thought that once you got this out of your system, you'd give up."

"Oh, give up the ghost?" Sarah mocked. "It's not that easy," she said, staring back at him. "It's not that clear!"

"Well, one's thing *is* clear, if you ask me. This is getting way out of hand. You care more about this…uh…apparition… than you do about your husband and kids." Carter stormed out and slammed the door behind.

Sarah ran after him, standing barefoot on the step. "Carter, come back. I'm just trying to sort this out!"

"Sort it out at home," he yelled over his shoulder. "I'll see you there." He got into his car, threw it into reverse, and screeched down the driveway.

Sarah went back inside. Terrence was nowhere to be seen. The comfortable Colonial ambiance was gone. For the first time, she realized her feet were freezing. She went upstairs, put on her contemporary clothes, and stared into the ivory-handled mirror on the bureau. "What's wrong with me?" she agonized, using her knuckle to wipe away the hot tears that burnt her eyes. Not getting an answer, she picked up her pocketbook, hurried down the stairs, stepped outside and locked the door behind. "Why do I keep coming back?"

Sitting in the car, she felt utterly empty. Chilled. Hungry. Alone. She tried to ignore the sinking feeling in the pit of her stomach as she stared out the window. Rolling clouds were coming in, heavy with the weight of snow. She pulled on her gloves and turned the car around. Unlike Carter, she was in no rush to leave. She knew that what waited at home would be stilted conversation and a cool rebuke.

Looking across the fields, she noticed the tops of the swamp maples whipping around. The birds must have sensed a storm coming in, because there wasn't one in sight. In fact, there was no sign of life at all. The sky was dark. The hills were dark. And all the joy in her heart was replaced by darkness.

The more her life spun out of control, the more Carter began controlling his. He started staying late at school and scheduling evening appointments.

That Thursday, after the last students had left, Carter raised the window of his stuffy classroom, hoping a blast of oxygen would drive out the stale air. He adjusted the chair behind his desk, sat down, and opened his laptop. Waiting for it to boot up, he reached for his cell phone and made a call.

"She went back to the house," he said in a near whisper, "and this time, she stayed all night. It was as if she couldn't leave, and now I'm getting worried. She's been out of it all week." He paused, fidgeting with a rubber band. After a deep breath, he continued, "I know. I know. But this is going further than we expected. She was just supposed to be a canary in the gold mine—brought in to sense something. Otherwise I would never have agreed."

Carter was getting upset, forcefully sifting through papers as he talked. It was obvious that the person at the other end had a different take on things. "Yes, I *do* feel better now that Sam's in the picture," he admitted. "It was brilliant to place her on the route where Sarah was putting out signs—but that's not a failsafe. Sarah is fragile now, and I don't want anything to happen to her. If it did, I'd never forgive myself."

He continued to tap his pen as he talked. "Sure, I saw Sam's article on the Durham site," he confirmed. "I know she's a pro. But that's no guarantee Sarah can handle it."

Just then, there was a knock on the door. Carter jumped. "Hey, there," a fellow teacher intruded. "Want to meet us in the gym for a little hoop?" Carter told the person on the phone he had to go and quickly shifted gears.

"Sure," he said. "What time?"

"Be there at six," his colleague said.

It was already four o'clock. Carter graded some papers, then called Sarah at her office to say he'd grab some food from the vending machine. Sarah was getting used to this routine, but she headed home to relieve the sitter and to make dinner for the kids.

"What's this, Mommy? Abby asked, holding up a small piece of paper as she walked into the kitchen. She held the page corner bearing the Colonial design.

"Where did you get that?" Sarah asked with more of an edge to her voice than she intended.

"I found it in your coat pocket, when I was looking for gum," Abby said sweetly.

Sarah composed herself. "Actually, it came from the house I'm selling. I think it's from a very old book."

"You're not supposed to tear books, you know," Abby said with great import.

"You're right," Sarah agreed. "It probably was an accident. Can you please put it back?"

Abby went off toward the coat tree in the entryway, and then down the hall to do her homework, but Sarah could still hear the television on in the next room. "Abby," she called, "Time to shut off the TV and get busy on your book report or you'll be working all weekend."

The nine-year-old called back. "I will in a minute, but there's some guy talking about that place we went."

"What place?" Sarah asked, heading toward the den.

"You know, where we saw the baby's grave," she said.

"The old Southbridge Cemetery?" Sarah asked, coming into the room.

The newscaster was still on screen. "Local authorities are unsure what caused the damage to the Covington plot, but many of the stones are broken and others upturned. Fortunately, our Boy Scouts have volunteered to set things right."

Sarah was immobilized. There was "her" headstone on its side. The camera moved to Molly, the librarian, a spokesperson for the Historical Society. "We're heartbroken that something like this happened. These old stones are part of our local and national heritage, and people are still interested in the Covingtons. Just the other day, we had visitors in town doing research on them."

"What do you think caused it?" Abby asked as she turned off the set.

"Maybe the frost," Sarah suggested. "Maybe vandals," she added as she walked out of the room. "Maybe a tremor in the Force," she said under her breath, borrowing a line from *Star Wars*.

Just then, Jared rushed into the kitchen. "Where's my Boy Scout cap? I need it for this weekend," he accused, as if his mother had taken it.

"On the table where you left it." Sarah called to him as he stomped into the dining room. "Why do you need it?"

"We're going down to the old cemetery on Saturday to set up the stones that were knocked over. Our troop leader said the newspaper will be sending a photographer, so we have to be in uniform. Tommy's mother will pick me up at 8:30."

Sarah shuddered at the thought of Jared walking among the dead she seemed to know so well. And, yet, she couldn't tell him not to go.

On Saturday, with Jared out, Abby at a friend's, and her husband on errands, Sarah lingered in the kitchen watching birds flit in and out of the feeders in their yard. In a few months, it would be spring, and the entire countryside would change.

Her thoughts were interrupted by the phone ringing. "Dr. Barrows? Why are you calling me?" Sarah asked, puzzled by the outreach. Hearing the reason, Sarah was apologetic. "Oh, I am so sorry. I completely forgot to send you my notes. Let me get them organized and I'll email them today." She hung up and shook her head as if to dispel the obligation. She had not been back to see Dr. Barrows since January 14th and weeks had passed since she spent that long night in the house. She had tried to jot down her recollections, but everything seemed unbelievable. How could she possibly write about it and retain a shred of dignity?

Sarah turned on her desktop, opened her email, summarized a few things, and hit Send. "Dr. Barrows will think I'm nuts—and I wouldn't blame her."

A few hours later, Jared returned, red-faced from the cold, but exuberant as he described their civic efforts. Washing his hands, he stopped and looked up at his mother, "Did you know they had a son with the same name as mine? Jared Covington. I set his stone back up and I felt like he thanked me. Weird, huh?" Jared kissed his mother on the cheek and hurried to his room. Sarah knew the feeling.

That week, the Randolphs called to say their financing was in place and that they could move to Purchase and Sale on the Covington property. They had scheduled a greenhouse vendor to show up the following Saturday. Could Sarah be there? Sarah was increasingly annoyed at the Randolphs' continued imposition, but the promise of a commission was greater than her irritation. Knowing she would be outside and not alone in the house, Sarah agreed, assuming she would not be swept away as she had previously been. She made it a point to tell Carter that a greenhouse rep would be there with her.

Carter could care less about the renovations but seemed more concerned about Sarah than before. Still, he didn't stand in her way. Thinking of Dr. Barrows, Sarah put a small tape recorder—a relic from her real estate training—into her pocket, hoping she would remember to use it. She assured Carter she'd try to be vigilant about the time and encouraged him to swing by, knowing full well he wouldn't.

The ivy along the road had long since dried up and blown away, leaving the old stone walls gray and barren. But, in the recesses of rock, where ice was starting to melt, there were the tell-tale signs of green shoots—a welcome sight this time of year.

The greenhouse company truck was already there when Sarah arrived, and the rep, waiting in the front seat, gestured a greeting with the brim of his cap. Sarah acknowledged and he stepped out. "So, you want to add a greenhouse in the back?" he asked.

"Well, not me. The new owners. I'm just the real estate agent," she explained as they walked around the house.

"Looks like a decent location," the rep said, zipping up his logo-imprinted jacket. "Ground is nice and flat, and you've got good drainage. No overhanging trees…lots of light." He made a sweeping gesture. "Do you know what kind they want?" he asked, pulling a brochure from his side pocket. "They gave me some specs and these models can all be sized."

"I'm not sure, but I'll pass this along," Sarah said, accepting the booklet. "I really don't know their budget, but I'm sure they'd appreciate a few recommendations and quotes for any custom work."

The rep's heavy Timberland boots made impressions in the squishy ground as they walked across the sleeping herb beds. "My grandmother's garden used to smell like this," he said with a bit of nostalgia.

"Thyme, I think," Sarah informed. "Smells great, doesn't it?" She inhaled deeply. Slowly she picked up another scent. "And lavender," she added, figuring they had brushed against the low, woody plants. Brochure in hand, she found a seat on the garden wall. She could hear the rep talking in the distance as he took notes. "This is such a good place for a laundry basket," she thought, looking around at the flat surface. A large brown ash basket sat next to her, filled with clothes sewn from unbleached cotton and homespun wool.

"Are you done yet?" a slightly impatient voice called from the house.

"Just a minute," she heard herself say as she stood up to drape a shirt over the cord that stretched between two sturdy poles. She had fashioned split pegs bound with wire at one end to hold each item in place.

Terrence was leaning in the doorway. "Like my handiwork, huh? Much easier than walking up to the trees." He looked self-satisfied as he admired the clothesline. Sarah smiled as she gathered the empty basket and headed toward the house. She did appreciate how handy he was—and how he tried to make her life easier.

"How's your arm," she asked, gently patting the spot where he had been shoved against a wall in confronting Bennington.

"Just a scrape, but worth every bit of it," he said.

"Guess we won't be seeing his Lordship for a while," she commented as they went inside.

Although spring was around the corner, the hearth was blazing, and the warmth felt good. "Terrence, can you sit with me for a minute?" she began, serious, folding her skirts under as she settled onto a straight-backed chair.

"What is it?" he asked, afraid something might be wrong. He pulled up a chair next to her, straddling it for balance, leaning forward, with elbows on thighs. He nervously ran his knife blade across a sharpening stone.

"Nothing bad. Just something unexpected." Then she giggled, "Well, maybe it *is* expected."

He looked over at her, intrigued, clearly taken with what he saw. Sarah was radiant as she sat in the fire's glow. Her hair tumbled down like fine silk, golden with just a touch of red. Her eyes were clear. Her skin, fair.

"I'm with child, love," she said, a Cheshire cat grin playing across her face. "We're to have a baby."

"Well, I'll be," he beamed, rightfully boastful, for he had done his part and done it well. "Come here," he said, extending his arms as she moved into them. He stayed seated and rested his head on her stomach.

"Ma'am. Ma'am. There's someone here to see you," the greenhouse rep called in Sarah's direction. She was still sitting on the wall, looking far into the horizon as warm sun pooled around her. "Ma'am, did you hear me? Are you OK?" the rep repeated louder, shaking her arm.

Sarah blinked several times. "Yes, I'm sorry. I just got involved looking at this," she muttered, holding up the brochure. "Who's here?" she more lucidly asked. The rep knew that Sarah had not been reading but thought it best not to pry. "A Dr. Barrows," he conveyed. "She wandered around back, but she's waiting at the front door."

"Darn!" Sarah stood up, unhappy that she had been tracked here. She was not ready to share the house—especially with a shrink—but she went to greet her visitor, determined to be professional. Both women stood there awkwardly, outside.

"Dr. Barrows," she politely said as she blocked the entrance. "What brings you here?"

"I'm sorry to intrude, but I called your house to talk to you, and your husband answered. He was worried. I told him I'd check in on you. Hope you don't mind my coming. Your notes were fascinating. I couldn't put them down. You know I've spent a lot of time studying this sort of thing." Dr. Barrows was unusually talkative.

"What sort of thing?" Sarah asked, not masking her displeasure.

"You know…phenomena…unexplained happenings… spiritual journeys."

"Then I'm not crazy or emotionally deprived?" Sarah asked, eyebrows arched.

"I don't think so. After reviewing your notes, I would say my initial hypothesis was wrong." Dr. Barrows admitted. "I believe you did see something—something concrete. What it is, I don't know, but you seem to be uniquely intuitive."

Sarah was surprised the doctor had changed her mind but liked this theory better than the other one.

"Why me?" Sarah asked. "Why not someone else? Lots of people have been in this house."

Dr. Barrows shook her head. "I can't explain it. If I could, I wouldn't need you."

"Need me?" Sarah questioned.

"Yes, need you…to keep notes, I mean…to document your encounters." The doctor cleared her throat. "That's the only way I can help you understand them." Sarah listened. The doctor seemed nervous.

"If you don't mind, I'd love to witness one of your episodes," the psychiatrist pushed, but Sarah didn't answer. "Could we at least go inside so I can see the setting?"

Sarah begrudgingly opened the door, figuring the sooner she did it, the sooner the doctor would leave. The two women sat opposite each other in rose-colored damask wing chairs as if on different sides of a boxing ring. Sarah spoke first. "I realize you want to observe what happens, but this is a rather private thing. Plus, I don't know what you'd be able to see." Then rather abruptly, she stood up. "Will you excuse me for a moment, I don't feel too well." Sarah headed to the bathroom, leaving Dr. Barrows to study her surroundings. When she returned, Dr. Barrows was walking around the room, putting a voice memo into her phone. "Where were we?" Sarah asked. She looked pale and shaken.

Not wanting to risk alienating Sarah, Dr. Barrows backed off. "I don't want to force you to do anything you don't want," she said with professional decorum. "And we don't have to do this now…just think about it. I'll call your husband and assure him you're fine." Sarah thanked the doctor for her concern and gladly watched the woman leave.

The greenhouse rep wrapped up his work, said good-bye, and, later that day, submitted a proposal. Sarah sent it to the Randolphs and called Carter to let him know she'd be home soon. "I'm in a workshop," he stage-whispered. "I'll call you back when I'm done."

Disappointed, she replied, "Nothing urgent. Just wanted to fill you in." Sarah was trying to include him, but there was only so much she could do.

Once home, she turned on her computer and went online.

"Barrows…Barrows," Sarah repeated, searching medical associations and professional journals. Sure enough, Dr. Barrows was there all right, just as Carter had indicated. She apparently was quite well-known on the speakers' circuit, especially within the paranormal community.

While online, as she often did, Sarah went to one of her favorite sites: Duke University. To her, this was home turf, ground zero, because that's where she and Carter had met. Just then, the phone rang. She closed her screen so she could concentrate.

"Sorry I couldn't talk earlier. I had signed up for an afternoon seminar," Carter said.

"Not a problem. I was at the house today," she volunteered.

"Yes, you told me. Remember, I sent Dr. Barrows out there?" Carter reminded.

Of course, Sarah thought. I'm not sharing anything new. Their relationship was still strained. "The greenhouse crew said the spot looks good. Some of the old herbs are even coming back," she said, making small talk.

Carter was not at all interested in the greenhouse and made it clear. "What did Dr. Barrows have to say?" he asked. "She left a message that you were fine."

"She said that after reading my notes, she believes her original hypothesis was wrong…that I probably *did* see something in the house. She said I was unusually perceptive… intuitive. I suppose that's better than being a loser in search of adventure, but it still sounded a little wacky."

"Maybe not so wacky," Carter replied. "Remember that time you insisted I change planes to Chicago? And sure enough, the first one crashed?"

Sarah *did* remember that incident, but she had chalked it up to coincidence. "That's just because I had that weird dream with grandmother in it, saying 'Don't fly.' Anyway, Dr. Barrows wants to watch me the next time this happens."

"Are you OK with that?" Carter asked, trying his best to foster a dialog.

"I don't know. We don't have a lot of time. The house closing is set for March 15th."

"Beware the Ides of March," he teased. This was the Carter she knew and loved. She wanted to tell him that Sarah—the original one—was pregnant, but she decided to wait. That evening, feeling a truce had been drawn, she told Carter about the impending birth. He resisted rolling his eyes. She worried he might ask if she had participated in the events leading up to it, but he did not. She wasn't sure if he didn't care or didn't want to know. Not wanting to upset him further, she said little more. They watched the late-night news and went to bed.

"Help her! Help her!" she screamed, waking herself up. "She's sick!"

Carter fumbled to put on the nightstand lamp. "Sarah, you're dreaming again. Are you OK?"

Sarah was sitting upright, trying to catch her breath, hand on chest to quiet her thumping heart. "I have to get back to the house. I have to do something," she said, jumping out of bed in search of clothes.

"Not now. Not at night," Carter insisted.

"Day. Night. What's the difference? It's all the same. Real. Not real. What do I know?" Sarah sputtered, frustrated and confused.

By this time, Carter was fully awake and trying to be the voice of reason. "Sarah, you can't do anything about this now. Why don't you call Dr. Barrows in the morning and ask her to meet you at the house? I realize you're not too keen on her, but that way at least I'll know you're not alone. Maybe you'll be able to resolve this once and for all. Now go back to sleep."

Sarah tossed and turned until 5 a.m. "This is ridiculous," she muttered, pushing her toes into her slippers. "I'm a grown woman...and," she suddenly stopped, "do I feel awful. I hope I'm not getting the flu."

Sarah was still under the weather when she called Dr. Barrows, but they decided to go to the house anyway. Sarah phoned her office to say she was sick and made herself some toast and tea. Cherry preserves seemed to help.

"Your car or mine?" the doctor asked.

"I'll drive," Sarah offered, not wanting to relinquish control, "Unless of course you need to go somewhere else from there." Dr. Barrows thought a moment and decided they could ride together. Sarah told herself to give the doctor a chance.

When they arrived, the house was damp, not yet having shaken off its winter chill. Sarah turned on the electric sconces as well as a table lamp. She nudged the thermostat upward and modern heating kicked in.

Sitting on the couch, Sarah apologized in advance. "I can't promise anything." Dr. Barrows said she understood. Sarah slowly stood up and began pacing the room. "I feel silly calling his name. He usually seems to know I'm here. But I did it once before and he appeared, so that might work again."

Dr. Barrows was fumbling with something in her pocketbook, only half-listening. "Nice perfume by the way," she said, not looking up. "What are you wearing?"

Sarah stopped walking. "Nothing. Carter doesn't like perfume. Allergies, you know," she explained. But, then, she realized the doctor was picking up the scent of something else.

"So, you smell it, too?" Sarah ventured.

"You mean that lavender-lemon? Sure," Dr. Barrows said.

"Well, that's it!" Sarah exclaimed. "I usually smell that first—before he appears. Sort of like people seeing flashes before a migraine."

"Interesting," Dr. Barrows commented, talking into her phone. "Olfactory stimulus," she stated before looking up. "And then what happens?" she prompted.

"Well, sometimes I just turn around and he's standing there. Sometimes I just feel him near me, but lately I've been able to move further away from him, and still be connected."

"That's a good way to put it," he said. Sarah looked up into two clear blue eyes.

"See," she said, glancing at Dr. Barrows, but the doctor was no longer there. The only thing left on the couch was a spool of thread.

"How's the sampler coming?" Terrence asked.

"Very slowly," Sarah replied, picking up her needlework. "But it's relaxing."

"You know we're meeting near the tavern tonight," he reminded her. "Paul and the men are coming in from Boston."

"Please be careful. People are getting suspicious."

"Why do you say that?" he asked.

"Well, the other day, when Mercy Biddle came over, she started asking the strangest questions…like whether I had heard talk of a Colonist uprising or whether I had seen a military map. Of course, I told her I hadn't, but she kept pressing. Finally, I just changed the subject to children, and she filled my ears for an hour." Terrence chuckled. They felt comfortable with each other. Their relationship was fluid and effortless.

Early that night, Terrence left for the tavern on foot, wearing simple farmer's clothing to avoid attracting attention. There, the perfect Tory, he ordered British-sanctioned East Indian rum, raised a toast to King George, and praised the Province of Massachusetts Bay as England's finest trophy. To his side sat a group of Colonial firebrands talking loudly about rebellion in South Carolina and cries of "No Taxation Without Representation" in Philadelphia. They purposely didn't look at him, nor did he acknowledge them. Polishing off his pint, Terrence tossed down a coin and left, planning to meet them later that night.

Just outside the tavern, Terrence felt a sword poke his back. He tried to turn around, but someone grabbed his arm. "Not so fast, good man," he heard from behind, though he could not see the face that belonged to the voice. "Where are you going?" the voice asked.

"Just to my homestead," Terrence stated, careful not to impart any emotion.

"And where might that be?"

"The Tory house down in Baker's Cove."

"Excellent! Our troops need a place to stay."

"I'm not sure our barn is big enough," Terrence replied, trying to stall.

"No matter," said the voice. "You'll just have to make room. You *do* know the Quartering Act became law last spring," the voice reminded. Terrence knew all too well.

His mind raced immediately to the arms stashed in his cellar. He reluctantly conceded.

"I'll tell my wife to prepare some tea and fixings," he said, hoping to get a head start.

"We'll go with you, sir" one of the commanders insisted, "and we'll leave word for our men to follow."

Terrence dared not turn around. He walked deep in thought, wondering how to warn Sarah about the potential danger.

"Sarah, we have company," he called as he opened the front door, his voice louder than usual. "Hope you're not asleep yet."

"Not at all. I'm working on my stitching," she said, standing to greet their guests.

She immediately knew from the blood-red uniforms that something was wrong, but she had assumed this role before and played along.

"I'll put on some tea," she offered, removing herself to the kitchen.

"We've got better brew," proclaimed one of the Lobsterbacks as he raised a flask.

"They'll be staying the night," Terrence continued in an even voice, "along with their troops. Can you put some fresh hay out in the barn, while I make sure the men are comfortable?" His blue eyes sent a cryptic message to Sarah.

She didn't need to be told. Her heart had just about stopped when she saw the guards flanking her husband, at which point she thought immediately of the arsenal beneath the first floor.

"Happy to help," Sarah said as she put on her wrap and stepped out the back door. She could hear other soldiers arriving and knew they would be occupied. But instead of going to the barn, she went into the basement and started pulling weapons through the bulkhead.

Loading the weapons into a wheelbarrow, she pushed it up the hill behind the orchard, to a small cave she had recently discovered. The cave was damp, but it would do. One by one, she placed the weapons against the interior walls and went back for more. After three additional trips, she rolled a rock across the cave entrance, obscured it with brush, and hurried down the hill to prepare the barn.

She was breathless when she returned to the house, her cheeks pink from the cold. But under her skin, she was burning and exhilarated. "Are you all right, Sarah?" Terrence asked, trying to read her expression. "I should have helped you," he apologized, "but I wanted to get these gentlemen settled." She knew he really wanted to keep an eye on them.

"I managed quite well," she said, breezing through the mudroom, brushing a loose strand of hair from her forehead. "The barn is ready for our guests."

By this time, the men were embroiled in loud and coarse conversation. She excused herself and went up to the third floor, carrying her stitching and a lantern into the tranquil space created by the Tory roof. She could hear the Regulars roaming around the house, opening cupboards, wandering down to the basement stairs. She was glad she had taken necessary precautions. It was quiet under the roof, and for a moment, she closed her eyes.

"Sarah! Sarah! Are you all right?" Dr. Barrow's voice broke the stillness. A few seconds passed before Sarah knew what was happening. She was being brought back to reality and she wasn't ready for it. She didn't want to leave, not now.

"I'm fine, but don't come up." Sarah pleaded. "The troops are in the house."

"What?" Dr. Barrows hollered, not heeding Sarah's request. Within seconds, Dr. Barrows was standing on the second-floor landing, looking up. "What happened to you? You just got up and walked away."

Sarah peered down from the third-floor eave, not saying anything. She glanced around for her stitching but couldn't find it. She was beginning to recognize the signs of transition and regretted she had no control over it. Sarah slowly stood up and walked down the stairs. "You look flushed. Do you have a fever?" the doctor remarked, holding her post.

"I'm fine. Go ahead," Sarah insisted, gesturing to Dr. Barrows to continue down. "It always takes me a minute to collect myself."

Dr. Barrows stopped on the main floor, looking back. "Does that mean you had one of your episodes?" she asked, not masking her enthusiasm. "What happened?"

"It's too complicated to explain and besides, I'm tired," said Sarah, joining her. "But I did something heroic. I'll tell you about it later."

Dr. Barrows decided not to push. She knew she had to win Sarah's trust.

After driving home, Sarah and the doctor went their separate ways: Barrows back to analyzing behaviors; Sarah back to life as a working mom. In the days that followed, Sarah was short-tempered and despondent. She missed the excitement and vitality she felt in the house. Work was unrewarding. Her home life was bland. With every nicety her husband tried, the more irritated she got. He brought her flowers, but she longed for milkweed pods. They went to fine restaurants, but she craved stew and root vegetables. The children noticed her moodiness, too, but she blamed it on stress. At Carter's prompting, Sarah got the physical Dr. Barrows recommended. No real problems; she had gained a few pounds, but those usually came off in the summer.

The weekend rolled around, and Sarah immersed herself in chores while the children played outside. "Spring cleaning!" she declared as she pulled the vacuum into their bedroom. Just as she went to plug it in, she was jarred by an unexpected ring. She followed the sound to a cell phone under the bed. "Oh, Carter will be lost without this," she thought, knowing he had gone to school for a science fair. "I'll leave him a message there," she decided as she picked up the phone.

"Knowing him, he won't have a password, but he'll have all his numbers alphabetized in Contacts," and sure enough, he did. Intending to scroll to Drake High School, she accidentally held her finger down too long and the menu opened on Duke. For some reason, one of the numbers caught her eye. It looked strangely familiar. After staring for a moment, she realized it belonged to the Randolphs.

"Why would Carter have the Randolphs' number?" she wondered, certain that she had never given it to him. "And more importantly, why would he file it under 'Duke'?" Sarah sat on the bed trying to think of a reasonable explanation. "Maybe I did give it to him once for an emergency," she considered, "but why would he keep it? And why would he keep it there?" Sarah kept staring at the digits. "Maybe this number once belonged to someone else we knew at college. But what are the odds…?"

None of these possibilities rang true, but then again, not much made sense lately. Sarah called the high school and left a voice mail for Carter saying she had found his phone. She figured she'd ask him later about the Randolphs' number. Reminded of their college days, she walked over to the bookshelf and pulled out their yearbook, hoping it might hold a clue.

Flipping through the pages, she found nothing enlightening other than photos of Carter and herself looking much younger and slimmer than she remembered. The book was stuffed with clippings and souvenirs. There were pictures of friends, a few movie stubs, and an article about Carter's favorite place: the famous parapsychology lab that been located on campus long before they met.

Carter had always been fascinated with the odd and unusual, but his professional pursuits had taken him down a more traditional path. While he may have secretly coveted tenure at a prestigious university or a career at a cutting-edge tech company, he seemed happy to be teaching science at the local high school.

As Sarah unfolded a yellowed newspaper page, she couldn't help but smile at the big dot pattern in the photos. "Life has certainly changed," she sighed. One story showed Carter and herself at a pep rally wearing oversized college sweatshirts and goofy grins. She spotted a recipe for their favorite pecan pie—hadn't made that in ages—and she stumbled upon the obit of a classmate, who had been killed by a drunk driver. She didn't know the fellow well, but she remembered his kid brother—devastated—being interviewed on TV.

Seeing no mention of the Randolphs or a record of that phone number, she returned the book to its place and finished cleaning the house. By the time the kids came in, she was wrist-deep in fruit salad.

Carter showed up later, bleary-eyed from judging entries at the science fair. Still, he couldn't suppress his enthusiasm for the best and brightest in the school. One child had built a model of the galaxy and developed a web site on black holes, another had completed a chick embryo project far beyond his years, and someone else had tested her entire family for ESP.

"How do you do that, Dad?" Jared asked, his ears perking up at the topic.

"Oh, there are some standard methods. One is a set of cards with different shapes and pictures. People are asked to identify the images without seeing them."

"We could try that with my Fish cards," Abby suggested, not waiting for an answer as she ran to get the deck. "I'll put the cards face down, and you tell me what they are. It'll be a game."

"I'm kind of tired, sweetheart," Carter said. "Try it with your brother." Jared made a face but agreed. Abby carefully laid out a salmon, seahorse, octopus, and whale face down on the kitchen table. Jared guessed a whale, seahorse, turtle, and mermaid. Abby tried again. Facedown, she placed a dolphin, eel, minnows, and swordfish. Jared guessed a dolphin, eel, striped bass, and shark.

They went through a few more rounds, but patience wearing thin, Jared let the cards fly across the table. "Hey, don't be mad. You got some of them right. Besides, it's time for dinner," Sarah said. "Abby, please help pick up the cards so I can set the table."

While Sarah was busy at the oven, Abby crawled under the table to retrieve the scattered deck. "And don't forget that mermaid under the chair," Sarah called over her shoulder. Abby reached for a card caught by the chair leg and saw that it was still face down. Lifting the edge, she noticed a scaly blue fin and flowing tresses. "But Mom, how did you know what it was?" Abby asked from under the table. Sarah couldn't hear the question and Abby didn't repeat it.

After dinner, Sarah planned to ask Carter about the familiar phone number in his cell, but they became involved watching a movie. She was going to mention it before bed, but Carter was asleep by the time she got there. She was ready to say something at breakfast, but mornings were always rushed. So, she said nothing, and the question festered in her mind. Of course, the longer she waited, the harder it was to address.

With the house closing near, the Randolphs were being allowed to ship some items in advance, and, as usual, they asked Sarah to sign for delivery. "Pain in the neck!" Sarah grumbled to herself, "but at least I'll be able to visit the house."

Midweek, the shippers called to say they'd be there that afternoon. Not wanting to repeat past errors in judgment, Sarah told Carter she might be late, *very* late…asking him to feed the kids and make sure they did their homework. Carter wasn't happy about it, but he promised to be home early.

Only a few patches of snow remained in the fields as Sarah drove to Baker's Cove. Returning geese converged in the old cornrows, where muddy ruts now replaced the once-tall stalks. Savoring some wormy treat, they pecked at the soil, oblivious to her passing car. Wisps of clouds stayed high in the otherwise clear sky, and she felt equally uplifted, knowing that spring was not far away.

The side door was unlocked when she arrived at the Covington house, so she walked in. She turned the corner and saw that the dining room table was set for six.

"We're expecting company, you know," Terrence reminded her. She was never tired of seeing his frame in the doorway. "Come here and give me a proper hello," he said, welcoming her with a kiss.

This time she didn't hesitate. It had been weeks, but being away felt like years. "You look as beautiful as ever," he said. "And how do you feel?"

"I'm fine," she answered.

"And the baby?" For a moment, she had forgotten that she was pregnant.

"Fine, too," she assured, glancing down at her rounding stomach, no longer concealed beneath her long skirts. "Starting to move."

"Excellent! Then let's ready ourselves for the festivities!" he proclaimed with a flourish reminiscent of a circus barker.

Sarah laughed—something she had not done for a while. "What's the occasion?"

"Completion of the new school," he answered with a wink. Sarah was puzzled, but soon learned more.

As far as the neighbors were concerned, a teacher was arriving in town to open their one-room schoolhouse. In typical fashion, he would stay with local families, who had school-age children, as room and board were part of his compensation. Since the Covingtons didn't have children yet, they had offered to host him until school began.

Sarah went about preparing dinner. Game was abundant in the surrounding woods and wild turkeys usually emerged at this time of year, so it didn't surprise her that a large one was roasting in a covered pan on the hearth. She brought potatoes and turnips up from the basement to boil and mash…pickled cucumbers and pepper relish to serve right from the jars. She gathered strips of dried fish and ham from the smokehouse to pair with apples and cheese as hors d'oeuvres. For dessert, they would enjoy the blackberry tarts she had made in the fall and frozen in tins out in the shed.

The pastor and two church ladies knocked on the door. Sarah removed her apron and went to greet them. Terrence was close behind. The women were accompanied by a quiet young man, slight in build, carrying a satchel and a lap desk. "You must be Mr. Hale," Terrence said, extending his hand. "You can leave your belongings by the door."

"I am, sir, I am…and thank you," the teacher replied, removing his hat and shaking Terrence's hand.

"Well, *do* come in," Terrence motioned to the foursome. "May I offer you some tea or brandy? The days are still chilly out here."

"Thank you, that would be grand," Hale replied, nodding toward the liquor bottle. Rubbing his palms together for warmth, the pastor also opted for the amber liquid. The two women joined Sarah in the kitchen for tea. They talked about a cargo of fabric expected on the next ship, seeds needed for planting, and a new litter of kittens down at the mill.

In the keeping room, the men discussed property and politics. Mr. Hale carefully concealed his allegiance when conveying news from the Southern Colonies, saying simply, "My young cousin heard some of the fiery speeches first hand. He said they caused quite a stir." Terrence wanted to learn more, but tempered his response as well, not sure how the pastor leaned. Ultimately, Terrence changed the subject to fishing—a universally safe topic with trout season approaching—and as expected, each man had a story about 'the one that got away'.

Dinner was bountiful, and the group ate slowly, savoring the occasion. When darkness fell, the guests excused themselves, thanking their hosts and wishing the teacher well. Once his escorts had left, Mr. Hale opened his lap desk and removed a roll of parchment, which he handed to Terrence. After a quick glance at it, Terrence tucked it safely into the pantry wall before showing Mr. Hale his room.

"I hope this is what you need," Hale said as he picked up his belongings.

"It's exactly what we need," Terrence replied. "Thank you."

Mr. Hale was not only an educator, but also a cartographer. His map calculated distances and charted landmarks between Boston and Concord, denoting road intersections and river ways on the route to Lexington. Word was that there would be 10,000 British troops stationed in the Colonies by year's end and Terrence wanted to be prepared.

Once the dishes were cleared and Mr. Hale settled in, Terrence and Sarah moved closer to the fire. Moonlight filtered through the branches, now beginning to plump out with buds, and quiet filled the room. "You'll spend the night, won't you?" Terrence asked her.

Two small flames danced in Sarah's eyes. She smiled. "I don't see how I can go."

Sarah woke up abruptly the next morning, while it was still dark. She didn't know whether she'd find Terrence or Carter at her side. Fact was, neither. A note on the nightstand read, "See you later, my love. I promised to help Joshua plow his fields."

Sarah got out of bed and looked down the road, expecting to spot him, but Terrence was long gone. Without a pressing reason to stay, she wondered if she could simply will herself to leave. Previously, a disruption had sent her back to reality: a voice, a noise, a knock on the door.... "But suppose nothing interrupts me?" she wondered. "Would I be captive in this house forever?"

Sarah didn't have much time to worry, because the delivery truck arrived momentarily. She looked down at her clothes and was happy to see that she was wearing gray jogging pants and a zip-up sweatshirt. As she opened the door, she heard one of the shippers say, "Sorry we're late. Big breakdown on the Pike." She peered around the doorjamb and saw a tall fellow rolling in a dolly stacked with large boxes. "Where do you want 'em?"

"How 'bout in the corner," Sarah said, gesturing to the side of the keeping room. She had no idea what the boxes contained or where they were supposed to go.

The tall mover was followed by a short one—a round, overweight fellow, who carried a smaller but bulky package. "Got 10 more just like this," he puffed as she tried to clear some space. With the boxes moved inside and the shippers gone, Sarah wrote a note to Terrence saying she'd be on her way. She had no idea if he would see it—or *could* see it—but she left it in the space under the Tory roof, which seemed to be a portal into his world.

By the next day, Sarah still hadn't asked Carter about the Randolphs' phone number, but since they were coming into town for the closing, she decided on another approach. She would casually bring up the subject of college to see how they might react. Picking them up at the airport, Sarah mentioned that she had unearthed her old yearbook from Duke. Mrs. Randolph laughed, rich and throaty, saying that long ago she had worked at Duke as a researcher in the science department. No secret there.

"Then you might know my husband?" Sarah suggested.

"Gosh, I don't think so," Mrs. Randolph remarked as if the notion were absurd.

"Well, I think he knows you; he was a science major there," Sarah replied, trying to make the conversation sound spontaneous and off-handed.

"What's your husband's name?" Mrs. Randolph asked.

"Carter. Carter Sutherland."

"*The* Carter Sutherland?" Mrs. Randolph exclaimed, as if finding a long-lost friend.

"Why the surprise?" Sarah asked. "He's got *your* number programmed into his phone." There was a hint of accusation in her voice.

"Oh, my goodness!" Mrs. Randolph clucked. "I'll be! I've talked to a young aspiring scientist named Carter Sutherland for years, but I never put it together. You see, we've never met...we just share information. I knew he lived near Boston, but I figured right in the city, not way out in the country. Isn't that funny?"

Sarah reprimanded herself for making such a big deal out of a seemingly benign coincidence. "How pathetic I am," she thought as she drove toward the County Courthouse. She chastised herself for not being more trusting. "Obviously, there is no great mystery here. Strange, yes, but not impossible."

Sarah sat patiently as papers were passed, and afterward, she congratulated the Randolphs on their new house. She dropped them off at the hotel where they were staying, then headed home, eager to tell Carter what she had discovered.

"Carter," Sarah spouted, as she rushed to greet him. "You'll never guess what I found out today!"

"That the moon is made of green cheese?" he teased as he hung his coat in the closet.

"No. That Mrs. Randolph knows you!"

Carter blanched, but with his face turned, Sarah didn't notice. Brimming with enthusiasm, she recounted finding the phone number, the conversation in the car and the small world irony of it all. "That's amazing," Carter said, concealing a look of relief. "So, *she's* my scientist friend back at Duke…" He paused to process the information. "She's a terrific researcher. Sends me a lot of material. Maybe she's got a new job up here."

"What does she send you?"

"Oh, articles, case studies, excerpts from speeches, stuff from the old lab…." Carter's voice trailed off as he rummaged in the kitchen for some cookies. He wasn't lying. He just wasn't telling the whole truth. "We'll have to get together once they move in."

With the Covington sale completed, Sarah realized that matters were out of her hands. She tried to focus on work but couldn't. Knowing the house was still vacant and that she had not yet returned the master key, she decided to visit one last time.

"I can't wait to see him," she thought as she stepped inside and walked around the delivered boxes. She called out a hello as if coming home from the office. No one answered. She tried again: "Terrence?" and started up the stairs. "Where are you?" Still no response.

She returned to the front room and sat on a bench, puzzled. The house was certainly quiet without him. She felt a twinge in her side and noticed the waistband of her long skirt had been extended with a piece of twine. "My God," she thought, "I really am pregnant." Maybe Terrence had gone to town for supplies or maybe into the city for business, she reasoned. Sarah touched the teakettle, and it was cold. She opened the back door and looked toward the barn. Someone was obviously taking care of the livestock. Then she spotted a newspaper on the stoop, held in place by a stone, likely put there by a well-meaning neighbor. She picked up the broadsheet and saw the headline.

"Suspected traitors captured by British," the large type proclaimed. Reading on, she quickly learned that Terrence was in trouble. The article described how a secret meeting of rebellious Colonists had been intercepted by Tory troops. Terrence Covington was listed among the suspected revolutionaries, now being held in custody.

Sarah grabbed her cape, bonnet, and basket, and then started down the path to the main road. There were no cars now, and pine trees had overtaken the fields in her contemporary world. This time she retained her historic identity even though she moved well beyond the confines of the house.

As Sarah passed the church, she smiled graciously and nodded to her neighbors. Some were sympathetic, some were skeptical, and some were downright hostile. "Good day, Sarah. We're so sorry to hear about your husband." "Hello, Mrs. Covington. Was your husband really cavorting with those rabble-rousers?" "Shame on you, Sarah Covington. Your husband should be hanged for treason against England."

Sarah held her head high as she walked past them.

She noticed two Redcoats standing guard at the meetinghouse where the suspects were said to be restrained. Walking behind the building, she attempted to see in, but the windows were too high. She noticed a row of barrels against the side wall, including eight hogsheads cut in half. She dragged five of the squat casks to the space below the window and turned them over to make a platform. On top of these, she added three more, creating a pyramid to serve as a ladder. Lifting her long skirts, she climbed up onto them and peered over the edge of the window sill.

There, below her, in the dim light she could see Terrence, hands tied behind his back, shoulder slumped against a wall, ankles loosely bound. His hair was matted, his beard grown in, and his mouth looked terribly parched. She felt tears well up in her eyes. His thigh had been slashed and his head bloodied. She couldn't tell how badly he was hurt but knew she had to get him out of there. She scurried down her makeshift ladder and returned the barrels to the row.

From there she went to the general store to buy some supplies and to hear the latest gossip. Townspeople were now openly berating British rule as oppressive and unfair, complaining loudly that their ties to the throne were too tight. "We purposely left England so we could have rights," one farmer was saying as he waited for molasses to be poured. "And now we can't even export our goods anywhere but there!"

"I hardly think we can keep paying prices like this for tea and sugar," an elderly woman lamented as a small block of black tea was wrapped up for her. "We can't even use our own currency."

"Join the militia!" yelled a boy from a porch across the street. "Sign up now to defend your land," he chanted, waving a piece of paper and a quill.

Sarah took it all in, keeping her eyes lowered. Then defiantly, she strode back to the meetinghouse and walked up to the guards. "Good day, m'lady," one acknowledged. "How may we assist you?"

"You seem to have my husband in there," she said, sizing up the Redcoat.

"And who might that be?" the wiry Brit asked.

"Terrence Covington," she answered, looking up to meet his eyes. "And I want to know when he'll be set free."

"He'll stay here until the facts can be reviewed," the man stated in a well-rehearsed reply.

"And how long will that be?" she challenged.

"Long as it takes," the other guard snapped, blocking her access with his torso. Somehow, the red wool jacket that had looked so dashing on Terrence seemed threatening now.

Sarah suppressed her fear and more forcefully insisted, "I want to see him."

"Not now. And besides, no women allowed," the first guard taunted, tightening the grip on his weapon.

"When, then?" she asked. "He's done nothing wrong," she started to protest, but knew her arguments would fall on deaf ears.

"We'll find you when he's ready to be released. Until then, go back to your pretty, little house in the Cove," the second guard instructed.

"You know where I live?" Sarah asked, alarmed.

"Of course," he answered. "We spent the night there in your gracious hospitality when we arrived."

Sarah thought back to the night when she had hauled weapons into the woods and laid out hay in the barn. "Well, I *do* hope you will expedite the situation in appreciation for that hospitality," she said with forced politeness, posing to accentuate her stomach. "We have fields to plow and livestock to tend. And I can't do it by myself."

Sarah turned on her heel and hurried down to the gristmill to think. The air was thick and sweet from the smell of grain. Although she couldn't see them, she could hear the resident cats mewing from the rafters. The mice didn't stand a chance. She found a bench in the corner and sat down, trying to calm her anger and figure out a plan.

When she finally stepped outside into the bright light, she knew what she had to do. First, she went to their neighbors, Jonah and Grace, to ask if they could look after the farm for a few days. "We're already doing that," Jonah said. "We started as soon as we heard Terrence was taken." Sarah was overwhelmed by the gesture. "Thank you. Thank you so much. Please help yourself to milk and eggs for your kindness," she encouraged. They agreed and urged her to get some rest. But rest was not in the cards that night.

At home, Sarah waited for total darkness to descend, then once again, gathered up her belongings. Using her tinderbox to light one of the candles in her basket, she walked through the woods parallel to the road, hiding behind buildings until street lanterns came into view. There she stepped out and fell in line with a group of revelers *en route* to the tavern. She hoped to go unnoticed, but a rakish fellow with a small, portable violin tucked under his chin—a *pochette* as it was called—pranced around her playing a version of *Highland Laddie*. "Won't ye join our party tonight?" he asked with a Scottish brogue thick as a fog on the moors. He was getting too close for her liking and far too familiar. Not wanting to be detained, Sarah rapidly shook her head no, pushed him away, and hurried along. She could hear one of the women mock, "Ain't she high and mighty?"

Sarah stayed focused on the mission at hand. Under the cover of a low mist, she slipped to the meetinghouse again and moved the cut barrels into position. On her tiptoes, she could detect guards standing across the room at the door. She could hear Terrence moaning below.

Reaching into her basket, she extracted a piece of paper torn from the newspaper that had been left at their door. Near the headline she had written, "I am here. – S." She rolled it into a tube, sewed a thread through it, and pushed it into the window, letting it drop slowly to the floor below. "Please, Terrence, see this before the guards do," she whispered, not so much for him to hear but for herself.

When Terrence noticed the white cylinder inching down before his eyes, he grabbed it with his teeth. Sarah released the string, which coiled onto the floor. Unclenching his jaw, Terrence guided the paper toward his feet. Placing one boot on each side, he unrolled it and knew that help was on the way.

Terrence didn't move for fear of drawing attention. Soon, a straight razor descended the same way. He retrieved it with his teeth and spit it over his shoulder, fumbling for it with his restrained hands and scooting into position to grab it.

Sarah knew it would just be a matter of time until Terrence acted. As nightfall deepened, Terrence used the straight edge to slice through the ropes that held his wrists. After working methodically for what seemed like hours, he felt one rope break. "Got it!" he muttered. Wiggling his finger through the open loop, he pulled his hands out and then cut the ropes that held his legs. With hands and feet free, he hobbled to the next man and slashed his ties, too, and in turn, that man did the same. Soon, one by one, each prisoner was released as if in a controlled domino spill.

Sarah could sense movement below although, she could not see very well. Luckily, the guards, deep in cards and conversation, could see no better. As the last man stretched his arms and shook out the kinks, Sarah climbed off the barrels and move them back in place. Then she headed to the livery. After unlatching the gate and letting the horses out, she reached for her tinderbox.

Just one spark was all it took to ignite the dry hay in the corral. Flames snapped to life and danced around the edges of the stable, licking at the posts, lapping at the dangling bridles, and erupting into a menacing blaze.

"Fire!" someone shouted from a storefront. "Fire! Get the horses!" someone else yelled. The guards flung the meetinghouse door open and ran across the street, filling buckets from the watering trough on their way. By this time, the prisoners were out the door and running in different directions. Discovering the horses were safe, the Redcoats spun around only to see the shadowy figures of men disappearing into the woods. "Get those bastards!" one of the guards ordered, as several sentries took chase.

Sarah and Terrence were close behind the escaping men, Terrence hobbling and wincing in pain. They looked back in time to see the framework of the coral collapse. "At least the livery was spared," Sarah thought, hiking up her skirts with one hand to run faster. Terrence clutched Sarah's other hand as they scaled the rise to the Whiting farm, slipping on the dew-damp ground, sliding back, and pushing forward again. They pounded on the door. Joshua had been a friend since childhood and was now a political ally. "Please let us in! We need a place to hide."

Sarah could see a lamp being lit in the back room, but it seemed to take forever until Joshua and his wife, Danna, cracked the front door open. Strong and comforting arms extended a welcome as blankets were offered for warmth. Soon the ripe smell of strawberry leaves and chamomile filled the air. Four cups of Liberty Tea were raised high in a toast of solidarity.

As calm settled in, Sarah recounted her adventure. After a second cup of tea, the Whitings ushered them into an alcove and told them they could stay there as long as they needed.

Sarah awoke, startled to be in a strange bed, but relaxed when she found Terrence at her side, asleep in his shirt. As darkness lifted, she could see the festering gash on his leg. She nudged him and whispered in his ear. "I need to clean you up. Your thigh isn't looking so good." He mumbled something about *her* thigh looking great, and instead, reached for her, pulling her toward him.

4

SAFE

As Danna prepared a morning meal, Sarah started a pot of water boiling and stepped outside to gather pine bark to add to it. She borrowed dry comfrey and chickweed from Danna's supply and found wild plantain growing behind the house. After washing Terrence's wound with her pinesap solution and drying it with a soft cloth, she applied a mash of herbs to it, a remedy she had learned from her mother. She wrapped plantain leaves around it to draw out the infection and used strips of muslin to hold the poultice in place. That evening she would repeat the process and again the next day.

"What smells so good?" the men asked as they bellied up to the table, heatedly discussing the injustices of the British King. Danna and the children brought over pitchers of milk, a crock of butter, and slices of warm ham. Quick biscuits, Johnnycakes, and jam followed. Danna ladled porridge into pewter bowls, while Sarah added a shaving of maple sugar to the top of each. There were three young ones clamoring for attention: Charles, Lydia, and baby Betsy. Seeing them, Sarah couldn't wait to have a family of her own.

The men railed loudly against the newly passed Declaratory Act that gave law-making power to the Crown. They knew it had been a shrewd power play by the British in retaliation for the Stamp Act repeal. Not to be fooled, Terrence and Joshua vowed to continue protesting and to rally others. Sugar and molasses were still being taxed along with coffee, wine, and printed fabrics. The British consumed great quantities of raw materials from America and sold the finished goods throughout Europe, while prohibiting the Colonists from free commerce. The Colonies were mandated to trade timber and iron only with England. There were even rumors of Colonists having to buy beaver hats made from their own pelts.

The men decided it was time to put a stake in the ground. With the Sons of Liberty established in Boston and a counterpart in New York, there was now a way to amplify their voice. A moonlight meeting would be held that night. Danna and the children spread the word as they walked through town with fresh-baked goods. Simple pastries decorated with an 'X' and furtive whispers conveyed the place and time.

Sarah stayed at the Whiting house that day, helping to repair clothing that had to last another year. Terrence and Joshua devised one plan after another, finding flaws, fixing them, and starting from scratch again.

Sarah watched from the next room as Terrence spoke with great animation. Daggers of resolution flew from his eyes as he championed his cause. "So handsome, so daring, so brave," she thought. "He doesn't even know he's a hero."

When night fell, and the moon rose, the men slipped out behind the paddock to a clearing near the pond. Soon others arrived and, with them, their oldest sons. Their voices were low and intense as the men plotted to protest the economic sanctions. "It's not enough to speak out. We need to intercept and destroy their goods," one of the men urged. "That will send a message they'll understand."

"Money and power, that's all that matters to them," someone else growled. "And we can rid them of both. But how?"

Terrence and Joshua had already given this some thought and shared their ideas with their neighbors. Seizing supplies in the city would be too dangerous with so many British troops stationed there. Warships were already guarding the Boston Harbor and strategically placed arsenals had been built to protect valuable inventory, but if the Colonists could follow the next mercantile shipment out of the city and into the country, they might be able to isolate it and capture it. That would require logistical precision.

Someone would have to learn when the ship was coming in and where it would be docked. Someone else would have to monitor the cargo handling to determine when it would deploy. Riders would be needed to escort it out of the city, unseen, to ensure that it was on schedule and away from British surveillance. Then it would have to be seized and destroyed.

William Smith volunteered to go into Boston with his sons. The boys, being of seafaring age, would chummy up to the sailors to see what could be learned. With family in the city, the Smiths had a place to stay.

A week later, they returned, brimming with news. "A cargo ship is arriving in a matter of days and will unload at the Long Wharf," William advised. "We have to move fast." Eldest son Tyler volunteered to take his wagon to Haymarket Square as if selling wares. His younger brother, Timothy, would join him there. Upon learning the schedule, Tyler would stay in place to gather additional information, while dispatching his brother by horse, west along the Post Road. Friends would be waiting for Timothy in the outskirts of town, serving as a relay team. They would split up—one rider spreading the word to residents and the other discreetly accompanying the cargo into the countryside. Timothy would return to Tyler should further communication be needed.

Meanwhile, a secondary plan of deception evolved, and Sarah was part of it.

At the first cluster of houses, a springtime fair would be staged as if it were the center of a larger town. People would come from surrounding areas to play their parts. Sarah and other young women would serve up food, while the older women sat quilting. The men would be engaged in sports of strength—log splitting and greased pole climbing. "We can play tag," one of the young boys suggested, "and the girls can roll hoops." "I play a mean whistle," an elderly gentleman offered. "And I can watch the babies," his wife volunteered. Soon, dozens of families were assigned roles and each person went home to gather supplies in preparation.

Six days later, Tyler Smith learned that the cargo ship had docked in Boston and that valuable mercantile goods were being unloaded. Timothy took this information to Ezra and Ezekiel, who were positioned in Waltham, waiting for him. "Gather as planned," Ezra yelled to citizens along the way, who in turn spread the word and summoned others. Ezekiel followed the cargo through the woods of Wayland and Sudbury, taking care to remain hidden.

As the drivers approached the eastern most homes, they could hear music and laughter coming from the fields. Pretty, young girls waved from the roadside. Ribbons, strung from the fence posts, fluttered in the breeze.

Sarah walked forward, offering fresh tarts and flasks of hard cider. "Partake in our celebration of spring?" she asked as the horses whinnied to a stop. The drivers climbed down and stretched their legs, eagerly accepting the sweet pastries and robust beverage. The guards slowly joined in. Little did they know that under the quilts and hidden in the water barrels were muskets, swords, and bayonets. They did not suspect that pie plates and petticoats contained ammunition.

A collection of villagers milled around the caravan, playing to the British ego. "What strong horses you have." "What fine wagons," the men commented. "What are you selling today?"

The young women flirted. "Are ye married, gentlemen?" "Want to come over for tea and company?" "Would you like me to mend that tear on your britches?" Flattered and amused, the guards relaxed.

Suddenly, the strongest men emerged from the crowd, each armed and determined. They circled the caravan and ordered the drivers and henchmen to step away. One by one, crates of fabric, belts and buttons, paper and dry goods, were unloaded and torched. Wine kegs were emptied. Sugar and molasses, spilled. British-made beaver hats, burned. And, when the ashes cooled, they were swept into the same barrels and dumped into the river.

The makeshift fairgrounds were quickly dismantled, and the crowds dispersed. The Brits were sent back to Boston at gunpoint, empty handed. What an embarrassment. They had lost their pride and their payload and, of course, there was no proof. The ersatz village didn't exist, and their material wealth now rested at the bottom of the Charles.

Terrence was certain British officials would never admit to being duped by a bunch of farmers, but he also knew the drivers and underlings would talk. Surely, the troops would be rankled by this story. And, if things played out right, the *Boston Gazette* would report on the incident, which would further fuel the Colonial flame.

Sarah was exhausted by the time they set up camp that night. As Terrence sat against a tree, she stretched out and put her head in his lap. His strong hands smoothed her hair and caressed her brow, easing away the strain of the day.

"Do you think it's safe to go home now?" she asked, longing for her own bed in their warm Tory house. "I heard that the Regulars have left town in search of the men who escaped."

"We can give it a try and see what happens," Terrence answered. "After all, we can't stay away forever."

She snuggled against him and he pulled her close, wanting to shield her from the night's chill.

A day later, they could see their house sitting safely on the horizon. The door creaked as they opened it and Terrence was quick to light a fire. Sarah filled the kettle and went out to the herb garden looking for signs of spring.

She could tell the thyme was perking up and she saw young chives poking through the mud. She thought of fresh onion soup and remembered she hadn't had lunch. That was all it took. Within seconds, she was on her way back to reality.

"Terrence! Terrence!" she cried as she rushed toward the doorway. "I'm going…leaving now…can't stop it… I love you..." she called, reaching toward him. He started toward her but couldn't draw her back.

The transition happened so fast, she felt cheated. She hadn't even had time to say a proper good-bye. Sadly, she knew that with the house sold, it would be difficult to return.

Dwindling rays of sun were disappearing behind the hills by the time she got home. Carter was already there. Apparently, her office assistant had phoned, wanting to know where she was, but she did not return the call.

A deep sense of loss engulfed Sarah as she tried to settle into her routine. She saw Dr. Barrows again, but all this did was rekindle her memories of Terrence. Despite her best efforts, Sarah moped. She went through the motions at work but was on the verge of tears every time she thought about what she couldn't have.

Finally, she made up her mind to go back to the property under the pretense of delivering a welcome basket. She found a perfect one at the market and loaded it into her car, retracing the route she knew so well.

Mr. Randolph answered the door. "Why Sarah! What brings you way out here?" he asked as he greeted her. But he didn't invite her in.

"Oh, we real estate folks just like to make sure our clients are happy," she lied, "so here's a little something from all of us at the office."

"Thank you so much. How lovely! Ann's not here right now and I'm in the middle of work, otherwise I'd ask you in."

He blocked the entrance.

"Maybe some other time," Sarah mumbled, craning to see behind him. She noticed that the boxes she had accepted were open. A computer and monitor were booted up next to what looked like some sort of vintage recording device.

Packaging for new digital equipment was torn apart. A video was playing with the sound turned down, but as she started to leave, she heard Mr. Randolph's recorded voice. "EVP One: Preliminary Electronic Voice Phenomena." Then she heard her own words very low, deep and slow, whispering, "Terrence, are you here?" The syllables stretched out as if to enunciate each letter.

"What are you doing?" Sarah asked. "I could have sworn I heard my voice."

"What do you mean?" Mr. Randolph replied, feigning ignorance.

"I think you've taped me in the house."

"Oh, that...." Mr. Randolph stalled, as he scrambled for an excuse. "I have to apologize for that. Our lawyer, you know... he's very judicious. He insisted we install a security system, so we had a video cam set up."

"I'm surprised you didn't mention it," Sarah replied, irritated. "Then I guess you know I've kept a good eye on the house," she said in a cool, professional tone. "I tried to check on it regularly," she added, hoping that nothing unusual had been recorded.

"Oh, we *know* you did," he assured, "and we appreciate that. Sounds like you were talking to yourself a bit, though," he chuckled.

"I guess I think out loud a lot," Sarah hedged.

At this point, she could do nothing, but make a quick exit. "Give my regards to Ann," Sarah called back as she headed toward her car, leaving Mr. Randolph standing in the doorway.

"I wonder what else he heard," she worried as she drove home.

The odd encounter with Mr. Randolph played in her head. She tried to recall what she had seen: Keyboard. Monitor. That old machine with the strange cylinders. She didn't know exactly what those were, but they looked vaguely familiar.

At home, Sarah paced around their den, walking once more over to the bookcase that held their yearbook. She kept sensing there was a deeper connection between the Randolphs and the school, but she wasn't sure what it was. She flipped through the pages and pawed through the items she hadn't looked at before. She saw a pressed flower that Carter had given her when they were young and in love, two cancelled concert tickets for front row seats, and a magazine article showing Carter and his colleagues in the psych lab. That's when she noticed it. Behind the table where Carter stood was something that looked like Mr. Randolph's old equipment. On the back of the clipping was the story jump, showing a picture of a researcher named Ann Dailey.

Sarah looked at the faces and lingered on the woman smiling up from her work. The pose reminded her of Mrs. Randolph reviewing the greenhouse plans. It didn't take long to make the mental leap. If Ann Dailey and Ann Randolph were the same person, then Carter and Ann were lying about knowing each other—but why?

Sarah recoiled, realizing the trust she held in her husband was being shaken. "I've been feeling *so* guilty about Terrence all this time and have been beating myself up over it, but apparently, Carter has secrets of his own." Sarah's emotional roller coaster dipped and hurled between hurt and anger. She grabbed the incriminating page and shoved the yearbook back onto the shelf. What was he hiding? And how long has he been hiding it?

The more she thought about it, the more upset she became. She threw on her coat and stormed outside, slamming the door behind. Walking nowhere in particular but walking fast, she headed for the Southbridge Cemetery. "It will be quiet there. I'll be able to think," she decided. "Maybe I'll go back to the Tory house and just stay for a while. I could slip in at night and not come back." Sarah was livid.

Hiding in the house would be foolish, her more responsible-self cautioned. "You have a husband and children," she heard in her head. Of course, she didn't want to desert them, but she had a feeling that something sinister was going on behind her back. She walked around the moss-covered headstones until she was calm enough to go home. When Carter returned that night, Sarah kept her distance.

"Are you OK?" he asked, feeling a chill in the air.

"Busy day, that's all," was her curt response.

"Want some wine?" he asked after he put down his briefcase.

"No—but I'd like a straight answer," she said, spinning around to make eye contact.

"About what?" he cautiously asked.

"About this!" she lobbed back, waiving the magazine page in front of his face.

Ever rational, he smiled as he took it. "Oh, that…why that's me when I was volunteering in the lab." He flipped the page over.

"I know that!" she snapped. "I want to know who Ann Dailey is!" Sarah said, pointing to the picture. Carter looked tired as he sat down. Sarah sat also, putting some space between them.

"She's Ann Randolph, right?" Sarah accused before Carter had a chance to speak. Carter said nothing but shook his head yes. "Well, why would you lie to me?" Sarah demanded. "You said you never met her. And she said she never met you."

"Sweetheart, I'm sorry. I'm *so* sorry. It was never important before." Sarah wondered why it was suddenly important now. Carter continued.

"Yes, I know Ann. We worked together back in college. And as I told you, we share information."

"Is that all you share?" Sarah needled.

"Yes. That's all we share. There's nothing between us. My God, she could be my mother!"

Sarah just stared at him. He was not at all comfortable with this conversation or the scrutiny.

"Ann's been able to continue a project I had to stop when we left North Carolina. In fact, she's spent years researching the topic. Mr. Randolph is a researcher, too. Together, they travel the world looking for paranormal activity. When they find a place with certain criteria, they stay for a while and monitor it. Sometimes they even move there."

"So?" Sarah prompted.

"So, they needed some help."

"And you're helping them?" Sarah asked, trying to understand the dynamics.

"Well, actually *you* are."

"What do you mean, *I* am?"

Carter was blunt. "They needed an objective observer. Someone who was particularly sensitive, intuitive. You're the conduit."

Sarah stepped back, appalled.

"I'm the *what*?"

"You were brought in to verify the location before they bought the old Covington estate…."

"Without telling me?"

By this time, Carter was pacing and apologizing profusely for being so thoughtless. "I know. I know. I should have told you, but that would have skewed the experiment."

"You put an experiment before your wife?" Sarah charged. "What kind of person are you?"

"Obviously, stupid and naïve," Carter admitted.

"That's for sure!" Sarah lashed out, her eyes squinting into narrow slits. "How could you do this to me?"

"I wasn't thinking. I was just looking at the science. We needed unbiased feedback, that's all. I never expected anything significant to happen."

"That's not my problem," Sarah snarled.

"I understand. But you're a natural at this sort of thing."

"What are you talking about?"

"Sarah, you may not want to admit it, but you are extremely in tune with your surroundings. You pick up things the rest of us can't begin to see or feel."

"Oh, come on," Sarah retorted, as if this were the most preposterous thing she had ever heard.

"Even the kids notice it. Remember that day they were using the Fish cards to test Jared's ESP?"

"Yeah…," Sarah said, thinking back. She didn't recall anything usual.

"Well, when Abby was picking up the cards that had fallen, she told me you reminded her to get the one under the chair."

"So?" Sarah asked, impatient at the line of questioning.

"She said your back was turned."

"That's not rocket science. If you drop 52 cards, one is apt to be stuck somewhere!"

"Yes, but she told me you knew which card it was—and it was facedown."

Sarah paused for a moment, trying to replay the incident. "It was probably just a good guess," she dismissed.

"There have been other times, too," Carter continued. "Many. I know because I've been writing them down."

"You've been keeping track of me?" Sarah exploded.

Carter knew he was digging himself in deeper and tried desperately to get out. "No, sweetheart...more of a diary...a journal...you know us scientific types. We take a lot of notes," Carter explained, trying to reason with her.

"Does that mean I have to watch *everything* I do from now on?" she raged.

"No, no," Carter assured, "it's just that I can prove you have... uh...a unique ability—and the Randolphs needed someone who could reach the other side."

"The other side? That sounds like hooey."

"It's not so far-fetched in the context of what they do," Carter explained more calmly. "They needed a channel."

"And that was me," Sarah said, bitterness lacing her words.

Carter looked ashen as he nodded yes. He saw their relationship unraveling.

"But you didn't even ask," Sarah said, not masking the violation she felt. "You just volunteered my services. You used me."

"I'm so sorry," Carter repeated. "The last thing I wanted to do was hurt you, and I certainly didn't want anything to happen to you. I just wanted to help my friends. I figured if you didn't know anything about it, you'd go into the house with an open mind and we'd get pure data. You'd say the lights flickered or you felt a chill, and that would be it. The Randolphs would move in, do their stuff, and you'd be out of the picture."

"But it didn't happen that way, did it?" Sarah sassed back. "I went there, I saw something all right, but I liked what I saw. And, now, I can't stay away. You played with my emotions. I've been nothing more than a lab rat!" Sarah stomped out of the room leaving Carter speechless. He could hear her car rev up and speed away. He picked up the phone and called Ann.

"I think she's heading to the house," he told his colleague, pacing in circles and running his hand through his hair. "She knows, and she's really pissed at me. You probably should leave her alone for a while."

Ann said something, and he nodded affirmatively. "Yes, I realize…it might not work now that you're living there…but she might have a better chance if you went away for a few days." By this time, Carter was speaking loudly, "But if something happens to her, I swear…."

His voice trailed off as Jared came running through the front doorway. "Dad! Dad! Guess what?"

"What, son?" Carter asked as he hung up the phone. He felt as if the wind had been knocked out of him.

"We went down to the old cemetery to check on the stones, and there were flowers on Sarah Covington's grave."

"That's nice." Carter commented, distracted. "Maybe they're from the Garden Club," he suggested.

"The Garden Club doesn't do that until Fourth of July, when it's warm. No, Dad, it was like she had a visitor."

"Hmmm. Maybe she did. The cemetery vandalism was all over the news. People might have come out to see it."

"Could be, Dad, but this was weird. There was a note with the flowers that said 'For my love. T.C.' and it was written in old brown ink, you know—fancy."

"Really?" Carter answered, now intrigued. "Maybe someone was just having fun with you guys."

"Yeah, maybe," Jared allowed as he headed down the hall.

Carter was left thinking about his conversation with Ann and was still rattled from his argument with Sarah. Figuring a walk would do him good, he called to Jared. "Can you watch your sister when she gets back from her dance lesson? I need to get some air."

"No problem," Jared answered, hardly paying attention.

Carter drove into town and parked his car near the old burial ground. The Minuteman statue gazed down on him. When he reached the Covington plot, he stepped carefully around the markers. The headstone for Sarah Hawthorne Covington was upright, as bare and untouched as the rest. Leaves had caught at the base and were trapped by the wind. An icy crust had formed over his son's recognizable footprints, but other than that, the area was deserted.

Carter suspected his son had inherited Sarah's unique ability to sense what others could not. He stood there for a while, wondering if someday he would lose Jared, too, to an attractive presence from the past. Carter returned home deflated and made dinner for the kids. Sarah didn't come back that night.

Although she no longer had a key to the Covington estate, Sarah suspected the bulkhead might be unlocked. As she drove past the house, Sarah could see that the Randolphs' car wasn't in the driveway. But, just to be safe, she continued a short distance beyond the house and pulled to the side of the road. She walked back through the woods, coming out behind the house.

Sarah tugged at the bulkhead door until it gave way with a painful creak. She propped it open with her shoulder, squeezed under it, then lowered the door above her head and crept down the wooden steps. The small flashlight she carried provided just enough light to show the way.

Sarah breathed in the damp earthiness of the underground chamber and remembered the first time she had seen muskets stashed there. Familiar blue and tan crocks lined the walls. She moved to the center of the house, ducking to avoid hitting the beams. She guessed she had about 3 inches between her headscarf and the ceiling. Clearly, she had already stepped back in time. With hand over mouth as if to muffle her own voice, she called out to Terrence. "Please, please hear me now."

Feeling a breeze in the otherwise still basement, she could see the flickering light of a lantern. Terrence was sitting on an overturned box, sharpening a blade, wearing the shirt she had made him. A tri-cornered hat rested on his knee, his British regalia, gone.

"Sarah, even if I can't materialize, I can always hear you," he said, ducking his head as he stood. "You're always with me."

Sarah rushed toward him, surprising him with her tight embrace. "Is everything all right?" he asked, returning her urgency.

"It's better now," she answered, not letting go. "I almost couldn't come back. The house is sold. My husband set me up. The Randolphs are studying us," she blurted out in one steady stream.

"Slow down," Terrence said. "Take a breath."

She nodded and calmed herself. "I've learned that we're part of a scientific experiment. Some sort of research. For all I know, they've conjured you up. You could be a hologram."

"A what?" Terrence questioned.

"Never mind. It's something new—like a picture that isn't there," Sarah answered with a tinge of exasperation, aware that she was melding her past and present worlds.

"I'm very real, I assure you," he said, leaning closer, piercing her with his blue stare.

"You certainly feel that way," she said, placing her hand where his chest showed.

"I've missed you," he said. She could sense a catch in his voice as he covered her hand with his. She could feel his heart beating. He certainly seemed to be among the living. His lips were warm as they encompassed hers, his scent filling the space. They still hungered for each other as they had months before. The room spun at such speed, she didn't notice the fieldstone pressing against her back or how her hair had come undone. She wasn't aware that their breathing was synchronized or that they collapsed against each other at the same time. All she knew is that she felt happy and fulfilled. She took a moment to steady herself before bringing her surroundings into focus. She eventually noticed Terrence sitting on the basement steps, grinning.

Sarah quickly buttoned her blouse and attempted to straighten her skirts. She started to ask about his meetings in Boston, but he stopped her. "Don't rush. I want to look at you...all messed up and naughty." She laughed, feeling childish and innocent, yet fully aware that she was anything but... She sat on his knee and he joked that she was getting too heavy to hold.

After a moment, he brought her up to date. "News from the city is tenuous at best. Residents are uneasy. Merchants are assembling to discuss their grievances. Publishers are voicing bold opinions. It seems like every day there's a new edict from the King to suppress us—and a new show of resistance. The British patrol the streets constantly." Sarah imagined the scene he described.

"The school...that's another thing. Mr. Hale has returned to Coventry to be with family in Connecticut. Ailing relative, it sounds. The women have been taking turns teaching classes. Maybe you could help, too."

"I'd be happy to do my part," Sarah offered. "Just tell me when."

"Let's plan for next week. Mercy Biddle has the children this week."

A wisp of current recollection flitted through Sarah's mind. "Do you think we have to stay here until then?" Sarah asked wide-eyed, referring to the basement. Terrence looked puzzled. "I mean, if we go upstairs, will the Randolphs see us?"

Terrence broke out laughing, then with a gentleness that came from love, he explained: "My dearest, it is highly unlikely that they will see or sense anything—unless you let them. They operate on an entirely different plane."

"They do?" Sarah asked as she followed Terrence upstairs.

She and Terrence stood in the main room and looked around. Boxes were stacked in every corner, along with books and crates, but the Randolphs weren't there. It was as if the present had invaded the past, yet everything else was primitive.

"I have no idea what that is," he said, pointing to the equipment— and of course, why would he? With that, the equipment faded away, but this brief overlapping of time made Sarah wonder if items from both realms could coexist.

"We have much to do—battles to fight and a war to win," Terrence mused as he stationed himself in front of the kitchen window, pouring a tankard of cider from a jug on the counter.

"Then you think we are definitely going to war?" Sarah asked, reaching for a handkerchief in the pocket that hung from her waistband.

"I think it is inevitable," Terrence solemnly replied. "I hear talk on the street and in the tavern. People are angry. They're joining forces. With each new law imposed, the British steal our rights as free men. We can't ignore it." Sarah mindlessly folded and unfolded the small square of cloth that was in her hand.

Terrence was somber as he continued. "Public opinion is finally turning in support of revolution and citizens like me," he said, motioning with the hat he held, "no longer have to pretend to be what we are not."

"Then we're in more danger than before," Sarah concluded, half to Terrence, half to herself.

"We have to be careful, that's all," he continued. So long as we meet secretly and keep our plans quiet, the British will go about their business with a lot of bluster, worrying more about squeezing money from us than anything else. But, one of these days, the fury will boil over and we will have to take a stand. Blood will be shed, and you must be forewarned…mine may flow with that tide."

Sarah wadded the little cloth into her fist, unnerved to hear Terrence talk this way. Only after seeing her pale did he realize he had said too much. "But that's a long way off, my love. I'm just saying we have to be ready."

Sarah and Terrence were each deep in thought as they ate their evening meal. When supper was done, Terrence went to the pantry, reached behind a wallboard, and took out the map Mr. Hale had brought. "I don't think I ever showed this to you. It provides strategic information," Terrence said, motioning for Sarah to come over. "At some point, we expect the British to amass their troops as they move inland from the harbor and retreat from New York and, when they do, we will be ready to confront them with force. This map identifies critical landmarks around Boston and Concord."

Sarah noticed Xs leading to North Bridge. "This house will become one of the base camps. We are storing weapons throughout the countryside and training a militia. John and Sam will be ensconced in Lexington for their safety. This is just the beginning of something much greater."

A sense of foreboding washed over Sarah. As she studied the paper, her eyes fixed on something far away. She thought she could hear the ratta-tat-tat of drummers and the voice of a commander summoning his troops into formation. "Father!" a little girl screamed as a Colonial soldier fell to the ground. Women sobbed, horses reared, and young boys picked up muskets. She saw blood in the snow and felt extreme hunger. She was cold, bone-chilling cold, cold to the point of death, as she saw a sick and starving Continental Army of 11,000 march through a place called Valley Forge. She couldn't discern all the faces, but she felt the pain. She shivered with them and writhed with gangrene. Her eyes burnt from the smoke of battle or perhaps the tears to come.

The image was startling and didn't dissipate for quite a while. Sarah silently worried about war as she carded wool in the firelight. When she finally went to bed, her sleep was disrupted by the sound of an owl hunting its prey. She could hear the shrieks and whimpers of what sounded like a rabbit. She tossed and turned, fearful for the young bunny being cornered and consumed by the great winged predator. In her dreams, the rabbit morphed into people she knew, cowering in the presence of a larger, looming danger.

When the next week was upon them, Sarah put on a clean dress to go to the school. Children were running around the fenced yard as she arrived but came to an obedient halt when she rang the bell. One by one, they filed in, all boys except for the small girl who was given permission to observe.

The days were still cool and one of the handymen had stoked the stove. Sarah noticed that the children, who sat next to it over-heated, while the others froze. She decided to do something different. She pushed the rows of benches back against the walls and told the children to sit on the floor in the middle of the room.

Although their ages ranged from 5 to 13 years old, they were glad to make the move. They watched inquisitively as she reached into her basket, producing the newspaper that had arrived those many weeks before. "Do you know this letter?" she asked the youngest one as she pointed to a headline. The longhaired boy proudly said, "B!"

"Good. And what is this picture?" she asked an older boy. He didn't know. "It's a drawing of a lion. Do you know where lions live?" Sarah continued. The children shook their heads no. Sarah walked slowly over to a globe that had been donated by one of the town's wealthier families. "Here" she said, pointing to Africa. Her father had shown her the same thing many years before.

"I don't see any lions there. They must be hiding," a smart-mouthed boy cracked. The class laughed, but Sarah wasn't flustered; she rather liked the exchange.

Tapping the newspaper illustration, she continued, "In this picture, the lion is shown to be very powerful. Look at the people next to him. They're quite small. What do you think it means?" One boy raised his hand: "I think it means that it takes a lot of little people to care for a big lion." Another boy disagreed. "No, the lion isn't friendly. He's going to step on the people and eat them."

Lydia Whiting raised her hand from the edge of the circle. "I can't see, Mrs. Covington."

"Then come a little closer," Sarah motioned. "You can sit right here on the floor next to me."

Lydia felt very special and sauntered up to the teacher. "My dad says the British are stepping all over us," she volunteered in a loud clear voice. Sarah wasn't sure how to respond. She knew she had to be neutral as she had children from both rebel and loyal households in her charge.

"That's not true," a voice boomed from the doorway. It was Lord Bennington, returned from his travels abroad, checking in on his youngest citizens. "Just like this lion, the British are helping the good people of the Colonies learn how to care for themselves," he said, removing his hat and revealing a freshly powdered wig. He was aware that his analogy would fly over the heads of the children but knew it wouldn't be lost on Sarah.

She stood to greet him, but he motioned her down. Unaware of her involvement in the recent resistance, he was polite and patronizing. Based on this behavior, she was sure he had no knowledge of Terrence's defection or incarceration—yet.

"There. There, good woman. These children have been hearing all kinds of rubbish in town, haven't they? Let's set them straight." Sarah stood silent as he muscled his way toward the circle.

Bennington moved a chair into the middle and like a kindly grandfather, summoned the children closer. "Let me tell you a story about a lion," he began, showing them the Royal Coat of Arms on the pouch he was holding. The children gasped at the colorful and mysterious decoration. He then recounted a tale of knights and dragons, princes and princesses, conveying all that was good and magical about his home in a land of castles.

The children sat wide-eyed, enraptured. Suddenly, Charles Whiting stood up and challenged, "Well, if it was so good there, why don't you go back and leave us alone?" He had clearly heard those words from his father.

Sarah was at first shocked and then concerned. She moved toward Charles as if angered, but more so to protect him. "Charles, that was rude. Go stand outside until class is done." As Charles left the room, the children followed him with their eyes.

By this time, Bennington had pulled himself together, determined not to be rattled by an errant child. "I must be going, Mrs. Covington. You *will* make sure these children get a proper education, won't you?" he asserted, sternly looking at her.

"I will certainly try, sir. But please realize, I'm just a substitute in Mr. Hale's absence." Bennington nodded a formal good-bye and started to leave.

Just then, there was a shot and a scream. Sarah could hear Bennington roar, "What have you done? Put that pistol down!"

Sarah pushed past the children, out to the street. There lay Charles, bleeding from his chest. Bennington had left his weapon outside and, curious about the pistol, Charles had picked it up. Charles was accustomed to his father keeping bullets in a separate pouch, but this weapon was loaded and it fired upon touch.

"Lydia, get your mother!" Sarah yelled over the hysterical children. "Tell her to come at once."

Sarah went to the fallen child and cushioned his head in her lap while keeping her hand over his wound. Bennington rode off, saying he would get help. That was the last they saw of him. As much as Sarah tried to keep the blood from spurting out, it pumped steadily, forming a small pool at the boy's side.

Two men came running from the gristmill and carefully moved the child into the general store. They assumed that Bennington had shot the boy. Sarah explained it was just an accident, a self-inflicted wound, but they doubted her, eager for someone to blame.

Danna was close on their heels, running toward her boy, gathering him up in her arms. If they were lucky, Charles would survive. If not, he'd likely be dead by daybreak.

With no doctor in town, Martha Quiggley, the midwife, arrived along with the barber, who owned the apothecary. They helped Sarah and Danna put the boy on a bench. Women brought over blankets, cloth, and pitchers of water.

Charles slipped in and out of consciousness as the midwife and barber cut away his bloodied shirt. His small chest heaved when they examined the wound. "Bullet is lodged here," the midwife confirmed, pointing to a spot below the right collarbone. "We'll have to get it out."

The barber applied a tincture to slow the bleeding and opened a flask of whiskey. "Get him to drink this," he instructed.

Danna took the vessel with a shaking hand and pressed it to her child's lips. Gasping for breath, he took a gulp, sputtered and lost consciousness. "My son. My son!" she sobbed as a bystander pulled her away.

Four strong men held Charles down as the barber doused the wound with water to flush away debris from the street. Once he could see better, he grabbed a set of tongs and worked at dislodging the persistent slug. Charles thrashed around, grunting and clenching his jaw around a dowel that someone had slid between his teeth. His mother winced.

Finally, the barber dropped the metal bead into a bowl and set it aside. Charles grew still, letting the dowel roll away. Martha tore a length of cheesecloth and wrapped it snugly around the child's chest and over his shoulder. "Give this to him for the pain," the barber instructed, soberly handing a small mortar of crushed powder to Danna.

Danna stirred the white stuff into a cup of water and forced a spoonful between her son's lips. Hours passed, and Danna didn't leave. Charles slept soundly but labored to breathe.

Sarah was numb. She stayed at a distance, not knowing what to do. If only she hadn't sent the child outside she agonized, he'd be alive and well now. "But if I hadn't removed him from the classroom, there's no telling what Bennington might have done," she reasoned.

Terrence and Joshua had gone to a cooper in the next town and had no idea what happened until Lydia saw them coming up the road. Breaking free of her mother, she ran to them, babbling about the day's events and they, in turn, followed her, running, to the store. Danna, color drained from her face, was sitting next to Charles. She told them the details while gripping her husband's powerful paw with her small hand.

Sarah saw Joshua, leaning over his first-born, sobbing like a baby. Seeing a strong man cry tore at her heart. No one said a word. Suddenly he pulled himself to his full height, stood back, and stepped away from his son. With muscles taut and eyes on fire, he vowed that he would seek revenge on the British—for every wrong they had caused or *would* cause, even if he had to die doing it.

"Are you with me?" he called, turning to the crowd that had formed outside the building. A smattering of "Ayes" arose. "Are we together in this?" he yelled again. This time the crowd echoed louder, "Aye! We are one!" From beyond the steps, Sarah could see fists clenched and muskets raised in unison. She knew Terrence's war would come to pass.

Sarah and Terrence walked home in silence until she spoke. "If something ever happened to our child, I don't know what I'd do. Children are supposed to outlive their parents, not the other way around."

"I know," he said quietly. Yet he had a different fear in mind: "If something ever happened to you, I don't know what *I'd* do."

116

The next day they learned that Charles Whiting had made it through the night and had awakened to find his parents sleeping next to him. Moments later, their neighbor Becca, arrived with Lydia and baby Betsy.

"He's awake! He's awake!" Lydia cried out, running to her brother, who was only one shade better than gray. "Can he come home now?" Lydia asked, optimistically looking at her parents.

"I don't think we can move him yet," Danna answered, smoothing her daughter's curls. "Let's see how he does as the day goes by, shall we?"

An exhausted Joshua and Danna were grateful as Becca opened her basket to offer them tea, cornbread, and pickled eggs. They were too tired to talk, but their eyes said everything.

With school cancelled, Sarah returned to town several times that day to check on Charles and to relieve Danna of her watch. Terrence remained in the fields with Joshua, trying to keep his friend's mind as busy as his hands.

When Sarah finally got back to the house, just as the sun began to set, she had a sense that something needed to be done, that she had somewhere to be. Charles kept reminding her of another boy…a son…*her* son…and she knew he was waiting for her.

For the briefest moment, Sarah remembered she was a visitor here and that she had to go home. Writing a note to Terrence, she promised she would find a way to return. Sarah now accepted the fact her life existed on parallel planes and that she would have to navigate between them. She sat in the rocking chair and picked up her stitching, forming a picture of that other boy in her head. Almost immediately, she felt herself drifting away.

As soon as she arrived in the present, Sarah knew she shouldn't be in the Randolph's house. She pulled herself together and quickly slipped out the back door, locking it as she went out. Hurrying through the woods that were starting to brighten with the rising sun, she headed down toward her car. She was surprised to see flashing blue lights and hear a police radio squawking in the distance.

There was Carter, talking adamantly, gesturing with his arms. He was pointing toward the house and then, in grand sweeping motions, to the fields across the road.

For some reason, he looked up and saw her standing there. Sarah could do nothing but continue to walk down the hill. She now remembered that he had deceived her, and she was reluctant to hurry back.

"You had us worried to death!" he called out, rushing toward her, not concealing his mix of frustration and relief.

"I'm sorry," Sarah answered, cool and distant. "I didn't mean to worry you. I, uh, went for a ride."

"I *know* where you went," Carter retorted. "And was *he* here?"

Sarah simply shook her head as if it were no use explaining. One of the officers, hearing their exchange, came over. "Was someone responsible for your disappearance, ma'am?" he asked, encouraging her to reveal any foul play.

"No, officer. Just a little domestic dispute. I needed to get away to think things out." The officer nodded, closed his notepad, and got into his car. Carter and Sarah stood there until the black and white disappeared around the bend.

"Do you want to see more of the house?" she tentatively asked, trying to rise above their disagreement. "The Randolphs aren't around."

"No way. I've had enough of this place," Carter said, making his opinion very clear. "Besides, the house has been sold and we have no business being here."

"You forget, Carter," Sarah snipped. "You made it my business." And, with that, they drove off in their separate cars.

Sarah's sister had been watching the kids, and upon seeing Carter's face, left without asking questions. Conversation at breakfast was stilted. When the school bus came, and the children were safely on it, Sarah turned to Carter. "I need a better explanation about what's going on with the Randolphs," she demanded.

"And I need more information about what's going on with you," Carter replied.

"Fine," Sarah agreed. Carter knew that if he didn't try to meet her halfway, his marriage would be in jeopardy. Perhaps it already was.

"We'll continue this conversation tonight, then?" Sarah pressed.

"Yes. Later," Carter promised, glad to procrastinate.

Throughout the day, Sarah replayed the shooting at the Colonial schoolhouse and the events leading up to it. Her thoughts drifted from incident to incident, person to person, until she stopped stone cold, realizing something even more ominous was looming on the horizon. The original Sarah had been pregnant and by all historic accounts, didn't live long after giving birth. Her pregnancy was, in fact, a ticking time bomb with Sarah Sutherland heading straight toward the death of her long-ago counterpart. Suddenly it seemed imperative to intervene.

The more Sarah thought about it, the more she feared that her historic death would affect her current life. What if she went back, died as the original Sarah, and couldn't return? What if she saved the original Sarah, but died trying? What if the original Sarah lived? What would happen to Terrence? The only reason he had found her in the first place was that he was looking for his wife, so would saving the first Sarah mean losing him?

Sarah felt herself hyperventilating. She was nauseous and dizzy. Perspiration began beading on her forehead; her palms were damp, her throat tight. Frightened and unable to control her panic, she called Dr. Barrow's office. "Can she see me right away? It's urgent," Sarah pleaded. Sarah waited for an answer, gulping for air. "OK. I'll be there within the hour."

The serene mood of the doctor's waiting room usually made Sarah relax, but this time when Dr. Barrows opened her office door, Sarah was scared. She sat down directly in front of the doctor's desk and began talking rapidly, fidgeting with a paperclip that was lying on the edge.

Dr. Barrows was concerned that Sarah's separation of past and present was becoming dangerously muddled. To mollify Sarah, the doctor likened going into the house to turning on an old radio, suggesting that Sarah was simply picking up signals on a different wavelength. The doctor reminded Sarah, in no uncertain terms, that she was not the wife of a Colonial farmer, wasn't pregnant, and certainly wasn't going to die.

Sarah didn't buy it. She had been feeling queasy recently and had put on a few pounds. "Could it be a symptomatic pregnancy?" she asked. The doctor allowed that it was remotely possible, but not likely. That wasn't enough to assuage Sarah's fears. She rationalized that if she could have a symptomatic pregnancy, then she could have a symptomatic death—and the thought was paralyzing.

Just then the intercom buzzed, and Dr. Barrows excused herself to the waiting room. Sarah sat there nervously looking around, trying not to listen to the loud voices coming from the corridor. She stared at the diplomas on the wall, studied the family photos on the bookcase, and tilting her head, deciphered the spines of medical journals propped up on the console behind the desk. That's when she noticed the open appointment book with a 7:00 p.m. entry scrawled in blue pen. Reading upside-down, Sarah saw that it said, "David Randolph."

She abruptly sat back. This had to be more than a fluke. But who was seeing whom and why? Was Mr. Randolph seeing Dr. Barrows for advice or had Dr. Barrows summoned Mr. Randolph for a consult? Then again, maybe this wasn't a professional meeting at all....

Dr. Barrows returned as Sarah was trying to process the information. "I could give you something for your nerves, but I don't want to impair your judgment," the doctor explained. "You'll need to be alert when you're at the house." What the doctor didn't say was that she was depending on Sarah's firsthand account.

"So, what are you telling me?" Sarah asked. "That it's OK for me to go back? That I should go back?"

"As long as it's well *before* Sarah gives birth. Just watch the timing and keep sending me your notes. How many more months do you...uh, Sarah Covington...have left?"

Sarah tried to calculate. "It's hard to say. Time there doesn't always equate with time here, but I'd say about 4 or 5 more months."

"Then sure, go back a few more times, gather what information you can, and share it with me. If the owners of the house understand that this is a medical situation, they probably wouldn't mind your visiting. Would you like me to speak to them?"

"Definitely not!" Sarah was quick to respond. "I want to talk to my husband first." Besides, she didn't particularly trust the Randolphs anymore.

"That's fine," Dr. Barrows said, clearing her throat and calmly closing her appointment book. "We'll figure out a way for you to cope with this."

The street noise was jarring as the sound of a jackhammer assaulted her ears. Sarah felt better having talked to a professional, but she wasn't convinced this doctor had her best interests in mind. In fact, she felt that Dr. Barrows was almost too eager for her to return to the house and began wondering if the doctor had her own agenda. All Sarah knew is that she was more often cast into the role of a researcher *for* Dr. Barrows than a patient. And, besides, if Dr. Barrows personally knew Mr. Randolph, there had to be more to the story.

After dinner, when the kids were doing homework, Sarah and Carter went into the living room for their dreaded heart-to-heart talk. A pronounced silence hung the air. Carter started by explaining that he had been a student when he first met Ann and David. They shared many interests, so they had stayed in touch. Knowing he had moved to New England, they had asked him to help find a location to study, aware that the area was rich in history.

"So, you were looking for haunted houses?" Sarah asked, not mincing words.

"That sounds like a bad movie," Carter admitted. "But yes. We wanted a site where the right elements converged...but not something that would draw attention. I told the Randolphs about the Covington estate. They liked that it was out in the country, away from foot traffic. And lucky for us, your office was repping it."

"But why didn't they just go to one of their psychic friends to test it out? Surely, in their line of work, they must know a slew of people," Sarah questioned.

"They wanted someone who belonged in the story…not a stranger, who might disrupt things. Since you're a real estate agent, you had the perfect cover. We decided they'd pose as buyers and bring you to the house to see if you sensed anything unusual. But you discovered a lot more."

"That's for sure," Sarah muttered. She hated being angry at Carter and was trying to give him the benefit of the doubt.

"Don't assume for a minute that I wasn't thinking about your safety, but I'm a scientist at heart and this could be quite a discovery," Carter continued. "Besides, we hired Dr. Barrows to be in the wings." As soon as the words left his lips, Carter wanted to take them back, realizing he was admitting to yet another deception.

"Dr. Barrows?" Sarah exclaimed. "You *hired* her?" Sarah was incredulous.

"Just as a precaution. I thought you might have guessed…I mean, didn't you think it was odd that you ran into her?"

"No. Things like that happen to me all the time," Sarah declared. She didn't tell Carter that she had seen Dr. Barrows that very afternoon.

"We made sure Dr. Barrows was planted right where you'd find her—or she was instructed to find you—just in case you needed help. She's there as a guide, a safeguard."

"And yet another thing you didn't tell me," Sarah lobbed back. Her hands shot up, palms open, in disbelieve.

"I couldn't. It was part of the plan—designed for your protection."

Sarah didn't want to interrupt him by saying she thought Dr. Barrows was hiding something, so she patiently listened.

"The Randolphs are extremely dedicated to their work," Carter continued. "Once they saw the potential in the house, they decided to move up here. I mean, it's not every day you find a center of paranormal activity and have a way to access it."

Sarah tried to understand his perspective, wanting him in turn, to understand hers.

"I'm hoping now that you know the context, you can forgive me and help them wrap this up. Then we can put this whole thing behind us," he pleaded, looking a bit like a lost boy. Sarah wondered how someone so smart could be so naïve.

"I'm not sure it's that easy," Sarah said, trying to explain. "You know you mean the world to me…the kids…our lives together. I wouldn't change that for anything, but I need to finish what I started. I think I was drawn to the house for a reason."

"I understand the intrigue," Cater allowed, perhaps sounding more condescending than he intended. "And I get it—he's handsome and brave."

"It's more than that now. I know I have something important do. I have to save Sarah."

"Then maybe you should become a nurse," Carter muttered, sarcastic, under his breath.

"That's not fair, Carter," Sarah accused. "You put this on me."

"I didn't tell you to start messing around with a ghost," Carter jabbed. "I can't compete with someone who's not there!"

"Well, maybe that's the precise way to look at it," Sarah retorted. "If this *is* in my head or in some other dimension, then no one *is* there. This would be my own private fantasy, wouldn't it? No harm. No foul."

Carter was quiet.

"You owe this to me," Sarah continued. "I have to go back, and I don't know for how long. I need you to cut me some slack and take care of the kids. I will return before there is any real danger." She went into the bedroom, threw some essentials into an overnight bag, and grabbed her keys.

Carter watched as she headed toward the door. "Be careful," he called after her, standing uncomfortably alone.

"I'll try."

✦ ✦ ✦

The road to Baker's Cove was deserted except for one pick-up truck coming at her. The only other company she had was the reflection of her high beams bouncing off a row of delineators. She slowed as she passed the house and tried to see if anyone was home. There were no lights on, but she parked beyond it and retraced her steps as before, looking over her shoulder to make sure she hadn't been followed.

Newspapers were piled at the bottom of the drive, so she figured the Randolphs were away. Their absence made her brazen.

She walked to the back of the house, noticing that the foundation for the greenhouse had been poured. Reaching for the bulkhead handle, she lifted it, slid under, crossed the basement and climbed up to the first floor. This time she didn't have to tell Terrence she was there. Lavender and lemon filled the air.

"I'm over here," he called to her, before she had a chance to speak. With one step toward him, her outfit was transformed into the garments of the time, her belly pulling the fabric tight.

"I had to come back. I've learned so much. Even my doctor is in on it. I think she's using me for her own gains. And Mr. Randolph…the doctor is meeting with him, but I'm not sure why."

Sarah was chattering at top speed when Terrence anchored her shoulders. "Pull yourself together, woman," he insisted. "None of that is happening here."

"I know, I know," she said, taking a breath as she folded into his embrace.

"Feel better now?" he asked, not letting go. His hands ran up and down the length of her back, exerting a slight pressure at the base of her spine. She was acutely aware of the heat between their hips.

"Much," she answered as she leaned her head against him.

"I'm so glad you came here tonight because something exciting is going to happen," Terrence said.

"What do you mean, *exciting*?"

"I mean we're going to test the British resolve," he replied, his eyes dancing with devious plans.

"And how are we going to do that?" Sarah asked, smoothing his shirt where her head had rested.

"Word is that several royal dignitaries will be coming to town to look at some land. We thought they could use a welcoming party." Terrence was having fun.

"I'm listening," Sarah said, her nose scrunching up with skepticism.

"We're going to assemble on the green—like we do in Boston—and hang King George in effigy from the big oak. That will be our Liberty Tree."

Sarah looked worried. "Isn't that dangerous? Being so bold, I mean?"

"Oh, just a little," Terrence winked, "but we want to see what they do. It's good to poke at them. Keeps them off-balance. Besides, there will be many of us and few of them…and with such prominent visitors in their entourage, the King's troops will most likely defer rather than cause a scene."

"Who's making George?"

"It will be a collective effort. Chances are if you stop by the Whiting's house in the morning, they'll give you something to do. You might take those milkweed pods," he said, pointing to the pitcher that contained her dry arrangement. "We'll need white hair," he gestured as if flouncing long locks. She enjoyed his sense of humor.

That night, the house ached as the wind whipped around it. Sarah could hear their cow, Madelaine, bellow when a branch hit the roof of her stall. Moonlight streamed in over the bed, making twiggy shadows on the patchwork quilt. Sarah slid further under the covers, letting the stress of her other life slip away. Turning toward Terrence, she absorbed his comfort and his warmth.

Sarah woke up early, not wanting to miss any of the activities at the Whiting's house. She sloshed cold water from the basin over her face, forcing her eyes open. Terrence was already feeding the chickens by the time she got downstairs, and a kettle of porridge was bubbling in a pot on the hearth. Even the simplest chores seemed to have meaning here.

When Sarah arrived at the Whiting's, an eight-pointed star was being cut for the royal insignia. Twine was being braided into epaulets and an ascot, fashioned from a remnant of silk, was taking form. The women welcomed her as if she were expected.

"Did you bring the hair?" Lottie asked. She was one those quiet types you'd never guess was a real organizer.

"Got it," Sarah said, pointing to her basket of milkweed tufts.

Several drawings of King George were hooked on a nail for reference. Soon, stockings had become arms and legs; a tablecloth became the body. Moss and hay were used to stuff the torso along with feathers from the coop. Red and black wools were selected for the outer garments and buttons were salvaged from old clothes.

Assembling these items was a sacrifice, because supplies were limited—and boycotts, prevalent. Merchants, craftsmen, and even young people had begun to forego British goods, choosing simple country attire over leather and lace. Wearing homespun cloth had become a sign of defiance and Sarah was all for it.

Working quickly, the women paused only to tend young children or beat down rising dough. Soon, a semblance of George sat on the table. The women leaned back, proudly admiring their handiwork. "Stunning," "Remarkable," "Outstanding," they told each other as they tucked George away in a potato sack.

Later that week, the church bell rang, signaling arrival of the King's emissaries. Sarah and Terrence watched as three ornate gilt-edged coaches appeared on the horizon. Each bore the bright Royal Crest—brilliantly painted on the slick black sides of the carriages. Twelve white horses halted obediently, their manes plaited and woven with gold ribbons. Three elegant couples and their attendants stepped out, assisted by the drivers.

Sarah was speechless at the grandeur in this otherwise modest town. The tavernkeeper scurried out to greet the entourage, bowing low and fawning over them. Behind him, his wait staff followed, ready to take wraps and offer libation. The group bustled their way into the building, aloof and preoccupied, as Colonists began to step into view. Soon, the green was churning with a crowd of seeming well-wishers.

Imperceptibly, the demeanor changed. One by one, members of the crowd started holding up signs that read: "No say, No pay!" "Free trade!" "Fair trials!" Hecklers began chanting, "Go back to England!"

Sarah could see Lottie remove George from her cart. Some of the older boys had already climbed the oak and looped a rope over the most prominent limb. George was tossed up to them and tied at the neck. The crowd cheered as his effigy swung from the noose. Someone with a drum began a pounding beat.

Hearing the noise, one of the coach drivers stepped from the tavern to see what was happening. Soon the entire entourage was on the porch craning to catch the action, staring, pointing, and gaping as a local farmer set George alight. Hoots and hollers arose from the field. Someone shot a musket into the air, spreading smoke like a blanket, over the scene. A line of guards quickly formed in front of the visiting dignitaries to create a barrier.

Another line of Regulars began advancing across the green with bayonets drawn. "On the authority of King George, we order you to disband immediately," their leader commanded. "Cease this assembly at once or we will take you into custody!" The demonstrators linked arms and stood firm.

"Try fitting us all into your shabby little jail," a voice taunted.

"One for all, all for one!" another voice cried out.

People who had been standing on the sidelines ran into the Common to join the others. Dogs began to bark, and children screamed, trying to find their parents in the melee. The drum beat persisted. Another shot rang out.

By this time, the visitors were nervous. Not wanting to risk bloodshed or an embarrassing incident, one of their escorts approached the commander.

The commander obediently nodded and called out, "At ease." The line fell back, and the men lowered their weapons. The crowd quieted as the commander stepped forward. "We will take our leave now and show our guests to a more hospitable location, but we will return. We know who you are, and we are prepared to tar and feather the instigators!" With that, he clicked his heels and turned away.

The crowd stood silent.

Sarah and Terrence could see the genteel British women lifting their skirts with gloved hands as they climbed back into the coaches. One dabbed her face with a hanky. Another attempted to tidy her hair. The distinguished gentlemen did their best to remain detached, but one couldn't resist throwing a look of disdain at the assemblage on the green. To Terrence, this sideways glance said it all: this humble, rowdy crowd—this riff-raff of villagers—had left an impression. Surely this story would be retold in pubs and social circles across the land.

Once the coaches were gone, the townspeople broke into cheers. George crackled like bacon in a pan until nothing was left but a smoldering belt and a scattering of metal. Sarah walked over to the pile of debris, kicking dirt on the buttons to cool them. She bent over, picked them up, and put them into her pocket…evidence of her enterprising spirit and a welcome addition to her sewing basket.

"Aren't you afraid?" Sarah asked Terrence as they walked home. He just shrugged. She had never seen anyone tarred and feathered, but she had heard it was a horrible experience.

When they got home, their thoughts were still on the green. While Terrence cleaned his musket, Sarah tossed leftover meat and vegetables into a kettle and poured corn meal batter into a pan. Soup and Johnnycakes were all she could manage. When supper was done, she went out to give Madelaine a fresh bale of hay and add water to her trough. The pump handle tended to be stiff when the weather was cold. As Sarah struggled to crank it, she felt someone grab her wrist. "Let me help you with that," a Cockney voice said.

She whipped around and found herself face to face with a British sentry. His hand tightened as she tried to pull free.

"Let me go," Sarah protested, struggling to get away.

"Not so fast pretty lady," he said, stepping closer, revealing a mouth of yellow teeth. The smell of whiskey hung on his words. Repulsed, Sarah turned her face.

"How about some sweetness?" he persisted, closing in for a kiss.

"Get away from me!" she hissed, trying to call for help. But the sentry's other hand clamped over her mouth and his body pushed her against the clothesline pole.

"Looking for those buttons?" the sentry mocked. "Let me lend a hand," he taunted, plunging his fingers far into her pocket, groping where he shouldn't.

Sarah tried to kick him but was trapped by her long skirts.

"I saw you on the Common today. All feisty and fired up. That's how I like my women. Brave and brazen. But not so tough now, are you?" he said as he shoved her to the ground. She could hear the crack of her skull as she fell against a rock. He stood above her, one boot on each side—her only view being up the inseam of his stained gaiters. Soon his weight was upon her, his grimy hand back over her mouth. Try as she might, she could not break free.

Straddling her, he took a knife from his coat pocket and toyed with it in front of her face. Her eyes darted back and forth, following the menacing blade.

"A lock for my locket," he teased, shifting his hand from her mouth to a strand of hair.

With that, she screamed—a terrifying caterwaul into the night—hoping Terrence would hear from within the house. The knife cut her cheek as she fought to roll over. But, she needn't have worried.

Within moments, the dull thud of a musket butt slammed into the sentry's head, sending him reeling. His knife landed with a plunk in the water trough.

Sarah attempted to stand, but when she noticed the blood spilling down her dress, she started to swoon. Terrence caught her and helped her to the settle inside their doorway.

"Stay here," he ordered as he ran back outside.

The sentry moaned, but Terrence couldn't tell whether it was from pain or drunkenness. Didn't matter. A length of hawser from the barn was all he needed to tie the soldier to the post.

Once inside again, Terrence hovered over his wife. "Sarah, Sarah…Are you all right? Please, please talk to me," he pleaded as she stared into the distance, dazed. He hurried to the bedroom and dampened a towel with water from the pitcher bowl, quickly returning to press it to the back of her head. She started to say something but began to faint again. Catching her, he sat beside her and guided her head to his lap.

He could see the slice oozing red on her cheek. "That beautiful cheek," he thought as he used his thumb to wipe away the blood. A bruise was already forming around it, puffing the skin into an angry pout.

"Sarah, please be all right," he whispered.

In time, her eyelids fluttered. "What happened?" she asked, groggy and squinting at the sconces. Remembering the sentry, she tried to sit up. "Is he here? Is he still here?"

"No, no…it's just me…he's outside, tied up," Terrence said, soothing her and leading her toward their bed. "You rest. I'm going to Jonah's to get help."

Sarah laid back on a pillow, her head wound now congealed. When she awoke, Terrence and Jonah were loading the sentry into a wagon. Jonah's wife, Grace, was at her side. "Here, drink this tea. It will make you feel better."

Sarah could smell the pungent scent of ginger. The back of her head ached, her stomach churned, and her cheek throbbed as she bent forward to drink. "What are they going to do with him?" she asked.

"Take him into town and deliver him to his superior, I think," Grace replied, smoothing the blankets around Sarah.

"If the troops hadn't stayed here, he wouldn't know where I lived," Sarah reasoned. "How dare they march onto someone's property whenever they want?"

"It's the law." Grace said, matter-of-fact. "But no use worrying about that now. Get some rest. We'll talk about it later."

"Bad law," Sarah thought, but she didn't have the strength to say it out loud. She leaned back again and fell asleep as Grace dozed in the rocker at her side.

On the edge of town, Terrence and Jonah steered the wagon to the officers' quarters. "Get your leader out here," Jonah demanded, pounding on the door.

"We have a present for him," Terrence added, holding a lantern above the unconscious sentry.

"Just a minute, mate," a sluggish voice said from within. A bleary-eyed British officer in long johns opened the door. "I'm in charge here. What is it?" he asked.

Terrence rolled the sentry out of the wagon and onto the ground. "This is what it is—a cowardly bastard going after my wife...coming to my home in the dark of night and attacking her!"

The officer was now fully awake and trying to put on some clothes.

"If this is how you fight your battles, then maybe we'll have to train our women to fight back," Jonah snapped.

"There must be some misunderstanding," the officer said, calling over his shoulder for help.

"Just stay away from my home and my family," Terrence threatened, moving closer and stretching himself to his full height, so he towered over the Brit. The officer didn't say anything; he just shook his head obligingly and backed into the building as two of his reports came out and dragged the sentry toward the door.

"And make sure this piece of dirt stays with you," Jonah added as he and Terrence climbed into the wagon seat and flicked the reins.

The first rays of sun were coming over the hills and a rooster was crowing when the two men returned to the Tory house. A weary Jonah and Grace went home, and Terrence walked inside.

5

CLOSE CALL

Terrence lay next to Sarah watching her breathe and, finally, stir. He got up to make her some tea and brought her the leftover Johnnycakes and jam. Still weak, she took a sip of the warm liquid. She spooned out a generous helping of blackberry preserves and spread it over the corncakes. Once consumed, she thanked him and went back to sleep. The next time she awoke, it was noon.

Terrence was sprawled out on a chair sleeping soundly when Sarah leaned toward him. "Are *you* all right?" she asked, jostling him.

He sat up, rubbed his face, and reached for her. "You had me worried last night," he said.

"I was petrified," Sarah admitted. He helped her to the chamber pot, aware that she walked more slowly these days.

"Is the baby all right?" he called to her.

"I think so. I can feel movement."

"We'll have to be more careful," he said, when she returned. "The British are everywhere and clearly they're not above accosting a man's family."

"They're not going to get the best of us," Sarah vowed, drinking the rest of her now-cold tea. "We're stronger than they think."

"Well, you look a lot better than you did before," Terrence said, examining the cut on her cheek. "Just a bit swollen there," he said, "Now let me help you with the rest."

"The rest?" Sarah puzzled, still subdued.

"Yes. Follow me to the kitchen. I'm going to wash your hair and examine the wound. Then we'll decide if we need to go to the apothecary."

Terrence propped a straight chair against the kitchen table and had her take a seat facing outward. After placing a cloth on her shoulders, he set their largest bowl behind her. In one hand, he held a pot of water warmed on the hearth and, in the other hand, an ivory comb. "Lean back," he said as he guided her head into position. Her long hair tumbled down so it touched the ceramic. The water ran clear at first, then red where it trickled over the cut. A pink pool formed in the basin. He removed the tangles as gently as he could, grimacing at the thought of her hurting her.

"Stay put," he instructed as he dumped the used water outside and heated more. Reaching for a square of soap, he carefully lathered and rinsed her locks. She could feel the taut muscles under his ribcage as he bent forward to gather up her hair. His sleeves, rolled to the elbow, revealed the raised veins that defined his arms. His hands, softened by the water, were warm as he carefully wrapped her hair in the cloth and secured it on top of her head. She closed her eyes as if in a reverie.

Sitting up slowly, she brought her head forward, still a bit dizzy. "That was incredibly relaxing, thank you," she said, holding onto his arm for support. He carefully combed her hair, separating it around the abrasion. The wound was raw, but at least it was clean.

Sarah stood in front of the rippled windowpanes, jockeying for the best reflection. "Oh, I look terrible," she sighed, touching the cut on her cheek. "But I guess it will heal. Besides, I'm not going far for a few days."

"Why's that?" Terrence asked.

"Because the women and I are going to send our own little message to His Majesty!"

"And what might that be?" Terrence asked, just happy to hear her talking.

"Well, there's a big stand of iris out by the stream."

"So?"

"You know we can't get West Indies indigo without being taxed." He nodded but didn't quite see the connection. "The women in South Carolina have been using their own recipe for dye," Sarah went on to explain. "Danna got it from her sister. It looks like we can turn white cloth blue by using iris and red oak or goldenrod and berries."

"Why do I feel like there's something you're not telling me?" Terrence teased.

Sarah offered a sly grin. She certainly *was* feeling better. "You know how much our town meetings irritate the British, right? And you know how women are usually excluded...."

"I'm listening," Terrence waited.

"We thought it would be fun if we all showed up dressed in blue at the next town meeting. Everyone knows we're boycotting English imports, so it will be pretty clear we don't need them anymore."

"And there's really nothing illegal about that, is there?" Terrence mused.

"No. Just a bit of passive resistance," Sarah smiled.

"I like that phrase," Terrence said, putting his arm around her. She realized the words had slipped in from her modern life.

They stood together, looking out the window as afternoon sun warmed the garden. Birds were lining up on the fence, gnats were swarming over a puddle, their hogs were in mud heaven, and their chickens were happily pecking at who-knows-what. All seemed right with the world and there was no way she was planning to leave this one just yet.

Later that week, Sarah and her friends gathered at the house with knives, scissors, and baskets, then walked with their children across the field to the stream. They decided to make a day of it and packed food to share under the trees. Leisurely spreading out along the banks, the women cut armfuls of iris, pausing in small groups to compare bouquets and inhale the delicate, frilly scent.

Conversation wasn't lacking. Sarah told her friends about the incident with the sentry. Someone else relayed a similar tale. The women expressed their concern and commiserated with each other. With the serious news behind them, their talk shifted to the mundane. "Did you hear the sermon last week?" one woman asked. "I nearly fell asleep," another answered. "Does your husband ever wash out his socks?" someone else questioned. "I fear not. He drops them on the floor," a different voice replied. The women laughed easily as they exchanged stories, songs, and advice.

The children stayed within sight, poking in the mud and breaking off skunk cabbage leaves. "Eew! Get away from me!" one of the girls cried as a boy ran after her with his smelly prize. Even when two of the children slipped at the water's edge, the women dismissed the dirty work ahead.

Three of the women strolled off in search of red oak to add to the dye pot. "Look what I found!" one of them exclaimed, holding up a clutch of dandelions. "These will make a fine salad tonight." Despite their gentle personas and pretty faces, within each heart lived the strength of sisters, wives, daughters, and mothers— women who would soon know the meaning of war. Some would be left to run their family farms, others would carry bandages to the front, and there were those who would disguise themselves as men to join the fight.

As the sun started to dip, the women and children walked back across the field, baskets brimming, and friendships renewed. They tied their bundles of iris with rawhide strips, hanging them flower heads down, from the sturdy beams of the Tory house. Tomorrow they would reconvene to render their bounty.

Getting the fire roaring was the first challenge. A damp spring had made even the most weathered wood tough to start, but soon, with snippets of straw and kindling, Sarah had a good blaze underway.

The women arrived on foot and by wagon, each armed with cloth and clothing. They reclaimed their iris and dropped the wilted bouquets, along with bark, into pots of boiling water, watching the petals melt into a steaming froth. "The water is turning blue!" one of the women announced with delight. They tested a piece of cotton, and the tone held nicely—like the color of sky. Wanting a richer hue, someone suggested adding beets, and within minutes, Sarah returned with a handful of bulbous, heart-shaped roots from the cellar. The claret red of the beets, when coupled with iris blue, produced a deep violet shade. Lottie tested this new batch on a skein of yarn and declared the results to be excellent.

A few hours later, sheets had become the color of plums and aprons, the tint of chicory. Linen that would be sewn into skirting, settled somewhere around the color of modern-day denim. Someone's faded silk scarf, brought from England, was left to soak overnight in hopes that it would turn navy.

With fabric squeezed, dripping, and hanging on the line, the yard was soon aflutter. The women leaned back and wiped their brows. "Good job," "Fine work," they complimented each other. Their hands were now blue, as were their wooden spoons, but it didn't matter. In fact, they laughed at the sight of themselves.

Sarah brought out bread, cheese, pickles, and smoked meat. Cold cooked potatoes were drizzled with vinegar. Apples, pared into pieces and dusted with cinnamon, sizzled in a pan. The house smelled sweet and spicy. The mood was jubilant.

During the next week, the women sewed furiously, ignoring other chores. They repaired old clothes, now dyed blue, and stitched new ones with periwinkle thread. As the town meeting neared, the women met at the general store, buzzing with excitement.

"Let's coordinate our arrival," Sarah suggested, understanding the importance of visual impact. "Anyone who needs something extra in blue can come see me. I've got plenty."

The British never liked it when Colonists assembled, but usually looked the other way. Until recently, the locals merely talked amongst themselves, but now, emboldened by Patrick Henry's "if this be treason" speech—news that caught like wildfire and swept up the coast—they started to organize in defiance. Petitions for independence were circulating. Smuggling, to avoid British trade regulations, was rampant.

The townspeople were eager to meet this time. Their short-lived optimism following the Stamp Act repeal had been replaced by outrage at the recently passed Declaratory Act. Not only did the Declaratory Act reassert Royal authority in making laws for Brits and Colonists alike, but it deemed all resolutions by the Stamp Act Congress—assembled in New York the previous fall—null and void.

Later that week the church bell rang, and families began their trek to the meetinghouse. Grown male children and grandparents stayed home to watch young siblings so daughters and mothers could attend. Sarah, Lottie, and Mercy appeared in bonnets of blue. Danna, Grace, and Rachel wore newly sewn skirts, deep as the ocean. Mary, Elizabeth, and Hattie sported aprons that spoke of mountaintops…and even women Sarah didn't know, joined the group.

Blue bows, blue blouses, and blue handkerchiefs appeared. Even the most shy and demure women were suddenly united by uniform. Each went out of their way to greet the Tory guards, nodding politely and sashaying in front of them just a bit flamboyantly. Soon a sea of blue had assembled on the benches and overflowed into the balcony. There was strength in numbers and power in unity. The men, wise to their wives' intentions, grinned at each other, enjoying the sour expression etched on the magistrate's face.

The meeting was called to order and questions were invited. One by one, the villagers stepped forward to express their concerns. Having a voice in government was foremost, along with objections to economic restraints. Each presenter was heard and, then, silenced by a Secretary, who made note of the issue. Delegates were assigned to form committees, but the Colonists knew that little progress would be made.

The women were particularly outspoken. Sarah noticed that the British officials were becoming increasingly annoyed as each lady in blue lobbed a volatile comment into the conversation.

"When do you expect your war debt to be reconciled, so we can be free of the tax burden wrongly levied on us?" one woman asked.

"How long must we continue to buy finished goods from England, when we could make those very things ourselves – and probably better?" another added.

"How can the King possibly think it right to have us feed and billet his troops, when we can barely take care of our own families?" a third complained.

At that point, a waiting page was summoned to the podium. Scroll in hand and, with great import, he read from the new Declaratory Act, which ended with a statement that cut to the quick:

"Be it declared that the said colonies and plantations in America have been, are, and of right ought to be, subordinate unto, and dependent upon the crown and parliament of Great Britain."

A hush fell over the room until in the far back corner, a farmer's wife stood up and called out, "No taxation without representation!" Heads spun around to see her. James Otis had expressed that very sentiment in Boston almost two years prior, but it was unusual for an average citizen, let alone a woman, to be so bold.

Soon, others were echoing her words. Their voices became a chorus and then a rally cry. Attendees filed out of the building, taking their chant into the streets. The British Regulars stood back, weapons poised, waiting for violence to break out. But not one bit of violence occurred.

Slowly the families dispersed, leaving behind a group of soldiers rattled by the hostile throng—a trend that was replicating throughout the countryside.

Sarah and Terrence were invigorated by the evening's events, talking vehemently about rebellion and love of country as they walked home. It was difficult to tell where political outrage ended, and passion began, but soon they were rolling across the floor in front of the fire—boots, bonnet, and britches thrown haphazardly around the room.

Terrence's long hair spilled over Sarah's face and hers fanned out like wings on the warm floor cloth. They were a collection of contrasts—his tan hands on her pale skin, her soft curves against his strong angles. Their lovemaking was as urgent and combustible as public sentiment. Soon they lay spent, gratified and too tired to move. Sarah pulled an afghan off the arm of a chair for cover. The next she knew, they awoke in the wee hours, chilled beneath the thin blanket.

The sky was milky gray as it tends to be at 4 a.m. and the house was cold. They ran in their skimpy wool wrap to the deep sanctuary of their bed. Morning came too quickly as far as Sarah was concerned and, although Terrence knew he had fences to fix and crops to tend, he was in no rush to leave Sarah's arms.

Under the covers, they relished the new day, talking about their unborn child and hopes for the future, listening to birdsong, watching sunlight dance on the walls. "You know I have to go home for a little while," Sarah said as she traced Terrence's lips. He held her hand there and kissed her fingertips.

"I know," he said, "as long as you come back." His sentence trailed off at the possibility that one day she could be gone forever.

"Oh, I will. I will," Sarah insisted, getting up to splash water on her face and run up to the outhouse on the hill. Terrence followed, and they walked back together.

"Let's see if I can control the transition this time," Sarah suggested as she prepared a morning meal. Soon she had a large omelet with chives cooking. "After breakfast, I'm just going to sit in that chair and think about my other life...as much as I can remember."

"I'll sit with you," Terrence offered.

So, after they finished eating, sitting side by side, Sarah slipped over the threshold, finding herself in that very same chair with her cell phone ringing.

"Uh, hello," she answered.

"Sarah, is everything OK?" the subdued voice at the other end asked. It was Carter.

"I tried to give you extra time…I didn't want to bother you… but I started to worry."

"I'm fine, really," Sarah offered without much emotion. "I'll be driving home momentarily."

"Good. Remember tonight is Parents' Night at the elementary school." Sarah had completely forgotten. Most schools held these events in the fall, but this school conducted a spring review as well. She said she would meet him there.

Before starting her car, Sarah sat behind the wheel thinking about the kids. Jared was doing alright in class, but he was already separating himself from the herd. He was well ahead of his grade reading level and he enjoyed learning about subjects most kids his age wouldn't consider. He recently had taken to wearing a black tee-shirt extolling French philosopher René Descartes. Carter had helped him buy it online and was amused by his son's choice, viewing it as a testament to his own love of math and science. "*Je pense, donc je suis*" was emblazoned on the front and "I Think, Therefore I Am" was translated on the back. Sarah, on the other hand, thought that Jared was sending her a message of encouragement about the existence of Terrence, suggesting that if she believed it, it was true.

Abby was less stable. Using her allowance to buy Kool-Aid, she had colored her hair purple. Sarah hadn't been around to stop it, but then again, it wasn't dangerous—just disruptive—which seemed to be a trend lately. Abby apparently had been acting up in school—refusing to take part in classroom discussions and doodling excessively. "While her graphic talent is impressive," her teacher wrote, tongue-in-cheek, "we'd rather limit it to art class." Sarah appreciated the teacher's gentle humor and knew they would have a good talk. As for lack of participation, Sarah was sure she could improve upon Abby's attitude by showing that speaking her mind in a constructive setting was far more productive than not. Maybe she would take her daughter to a debate or a town meeting....

While thoughts of the kids occupied her mind, Sarah remained uneasy about seeing Carter after their blow-up the other night. She knew they had to put their differences aside for the sake of the children and hoped he would agree. After all, she and Carter were the adults here. Taking a deep breath, she switched the ignition key on, made a U-turn, and drove down the driveway. The day was fresh, but she was tired. How long could she go on being two places at once?

After work, Sarah met Carter in the school lobby. Their exchange was cool but civilized. Attending Abby's class was easy—all in one room—so they went together. Covering Jared, however, required tactical precision. Carter tended to avoid math and science in the interest of objectivity, so Sarah covered those subjects. He took English, Art, and Phys Ed, forfeiting American History, which Sarah wanted.

Jared's history teacher was very conventional and taught by the book. Sarah remembered those kinds of classes. Never her favorite. She greeted Mrs. Rooney with a smile and took Jared's seat in the front row. The teacher explained they would be holding a year-end Colonial Fair and that the children would assume appropriate roles—the boys as farmers and fighters, the girls as housewives.

Sarah listened politely, but just couldn't agree. "I hope you won't leave our girls out of the equation entirely," Sarah objected. Sensing a need to explain, she added, "I've been reading a lot lately and it looks like women took a much more active role than we think."

Mrs. Rooney was surprised to be challenged so overtly, but she recovered quickly. She offered to catch up on some reading herself and said she would certainly assign some heroine roles—at least one Molly Pitcher and one Deborah Sampson among the troops.

Sarah knew she should stop while she was ahead, but something prompted her to continue. "Well, I was hoping we might also include some local women who took part in the Revolution. The cemetery's full of them." By this time, several parents were furrowing their brows and looking at Sarah. She noticed Harry from her office sitting in the back of the room, rolling his eyes. His daughter was in Abby's class.

Mrs. Rooney curtailed the dialog by saying, "That's a good idea. We'll check it out," and without breaking pace said, "Next."

As Sarah left the room, she could feel stares boring into her back. She overheard several women talking in the hallway. "What's with her?" someone stage-whispered. "Overreacting, wouldn't you say?" someone else muttered. "You think?" a third groaned.

Sarah tried to ignore the negative comments but felt compelled to turn around. Maybe it was the events of the day or the frustration of leaving unfinished business in the past, but she stepped up to the women and looked at them square in the eye.

"All I want to do is make sure our gender isn't slighted by some skewed account of history. I don't know what you were taught, but I was taught that men did everything and that's not the case." The women were too surprised to say anything.

When Carter and Sarah met back in the lobby, he had already heard that some woman had been sounding off about the history curriculum. "That wouldn't be you by any chance?" he asked, weary of the drama that surrounded Sarah these days. Sarah dismissed the comment as if swatting at a fly and flatly said, "Not a big deal. I'm tired. Let's go home."

At home, they paid the sitter, foraged for food, checked their email, and settled down to decompress. Sarah was grateful for this routine, because it meant she didn't have to think. Soon her eyes batted closed and she found herself asleep on the corner of the couch.

"Let's head to bed," Carter suggested, patting her ankle.

"Sounds good," Sarah mumbled, stretching as she stood.

Teeth brushed and pajamas on, they gave each other a quick kiss and said, "Good Night." Their conflict wasn't resolved, but it was on hold.

The next day at work, Harry couldn't help but rib Sarah. "Hey, Miss History Buff, you sure gave that teacher an earful on how to run her class."

Sarah glanced up from her desk, ready to bite, but she decided against it. "Come on, Harry, I'm busy," she said, trying to look as if she were reading. Not wanting to wait for his response, she picked up the phone and punched in some numbers. Without thinking, she had called the Randolphs.

"Hello," Ann said, exuding her southern charm. That snapped Sarah back to attention.

"Oh, Mrs. Randolph. It's Sarah. I'm sorry to bother you. Wrong number…Force of habit."

"It's lovely to hear from you, dear. How is everything?" Mrs. Randolph replied in her lilting voice.

"Fine," Sarah said, not wanting to reveal the truth. She had no idea how much Ann knew about her personal struggles, but she suspected Carter had kept his colleague apprised. Still, Sarah felt better making small talk. "Are you enjoying the house?" she asked.

"It's amazing," Ann gushed. "Like living back in the 1700s… but with all the modern conveniences."

"It *is* rather impressive, isn't it?" Sarah agreed.

The phone line went silent. For a moment, Sarah thought Ann had hung up. "Mrs. Randolph?" she tested.

"Oh, I'm still here, Sarah. I'm just not sure how to broach the subject."

"What is it?" Sarah asked, keeping her voice low so Harry couldn't hear.

"Well, I think you know that Mr. Randolph and I are researchers, parapsychologists to be exact," Ann continued.

"Yes, Carter mentioned that when we realized you knew each other." Sarah intentionally downplayed the significance.

"Well, Carter and I have been talking. He told me how upset you were to be…shall we say…*drafted* for our project. I must apologize. We never expected such profound results."

Sarah had to be careful. She was still angry at being presumptively cast into this role, but the Randolphs were, above all else, clients. Sarah appreciated Ann's directness and thought it best to respond in kind.

"Well, I have to admit, I wasn't very happy when I learned that Carter had volunteered my services without telling me, but I *am* fascinated by the subject."

"As are we!" Ann effused, but pulled back slightly. "I don't want to push you, dear," she continued, "but you do have skills we find very valuable."

"So, you don't think I'm nuts if I say I've conjured up Terrence Covington?" Sarah joked.

"On the contrary," Mrs. Randolph insisted, dead serious. "We've been doing this for years and, if a little ridicule were going to deter us, it would have happened long ago."

Ann was being nice, and Sarah could see why Carter liked her.

"Well, maybe we *could* get together sometime and talk. I feel a little foolish, but I've gotten rather caught up in the (she paused to choose her words carefully) happenings at your house. In fact, I've had an overwhelming feeling that I need to return." There. Sarah said it.

She could sense that Ann was listening closely, maybe even taking notes. "That would be fine," Mrs. Randolph offered. "Maybe we could all learn something new."

Sarah found Ann's tone comforting. "I guess Carter has told you that I'm sort of...uh, 'taken' with young Mr. Covington," Sarah quietly confided.

"He did," Mrs. Randolph acknowledged.

"And did he tell you I've become quite a Patriot myself?"

"That, too," Ann answered. Sarah could sense a smile in her client's voice.

"Isn't it wild?" Sarah exclaimed, welcoming the empathy of a female ally. "I'm a happily married, modern woman."

"Sarah, you've embarked on an adventure most of us will never experience. For you to explore it and enjoy it is totally understandable. Even Carter—as a scientist—realizes that. As a husband...well, that's another story. Emotions are tricky stuff," Ann counseled.

Talking together cleared the air and Sarah agreed to come to their house on the weekend, with or without Carter.

When Sarah put down the phone, she could see Harry straining to eavesdrop. Deciding to take the bull by the horns, she said, "That was Ann Randolph. I actually called her by mistake, but they like the house and are doing fine."

Harry grunted. "Spooky old place, if you ask me."

"You don't like antiques?"

"They give me the willies. Probably haunted."

"Why would you say that?" Sarah asked, trying not to be defensive.

"Just looks it. You know, I went to that first open house, too."

Sarah had forgotten that Harry had been at the initial agent briefing. "Really?" she asked in her most innocent voice, adding, "I didn't sense anything strange."

"Funny, of all people," Harry huffed.

"What do you mean?"

"Well, you have a knack for these things, don't you? A sixth sense…a little ESP and all that bunk?" Harry taunted.

Sarah was stunned. Was it so apparent to everyone but herself? "I don't know. My husband says I've got women's intuition."

"Come on. Quit denying it. You always pick up the phone before it rings. You tell us a house is going on the market before it hits the papers. You just act that way."

"I do?" Sarah asked, genuinely surprised. Maybe there *was* a reason Carter had chosen her to help the Randolphs. "I'll have to pay more attention."

"Yeah, do that," Harry called over his shoulder as he grabbed his coat and walked out.

Sarah sat in the office, alone at her desk. Emotions careened through her head. She was irritated by the encounter at the school, relieved by her conversation with Ann, and shocked that Harry—plain, crude, brusque man that he was—had been so observant.

The morning went by quickly as Sarah updated her accounts and pulled pertinent market reports. When she looked up, it was time for lunch. Her colleague, Jen, had just walked in and could cover the phones. Remembering that it was warm and sunny outside, Sarah carried her lunch bag to a park bench not far from the center of town.

As she ate, she watched the squirrels search for acorns. A flock of geese flew overhead toward the northern sky. She relaxed as she scanned the horizon, now budded and alive.

Looking past the iron fence near the church, she noticed a woman standing at the cemetery gate. She wore a long blue skirt and had her light hair piled on top of her head. The woman bent over one of the graves to touch it, then slowly straightened and turned her back on it. She moved toward the fence and stared at Sarah. The woman brought both arms forward and up into the air, as if to grasp an invisible object. Figuring the woman was praying, Sarah averted her eyes. When she looked back up, the woman was gone.

Sarah thought nothing of it, returned to her office refreshed, and pledged to eat lunch outside again.

The next day, the sky was overcast, but not enough to rule out a picnic. As Sarah savored her sandwich under a tree, she admired her favorite landmarks. She gazed across the lawn to the little ice-skating rink, now melted and serving as a duck pond. She studied the Minuteman statue, a tribute to the town's native sons. Her eyes wandered to the old church with its graceful weeping willows whose branches swayed in a quiet sob. She was surprised to see the same woman visiting the cemetery again.

As Sarah observed the scene, the woman went through similar motions. She bent over a grave, stood up, turned her back on it, and took a few steps forward, raising her hands as if to reach for the Almighty. This time Sarah didn't look away. The woman completed the motion, brought her hands down and in toward her chest. Sarah stopped chewing and simply stared. The woman nodded several times with her fingers intertwined on top of her collarbone. Sarah assumed she was crying. Feeling guilty about intruding on the woman's grief, Sarah finished her sandwich and started to leave. Glancing over her shoulder, she couldn't help but steal another look at the cemetery. The woman was focused on Sarah, saying something, but too far away to be heard.

Intrigued, Sarah turned back and started walking toward the woman. Tripping on a root, Sarah uttered a few choice words and looked down to see what had snagged her foot. In that split-second, the figure vanished. Sarah blamed herself for scaring the woman away. "Nothing like a tirade of four-letter words to ruin a tranquil mood," she said, not sparing any sarcasm on herself. With the woman gone, Sarah retraced her steps and returned to work.

Throughout the otherwise dull afternoon, the image of the woman lingered…sad and frail for her young years. Sarah decided to reach out to her if nothing more than to share a kind word. After all, Sarah was feeling a loss of her own, being away from the house and the man who held her heart.

Lunch hour didn't come fast enough the following day. This time, she didn't wait for Jen to return. She left Harry by himself and put a note on Jen's desk. In the park, Sarah assumed her usual spot—on a solitary bench beneath the spreading oak.

Squirrels chattered loudly and ran in circles as she ate. Beds of Lily-of-the-Valley perfumed the air. She noticed pink azaleas in full bloom at the park borders and tufted clouds catching in the church steeple. Sarah's eyes roved to the graveyard, but it was deserted. Disappointed, she felt as if she had been stood up for an important date but knew if she walked over there, she would not be disturbing anyone. Sarah finished her sandwich and crumpled up the paper, tossing it into a wire trash bin on her way to the cemetery gate. The grounds inside were empty, the headstones undisturbed. She wondered whose plot the woman had been visiting.

As Sarah moved between the rows, she felt someone tap her on the shoulder. She quickly spun around and saw the familiar woman kneeling near one of the mossy stones on the other side. A cold current of air kicked up from nowhere. Sarah started moving toward the woman, but before she could say anything, the woman stood up, faced her, and went through her routine: hands upward, pulled to chest, nod, nod, and eyes lifted. This time, Sarah could see her clearly. The woman stared back at Sarah and mouthed two words. Sarah strained to hear but couldn't. The woman's lips formed the words again. "Help me. Help me." It was then that Sarah realized the woman wasn't speaking out loud.

Transfixed, Sarah couldn't move. A shiver ran across her shoulders and down her spine. The woman was beckoning her, encouraging Sarah to step forward. Studying the woman more closely, the hair stood up on Sarah's arms. The woman's skirt was strikingly similar in appearance to the one she had colored with her Colonial friends…and the woman's hair was golden-red like Sarah's in her youth. At her throat was a locket that Terrence had given her shortly after they became engaged and, on her finger, the heirloom Covington ring.

Sarah's heart began to pound. She could hardly breathe as she stared in disbelief. She had been watching herself as Sarah Hawthorne—that is, Sarah Covington—so many years before!

Sarah's hands moved automatically to her mouth to stifle a gasp. She backed away from the woman and once she had put some distance between them, turned and ran through the park. She rushed into the office and made a beeline to her desk, trembling, too afraid to say anything. "Everything all right?" Jen asked.

Sarah nodded, reaching for her cell phone. "Are you sure?" Jen asked again. "There's no color in your face." Jen didn't push for more information and Sarah didn't volunteer any. The office was quiet, and Sarah was sure Jen could hear her unsteady breathing. Sarah hurried into the vending room, out of earshot.

Dr. Barrow's number was programmed into Sarah's cell and she didn't hesitate to use it. "I need to see her as soon as possible," Sarah demanded. She purposely didn't say Dr. Barrow's name for fear of being heard. "Yes, I can be there at the end of the day." Even though Sarah had doubts about the doctor's personal agenda, at least this woman was trained in this sort of thing.

The doctor's waiting room was empty when Sarah arrived. "Dr. Barrows?" she called. The receptionist had already left, "Dr. Barrows?" Sarah repeated more loudly.

"Sarah, come in," a warm voice called from the back room. "I'll be right with you. Help yourself to a beverage."

Sarah didn't want anything to drink, so she stood there, rocking on her heels.

Dr. Barrows came out to greet her, lightly touching Sarah's arm. "How are you doing tonight?" Sarah shook her head as if to say, "Not so great," but didn't speak.

Once seated, she looked up at Dr. Barrows and said in an unusually shaky voice, "I've just had an experience that scared the hell of out me. None of this romantic stuff in the house. I've just seen the ghost of Sarah Covington in broad daylight!"

"Tell me more," Dr. Barrows said, leaning forward, eyes darting like little ferrets on the loose.

"It was like seeing myself 250-some years ago!" Sarah blurted out. "Crystal clear."

"And where was this?"

"In the old cemetery in town."

Dr. Barrows nodded.

"The woman looked just like me. It *was* me!"

Dr. Barrows studied Sarah for a moment, then uttered a single word: "Doppelgänger."

"What?" Sarah asked.

Dr. Barrows reached for a book from the console behind her desk. "A sense of encountering oneself," she said as she flipped the book open to a marked page.

Sarah was surprised. "Is it that common?" she asked, looking at the grotesque black and white etching of mirror images.

"It's common enough that there's a name for it…comes from the German for 'double walker'. Some think that seeing one's phantom self is…" Dr. Barrows stopped, realizing she had said too much.

"Is what?" Sarah pressed.

Dr. Barrows sighed: "A harbinger of death."

An awkward silence followed, but Sarah felt confident that this death would not be hers in the here-and-now, but rather, in her previous life—something she already knew.

"Then what should I do?" Sarah asked, half-thinking out loud.

"You won't have closure until you resolve things," Dr. Barrows advised, "and now that you've experienced a doppelgänger, don't be surprised if it happens again." Sarah could detect a hint excitement in the psychiatrist's voice.

"So, should I confront it? Ignore it? Go back to the house?" Sarah asked, almost afraid to hear the answer. The idea of seeing Terrence was one thing but facing one's own mortality was something else.

"What do you want to do?" Dr. Barrows asked, deflecting the question. The doctor followed her statement with some throat clearing which Sarah had begun to suspect was like a poker tell—a manifestation when the doctor was fudging the truth.

"I want to help the original Sarah. I want her to live. I want to spare Terrence the pain of losing his wife." Sarah said, "But I'm terrified at the idea of dealing with a…uh…ghost."

"And yet you are totally comfortable with Terrence," Dr. Barrows noted, her eyes asking why.

"But that's different," Sarah quickly defended. "There's nothing ghostly about him. He's warm, tangible, and when he talks, I hear him. Besides, he's not intruding on my life. If anything, I'm intruding on his."

Dr. Barrows smiled. "Then maybe you should go back and try to fix things in hopes that your counterpart Sarah survives."

"You mean go back and save her life? *Can* I?" Sarah asked. She had seen more than her share of time warp movies and had grown to believe one couldn't—or shouldn't—mess with destiny.

"I don't know, but you could try," the doctor suggested.

Sarah began to process this notion.

She had wanted to do this all along but thought it impossible. However, hearing the doctor say it somehow made it plausible. Sarah sat there wondering if Dr. Barrows was humoring her, but the good doctor wasn't smiling now. If anything, her eyes were glued on Sarah, dilated as if trying to see into Sarah's dark, alternate world.

"I'll think about it," Sarah conceded. "I will need things— modern things—and I'm not even sure if I can transport them across time barriers. Suppose I introduced something contemporary that didn't belong...what then?"

Dr. Barrows didn't have an answer, but she was extremely interested to learn that Sarah would be visiting the house on the weekend. "Keep me posted," she told Sarah. "I would love to hear about your visit there...or any further *visitations* elsewhere." Dr. Barrows, proud of her wittiness, accentuated her play on words.

Sarah agreed, trying to find some normalcy in their conversation, but there was none. "I'll let you know what I decide," Sarah assured. She paused a moment, wanting to ask the doctor about Mr. Randolph, but refrained.

6

SECRETS IN THE WALLS

That weekend, just as the morning sun lit up the bedroom ceiling, the phone rang. Not fully awake, Sarah fumbled to grab it.

"You'll never guess what happened!" Ann squealed into Sarah's ear. "They found a shoe!"

"A what?" Sarah asked, wiping sleep from her eyes with one hand and holding the phone at arm's length with the other.

"The workmen just found a concealment shoe in the roof where they're fixing the rafters," Ann burbled.

Sarah had heard about concealment shoes, but had never seen one. She had read that dozens of shoes had been found in old houses in New England, stemming from a belief that an old shoe, retaining the energy of its owner, could ward off evil spirits. Usually women's and children's shoes were used, but sometimes other prized possessions like spoons or toys, were also concealed in the walls.

"Are you there?" Ann asked in response to Sarah's silence.

"Uh, yah," Sarah said, trying to wake up. "That's amazing."

"You'll want to come over and see it!" Ann insisted. "Besides, a hold will be put on any renovation until the local historical and archaeological societies can do their thing."

"I'll be over as soon as I can," Sarah said, reaching for her bathrobe.

When she arrived, the house was crawling with people.

"It's up here," one of the workmen said, pointing to a small nook under the Tory roof. "I almost missed it; it's tucked so far back."

Sarah climbed the ladder to get a better look. There, nestled in a dark corner, was a woman's damask shoe bearing a low French heel and tapered toe. The rosy color had faded into a rusty brown, but she could see the careful stitching and floral pattern that had once given the shoe value. She noticed worn silken bands across the arch, held in place by a slightly pinker rosette at each side.

Mr. Blackthorn from the Archaeological Society had just landed so Sarah backed down the ladder. Confidently, he scaled the rungs. "Yup, yup…I'd say what we have here is an old Colonial shoe imported from Europe…King Louis heel," he said, peering into the corner with a high-powered flashlight. "Looks to me about 1750, 1760 judging by the point of the toe. I wouldn't be surprised if it were made by the Georgian Cordwainer, James David, from Aldgate, London."

Blackthorn climbed back down and turned to the crew. "Let me get my photographer up here," he said, then addressing the foreman: "I assume you still have to get in here to fix the roof?"

The foreman nodded yes.

"Well, we have to preserve the integrity of the setting, so we can document it properly—that is, before you move anything," Blackthorn explained with authority. "We'll also want to see if there are any other artifacts up there, but we'll try to be out of your hair by Monday. And if no one minds, we'll take the shoe with us for analysis." No one objected.

While the foreman wasn't happy about the interruption, he realized the importance of the find. "Take the rest of the weekend off, boys," he yelled to his crew, gesturing to their respective trucks and a company van. He looked at Mrs. Randolph and reminded her, "I'll do the best I can, but under these circumstances, you can't hold me to the original deadline." She said she understood.

As the foreman backed his SUV out of the drive, Sarah edged closer to Blackthorn who was busy taking notes. "Who do you think this belonged to?" she asked, hoping to gain some insight, although she suspected she already knew the answer.

Blackthorn, mildly annoyed at the intrusion, responded with practiced politeness. "Probably the lady of the house," he said, returning his attention to his writing. "I'd say it was put there around the time of the American Revolution, after the shoe had been well-worn. New shoes were too expensive to use for concealment."

"So, it would have belonged to Sarah Covington, wife of the grandson..." Sarah ventured, almost afraid to say the name out loud.

"Sounds right," Blackthorn confirmed, adding with a snicker, "Hope she's not mad."

"What do you mean, 'mad'?"

"Oh, one of my silly beliefs, I guess," Blackthorn said, looking up and speaking more patiently. "You see, we just disturbed a resting place of sorts...." His thoughts trailed off. "There's no scientific proof, of course; just a spiritual thing I try to avoid. I prefer to respect the dead."

Sarah thought about the upturned gravestones, the woman in the cemetery, and now this.... "Ann, I'll come back at a better time," she said, forcing herself to use her client's first name. Sarah hurried to her car and once buckled in, glanced up at the Tory roof, now covered by a blue tarp. "Oh, Terrence," she said out loud, "What have we done? We seem to have unleashed the past."

Arriving home mid-afternoon, Sarah found Carter in one of her favorite places...sitting on the floor near the bookshelf where their college memorabilia was stored.

"It's strange," he remarked before saying hello to her. "Despite all of Ann's and David's work, I don't see anything about them. There's nothing that acknowledges their achievements other than that clipping you found of Ann as a researcher in the lab. No published papers. No honorary degrees. No speaking engagements."

"Have you tried LinkedIn?" Sarah suggested.

"Was going to do that next," Carter said, walking over to his desktop.

Sarah put down her pocketbook and took off her sweater. She poured herself a glass of iced tea and joined Carter, watching over his shoulder as he searched for the names he knew.

"Nothing. Nothing at all," he said, looking up at her, puzzled. "They have no profiles. No press."

"Maybe they're just not into social networking," Sarah suggested, remembering how disengaged they had been when purchasing the house.

Carter proceeded to Google them, but other than finding past addresses, he discovered nothing about their professional lives. "You would think that two people of their stature, with their scope of expertise, would have gotten some recognition," Carter persisted.

Sarah pulled a chair next to him to be closer to the screen. "Maybe the Randolphs are just private people," she suggested. "After all, not everyone takes their line of work as seriously as they do. Maybe they just didn't want to be in the limelight."

Carter continued to search online as Sarah stepped away to sort the afternoon mail. "Then again, maybe they're not who you think they are."

When Carter didn't answer, she glanced over at him and saw him staring at her as if a lightning bolt had hit the floor. They decided to devise a plan that would allow Sarah to investigate further without raising suspicion. With luck, she would be able to unearth some truths about the Randolphs—and she might even be able to see Terrence again.

The next week, Sarah let her colleagues know she was heading to the house to gather information for a blog post. When Sarah arrived, Mrs. Randolph was outside talking to the foreman, hand shading her eyes from the sun as she looked up toward the roof.

"I don't want to change anything about that," Sarah could hear Ann saying. "It seems to be the essence of the house."

The foreman nodded in agreement, mentioning something about the roof adding character. He assured her they'd work only on repairs that were historically correct and would do nothing to modernize the façade.

"Sorry to interrupt," Sarah called as she walked purposely over to the duo, "but I'd love to take some photos. I'm writing an article for our website about the concealment shoe and thought it would be nice to show your renovations, if that's OK. I won't be long or in your way."

"That's fine," Ann said, looking at the foreman for consensus.

"Jim," he said, extending his hand to Sarah. She offered hers. "No problem. Just be careful if you go up the stairs. We're reinforcing them, but we're not quite done," he cautioned. He paused a moment. "Come to think of it, if you want to go up there now, this would be a good time since the guys are on lunch break."

Sarah gave him a thumbs-up and hurried toward the house. Once inside, she felt a refreshing coolness that countered the early summer heat. Knowing that Mrs. Randolph was still outside talking, Sarah softly called out, "Terrence? Are you here?" as she climbed the stairs and approached the eave.

The air got increasingly hotter the higher she went. She put her camera down on the cot, so she could pry open the window. Looking across the road, she heard splintering wood and saw a massive pine crash to the ground, sending a plume of needles skyward. Terrence and Jonah had driven their workhorses into the field and were rolling the fresh timber onto a sledge. "Gee-Hah," she could hear them yell as the mighty animals, four-in-hand, strained against the rope. When the load started to move, jubilant hoots arose. Soon the tree was making its way down the road, bouncing behind 16 mighty hooves.

Sarah turned away and picked up a Bible that had been left on the nightstand, hoping for spiritual guidance in preparation for the birth of her child. The leather of the book cover was soft to the touch, and the pages smelled pleasantly musty. Engrossed in her reading, she didn't hear Terrence arrive until he called up the stairs.

"Sarah, did you see the tree we dropped?" he yelled. "That will be our own Liberty Pole here in town."

Easing down the stairs, protecting her rounded stomach, she asked where the pole was going to be placed. "Not sure yet," Terrence replied, "but you can be certain it will be front and center," he said, grinning. "Especially since we're supposed to save these pines for his Majesty's masts," he added with a wink. "But, hey, my land...my tree, wouldn't you say?"

Sarah smiled, but she was worried that Terrence was inviting trouble. "Maybe you should wait a while before you raise it," she suggested.

"Don't worry. Prepping it will take time. We still have to mill it and clear the space."

As Terrence talked, Sarah busied herself in the kitchen. She had found watercress growing in the stream on their property and set about trimming it. Terrence playfully stuck his fingers into the bowl of water she was using, flinging some droplets at her cheek, then drying his hands on her skirt. Despite her feigned annoyance, she enjoyed the attention. "Want to see something?" he asked.

"Sure," she said, following him out of the house toward the shed. She was happy to be free of kitchen duty.

"You can't look yet," he said, guiding her into the doorway. He took her hands and placed them over her eyes. "Not until I'm ready."

She could hear something heavy being moved...something scraping and then creaking.

"OK now," Terrence said, helping her hands drop. There in the center of the small room, sitting in a beam of light, was a carefully crafted cradle on which had been etched three birds—two large ones and a small one. The symbolism wasn't lost on Sarah.

"It's beautiful," she whispered, tears coming to her eyes. Bending down, she rocked it wistfully, and then stood to give him a kiss. "When did you have time to make this?" she marveled.

"Oh, I have my ways. Besides, we're going to need it soon."

Sarah wanted to share his exuberance, but guarded against it, knowing how risky birthing could be. "To think, by fall we'll have a little person of our own," she said, quietly soaking in the scene. Particles of dust floated aimlessly around Terrence, suspended in the narrow channel of light. There wasn't a breeze to be felt. In fact, the shed was stifling.

"Air!" she thought. "I need to get some air," she said, trying to force the window open further.

"Everything OK?" the foreman called up the stairs. It took Sarah a moment to come to her senses. "Yup, fine and dandy," she called back. "Just want to get one more shot of the view."

With that, Sarah took a picture and came quickly down the stairs. "Wicked hot up there," she said, wiping her forehead."

"Tell me about it," the foreman said, leading to a protracted pause.

"Gotta ask you something," he continued, taking off his cap and running his fingers through his buzz cut. Sarah waited as he went through the motions.

"How well do you know the Randolphs?" he asked.

"Well enough. Why?" she answered, explaining that they had a business relationship.

"Well, something's hinky with them, I think," he replied. "They've got all this recording equipment and a printer that's running off diplomas or something."

"Diplomas?"

"Yeah, like the kind you see in a doctor's office. You know, certificates, credentials…"

"Hmmm, that's strange," Sarah allowed. "I gather they're rather accomplished, so maybe they're just scanning their old degrees?"

"Didn't look like that," Jim continued. "Looked like they were Photoshopping some stuff together…you know, like a university seal…a fancy border…and signatures."

Sarah didn't expect him to know much about computer art programs, but before she could respond, he jumped in. "Bet you didn't think I knew about that stuff," he grinned, "but don't be fooled by this blue collar. I was a graphic designer before I got into this line of work—just had to make a better living."

Sarah smiled. She liked the guy…and now she was even more intrigued about the present owners. She said she'd ask her husband about the Randolphs, since he knew them better. Then she took a few exterior shots and headed home.

"Carter, can you do me favor?" Sarah asked as she set the table. "The next time you talk to the Randolphs, can you see if they're setting up an office or going into business…something where they'd want their diplomas hanging on the wall."

"Sure, but why?" Carter asked as he brought a pitcher of water to the table.

"Just curious. Something isn't adding up," Sarah said, conveying what the foreman had seen.

The next day Carter called Ann and casually inquired if they were opening a practice. "As a matter of fact, we are. Life coaching and leadership training. Figure we know a thing or two about human behavior with all the research we've done. Why do you ask?"

Carter covered his curiosity by saying that Sarah had mentioned there was great office space in the house. He also used the opportunity to tell Ann that he needed to move on to other things. He explained that his involvement in their project had almost destroyed his marriage, and at the very least, had left raw wounds.

Clearly, Ann wasn't ready to dissolve their association yet and deftly changed the subject. "You know, Sarah was over here the other day," Ann stalled, not acknowledging Carter's attempt to distance himself. "She had her camera and was taking pictures of the renovations. Wonder if it ever occurred to her to photograph that ghost of hers…."

Carter felt strangely defensive. "Oh, I don't think she would do that even if she could. She's in awe of the experience and wouldn't want to cheapen it. To her, it's something very pure."

"That's too bad," Ann said. "A nice ectoplasmic orb would certainly enhance our paper." Sarcasm was out of character for Ann, but Carter chalked it up to stress. He tried shifting the focus.

"Then you *are* going public with your findings?" he asked. "Do you have a publisher or are you self-publishing?"

"Neither initially. First, we're obligated to turn our research over to our funder. Besides, we can't do anything without Sam Barrow's report."

"I didn't know she was contributing. I thought she was just on the sidelines for safety," Carter replied.

"Hmmm, didn't I mention that? Guess it slipped my mind. It's part of our agreement," Ann explained. "Sam's wanted to collaborate for a long time. She thinks academic exposure will help secure backing for a state-of-the-art psych lab."

"So, she'll be sharing your credit?" Carter asked, knowing how competitive academic peers could be.

"Well, we'll see about that," Ann snorted. "We were thinking more like 'Foreword by the esteemed Dr. Barrows….'"

Carter chuckled. As fascinating as this experience had been, he was going to be very glad when it was over. With that, Carter concluded the conversation and said he'd be in touch.

A week later, Sarah arrived on the construction site, pleased to see the roof unencumbered by a tarp.

"Hi, Jim," she called across the yard. "Mind if I snag a few more shots? You guys really got a lot done."

"Sure. Come around back. I'll show you the greenhouse." Sarah watched as Jim ambled forward, fit and tanned from the sun.

She walked toward him, impressed by the greenhouse frame that now sprung from the back of the house. Large panels of glass leaned again the wall, reflecting sunlight in an uncomfortable glare.

Jim moved into shaded space to make talking easier. "Yup, it's coming along nicely," he said, proud of his crew's work. "And the Randolphs *are* going ahead with an office in the wing. They've had us lay in a walkway around the side of the house." He pointed in the general direction. "Guess they'll be putting out a shingle soon."

"Yeah, about that…" Sarah continued. "My husband asked them, and it sounds like they're going to specialize in life coaching and leadership training."

Jim shook his head. "Beats me," he said, "I'd question their intentions and their qualifications, but hey, I'm just here to build things." He shrugged and started toward the greenhouse frame. "By the way, you can go anywhere you want today," he called over his shoulder. "The Randolphs are gone and this is the only hard-hat zone on the property."

"Super," Sarah yelled back as she started to walk around the house. She enjoyed entering through the front door, being welcomed by the great room as she had the first time she visited. The scent of firewood still lingered, and the hush of history surrounded her. She looked down and was happy to see that her long skirt was made of cream-colored muslin, lighter weight for the warm weather.

"Sarah!" Terrence greeted her urgently, closing the cupboard door and tossing some salted meat into a leather pouch on the floor. She noticed a bedroll filled with clothing, a flask, and his musket laid out next to it. "I was about to leave you a note. Several of us are going 'cross state to talk with the folks in Stockbridge."

"Stockbridge?" Sarah asked, recalling a town by that name in Western Massachusetts.

"Yes, to the Mahican Mission out there," he replied, scanning the room for his hat. "Word is that the Stockbridge Indians will support us if we fight the British."

"But I thought the Natives were siding with the Brits," Sarah found herself saying, as if versed in the politics of the time. She spotted his hat on top of the hutch, stretched to reach it and put it on his head. He subconsciously adjusted it to a rakish angle.

"They are—in New York and parts west—where they want to protect their lands. But these people broke off and moved east. I want to strengthen those ties now, before we need them," he explained. "We're bringing out some provisions from Boston."

"When will you be back?" Sarah asked, trying to hide her disappointment as she heard the coach pull in.

"It won't be long. Maybe 10 days," Terrence answered, grabbing his supplies and heading toward the door. Realizing he had been self-absorbed, he stopped, put his things down, and walked back to Sarah, pulling her up into his arms for a deep kiss. He could feel her fuller form against him and took comfort in the promise of a family. "Don't miss me too much," he teased, forcing a smile onto her otherwise glum face. "I trust you'll keep yourself busy," he said, looking around the room.

"That I will," Sarah said, hands on hips, resigned to a productive week of housework. With that, he picked up his gear and was out the door. "Be safe," she whispered as she watched him from the threshold. She saw the coach driver slap him on the shoulder in a brotherly fashion and someone from within extend a welcoming hand to assist with his gear. Soon Terrence and his fellow travelers disappeared into the landscape.

After Terrence left, Sarah went outside to feed their livestock and weed the newly planted carrots. She laughed at herself as she squatted ungracefully between the feathery rows, trying to maneuver around her growing stomach. With Terrence away, this would be a good week to make soap. Ordinarily she'd wait until cooler weather, when the hogs were slaughtered, but with a baby to care for in the fall, she knew she wouldn't have time. Besides, they had plenty of lard left from last winter.

Sarah hummed as she puttered in the backyard, preparing her work area. She brought out a bench from the kitchen, her largest kettle, a long-handled wooden spoon, pewter ladle, small pail, and cloths for clean-up and protection against the heat. She searched the orchard for kindling and set up the firepit. She hung the kettle above it, hooking it onto a chain suspended from the tripod that Terrence had built. She dragged a vat of animal fat from the smokehouse and retrieved several flat wooden trays from the barn to use as molds.

"Come all ye fair and tender maidens...Be careful how ye court young men... they're like the dew on a summer's morning... first they're here, then gone again....".

Her clear voice cut through the hay-heavy summer air. The old English ballad, haunting and sad, competed only with birdcalls and the sound of the distant rushing stream. Sarah worked until the sun set low in the sky, planning to make the lye and render the fat the following day.

Glad to be back in the coolness of the house, Sarah poured a large tankard of water, slathered a thick slice of bread with honey, then settled into a rocking chair to relax. Her mind drifted between the peacefulness of their country life and the threat of revolution. She smiled as she thought of Terrence—rugged, dashing Terrence—and the cause he held so dear. His arguments against the British certainly made sense and as she recounted them, recalling the injustices imposed on the Colonies, phrases started to form in her mind.

Moving to their small writing desk, she sat down on the straight-backed chair and fetched a freshly cut quill. She carefully pulled a single sheet of paper from the Rittenhouse box, prized Colonial stock couriered up from Pennsylvania. Flattening the cotton and rag fiber with her fingers, she dipped the quill into a well of brown ink and wrote in a flourishing hand:

"We have been often told that if we do this thing, or do not do that, we shall be thought ungrateful and disobedient to the King and Parliament who serve powerfully to influence people so loyal and dutiful as his Excellency must certainly know we are...but it is a pity that this should be held as a rod over us."

She went on to outline why domination by England was wrong and how the Colonies could reach their fullest potential only by being independent. Her thoughts flowed easily into the night as she explained that with loyalty must come self-worth, the freedom to earn income, the ability to own land, and the right to participate in government. Sarah paused briefly only to light the sconces after which she quickly returned to her quill, intent on not losing her train of thought. Hours later, she awoke with a start, her head down on the desk. The sconces had since died out, leaving the room lit by a full Flower Moon. She shuffled up the stairs to bed, falling on top of the covers, too tired to put on a dressing gown. Awakened by Madelaine's demand for milking, morning came too soon, and with it, the chore of soap-making.

Wanting to work in the cool of the day, Sarah skipped breakfast and instead, dragged the potash hopper out of the shed, topping it off with last week's cooking ashes and placing a cask under it. There was enough water in their rain barrel to start the lye-making process, so Sarah scooped the first pail of water out and poured it carefully over the ashes, averting her eyes to avoid the dust and fumes. She poured several more pails of water on top of the blackening mound and watched the dark liquid trickle into the container below. From the vat of lard and cooking oils, she ladled the greasy mixture into the kettle. She lit the fire under it, using her trusty tinder box, and began to stir. The stench of boiling fat made Sarah wretch, but by chewing on a spring of mint, she quelled the urge. That gave her an idea.

She gathered some handfuls of mint, along with sprigs of lavender, and set them out to dry. Once the lard had transformed to liquid, she wrapped her hands in the cloths and carried the lye water to the kettle, trying not to slosh it onto her skin or clothing. She slowly poured the lye into the liquid fat, stirring constantly, stopping only to wipe her brow. A half hour later, the mixture started to trace, turning thick and milky. A stiff froth began to form around the edges. She remembered a trick her mother had taught her and hurried to the brine barrel for a cup of salt to harden the soap. She tossed in the salt, added the herbs and stirred again.

When the additives were dispersed, she ladled the creamy mixture into the flat boxes to cool. What resulted were blocks of soap that rivaled the finest scents from Europe. Satisfied, she brought her stash inside and returned the supplies to their rightful places. She would turn out her soap the next day, cut it into bars, and let it set for several weeks.

The following day, with soap cut and arranged on the counter, Sarah was restless and anxious for Terrence's return. To dispel her nervous energy, she walked into the field and observed the changing countryside. Stopping to shake a pebble from her shoe, she noticed a round object on the ground. She picked it up and saw that it was an old musket ball.

How she knew this, Sarah wasn't sure, but she liked the feel of it in her hand and let the smooth weight warm to her touch. She took this find as a sign to head back into the house and when she did, she plunked the bead into a bowl. The sound reminded her of dropping coins into the bin at a tollbooth—a turnpike tollbooth in modern New England.

It took little more than that to send her back to the present where she waved good-bye to the construction crew at the house, not sure if she had been there a single afternoon or a week.

At home, the kids and Carter were on their best behavior. No one mentioned how long she had been away. No one asked what she had done. That night she told Carter about her soap-making experience and he seemed to enjoy it, mostly, she thought, because Terrence wasn't there. Carter mentioned that he had talked to Ann and confirmed that the Randolphs were indeed planning to publish their findings.

"I hope they don't use my name," Sarah grimaced.

"Why?" Carter asked. "I thought you were interested in the subject."

"I am, but I'm not sure I want to be associated with it. Besides, that sounds kind of commercial, like I'd be selling out."

"That's what I told Ann when she asked about your taking pictures of Terrence," Carter said, looking for validation.

"I'd never do that! Besides, I was under the impression that all this was for academic research, not fame and fortune."

"Well, you could tell the Randolphs that you did your part and want to wrap things up. I pretty much told them that myself," Carter said.

"Do you think they'd go for it?" Sarah asked, then paused. "But even if they did, Dr. Barrows can be persistent."

"That's probably because she's contributing to their paper."

"She is?" Sarah asked. "I thought she was just there for my mental health."

"She was," Carter allowed. "But apparently there's some other arrangement I didn't know about. Took me by surprise, too." Sarah scowled. At least now, she felt Carter was on her side. "Why don't I go with you to talk to the Randolphs," he offered. "That way we'll kill two birds with one stone—see Ann and help bring this whole thing to a cordial close."

"That would be great. Thanks," Sarah said, planting a kiss on his cheek. "As much as I want to prolong my other life, I don't want the Randolphs to be part of it. And I certainly don't want Dr. Barrows profiting from it."

Later that week, Carter called Ann to see if they could both come over. "Sure, why don't you join us for lunch on Saturday," Ann suggested. "That will give us a chance to catch up on old times and explore new ones."

That Saturday, Carter and Sarah dropped the kids off at her parents' house and continued to Baker's Cove. The day was seasonally warm and with the car windows open and radio blaring, they felt like teenagers out for a joy ride.

Parking on the roadside, they walked quietly up the drive. The side door was slightly ajar, but, just as they were about the knock, they heard the Randolphs talking.

"So, J.B., what do you think about the latest recordings?" Ann asked. "I thought I heard something viable."

"J.B.?" Sarah mouthed to Carter. He pantomimed confusion with his palms up.

"I honestly don't know, Louie," Mr. Randolph answered. "I'd like to try the Zener cards on her. I think she'd be responsive."

"Sometimes I wonder when Louisa became Louie," Ann sighed, shaking her head with feigned annoyance, as she puttered around the room. "But yes, I think she's ready."

"Louisa?" Carter's lips formed the syllables as Sarah shrugged.

"If we can't explain the Psi in some concrete way, I doubt anyone will believe us," Mr. Randolph cautioned. "We need hard evidence."

"True. Not having measurable results is problematic," Ann agreed.

Carter looked at Sarah with his hand poised over the knocker.

"What's going on?" Sarah whispered.

"I haven't a clue," Carter whispered back. "It's almost as if they are role playing."

"Do you think we should knock or just wait? We're probably a few minutes early," Sarah said in an almost imperceptible voice.

"Let's wait. We wouldn't want to embarrass them," Carter suggested, knowing full well they both wanted to hear more. Sarah peered through the opening. Mr. Randolph was absentmindedly shuffling a deck of cards as he talked with his wife. Sarah could see circles, squares, stars, crosses, and wavy lines flash by, before the cards were tapped into place.

"I must say, you look mighty fine with that new haircut, J.B." Ann said, acting coy and unlike her usual self.

"And you look darn pretty in my favorite dress, my dear," Mr. Randolph replied. "Is that the necklace I got you?"

Sarah stood there with her mouth open. There was Mr. Randolph, who usually concealed his bald spot with a bad comb-over, now wearing a thick peppered wig parted on the left. Mrs. Randolph flitted around in a vintage printed shirtwaist dress accented with a modest string of pearls, eyeglasses suspended from a cord. Sarah had never seen Ann wear glasses before.

As soon as Sarah stepped back, Carter peered in.

"Oh, my God. What are they doing?"

"Practicing for a play?" Sarah suggested.

"Yeah, right," Carter answered, not masking his sarcasm. "Looks to me like they're off the deep end."

Sarah and Carter could hear a grandfather's clock chime noon and took that as their cue. Apparently, so did the Randolphs, because when the Sutherlands knocked a few minutes later, everything was in order. Ann was dressed in casual capris and David sported his usual receding hairline.

"It's so nice to see the two of you together," Ann gushed, clasping Carter's hand between her own, "and you look well, Sarah... it's always a pleasure."

"Come on in," Mr. Randolph called from the corner of the room, adjusting what seemed to be a very small microphone clipped to the edge of his desk. The stack of cards was tucked away to one side, a book on the theory of parapsychology neatly placed on the other. He gestured for Sarah and Carter to take a seat. Sarah couldn't help but look for signs of Terrence, though it would be problematic if he appeared.

Ann had prepared a lovely spread of leafy sandwiches and diagonally cut wraps. She brought out bowls of sliced fruit, green salad, and a platter of garnishes. There was a pitcher of iced tea, bottles of water, and cans of soda on a serving table against the wall. A plate of brownies was piled high for dessert.

Soft jazz played in the background, and diffused light filtered into the room. The mood was relaxed as they made small talk and enjoyed the meal, although Carter and Sarah couldn't forget what they had just seen.

"Looks like you've really settled in," Carter commented as he pushed back his chair, hoping to learn more about their new venture.

"Indeed, we have," Ann agreed. "David has been redoing the wing to accommodate an office and we'll be announcing our practice shortly."

"You mentioned something about that. Life coaching, was it?" Carter asked, trying to be casual.

"Yup, that and leadership training, maybe a little behavior modification, too," David replied. "They seem to go together."

Sarah and Carter nodded appropriately, still trying to figure out who J.B. and Louisa were.

"Want to see the office space?" Ann offered, standing up once the meal was done. Sarah and Carter padded behind her down the wing that smelled of sawdust and fresh paint. Mr. Randolph was a few steps behind them, trying to catch up.

"We've removed a couple walls and created a side entrance," Mr. Randolph explained as they strolled into a large room. "And we've put in a brick walkway around the house."

"Not that we expect a lot of foot traffic," Ann piped in, suspecting they might have needed a permit, but Sarah didn't bite. Instead, her eyes were fixed on a wall of polished wooden frames that held psychiatry degrees and professional certifications from prestigious universities.

"I didn't know you both held doctorates," Sarah commented, realizing she had been staring slack-jawed at the excessive display.

"Oh, yes. David and I have been around," Ann said, nonchalantly running her hand over a marble tabletop.

"It seems like you've gotten some exceptional press," Sarah added, looking at magazine articles and newspaper reprints preserved between sheets of plastic.

"We have," Ann confirmed, obviously unaware that none of this showed up online.

"That brings us to the reason we wanted to see you," Carter said, breaking an almost wistful spell.

"We'd like to wind things up," he said, not being one to beat around the bush.

"Why would you do that? We're just getting started!" Ann protested as she hastily ushered the twosome back down the hall.

Sarah initiated the explanation. "I think by now you have enough information to establish a premise and I'd like to keep the rest of my experience private. I'll be approaching a very emotional time in the lives of the Covingtons and I don't want to exploit it."

"We'd never do that, dear," Mr. Randolph said, looking at her from across the room. Sarah was certain he didn't even realize how condescending that sounded.

Carter, trying to preserve their professional rapport, quickly added, "Oh, David, we weren't implying that you would do anything irresponsible, but, you know, sometimes information like this falls into the wrong hands. We just don't want to read about it in the tabloids. What Sarah has experienced is pristine and innocent."

"Well, it sounds a bit juicier than that," Ann retorted, with more of an edge than usual.

"Only if you think of it that way," Sarah said in a soft voice, eyes cast downward. "Really, it's a love story."

Ann changed her demeanor surprisingly fast and went on the attack. "Look, Sarah, I realize this is all lovey-dovey to you, but for us, this is our life's work. We need proven facts and statistical data to be respected and to generate funding for our research. Believe me, we're not getting rich on this, but there *are* operating expenses that must be covered. We've made promises to clients and we're up against some tight deadlines. I don't feel like our work here is anywhere near done."

Sarah was stunned to see this side of Ann.

"Calm down, Louie," Mr. Randolph said, putting his hand on Ann's shoulder.

Sarah and Carter glanced at each other, recognizing the name they had recently heard.

Mr. Randolph realized his slip and tried to recover. "Oh, pet name," he bluffed, then quickly changed the subject. "Why don't we agree to a couple more sessions in the house, so we can at least observe what happens. I'm sure Dr. Barrows also wants to carry this through to the end."

"To the end?" Sarah asked.

"I mean, to its natural conclusion," Mr. Randolph hedged. "According to historic accounts, that would be when Sarah has the baby and…err…passes on."

"A lot can happen between now and then, so don't count on it," Sarah shot back. Then remembering she needed the Randolphs' cooperation to access the house, she reluctantly backpedaled, "Though if you really want to watch, I guess I can't stop you.

After all, this *is* your house. But I'm not doing this you or your research and certainly not for the good doctor. This is for me—and for Terrence." Emboldened, she added, "And what's with you and Dr. Barrows anyway?"

"What do you mean?" Mr. Randolph replied, uncomfortable with the direct question.

"Well, I know you hired her to monitor me, and I didn't like that to begin with, but I gather she's met with you recently," Sarah said, eyes drilling through Mr. Randolph.

He seemed rattled.

"I just wonder who's consulting whom or are you simply comparing notes?" Sarah asked, knowing she had invited an elephant into the room.

"We all meet from time to time to discuss the project and how we're going to present it, that's all," Mr. Randolph deflected.

"When was this?" Ann asked, inserting herself into the conversation.

"A couple weeks ago, as far as I can tell," Sarah answered, not waiting for Mr. Randolph's reply.

"Guess I wasn't part of *that* meeting," Ann huffed, shooting a sharp look at her husband. Mr. Randolph was exasperated: "Ann, nothing's going on that you don't know about."

By this time, Sarah and Carter were eager to leave, not wanting to be caught in the middle of a family fight.

"Let me think how to proceed," Sarah said, regaining her composure, as did Ann. "We can connect next week."

"I'm sorry this got a little heated," Ann said, returning to her charming self. "We're just so passionate about what we do."

"We understand," Carter replied, extending his hand, hoping to smooth things over. Sarah just nodded politely and thanked them for lunch.

Back in the car, Carter turned to Sarah: "OK. Something's not right here. Do what you have to do, but let's start putting some space between ourselves and these two."

"You betcha, J.B.," Sarah teased.

"Not funny," Carter mouthed as he put the car in gear.

Once home, they sank into the couch. "Looks like we've got an hour before picking up the kids," Carter said.

"That's good, because this whole role-playing thing has really creeped me out." Sarah shuddered.

"And that's coming from someone who hobnobs with ghosts," Carter jabbed. But this time his tone was kinder than before.

"It's not the same," Sarah insisted, glad that they could finally joke about it.

Then almost simultaneously, they said to each other, "Are you thinking what I'm thinking?" They both dashed to the desk and Carter booted up the computer, entering "J.B. and Louisa" into the search bar.

"Holy cow!" Carter said. "Look at this!" There was an immediate hit: "Joseph Banks Rhine" from Wikipedia; then "J.B. Rhine (deceased)—The Parapsychology Association", then "History—Rhine Research Center." The last listing was from rhine.org and began, "When Joseph B. and Louisa Rhine joined Professor William McDougall at Duke University in 1927, the field of investigation into psychic phenomena was known as psychical research."

That was all they needed to see. A subsequent listing for a "Guide to the Louisa E. Rhine Papers, 1890-1983—Duke" chronicled the works of J.B. and Louisa Rhine. Now the play-acting that Carter and Sarah had witnessed was starting to make sense.

The Randolphs were obviously enamored with the Rhines, but lacking credentials of their own, they "borrowed" a few from the famous pair. Following in the Rhine footsteps, the Randolphs showed up in the appropriate places, mingled with others in academic circles, attended professional conferences, and participated in theoretical conversations, all while attempting to recreate early parapsychology experiments and add new findings to the field. No one seemed to question their credibility, and prior to now, they had operated under the radar.

"Then is this a sham?" Sarah asked Carter, trying to separate fact from fiction.

"I'd say yes and no. I really don't think the Randolphs are trying to hurt anyone…and they *do* have some training in psychology… but based on what we saw, I think they have bigger problems."

"You mean they not only want to *be* the Rhines…," Sarah said, looking at Carter, "but…."

He finished her sentence. "They think they *are* the Rhines."

Just when and where the Randolphs lost touch with reality is unclear. On the surface, they seemed perfectly normal. Their research methods were meticulous, their writing, well-structured; even their skill set was appropriate for therapeutic counseling— but if they were planning to pass themselves off as doctors and potentially write prescriptions—they'd be practicing medicine without a license.

Sarah and Carter weighed the moral dilemma as they rode to pick up their kids. Neither wanted to be implicated in some sort of fraud, but they didn't feel right snitching on the Randolphs either, especially since proof of malpractice was lacking.

During the following week, Sarah stayed clear of the Randolph's house and Carter kept busy around their own. But by the next weekend, Sarah was anxious to go back.

"Terrence will be returning soon," Sarah said on Saturday morning as she poured herself a steaming cup of French Roast.

"And you know this how?" Carter asked, not quite able to mask his jealousy.

"I can feel it. I can't explain," Sarah said. "Besides, he was away when I was there last, so he should be back by now."

"Then I supposed you need to go," Carter said, resigned but not happy about it. "Just be careful with the Randolphs. I doubt they would do anything intentionally dangerous, but they may be unpredictable."

Later that day, Sarah called the Randolphs to say she'd like to visit again and agreed to share her experience. When she arrived, Sarah recognized the equipment she had seen before, the day she had gone to the house on the pretense of delivering a gift basket. Now, the equipment was out in plain sight.

Jill C. Baker

Sarah put her duffle bag on the floor. "No guarantees," she said as she looked around. Mr. Randolph assumed a professional pose at his desk, adjusting dials and testing sound levels on a box with cylinders. Sarah could hear Ann saying good-bye to a client in the hallway, confirming their next session and offering to call the pharmacy.

"Where do you want to be?" Mr. Randolph asked Sarah.

Before she had a chance to answer, Ann appeared. "Why don't we let her walk around," Ann suggested, entering the room with a sweeping gesture. "We don't want to interfere."

"That sounds good," Sarah said, trying to make the best of the situation. "If I wander off or zone out, just leave me alone. I might go through the motions I'm experiencing—you know, like a dog chasing rabbits in his sleep—or I may not. I really don't know what happens, and I'm not sure what you'll be able to see."

Mr. Randolph assumed the kind tone he often used. "We're not going to make you do anything you don't want, Sarah. We just need evidence."

Sarah noticed he had slipped on a sports coat with a white pocket square, reminiscent of the J.B. Rhine photo she had seen online. "I know. I'm eager to learn what you discover," she said. Sarah purposely did not reveal that she was aware of their identity issues.

Ann adjusted the video cam and donned a headset. She was wearing a short-sleeved blouse and had her hair trimmed around her face. She looked lot like Louisa did in the old pictures. "We're ready anytime you are."

"Mind if I use the bathroom room first?" Sarah asked, heading toward the hall.

"Not at all," she heard Ann say.

Once inside the lavatory, Sarah knew something was about to happen fast. As she dried her hands, she felt two larger ones on her shoulders. She leaned back into them. There was Terrence looking appealingly disheveled as he spun her around.

"Where have you been? I've missed you so much!" he said, pinning her against the sink and kissing her neck. He wasted no time in cupping her breasts. Clearly, he had been thinking of her while he was away.

174

"And where have you been?" she asked in return, hooking her leg around his to bring him closer.

"I just got back this week, but you weren't here. I saw the soap you made, so I know you had stayed a while," he said. She felt his hands working the buttons on the front of her dress.

"I did, but I had to leave...I mean, something triggered me to leave faster than I planned." She reached for the flap on his britches. By this time, Terrence had undone her apron and was lifting her skirt.

"I found a musket ball and that..." she started to say, but she was silenced by his mouth.

"Mmmm...tell me about it later," he said, as his blond hair swept across her face.

Sarah lost track of the people waiting in the other room. She forgot why she was there. All she could do was respond to his touch and encompass him. The scent of lavender and lemon was intense in the small enclosure. Her head spun. They didn't let go until there was no more desperation between them.

"Welcome home, Mr. Covington," Sarah said, trying to catch her breath.

"Good to be back, Mrs. C," he answered, followed by a "Whew!"

They laughed as if they were naughty children. After neatening their clothes, Terrence led Sarah to the front room. Mr. and Mrs. Randolph were nowhere to be seen. He walked over to the desk and returned with a sheaf of papers in his hand. "You didn't tell me you could write so well."

"Oh, my father taught me – penmanship and prose. I didn't mean to use so much paper, but I had all these ideas in my head. I had spent the day outside and when I came in, I started thinking about you and the British.... I hope you don't mind."

"Mind? Are you daft, woman? This is just what we need. A fresh voice to fuel the revolution!"

Sarah furrowed her brow as if to ask, "What are you talking about?"

"I must get these to my friend, Ben Edes," Terrence continued. "He publishes the *Boston Gazette*, and he'll want to see this. He may even be able to use your words."

Sarah was flattered, but mostly happy that Terrence liked what she had written. Over dinner that night, he talked about Stockbridge and what he had seen. It seemed that anti-British sentiments were not too different in that part of the state than on the coast—just expressed with fewer Redcoats hanging around.

As the conversation dwindled and Sarah rose to clean the dishes, she decided to broach a more difficult subject. She had found that with an extreme amount of concentration, she could draw thoughts from both time realms.

"Terrence, I've been thinking...."

"Yes, clearly...," he teased, referring to her volumes of writing.

"No, I've been thinking about us and the baby. I want to try to change what happened before."

Terrence looked startled. "How would you do that?"

"I'm not sure," Sarah said, "but it could mean that the original Sarah might not have to die."

Terrence's eyes widened. "But how is that possible? What would you do?"

"I have an idea," Sarah said, "though I'm not sure it will work. I will need to be able to transport things across the time barrier."

"All right...," said Terrence, drawing out the syllables.

"The bad thing is," Sarah said as she felt a lump rise in her throat, "I might have to say good-bye to you in my present life, so you can have me in the past."

Terrence looked grim. "Suppose it doesn't work," he pressed. "I can't bear to lose you twice!"

"I'm not sure we have a choice," Sarah answered. "Time is fleeting and soon the baby will be due. I'm sure there's going to be some sort of reckoning ...a convergence of the ages."

They stood in silence. Terrence finally said, "Well, what do you want to bring across the divide?"

"I was thinking I could test the musket ball I found," Sarah said, going to the bowl where she had placed it. "It's small and durable...and it fits in my palm." This time she was careful not to let it plink against the sides.

As she put the ball into Terrence's hand, she sensed that a memory accompanied it. He picked up the pellet with two fingers and held it high to get a better view.

"Looks like this came from the old matchlock my father had. Couldn't shoot worth a damn but it was sure fun trying." Terrence smiled and handed it back to her.

"Last time when I dropped it into the bowl, I transitioned. The sound reminded me of a toll booth."

"A what booth?" Terrence asked. Once she explained it, he liked the idea of a road paying for itself. "I'll have to remember that once this new country gets on its feet."

"Yes, feet...," Sarah said as she envisioned the Randolphs standing in the house, waiting for her. "I have to get back to the people who are studying me," Sarah said. She wrapped her left hand around the little sphere and walked back toward the bathroom.

"Sarah, be careful," Terrence said as he reached out to touch her. But, by that time, she was gone.

"Sorry I took so long," Sarah said, returning to the front room.

"Oh, you weren't long," said Ann, training the video cam on Sarah. They sat on the couch for a while and then Sarah paced around the room. She went back the couch and then tried sitting in the wing chair.

"I don't think it's going to happen this time," Sarah said, not letting on that she had already seen Terrence. "I'm so sorry, but I'll have to come back and try again."

"That's too bad," Mr. Randolph said, handing Sarah her duffle. "Guess you won't need this today."

Sarah thanked him as she draped the strap of the nylon bag over her right shoulder. Once at the car, she put the duffle down on the ground and reached into her right pocket for the keys. As she uncurled her now sweaty left palm, she saw the perfectly round musket ball preserved in its entirety. It had successfully traveled with her.

7

TESTING THE BOUNDARIES

"Carter, you'll never guess what I can do!" Sarah said, bounding into the house.

"Glad to see you, too," he said, looking up from his computer, implying that she hadn't even said hello.

She held out her hand with the musket ball in it.

"I can bring things back from the past," she proclaimed. "You know what that means?"

"Um, that you can open an antique shop?" he sassed.

"No, it means that I might be able to save Sarah's life," she said, as if this were the most logical thought in the world. "If things can travel back here with me, they should be able to travel the other way."

"Cool," Carter said, thinking about the science of it. He was trying very hard to remove emotion from the equation. "Have you told the Randolphs?"

"No, are you kidding?"

"What about Dr. Barrows?" he asked.

"Definitely not—and that's a whole other thing. She keeps pressing me for updates. I bet she's texted me 12 times this week," Sarah complained.

"Can't you just send something along to stall her?"

"I'll try… Did you find out anything else about the Rhines?" Sarah asked.

"I'm still poking around. They were a fascinating couple. Father—and Mother, I suppose—of Parapsychology. Published a lot of stuff. I'm sure the Randolphs have read it all." Carter answered, pausing to ask, "Speaking of which, how are they doing?"

"Acting pretty 'Rhiney' if you ask me," Sarah allowed, "and apparently they *are* starting to take on patients. I overheard Ann talking to one of them, saying she would call in a prescription."

"That's bad," Carter replied. "Did anything else happen while you were there?"

"I saw Terrence briefly, but they didn't see him. I had stepped out of the room." Carter was glad her encounter with Terrence had been short. He didn't ask more about it and she didn't elaborate.

"Well, maybe we can put this behind us soon," Carter said, hopeful.

"Soon maybe, but I will need to go back to test item transport… and I want to see what happens with my writing," Sarah said, combining both timelines as she spoke.

"Your writing?"

"Oh, yes. Apparently, I had quite a gift for political commentary back in the day," Sarah said, head in the fridge looking for something to drink. A can of Diet Coke fizzed as she snapped off the tab. "We're going to send it to the newspaper."

"I look forward to reading it" Carter said, tongue-in-cheek. "I'm sure I can sign up for 1766 home delivery."

"Give me a break," Sarah said, rolling her eyes. "You know I'm trying to figure this out." Carter eased off.

"So, you'll send Barrows something to chew on?" he reminded.

"Yeah, I'll write up something now," Sarah said, taking her soda to the table and opening her laptop. She typed a few details—minus the juicy parts—and hit Send, hoping her synopsis would suffice. A few days later, Sarah called the Randolphs to schedule another visit.

"Come in, Sarah," Ann greeted from the doorway. "We're all ready for you." Her over-the-top enthusiasm was irritating, but Sarah viewed it as part of a job to be done.

"Hi, Ann." Sarah forced herself to smile as she purposely used her client's first name. "Where do you want me to sit?"

"On the couch is fine," Ann replied, looking over at Mr. Randolph, who was in position near the audio equipment. He angled the microphone on his desk, hoping to capture the room tone and Sarah's words. "Can you hear her?" Ann asked.

"Say something, Sarah." Mr. Randolph adjusted his headset and wiped his brow. The day was warm, and the house was stuffy despite the open window.

"Testing one, two, three," Sarah obliged, fingering the musket ball she had concealed in her left pocket.

"Did you want something to drink before we start?" Ann offered. "Soda, lemonade, water?"

"Oh, lemonade would be great," Sarah answered, trying to relax. She let the little globe roll around in her palm.

"I made it myself," Ann called out from the kitchen.

"I thought so…. I can smell the lemons."

"Can you?" Terrence asked, holding up a jar with an ornate red and gold label. "This came all the way from England," he said. "Marmalade from the old country." Sarah couldn't tell whether she was inhaling the scent of citrus that surrounded him or getting a whiff from the jar.

When she went to take a closer look at the marmalade, she felt the weight of something in her left hand. She was holding the musket ball she had brought from the present. "Yes!" she thought, issuing a fist pump before assuming her demure Colonial persona. She dropped the little ball into the pocket that hung from her waist—a waist, she noticed, that was almost completely gone—and continued the conversation.

"Where did you get this?" Sarah asked, looking up from the preserves.

"From my Aunt Charlotte," Terrence said. "She put it on the ship that just came in. Seems that she knows the Captain *quite well*"—his eyes implied hanky-panky—"and I guess she figured he'd have no problem smuggling in a little booty for her favorite nephew."

"Yummm," Sarah said. "I'll make some fresh bread to go with it."

"While you're at it, think about joining me in Boston next week—that is, if the trip isn't too much for you. You really should be the one to give Edes your writing. After all, you did the work. Besides, it could be a holiday for us before the baby arrives."

"Would he be receptive to that?" Sarah asked, well-aware that young men at 16 had more clout than most women twice their age.

"I think, under the circumstances, he will be very agreeable and most appreciative. Besides, I'd like you to see what goes on when I meet up with Sam and the men. It can get rowdy, but I'm sure it will inspire more of those feisty words," Terrence teased. "Do you think you're up to it?"

"If we go by coach, probably, especially if we stop along the way."

To say that it wasn't hot and uncomfortable would be a lie, but they traveled early in the morning and late in the afternoon to avoid the noon sun, stopping to eat a mid-day meal in a wooded area along the Boston Post Road. Pushing back sleeves and unbuttoning collars, they welcomed the cool shade.

Maples rose high in a canopy high above, and pine needles made a thick carpet below. Fern fronds, like neon ostrich feathers, grew over birches that had fallen in last year's storms. The air carried a hint of moss, roses, and mushrooms—nature's opiate—deep, earthy and intoxicating. The crock of cider they had brought was still cold and refreshing; the bread and cheese, filling.

Sarah watched from the woods as Terrence strode into the bright open field, setting off a cloud of grasshoppers that lifted skyward, before settling down again. That telltale twitch along his jaw belied his eagerness to leave. Walking up behind him, she slipped her arms around his torso, putting her hands into his pockets, over his hands, and suggested they move along. She stalled a moment, enjoying the feel of her cheek against his back.

As evening fell, Terrence instructed the driver to pull in at one of the hostelries that dotted the highway. Country inns were like beacons on the dark landscape. Their inviting glow could be seen for miles away and the lively music that drifted from their windows made for a cordial welcome.

Sarah and Terrence went immediately to their room to freshen up, but soon returned to the lobby to ask about food. In deference to Sarah, they avoided the tavern where a toe-tapping fiddler and lewd limericks triggered peals of laughter from the crowd, opting instead for a quiet alcove off the main dining room. How good it was to have someone else prepare the meal, Sarah thought, as she dipped her spoon into a bowl of thick lamb stew. Terrence kept looking at her in the yellow light and smiled.

"What?" Sarah asked him, catching his gaze.

"I was thinking how beautiful you are and how lucky I am," he said, sitting back in his chair, adjusting his waistcoat. Leaning forward, he picked up his tankard of ale to toast their child-to-be. Sarah held up her goblet of cold water, watching a chunk of ice float in the middle, grateful for the annual ice harvest on the lake behind the inn.

"To our future family," Sarah said, each sipping from their respective vessels. That evening, despite fatigue, they loved each other to the song of crickets and the next morning, continued their journey.

Sarah had not been to Boston in ages and had been much younger when her father first showed her the bustling harbor with its tall ships. She remembered the mélange of odors—fish, firewood, sweet pastries—and the crooked cobblestone paths that set her off-balance and hurt her feet. But, this time, she leaned on the arm of a strong, handsome man, who protected her from obstacles and careless passersby, a proud American, who tipped his hat to well-dressed Brahmins and stepped aside for boisterous children.

Terrence and Sarah unloaded their belongings at the home of family friends and went out to explore the city. Terrence steered her to the corner of Essex and Orange Streets, where people milled around a magnificent elm festooned with flags and banners. "This is the Liberty Tree I mentioned," he explained, looking at Sarah for a reaction, but her gaze was fixed on a frayed rope that once held the effigy of a stamp collector.

"Good day, Sheriff Greenleaf," Sarah heard Terrence say. She turned around to see an official-looking gentleman holding a pouch stamped with the words "Suffolk County."

"What brings you to town, Mr. Covington?" the sheriff replied, tipping his cocked hat, seeming to be overly genteel.

"A holiday for my lady," Terrence answered, at which point Sarah assumed a wifely pose, hands atop her belly, politely smiling.

"I see the tree is looking as grand as usual," Terrence commented as he put his arm protectively around Sarah. He knew that Stephen Greenleaf tried his best to keep the peace, but Terrence resented the sheriff for censoring what could be displayed.

"Yes, wonderful specimen," Greenleaf remarked, looking up into the verdant boughs, staying clear of any volatile conversation. "Well, you two have a nice day," he offered, and with a brief nod, turned and walked away.

"How do you know him?" Sarah asked as they strolled toward Faneuil Hall.

"Oh, he and I met about a year ago," Terrence let on, a wry smile playing around his lips. "We were both at the Stamp Act protests last August, but let's just say, not always on the same side of the street."

"Terrence, you worry me," Sarah scolded. "I fear that someday you're going to be seriously hurt—or worse."

"Not to worry now, my love," Terrence countered, taking her hand as they maneuvered through the busy marketplace.

Sarah realized she was hungry and convinced Terrence to sample the wares. Going from cart to cart, rather than stepping into a dining establishment, was an adventure she welcomed. There were meat pies and roasted potatoes intended to be eaten with the fingers; hasty pudding and sweet cornmeal served in pewter bowls to be returned; hearty breads and maple cake cut into fat wedges; steaming cauldrons of fish stew and baskets of greens. There were even bottles of fox grape wine, carefully labeled "Vitis Labrusca—American grown," set up near a sign that said, "As Proffered by *Poor Richard's Almanack.*"

This freewheeling escape was good for them and, later that afternoon, when they met Edes at his office near the old North Church, they were refreshed and energized.

As Terrence lifted the heavy brass knocker, Sarah could see a Sons of Liberty flag through the window. She had heard that the vertical red and white stripes represented the first nine Colonies to protest at the Stamp Act Congress.

"Rebellious Stripes," Terrence stated, seeing Sarah's interested expression. "That's what we fly on the Liberty Tree when we want people to gather."

A congenial fellow in his early thirties opened the door. "Welcome to Edes & Gill," the man said, extending his hand to Terrence and nodding in Sarah's direction. Sarah introduced herself.

"How's my favorite agitator?" asked Terrence, flashing his winning smile as he clasped Edes' hand.

"Never better, brother," said the printer, indicating they should all sit at the long table.

"And your wife?" Terrence asked as he pulled out a chair for Sarah.

"We've just celebrated our twelfth anniversary," Edes answered, taking a seat.

Sarah glanced around the room. Newspapers were stacked on every available surface. Towers of the *Boston Gazette* leaned against piles of the *Country Journal*, edging out samples of the competitive *Boston Evening Post*. The air smelled of ink and paper, acrid, but not entirely unpleasant. She could see rows of wooden letters fitted tightly into trays. An unfinished row sat in a composing stick at the end of the table near bins of neatly organized wooden type. On the wall was a chart of Caslon faces and point sizes, the preferred font of the day.

"What brings you here?" Edes asked. "Other than to cause trouble?"

"No, no, I'm on good behavior this time, but my wife has something for you. Turns out, she's a bloody good writer and I thought you might be able to use her work."

Sarah carefully took her sheets of paper out of an envelope and pushed them across the table.

"Uh-huh. Uh-huh," Edes said as he quickly read her words. "Yes! Yes!" he muttered out loud. Without looking up, he flipped to the next page and the next, pounding the table when he was done.

After a prolonged pause, he turned directly to Sarah. "Well, good lady," he said with a pleased smile, "I think we have a future Martha Wadsworth Brewster here."

"I'm afraid I don't know who that is," Sarah confessed.

"Oh, we published her about 10 years ago. She's a poet and a writer...the first American-born woman to publish under her own name. A whole different genre, but you can be assured, we are not afraid of the female voice."

Sarah's eyes were wide as she looked at Terrence, hand to mouth to stifle her excitement.

"Then you think this is worthy of publication?" Sarah timidly asked.

"Absolutely," said Edes. "And we should discuss how we want to use your talents in the future...perhaps anonymously at first, then maybe in your own hand."

"I'm not looking for fame or recognition," Sarah said, "And the last thing I want to do is endanger Terrence."

"We'll give it some thought," Terrence replied, looking at Sarah, "but, in the meantime, do we agree that this is too good to wait?"

"Definitely. This will go to press in July," Edes confirmed, "Carefully disguised."

"That's wonderful. Thank you so much. I am most appreciative," Sarah said as she gathered her skirts to rise.

"It is I who appreciate *your* contribution," Edes said, bordering on the gallant.

"See you tomorrow night?" he asked Terrence in a more collegial tone. Edes was a Son of Liberty, too, and one of The Loyal Nine, an even more incendiary and surreptitious group.

Terrence nodded yes, "Absolutely," and closed the door behind.

Terrence couldn't have been prouder of Sarah as he ushered his wife outside. The air was cooler now and smelled of ocean, and they found it invigorating. Street lamps were being lit, their oil emanating a warm glow, but people were still milling around, enjoying the salty breeze that came in off the shore. Suddenly there was a jagged streak of lightning, and then a boom. Torrents of rain began to fall, first splattering the ground and kicking up small puffs of dust, then turning into blinding sheets of water that swept across the brownstones like a large eraser.

Terrence immediately put his hat over Sarah's head and steered her down the street into an alleyway. Breathless, she couldn't move as fast as she did when she was 20 pounds lighter, but she managed to keep up with Terrence—and like two wet dogs, they ducked under the protection of the overhanging roofs. Lacking downspouts, water rushed down the sides of the buildings and splashed back at their feet. Sarah found herself hopping to avoid fast-forming puddles as Terrence tried to shield her with his body.

Electricity sparked and sizzled across the horizon, lighting up the harbor as if by a flare. Sarah could feel her heart thumping with every clap of thunder.

"Are you all right?" Terrence asked, wiping water out of his eyes. Sarah shook her head yes, but she couldn't stop shivering. A crack of lightning followed by a louder peal of thunder sent them further into the recesses of the alley.

"Terrence, I'm not sure I'll be able to stay," Sarah suddenly said.

"We can leave once the rain is over or certainly by tomorrow morning if you want," he said.

"No, it's not that. Something is pulling me back now. I don't think I can stop it," and, with that, Sarah found herself rushing over to Mrs. Randolph who was kneeling next to her husband, supine on the floor.

"Quick, call 911," Ann commanded. "Something is terribly wrong!"

Sarah did as she was told. Within minutes, she could hear the wail of an ambulance approaching. "I'm sorry, Sarah," Ann said, frazzled and impatient, "We'll just have to do this another time."

"Of course," Sarah said, aware of the emergency. Apparently, the Randolphs had seen nothing of her experience.

"I don't know what happened," she could hear Ann saying to the EMT. "We just sat down with a guest and then suddenly David keeled over as if he were shocked or having a heart attack."

"We'll stabilize him. You follow us to the hospital."

"Did you want me to drive you?" Sarah offered, but Ann shooed her away.

"You go home. I'll let you know what happens," she called over her shoulder, grabbing her keys, and heading out. "Just lock the door behind you."

Once again, Sarah was alone in the house, head reeling from what had just occurred. She walked over to Mr. Randolph's equipment and touched the headset. No heat. No smoke. Nothing seemed out of the ordinary. She turned the dial to the Off position and watched a small green light fade to black. She briefly wondered if the electricity from that long-ago storm had somehow been transmitted.

Despite her concern for Mr. Randolph, Sarah was intent on joining Terrence at the Sons of Liberty meeting. Unfortunately, he

Jill C. Baker

was far from the house. She had never tried reaching him at such a distance, but she sat down, deciding to visualize him where he last stood, drenched, and crouching, in an alleyway in the North End of Boston. Mentally, she recreated his clean-shaven face, neck scarf, fitted waistcoat, long shirt tucked into button-front breeches, fine linen jacket made especially for summer and of course, those crystalline blue eyes. Looking at her feet, the stockings and shoes she saw were wet, at which point she knew she was back at his side.

"What were you saying about leaving?" he asked. "I couldn't hear you over the noise."

"Oh, nothing," Sarah said. "I had to go back for a moment, but I was able to return."

"I'm glad," Terrence replied, setting his hand on her shoulder.

"Looks like the rain is letting up," Sarah observed as they peeked around the brick wall.

"Yes, finally. Let's go back to our room and dry off."

Inside the stately town house, Sarah and Terrence peeled off their wet garments and put on their spare set of clothing before joining their hosts, Mehitable and George, in the library. The hallway to the library was replete with tapestries and oriental carpets. Heavy burgundy drapes were tied back with braided gold cord, each anchored by a disk of aquamarine pressed glass. Massive oil paintings, set into deep gilt frames, marked strategic points along the corridor. Ornate plasterwork embellished a ceiling dome where cherubs cavorted against an interpretation of sky and clouds. Quite a change from simple country life, Sarah thought, as she adjusted her gown, smoothed her hair, and placed her hand on Terrence's forearm.

"I'm so sorry you got caught in the rain," Mehitable said, graciously handing Sarah a steaming cup of tea. George passed a cup to Terrence as well. Sarah thought these people might be Loyalists—they certainly had the air of Old England—but as they talked with Terrence, it was clear they knew of his underground activities.

"I'm told the Green Dragon's been sold to the Freemasons," George said, aware that the prominent landmark was home to both the Boston Caucus and Sons of Liberty.

188

"I gather…St. Andrew's Lodge," Terrence said, emptying his cup and holding it up for a refill. "Guess we'll see if we're still welcome tomorrow."

"You can stay here with me while Terrence goes about his business," Mehitable offered, looking at Sarah as the men talked about the mounting discontent.

"Well, actually, she'll be coming with me," Terrence interjected, leaving George and Mehitable aghast.

"That's no place for a woman," George sternly reprimanded.

"But it *is* for a Patriot," Terrence retorted, "and Sarah is definitely that." Sarah was surprised and delighted at his endorsement.

"I don't think you can just walk in the front door, dear," Mehitable warned. "It's a men's den and you'll surely want to cover your ears. I've heard horrible stories about the language and behavior there."

"No worse than the fiery speeches we're hearing out in the country," Sarah replied. "But fortunately, I can now do something with that rhetoric." Her hosts were puzzled.

"I introduced Sarah to Ben Edes today," Terrence explained. "She's going to be writing for him—for the Colonial press."

"Well, I'll be!" said George. "That's excellent."

Sarah beamed with pride as the conversation continued, in which—for once—she was equally included. The foursome eventually reconvened in the dining room around a great table laden with platters of roast beef and sumptuous pairings, after which snifters of brandy were passed around along with small, buttery pastries filled with jam. Warm, full, and happy, Sarah and Terrence excused themselves, returned to their plush room and fell easily to sleep, waking much later than they had planned.

After a light lunch, they headed toward Union Street and the Green Dragon Tavern. As they approached the building, Sarah could see the copper beast hanging above the doorway, its metal scales corroded green from the briny ocean air. She immediately knew where the establishment had gotten its name.

Sarah was dressed in barmaid's attire, thanks to some creative assembling by Mehitable. Terrence entered first through the center doorway and as instructed, Sarah waited by the door at the left side. Quickly ushered in, she was pointed to a galley where other servers waited. The counters were lined with trays of tankards ready to be filled.

"What ye doin' here, missy?" a woman of great girth queried. "Haven't seen ye around these parts."

Sarah kept her eyes down and her voice low. "Just trying to pick up some coins," she said as she lifted a tray and turned toward the main room. Terrence apparently had an 'in' with the manager.

Soon a stampede of first arrivals made their way down the narrow stairs to the basement. Sarah immediately followed with a round of biscuits and beer, quickly retreating to the first floor once the drinks had been served. She didn't dare look at Terrence and he ignored her as well.

Another group of men joined moments later, brimming with bluster and bravado.

"Hey, Paul, you rascal. Finally made, it I see," she could hear one of them bellow.

"John, my man," a disembodied voice acknowledged. She wasn't sure if that was Hancock, Lamb, or Adams, but she had a feeling all of them were there. She knew that roll call would never be taken nor names written down, because most of the men were charged with civil disobedience or treason and did not favor their attendance recorded. Secrecy also meant that Sarah's witnessing the event would never be documented. Exactly what she wanted.

"It's come to my attention that our brethren in other cities need our help," the leader of the group announced as the room quieted. "How can we lend our support?"

"We have horses, guns, and the power of the press," someone said. "We can rally anywhere, anytime, and get the word out to supporters."

"We can pool our intellect and help them strategize," another voice said. "And stand beside them," someone else added.

"Too many people are growing complacent after the Stamp Act repeal," one man complained. "We've gotta fire up those slackin' bastards," a different voice growled. Loud cheers arose.

190

As heated discussions boiled, Sarah slipped in and out of the Long Room with ale and hard cider, beef jerky and dried fish strips. The salty snacks inspired additional drinking, which the tavern owner liked. It was only once, when she felt a hand pat her backside, did she hear Terrence say, "Leave the wench alone and let's get back to business. How much time do we need to get to Egremont?"

Sarah had heard that General Gage's army was pillaging and burning homes in the western part of the state and that some citizens in Great Barrington were being removed bodily from their houses. Surely, the Sons could send a message, if they gathered there, she thought.

"It's the Quartering Act that's getting New York up in arms," someone else was saying. "We'll need to get down there, too. That's an important line of defense for us."

Sarah could feel the excitement building, and the bolder the conversation got, the more energy was emitted. Swearing about Parliament, roads, and taxes only begot swearing about mercantilism, legislation, and lack of representation. F— this, Bloody— that. Sarah tried to close her ears, but at the same time, she was amused by this big bunch of bad boys, who took such delight in rabble-rousing.

She could see why the Sons walked a thin line between being hailed as Patriots and being cursed as scoundrels. Many of them had been recruited from the docks and were as salty as the sea. Others had been charged with crimes she couldn't imagine. But, among this unruly mix of dissidents were also statesmen, orators, philosophers, and visionaries.

More beer, bread, baked beans, and thick clam chowder. The night didn't end until the last man stumbled up the stairs and Sarah's rotund co-server slumped spread-eagle on a low stool.

"Will that be all?" Sarah asked as she removed the last of the tankards from a vat of hot water and set them out to dry.

"All for tonight," the other woman answered. "Go find the Mister and he'll pay your wages."

Sarah nodded thanks.

191

"Will I see ye tomorrow?" the big woman asked as she hung her apron on a peg.

"I think not," Sarah answered. "I have to go home, but this was excellent training as I'll be working at the pub there," she lied.

"Glad t' help," her co-worker said, blowing out a candle and pulling the wooden door shut behind them. "Do ye have a place to stay?"

"Staying with friends," Sarah answered, not wanting to provide too much information. "One of them is coming to meet me in a few minutes." With that, the big woman waved good-bye and waddled into the narrow street where she was swallowed up by the encroaching fog. Sarah waited in the shadows and thought about what she had seen.

Moments later, Terrence was at her side. "What did you think?" he asked. "Did you get some ideas for Edes?"

"Oh, yes, many," Sarah confirmed. "I've got some great ammunition for my next article."

"Good," said Terrence. "Then let's get some rest and head home first thing in the morning."

Thanking Mehitable and George and, accepting a basket of smoked meats and bread for the road, Terrence helped Sarah into their coach and cued the driver to leave. She was heavier now, and the seat offered welcome support. They stayed overnight at the inn they had enjoyed before, and the next day, moments after the coach dropped them off at their house, Sarah returned to modern times, assuring Terrence she would be back.

When Sarah arrived home, Carter was pacing. "I heard what happened to David. How terrible," he said as soon as she walked in the door.

"I know, I was there," Sarah said, "at least for part of it."

"What do you mean?" Carter asked. "I thought you were at the house."

"I was, but apparently I transitioned just before this happened. I got back in time to call 911."

"Do they know what caused it? I heard he had a pacemaker."

"I didn't know that," Sarah said. "It was a very hot day and he seemed stressed."

"How did Ann handle it?"

"She tried to hold it together but was clearly rattled. What do you expect?"

"I don't know," Carter said, "but when she called here afterward, she was just plain nasty. She said this was all *your* fault."

"My fault? I have no idea what she's talking about. I didn't do anything to her husband."

"I know, but something's going on. She kept mentioning deadlines and the pressure they're under for funding…then she said I wouldn't understand."

"That's funny," Sarah commented as she sat down and took off her shoes. Did she imagine it or were her feet sore from walking on cobblestone? "The only pressure I've seen on the Randolphs is their eagerness to prove people can talk to the dead—while pretending to *be* the dead." Sarah was cynical.

"Well, maybe we should check on David anyway. After all, they're still colleagues of mine and clients of yours," Carter reminded.

The following evening, Sarah and Carter went to the hospital where Mr. Randolph was resting in bed, recovering from heart surgery. However, instead of seeing Ann at his side, they saw Dr. Barrows dressed in a trim charcoal gray pantsuit, white blouse, and heels, giving her a few more inches of height than Sarah remembered.

"Don't fail me now, David," they could hear her saying. "I'm counting on you to deliver."

Sarah and Carter tapped on the open door and Mr. Randolph motioned for them to come in. "You know Dr. Barrows, right?" he said, making a gesture of introduction. He looked agitated.

"I do," said Sarah.

Carter extended his hand. "Good to finally meet you. Thank you for being here. I've followed your work."

Dr. Barrows nodded briefly, but Sarah could sense that something was wrong. It seemed as if the good doctor and Mr. Randolph had been arguing.

"Where's Mrs. Randolph?" Sarah asked.

"Cafeteria," he answered, eying the hall. "She'll be back in a minute, so please stay."

Dr. Barrows picked up her purse and turned to leave. "Glad you're feeling better, David," she said in a cool, almost aloof, tone. She cleared her throat and smoothed her suit. "You should get some rest. I'll be in touch." She acknowledged Sarah and Carter, then hurried out the door.

Sarah couldn't help but notice that Mr. Randolph's pulse rate was making small peaks on the monitor as the steady beep-beep-beep picked up pace. He kept forming his hand into a fist and releasing it.

"We just wanted to see how you were doing," Carter explained. "We won't stay long."

"That's fine and much appreciated," Mr. Randolph said, appearing tired. "Who would have thought I'd end up here?" he muttered. "I just had a physical."

Within minutes, Ann returned to the room—a dervish of activity—arranging flowers, plumping his pillow, bringing him a newspaper. "They shut off the lights pretty early," she said, looking over to Sarah and Carter in a not-so-subtle hint.

"Oh, we'll be going in a moment. We just wanted to check in," Carter explained and then added, "Maybe this is a sign we should curtail our efforts."

"I'm beginning to think so, too," Ann said, resigning herself to a change of plans. "You know, it's such a shame after all our hard work. All we wanted to do was show that people could cross the barrier between life and death—prove that it *can* be done," she emphasized.

Carter nodded, accepting the sincerity—if not the recently odd behavior—of his friend.

"And all I want to do is prove *how*," said Dr. Barrows from the doorway, her voice sounding decidedly different.

Sarah and Carter whipped around. Sam was standing there with a pistol trained on the foursome. Sarah immediately clutched Carter's hand as Mrs. Randolph moved protectively in front of her husband's bed.

"I hate to do this, friends and colleagues, but I need you to sit over there," Barrows said, pointing with the weapon to some chairs on the other side of the room. "I've got a few things to figure out," she said, moving behind them, gun poised. Her speech was void of emotion; her eyes, calculating.

Just then, a cheerful nurse came in to check on Mr. Randolph. "Everything all right in here?" she asked as she took his temperature and refilled his IV bag. Noting his accelerated heart rate, she advised, "I think we need some quiet time. Your visitors can wait in the lounge if they'd like."

Ann, Sarah and Carter sat stiffly, keenly aware of the pistol aimed at their hips. One shot to the spine could paralyze any of them.

"Yes, why don't you do that," Mr. Randolph suggested, trying to get the group safely into a public area. "I'll just stay here and read a little," he feigned, fully expecting to call Security.

"Sorry, but we need to borrow you for a moment to change your dressing," the nurse corrected as two orderlies entered the room. "It won't take long."

"But, I need to do something first," Mr. Randolph started to say. "I have to…I must…." Sarah could see his energy wane as he was lifted onto a gurney.

"Not to worry," the nurse said, noticing Sarah's concern as the aides wheeled him into the hall. "We'll have him back in a jiffy."

"We'll leave now," Dr. Barrows said to the nurse, ushering Ann, Carter, and Sarah along, so they moved as a single unit, down the corridor.

"You can come back later," the nurse called after them. Ann said thank you but was afraid to say anything else.

"This time, we're all going to the house," Dr. Barrows stated, her cool demeanor turning to ice, "and I'm expecting to see some remarkable results." The threesome looked at each other realizing they had no choice but to obey.

"You drive," she said to Carter. "Your car," she said to Ann.

Barrows continued to press her gun between Sarah's shoulder blades as they made their way toward the parking garage and to Ann's vehicle. "Keys," she demanded. Ann tossed them over to her. Carter and Sarah stood silent, breathing in short halting puffs.

"Put your phones on the ground," the doctor instructed as she walked around and opened the car doors. Three cells were laid painfully on the concrete floor, side-by-side, along the white line that separated the parking spots. She handed the keys to Carter. "Get in. All of you. I'll ride up front."

Aware that a pistol was now pointed at Carter's ear, Ann and Sarah obligingly climbed into the back seat. "You know, I have no problem shooting this man; he's of little use to me," Barrows reminded, as she slid into the passenger seat. She leaned on the armrest and turned around to get a better look at the cowering women behind her. "So, it would be wise to cooperate." Her stare was piercing and her tone, acerbic.

"But why are you doing this?" Ann asked. "We're happy to share credit for our work. We'll even share our funding if you want."

Barrows huffed. "I don't want a by-line on your measly report or a piece of your meager budget. I think bigger than that." Her comments were demeaning, surgical —precise and cutting. Ann seemed hurt.

Carter pulled out of the lot. "Then what do you want?" he asked, hands clenching the wheel. He felt surprisingly betrayed by this person he had respected.

"What do I want? What *do* I want?" Dr. Barrows said, changing the emphasis on each of her words, a chortle following her contemplation. "I want ten million dollars for writing a 'How To' manual."

"Ten million dollars?" Ann asked. "But we're just going after $100,000 in funding."

"Oh, I know. A few grand doesn't interest me in the slightest. It will take millions to build a state-of-the-art psych lab, to create a brand, and to start selling the proprietary knowledge I will soon possess," Barrows sniffed.

"How are you planning to get that kind of money?" Carter challenged.

"I'm going after the award from the brother of that kid who was killed."

"What award?" Carter asked as he steered the car along a curve.

"You know, the Lange Prize…Stuart Lange. His older brother was killed when you were in college." Carter remembered the incident and Sarah recalled looking at the clipping in their yearbook.

"What's Stuart got to do with this?" Ann asked.

"Oh, he's a man of means now. A little eccentric, but very rich. Owns a slew of companies, likes to tinker in the trades and has a bunch of VC money to invest," Barrows replied, not letting the gun move from Carter's head. "But none of that can replace the brother he lost. Misses him terribly."

"And…?" Ann prodded, trying to understand what was going on.

"And he's put up 10 million dollars for anyone who can show him how to talk to his brother—his dead brother, I mean." Barrows paused to clear her throat. "Lucky for me, someone here knows how to do that."

There was a prolonged silence until Sarah spoke. "You think *I* can show you that?"

"I'm sure you can," Barrows said in a tone that Sarah had never heard from her before. "And if *you* can do it, *I* can do it."

"I don't think it works that way," Carter interrupted.

"No one asked you," Barrows said, shutting him down with a phrase. Carter went mute.

He could see the Covington house in the distance and, when he pulled into the drive, he wished the familiar black-and-white cruiser were on patrol, but no police car was in sight. No neighbors. No luck. Just three scared people being held at gunpoint in a dark car on a back road.

Barrows ordered Carter to get out and open the side door of the house. She kept her weapon drawn on the women in the car. "Brass key with the lettering," Ann called to Carter, knowing he had no idea which key would work.

"Get on with it, and don't try being clever," Barrows threatened.

Carter didn't think Barrows would shoot Sarah or Ann, as they were her bread and butter, but he couldn't take any chances. He turned the key, but the door resisted. Only after a kick to the bottom did it push in. Barrows ordered the women out of the car and instructed them to stand at Carter's side. "Get in there and be quiet," she said, forcing all three into the mudroom. As soon as Barrows set foot on the floor, Sarah sensed the house recoil. "Now I want you to conjure up your damn ghost," Barrows said, zeroing in on Sarah.

Although it was summer, the house was cool and damp. Sarah felt a suffocating stillness she had not previously noticed. The drapes hung like shrouds, and oblique shadows cut across the sitting room, creating angles and dark corners in areas that had once been soft and inviting. The graceful rose damask wing chairs that had always reminded her of archangels, seemed to resemble gargoyles now, hunched in the presence of evil. The pendulum of the grandfather's clock swung steadily—a ponderous heartbeat. Sarah noticed Carter trying to assess the scene, surely wondering why she had found this house so enchanting.

"On the couch, all of you," Barrows instructed, detached and expressionless. "Remember, the more you help me, the better it will be for you." Sarah knew Barrows would use all the tricks in the book to psych them out, and she vowed not to fall for any of them.

"I'm not sure I can do this," Sarah said, tears coming to her eyes. "It usually happens when I'm relaxed."

"Well, relax then. Have a drink. Take a toke, whatever," Barrows bullied, letting her professional demeanor slip.

Sarah and Ann looked at each other, not sure how to respond. Barrows struggled to open a window, rattling the glass and forcing the wooden frame up the cord with an excruciating screech. The sound of crickets drifted in along with the radio of a passing car. The bass notes blasting from a woofer thumped in their chests.

An imperceptible breeze carried with it the smell of leaf mold and warm earth. The air was thick with humidity.

"Now!" Barrows demanded, moving the gun to Carter's neck. His hands were clammy, and he shivered at the feel of cold metal on his skin.

In an exaggeratedly eerie voice, with arms outstretched, palms up, Sarah began to chant, "Terrence. Oh, Terrence. Come to me...." Was it her imagination or did the house shudder in response? Carter looked sideways at her, realizing she was putting on a show.

"I can feel your presence now," Sarah continued as if hosting a séance. "Join me from the other world and be one with me," she said, rotating her head as if falling into a trance. Even Ann was suspicious, aware that Sarah had never acted like this before. Barrows, who knew Sarah had previously summoned Terrence, had no reason to think this wasn't the norm.

By this time, night had extinguished the last remaining rays of day. Sarah could hear a dog barking in the distance and the whirr of a helicopter flying overhead. Barrows flicked on the sconces, keeping her pistol drawn. The electrified flames were mirrored in the rippled windowpanes, their usual playful dancing now devilishly cavorting. Sarah tore her eyes away and slowly walked to the middle of the room.

"What's happening?" Barrows hissed, "Tell me!" The grandfather's clock chimed 9:00.

"Not much," said Sarah, coming out of her fake stupor. "I'm not getting anything."

"Well, try harder," Barrows growled. "What do you do? Close your eyes? Count backward? Hypnotize yourself? Say a magic word?"

"None of that, really," Sarah explained, "it just happens."

Carter and Ann watched silently, trying to calm themselves, as Sarah sat motionless, head down, hands folded in her lap. Barrows glowered, tapping her foot impatiently.

"Well, maybe we should set up the room like we did before," Ann suggested, wanting to appear helpful. "I'll hook up the headphones to our low frequency recorder to see if we can hear any abnormalities." She looked at Sarah and then at Barrows. "Sometimes these things manifest themselves aurally."

"Put it on speaker," Barrows said, not wanting to miss anything and not trusting Ann.

"Sure," Ann said, going over to the desk where David had sat.

"Now be quiet," Barrows said, hushing everyone with the fingers that didn't hold the gun.

The threesome sat stock-still as Barrows paced. The only noise they could hear was ambient room tone coming across the amp with a whoosh-whoosh reminiscent of an ultrasound. Carter's eyes darted from floor to ceiling as he contemplated ways to escape.

"I have to go to the bathroom," Sarah announced, hoping to break from the group.

"Is there a window in there?" Barrows asked. "I don't want you jumping out." If this were an attempt at humor, it fell flat.

"No," Ann answered quickly. "You can see for yourself."

"No need," Barrows said, moving to a position between the main room and the narrow hallway. "But be quick about it," she said, her gun following Sarah before returning it to Carter and Ann.

Carter and Ann looked at each other, hoping Sarah had a plan. Moths had gathered on the window where the sconces sent their light, creating a pale mosaic against the black background. A June bug persistently batted the screen. Carter and Ann could hear fire engine sirens in the distance, getting fainter as they drove further away toward town.

With the bathroom door closed, Sarah summoned Terrence, hoping her concentration would work. "Help me," she pleaded, explaining what was taking place.

"I'm not sure how..." he said, appearing from nowhere. His brow furrowed as he chewed the inside of his cheek. "Unlike you, I can't cross over." Seeing Terrence trapped this way was disconcerting.

"I know, I know," Sarah said bracing his arms, "but this woman has a gun and there's no telling what she'll do."

"Let me think," Terrence replied, running his hand through his hair and over his chin. "You go back, and I'll figure something out."

Within minutes, Sarah returned silently to the couch. "I have to do the same thing," Ann said, glancing toward the bathroom with some urgency.

"Be fast," Barrows said, keeping her gun trained on Ann.

With Ann out of the room, Carter tried to engage Barrows. "Sam, I had no idea you were going after the Lange Prize. I didn't even know it was real. I thought it was just an urban myth in the weird science community."

"Hardly," Barrows answered, alternating her focus between the couch and the bathroom hall. "All I had to do was convince this fellow that I meant business. Getting my application approved was a no-brainer."

"What do you mean 'approved'?" Carter asked, trying to understand the dynamics of this high-stakes game.

"I mean I had to give this guy a reason to believe I could deliver and then it was full-tilt boogie. That's why I sent him out here."

"Out here?" Sarah asked.

"Stuart's Inspections?" Barrows replied, annoyed at the question. "You know, to see for himself."

"But I thought the Randolphs arranged that," Sarah said.

"Pull-ease," Barrows replied, turning the word into two syllables. "I'd be a fool to leave this in the hands of Ann and David...or should I say, Louisa and J.B. Nice people, but come on...."

"So, you know?" Sarah asked, surprised.

"Of course, I do. You don't seriously think I could hang around these two all these years and not notice their delusions," Barrows said, as if offended. Carter and Sarah shrugged.

"I mean, who wears shirtwaist dresses, a white wig, and dabbles with equipment from the fifties?"

"I don't know..." Sarah started to say. "I just thought they were trying to recreate the original experiments," at which point Carter finished her sentence... "and just got carried away."

"Highly unlikely," Barrows said with a distinct air of superiority. "I know they're practicing without a license. That's my ace in the hole. I plan to use their research, add mine to it, and walk away with the Lange Prize. If they don't co-operate, I'll turn them in and access their files anyway.

"So, this is all about the money?" Carter asked.

"More about the power," Barrows corrected. "With that kind of seed money and the knowledge I'm about to receive, I will hold the keys to the kingdom. Living and dead."

"But the Randolphs could turn you in just as easily," Carter postured, trying to exert some leverage. "Stealing their work, ethics violation, breach of contract...kidnapping." Carter emphasized the last word.

"Who would believe them?" Barrows challenged. "No credentials. Mentally unstable. Out of touch. Nope, my priorities are with making Stuart happy and that's where I need you."

Sarah didn't have to say anything to Carter. They both knew that Barrows wouldn't need them much after that. As Ann rejoined the group, the grandfather's clock struck 10:00. Barrows was getting antsy. Her usual calm demeanor was being replaced by tension that played out in her shoulders and in a tic at the side of her mouth. Ann rolled her head to loosen her neck muscles and rotated her shoulders as she waited.

"Keep stalling," Carter told himself as he thought about the hospital they had just left. He knew it was getting late and David would surely be back in his room. He must certainly have notified Security by now.

"Try again," Barrows suddenly said, pointing the gun at Sarah. "You said you smell lavender and lemon when Terrence is near. Well, I'm getting a whiff of something pretty delicious."

Sarah wasn't sure whether Barrows was really detecting anything or just toying with her. After all, Barrows was skilled at mental manipulation. Afraid that Terrence would manifest himself, Sarah asked if she could sit behind the room divider. "So long as I can watch you in the mirror, fine," said Barrows, allowing Sarah to open the ornate Oriental screen and pull a chair behind it. The screen smelled musty and was rheumatic as she unfolded it.

Sarah didn't know if Terrence could be seen in mirrors, she had never really noticed—but this set-up seemed somehow safer and more private. She sat quietly and gazed at the black and gold mural of cranes and bamboo shoots, stomach rumbling, mouth dry. They had planned to go out for dinner after the hospital visit, but obviously, they didn't make it. Thank goodness, her sister was staying with the kids and could sleep over.

By this time, Ann was dozing off on Carter's shoulder, the circles under his eyes getting darker with each passing hour. "We need some water," Carter finally said, "and some food."

"Can't promise much," Barrows responded, poking Ann with her gun. "Maybe Louie, here, can rustle something up." Ann looked mortified at the disclosure.

"I'll see what I can find," she mumbled, heading to the kitchen.

"In there with her," Barrows said to Carter, prodding him with her weapon. Barrows' heels slapped the floorboards; they squeaked in protest.

Sarah could see the activity from her vantage point behind the screen, but didn't dare move. She didn't try to contact Terrence, either.

A few minutes later, the threesome emerged from the kitchen, Barrows walking behind, gun in position, as Carter and Ann carried plates of ham sandwiches and glasses of water into the main room. Barrows called to Sarah, "Come over for food." Sarah was happy to leave her post and willingly joined the group. No one talked. Other than the occasional creak of the walls settling, there was no sound. She had never realized that this location was so isolated.

"Put on the TV. I want to see the 11:00 news," Barrows ordered Ann, reaching for a half sandwich with one hand, holding her gun with the other. Ann opened the door of a vintage hutch and revealed a flat panel screen, which she resuscitated with the press of a remote. A female news anchor was stationed in front of the local hospital.

"Turn it up," Barrow instructed, and Ann complied.

"A significant power outage hit County Hospital early this evening, which the Police say was a diversion for an attempted drug robbery. Shots were fired in the hallways, and authorities confirm there have been several casualties. Names are being withheld until families can be notified. More as soon as we have it."

Ann felt an icy draft sweep across the room. She doubled over as if the air had been punched out of her lungs. A wave of nausea rose in her throat and she started to shake, certain that David was dead or dying. Tears spilled over the lower rims of her eyes as she looked for a way to leave. "I need to get to him, please," she said, more desperate than Sarah had ever seen her before.

Barrows moved in and put the gun over Ann's lips. "Shhh," Barrows whispered as if soothing a child. Ann cringed and pulled away. "I think it's too late," Barrows said, failing to conceal a perverse sense of glee.

Carter put his arm around Ann's shoulder. "I'm so sorry. Maybe he's OK." Ann shook her head no. Sarah knew she was right. Barrows shut off the TV.

"Well, isn't that convenient," she said, pointing out the irony. "The one person who could interfere is most likely out of the picture. Guess that leaves us plenty of time to trip down Memory Lane and find Mr. Wonderful." Her sarcasm was biting. She used her pistol to gesture at Sarah. "Funny thing about death," she said, letting a faraway look float across her eyes. "There's no telling when and where death will occur." Sarah tried to retreat into her own bones, not wanting to hear Barrows' philosophy. "Isn't that the beauty of it all? The randomness, the spontaneity," Barrows said, as if recalling a journey that she had previously taken—or hoped to take. She suddenly snapped out of her wistfulness and stared at Sarah. "Keep trying," she demanded. Sarah could hear water dripping in the sink almost as if the faucets were crying.

Seeing Ann at her most vulnerable, Barrows moved closer, delighting in the power she held. "I wonder what it was like for David. Dear David. Did he see the gunman coming or was he taken by surprise? Do you think it was a quick kill or slow and painful suffering until he bled out on the hospital sheets?"

"Stop it! Please, stop," Ann begged, not wanting to think about the gory details, not comprehending how a former colleague could be so cruel.

While Barrows tormented Ann, Carter and Sarah exchanged glances. Carter was getting concerned. "How many people come this way?" he whispered, realizing they were on the far outskirts of town.

Sarah said under her breath, "Not many, but don't worry. Someone will find our cars and phones at the hospital, and I'm sure my sister will eventually call the police. They'll be looking for us soon."

"But that could take hours," Carter mouthed to her. "And we might not have hours."

Just then, there was a knock at the door. "Is everything all right?" a male voice called. The voice sounded familiar, but Sarah couldn't place it.

"We're fine, why?" Ann answered with a slight quiver in her reply. A gun pushed Ann forward to open the door. Jim, the construction crew foreman, was standing there.

"I know it's late, I'm sorry, but I was driving by and saw your roof light flashing like crazy. I just wanted to make sure we didn't leave wires exposed when we were up there."

Ann listened, afraid to respond.

"You know, there was a big blackout in town—transformer blew. Then there was a shooting at the hospital. Crazy night," Jim continued. "Crews are all over the place putting out fires from the power surge and investigating the crime scene."

Ann could have kissed Jim for showing up. Now if only she could signal him about their predicament. "You're welcome to check out the wiring if you want," she said, motioning to the stairwell. "I did change that bulb in the lantern like you suggested."

Barrows was getting uneasy with all this small talk but didn't want to draw attention to herself. She kept her gun in hand and slipped it casually into her suit jacket pocket. Ann introduced Jim as he went through the room. "You know Sarah. This is her husband, Carter, and my collaborator, Dr. Barrows." Jim nodded a polite hello and proceeded up the stairs.

Sarah immediately thought of Terrence and the Sons of Liberty talking about using lanterns in the Old North Church to signal a British invasion. Could this be Terrence's handiwork?

When Jim came down, he was shaking his head. "Darnedest thing. The wires seem fine. I think the problem is with the lantern itself. Unfortunately, I couldn't get it off the chain—the links are too thick. But I can have my guys swing by in the morning with cutters, and they'll bring it back to the shop. I can get you a temporary fixture in the meantime if you'd like."

"That would be great," Ann said, encouraged that someone would be coming back. Sarah kept looking at Jim. If in fact she did have psychic abilities, now would be the time to use them.

"Oh, Jim, before you go, I meant to thank you for letting me take those shots of the concealment shoe," Sarah said, channeling her thoughts to Jim in a nonverbal way. "Concealed weapon, not shoe. Real shots, not photos. Barrows has a gun."

Barrows had no idea what Sarah was talking about and didn't like being kept in the dark. "What's a concealment shoe?" she asked, only superficially interested in the topic, but wanting to understand the conversation. Ann explained, while Sarah continued her mental telepathy.

"My pleasure," Jim said and then paused for a moment, cupping his forehead. "Woah. Excuse me. Bad headache. Long night."

"I've got some pain-killer in the bathroom," Ann offered. She glanced at Barrows for permission to leave and the doctor gave her an imperceptible nod. Ann hurried to the bathroom cabinet and grabbed the marker she used to touch up her shoes. "Help," she wrote on the blister pack before handing it to Jim. If he saw the word, he didn't indicate. He just said, "Thanks. I've got water in the truck," and headed out the door. Ann purposely left it unlocked.

"What now?" Carter asked as the clock chimed midnight. He could hear Jim's oversized tires crunch on the gravel as the vehicle pulled away. The soft whoo-whoo of an owl emanated from the woods.

"We need Sarah to summon that ghost of hers, even if it takes all night," Barrows said to the group, motioning Sarah to get back behind the screen. "I want a step-by-step description of how you make contact," Barrows called toward Sarah's small sanctuary.

"And you," Barrows waved her gun at Carter. "You're the science teacher. Do something *scientific* to help us see this ghost."

"That's not my area of expertise," Carter said, "but I've heard that some manifestations show themselves as luminescence. Maybe if we could find a black light, we could see it better."

"Who the hell has a black light?" Barrows mocked. "Think of something else." Carter sat down and steepled his fingers as Barrows pounded on the screen that obscured Sarah.

"You're not trying hard enough, missy. If you don't show me how you do this, I'm going to have to hurt your husband." Barrows leered around the screen at a terrified Sarah. Sarah wondered how someone who had been so compassionate before could be so cruel now. She moved her hands over her eyes as if to deepen her concentration.

The room was mute except for the grandfather's clock that chimed solemnly on the hour: one, two, three gongs. The reverberation rang out until it dissipated into the thick air. Ann was losing hope that Jim had seen her note.

"I need caffeine," Barrows said, looking at Ann. "You have coffee, don't you?"

Ann stood up to accommodate. "I'll make some," she said, unlocking the back door on her way to the kitchen. Sarah could hear the pipes clang, irritable, as water pumped through the vintage plumbing. Soon the addictive fragrance of coffee was wafting into the sitting area.

"Pour me a cup," Barrows instructed, walking toward Ann, gun raised. Ann handed Barrows a steaming mug, resisting the urge to throw it at her. "Ah, that's good," Barrows said, letting the hot liquid settle in her chest. It was clear she wasn't sharing any.

"I need a break," Sarah said, emerging with a yawn. She arched her back to stretch out the kinks.

"Me, too," said Carter, as he nodded toward the bathroom. Damn, he could really use a cup of coffee.

"Five minutes," said Barrows, keeping her gun trained on him before rotating her body to cover Sarah. The clock chimed 4:00.

"We're not getting anywhere," Carter appealed to Barrows as he returned to the couch, hoping fatigue would lessen her resolve. "Maybe we can all get some rest and continue in the morning," he suggested.

"Unfortunately, I don't have that kind of time," Barrows insisted. "Stuart is expecting to see a demo before noon. That gives us 7 hours, max." She held the gun on Carter and ordered him to extract three plastic ties from her tote. "Bind their feet and then bind your own," she said, gun following his moves. "Only temporary," she remarked over her shoulder as she went down the hall to use the facilities. "I *am* civilized, you know."

The group wasn't so sure. There seemed to be something ominous lurking behind Barrows' eyes and a compulsion that was driving her brain. The smell of coffee continued to tantalize them.

When Barrows returned, she took a penknife from her pants pocket and slashed the ties as promised, then picked up her weapon and trained it on Ann. "Get coffee for everyone," she instructed. "As I said, I *am* civilized." A moment later Ann appeared from the kitchen with 3 large mugs on a tray. She set it on the table and Sarah pulled up a side chair. Three hands immediately grabbed for the hot liquid. Relishing the infusion of caffeine, Sarah drank slowly and gazed out the window. She noticed that the sun was starting to color the hills. Birds had begun their morning serenade, and there was a coolness in the air.

As time ticked down, Sarah rocked at the edge of her chair, chewing her nail. Carter and Ann had returned to the couch and alternated between sleep and wakefulness. It was about this time that Barrows changed her tactics. She no longer moved quickly or barked out orders, but rather, she moved in slow, deliberate motion. Maybe she was tired or perhaps this new approach was intentional, but the effect was even more chilling. She walked up behind Sarah and leaned into her ear, so close that Sarah could feel Barrows' breath. "You *do* understand how important this is, right?" Barrows said through gritted teeth. Sarah nodded affirmatively, pulling her lips inward to control her emotions. "Good," Barrows replied, clasping Sarah on the shoulder to exert pressure. Sarah found Barrows' stealth more frightening that her bluster.

At the stroke of 5:00, Sarah could see Barrows' fingers starting to cramp. She watched as the doctor shifted the gun from hand to hand, making fists and shaking them out. Sarah wondered if she could get away during this momentary distraction. But Barrows was quick to recover. "Show me how you do it," she repeated, using both hands to steady her gun as she aimed it at Sarah's forehead.

"Please, Sam, this is not like you," Carter tried to reason. He stood up and moved closer. "You're a professional, a well-respected expert." Ann pulled him back.

"You don't know who I am," Barrows snarled. "I'm a damn good actress, that's all."

Sarah retreated to her enclosure behind the screen. She could hear the newspaper carrier stop at the end of the drive and throw a paper toward the house. "Maybe I should try to summon Terrence after all," she started to think, "But I still couldn't explain how I do it." Barrows turned off the sconces and checked her cell.

"Stuart is getting anxious," she said. "We're going to have to do better." She stepped behind the screen and invited Sarah out in a voice so polite that it was unnerving. "Please, dear, stand next to me." Sarah obliged, trying to stop the wobbling in her legs. "You know, I'm not one to accept failure," Barrows stated, as she walked around Sarah, looking her up and down. "I simply need to know your secret. It's for the betterment of mankind." Sarah felt like a gazelle being stalked by a lion. Her feet were lead, weighted to the ground. Barrows came up behind her and reached around to Sarah's cheek, gently brushing her hair away from her face. "What beautiful hair you have," Barrows purred, caressing it, getting lost on a tangent that seemed to please her—then without warning, she grabbed a clump and yanked. "I mean it!"

Sarah whimpered and said that she would try harder. Carter clasped his hand over his mouth, eyes wide, then lunged forward. Ann looked horrified as she impulsively put out her arm to restrain him. The pendulum on the grandfather's clock continued its repetitive arc, chiming 6:00 and, then, 7:00.

The air was starting to warm as it often does on a blistering day. Ann could hear the trash collectors come up the road and continue past the house. She wondered if they thought it odd that she had not put out the recycling bin.

Sarah paced around the room, following the lines of the floorboards and walking the perimeter of the space. "I'm not sure what I can tell you," she said to Barrows, feeling a sense of futility. "I don't think I do anything special to make this happen." This was not the response Barrows wanted.

Just then, an upbeat voice called from the back entrance. "Crew's here!" Jim yelled. The sound of sliding van doors could be heard in the driveway. Sarah could see several workers pulling a ladder and tool box from the vehicle but noticed that Barrows hardly gave them a glance. Only then did Sarah realize that one of the men was the police officer, who had knocked on the door during that rainstorm when she first stayed at the house. This time the cop was undercover, dressed in faded jeans and a black construction company tee shirt, a Red Sox cap set low over his eyes. Sarah noticed that a boxy vehicle was parked behind the trees. Six men in full body armor jumped out, snaked toward the house, and split up SWAT-style to assume strategic positions. She purposely looked away.

"We've only got 3 hours to do this and do it right," Barrows pressed, clearing her throat and aiming at Sarah. When Sarah glanced up, she could see the officer standing behind Barrows at the back door, Glock in hand. He silenced Sarah with his eyes.

"You actually have a lot less time," he said, stepping forward. Barrows spun in the direction of the voice, momentarily distracted. In that split second, two SWAT officers armed with SIG Sauers barged in the front door and tackled her, prying the pistol from her fingers and forcing her to the floor. Face down she kicked wildly and protested loudly, spewing obscenities as her spiked heels sliced the air. One of the men straddled her, wrenching her arms behind her back. As cuffs were being locked into place, she fumbled for the knife in her pants pocket, but couldn't reach it.

"Don't even try," a second voice commanded. Carter could see an armed SWAT officer, wearing kneepads and an empty holster on his leg, emerge from the hallway as one of the arresting officers pocketed the knife and continued to frisk her.

"I'm a doctor," Barrows yelled. "These patients were violent. I had to subdue them. I'm licensed to carry." Sarah and Carter were speechless—stunned that Barrows could lie so glibly. Ann froze in place.

"We know who you are, and we're taking you in for kidnapping," the officer stated. "One of these gentlemen will read you your rights."

"But I have very important work to do," Barrows sputtered as she was taken away. Ann remained speechless as she sat on the couch watching the scene unfold.

"Are you Ann Randolph?" the lead officer asked, looking at her, holstering his weapon but keeping his hand on it. Ann nodded yes, her lip twitching ever so slightly.

"Ma'am, we have a warrant to search these premises. We have reason to believe that you're running an illegal medical practice here and we are bringing you in for questioning." One of the uniformed men slipped behind Ann. Sarah could hear handcuffs snap around Ann's thin wrists and imagined those ever-manicured nails being gathered into a red bouquet.

The officer looked at the duo sitting on the couch as Ann was patted down and ushered out the front door. "You two all right?" Sarah and Carter nodded yes, not quite finding words. Their hands were cold, color absent from their faces. "You weren't roughed up, were you?" Carter uttered a raspy 'no.'

"Well, you go home and get some rest. Then come by the station later today to file a report." They agreed, still not moving.

Around her, Sarah could feel an invisible weight lifting and a subtle exhale as the house released its villains. She could sense the timbers relax and the air clear.

"I knew something was hinky here," said Jim, grinning, as he sauntered into the room. "Especially when Ann told me she had changed a light bulb that I had just replaced. Then I got this weird picture in my head of a hidden gun. Don't know where that came from." The corners of Sarah's mouth turned upward. "But when I saw the word 'Help' on the pack of painkiller, I had no doubt about it," Jim continued.

Sarah and Carter stayed seated, trying to process what had occurred. A beam of sunlight caught the crystal decanter on the sideboard and bounced small rainbows around the room. To Sarah, they looked like smiles.

"Luckily, I ran into these guys coming back from that mess at the hospital," Jim explained. "That's when I flagged down my friend, Mike." The undercover cop nodded as if to introduce himself.

"I can't thank you enough," Sarah said, standing, looking between Jim and Mike. Carter got up to shake their hands.

"Unfortunately, our car is at the hospital," Sarah said, trying to figure out how to get back. "Along with our phones."

"Or what's left of them," Carter remarked, assuming they had either been broken or stolen.

"No problem," Jim said, "I'll give you a lift."

"That would be great," Sarah replied, glancing back at the wing chairs, now returned to their angelic state. She closed the windows, locked the back door, and secured the front one after the group stepped outside. As they walked toward the van, Sarah could hear the crackle of two-way radios in the distance. "May I use your cell to call my sister?"

"Sure thing," Jim said, handing it over.

"By the way, you don't have to take down that roof lantern to fix it. I think if you check it again, you'll see that it's just fine," she added. Jim looked puzzled.

Carter interjected, "Trust her on that one. She has a knack for these things."

Sarah eyed Carter with affection, made her call, and took a deep breath. She had one more thing to do.

8

HOME FREE

Sarah phoned her office as soon as they got home to say she had to deal with a legal matter and would not be in. Knowing the kids were at day camp and that her sister would transport them, Sarah and Carter fell asleep on top of their bedspread. They awoke to the sound of children clamoring up the stairs. Joyous hugs followed as Sarah and Carter told the kids a version of the truth, explaining that they would all be going to the police station soon.

At the station, Sarah and Carter alternated between watching the children, filling out paperwork and reclaiming their cell phones, which against all odds, had been returned, intact. Jared and Abby thought it was cool to hear APBs coming in and BOLOS going out. Their parents thought it was cool to simply be alive.

During the following week, Sarah and Carter kept to themselves, looking for things to discuss other than their harrowing experience. They were saddened to see David's name listed in the newspaper as a casualty from the hospital shooting. His obituary was lengthy and touted the patents he held for several scientific devices.

213

While investigators removed boxes of evidence from the house and closed the crime scene, Ann retained one of the best attorneys in the state. Due to David's death and the non-violent nature of the charge, she was released on her own recognizance to make funeral arrangements. Bail was paid by David's family on the condition that Ann would stay with them until she was arraigned. That made the news. The Barrows story did not, which led Sarah and Carter to believe Sam had more influence than they originally thought.

Escorted by her attorney and an Officer of the Court, Ann was delivered to David's family. In the following days, she called each of her patients personally to explain the office would be closed for an indeterminate time, encouraging them to seek counsel elsewhere. She then put similar messages on the office phone, website, and email account.

During this time, Ann sent a notarized letter to Sarah giving her permission to use the house. In it, she told Sarah where a spare key was stashed and encouraged her "to continue their work." Sarah read the letter several times, then set it aside, staring at it in silence before looking up at Carter.

"I know you have to go to the house," he finally said. She shook her head yes. "Be quick and, be careful," he cautioned.

"I don't know about quick, but I will be careful, and I will be back before the baby is born," she assured.

Gathering a change of clothes, an apple and a granola bar, Sarah headed out the next morning, trying to dispel the uneasiness that gnawed at her insides. When she entered the house this time, she noticed the items left in haste. She tidied up the kitchen and stacked the papers that were spread on David's desk. Moving the Oriental screen that had been her shield, she folded it accordion-style into itself and leaned it against the wall. She set aside mail that had arrived for Ann, planning to forward it later.

"You look deep in thought," Terrence said, slowly strolling toward her.

"It's you! I'm so glad," she replied, flinging herself into his arms, aware that she had just one petticoat under her dress to allay the heat.

This time Terrence was reserved and appeared skeptical. Holding her at bay, he asked, "So what did you tell them? Did they hurt you?"

"I told them nothing, showed them nothing, they didn't hurt me, and your signal in the roof saved our lives," Sarah said in one long breath.

Terrence looked visibly relieved. "That's good to hear. I would not want some greedy interloper corrupting what we have."

"Nor I," said Sarah, going to the window, looking over their lush piece of land.

"Some of the crops are in," Terrence said, as if continuing a casual conversation. "Want to go see them?" Sarah grabbed a bonnet, paring knife, and basket, happy to be back in her second home.

The meadow was alive with summer sights and sounds: crickets, bees, and an occasional dragonfly made their presence known. An acre of blue flax swayed in the breeze, turning the field into sky. Sarah walked slowly, keenly aware of her added weight as Terrence protectively took her hand to help her over the unevenly plowed rows.

Bending at the knees to extract a small fruit from the hay, Sarah knew that strawberry season had come and gone, leaving the intoxicating smell of fermentation on the ground. A stand of blackberries was beginning to ripen, showing off shiny red corpuscles among the fuzzy green knobs. Soon these would be plump and fragrant.

Bean vines curled up the pyramids of branches that Terrence had lashed together, their delicate white flowers hiding under a cool cover of leaves. Embryonic beans dangled as if by thread from the fading blossoms, indicating they would soon need picking. Corn towered over the other crops, tassels aimlessly swaying in their quiet act of pollination. Squash plants, bursting with orange blooms, spread beneath the corn stalks, smooth yellow globes starting to form. The plot half-planted with carrots was almost ready to harvest.

Sarah looked at the earth's bounty and at Terrence, grateful and satisfied with both gifts. "There's a lot of work to be done," she observed as she adjusted her bonnet. "We'd better get busy."

"I wanted to talk to you about that," Terrence interrupted as they turned toward the house. "I need to go back to Stockbridge. With the Pontiac uprising under control, General Gage is bringing his troops in from the frontier. We expect they'll overrun the western part of the state and wreak havoc."

"So that means you won't be here to help me?" Sarah asked, a look of exhaustion coalescing on her face.

"Well, only for a short time, but I've asked our neighbors if they would lend a hand and they're ready to come over when you need them.

Sarah was disappointed that Terrence would be gone, but she made the best of it. "I'll miss you and so will our little Covington," Sarah said, patting her belly, trying to smile as they walked back to the house.

"Think of it this way," he consoled. "With troops stationed here, they'll need food and clothing, so, while we might not like it, we can at least profit from it."

"That's true," Sarah said, sinking into a wing chair, already thinking what she might sell to the Brits. She removed her bonnet and pushed the damp hair off her forehead. Her cheeks were flushed; her throat, parched.

Terrence brought her a cup of water. As a tea-guzzling, rum-swigging native son, drinking plain water seemed odd, but he was happy to accommodate. "You look uncomfortable, love."

"Just warm," Sarah said, "and fat."

Inspired by a thought, Terrence jumped to his feet. "I have an idea I think you will like."

"What is it?" Sarah asked, trying to be receptive, but too tired to show much enthusiasm.

"You're coming with me to the river. I'll get the cart."

"Oh, I'm not sure I want to move. Besides, it's cooler in the house and I don't have anything light or big enough to wear."

"I wouldn't worry about that," Terrence said, blue eyes sparkling. "We'll go slowly and avoid the ruts," he assured. Sarah was too weary to argue.

Climbing into the cart, Sarah removed her head cover and let the wind blow through her hair. Terrence took his hat off and did the same. They felt better already. Relaxed conversation followed, along with a ditty Terrence had heard at the tavern. Sarah couldn't help but laugh at the bawdy limericks.

With inhibitions gone, the rest was easy. Finding a grove of willows, Terrence brought the horses to a stop, so they could drink in the shade. He and Sarah laid out a blanket for shoes, stockings, and outer garments. Now barefoot, they walked gingerly along the pebbly banks to where a beaver dam had trapped the water.

"I dare you," Terrence teased, pulling at Sarah's petticoat. "I dare you," Sarah teased in return, snapping the laces at the back of his britches. Then, without a word, they both raced to strip off their clothing, hurrying to step out of linen and ruffles, cotton and wool, freeing their arms from long sleeves, and leaving the last of their encumbrances in a damp heap among the reeds.

Cool currents of air offset the mid-day sun as they eased into the water, an audible "Aaahh" escaping from each. "Go under," Terrence said, "and I'll meet you there." Sarah had never kissed anyone under water. She sputtered to catch her breath as she broke through the surface.

What a glorious day it was! All the stress of work and war was washed away in the clear, cold water. Sarah felt weightless in body and mind. They splashed, swam, and floated, laying back to watch the clouds form animal shapes. They dove, eyes open, to find smooth stones at the bottom. They laughed and lingered on the shore to warm and loved each other on the blanket, returning once more to their deep baptismal for another dip.

Refreshed and restored, they rode back to the house, lightly clad, boldly breaking most cultural taboos. They didn't care. The sun dried their hair and tanned their skin. Their feet rested on the warm wooden planks of the cart and they both wiggled their toes as they walked on the moss along the path to their door. That night, Terrence packed for his journey and Sarah thought about the first harvest. This separation would be their longest to date.

When Terrence arrived in Stockbridge this time, the town was bustling. He was greeted at the coach stop by a dark-skinned boy with a wagon, who offered to take his bags to the Mission House. Agrippa, as the boy was called, lived with a free black family and was fascinated by military maneuvers. Terrence bought him a molasses candy and with that, a bond was struck.

A group of Stockbridge Indians was assembled on the corner, talking loudly in a mix of Muhhekaneew and English, discussing the pros and cons of General Gage's treaties with the Pontiacs. Terrence didn't know the native tongue, but he gathered that Mahaiwe was "the place downstream," and that meant returning troops would soon be marching into Great Barrington.

As Terrence later learned, the entire area was amidst a land grant dispute, which made these small towns particularly vulnerable. So close to Connecticut and New York, their borders were sketchy, their ownership unclear, and their allegiances, lax. The one thing Terrence was sure of this time, that if threatened, he would not hesitate to use force to fend off the British.

News of skirmishes along the western border was a popular topic of conversation at the general store where Sarah shopped. She noticed that anger seemed to accelerate with the summer heat. The store quickly became a forum for villagers who wanted to vent their feelings about the British and share their vows of resistance. She became a regular visitor.

The next Sunday, at Sarah's request, neighbors arrived to help with the crops. The processional was overwhelming. Sarah felt tears of gratitude come to her eyes as she watched the parade of people walking toward her house armed with rakes, hoes, and scythes. Strong men steered muscular horses across the fields, each team of two pulling a wagon to be filled with flax and grain. Children brought baskets to gather beans and berries, and women, with seed-filled pockets, carried sweating jugs of switchel to quench their collective thirst.

The afternoon passed quickly, and they worked until the last rays of sun cast the ground red. Promising to share the rewards of their labor, Sarah sent her helpers home, gazing at the newly weeded rows and turned top soil where late-season carrots were now sewn. Several women returned the next day to help cook down the berries and put up the jam. Beans were blanched and salted, other laid out to dry for soups and seeds. Corn could wait.

The next time Sarah went to the store to trade eggs, she saw men gathered at the blackstrap molasses cask, nibbling on dried codfish, drinking rum, and poring over a newspaper. Recognizing the publication as one of Edes' editions, she craned to see what they were reading. "Look at this," one man said, pointing to a paragraph on the page. "That's the way to put it!" Someone else chimed in: "Hah! Gage hates talk of democracy. Just wait 'til he reads this!"

Sarah edged nearer and saw her own words embedded in the column. How 'real' they looked in print. How empowered she felt contributing to the cause. Were it not for her father's insistence and his patient, stealthy instruction, she would never have learned to read and write, let alone express herself so eloquently.

Sarah quietly backed away, suppressing a grin. She clutched the handle of her egg basket, pledging to publish more of her ideas. That evening, she grabbed a fresh quill and paper—and deep into the night—argued why Colonists were justified in refusing to quarter troops.

Terrence settled in at the Mission House where an interim pastor and his family lived. He used his time to get to know the neighbors and assess the political climate. Agrippa tagged along, asking questions and offering to help. The seven-year old told wild tales of his father being an African prince before being taken to America. He explained how his father had died young, and how his mother, unable to care for a child alone, had sent him to live with Joab and Rose who were previously owned by missionary Jonathan Edwards.

Agrippa talked about worshipping at the Congregational Church and the many interesting people who lived in Stockbridge, but mostly he talked about war and how he would grow up to be a great soldier and lead men into battle, at which point, Terrence smiled and patted the child's head.

The impending British invasion was palpable. In this otherwise quiet village, doors were now locked at night and young children kept close to home. Men carried muskets in their carts and women learned how to shoot. Neighbors gathered frequently at the meetinghouse to plan retaliation.

One afternoon, when Terrence was at the farrier getting his horse shod, Agrippa came running over. "Mr. Terrence, Mr. Terrence," the young boy prattled. "I heard something important…."

Terrence affectionately looked down at the lad. "What is it, son?"

"Gage's troops are coming. Indian scouts spotted them at the border."

"Do you know where they're heading?"

"I don't know, but I think they're coming up the river. We could line the banks to show our strength."

"That's a good idea," Terrence agreed, surprised at the child's strategic thinking. Little did he know that Agrippa Hull would indeed grow up to serve in the Continental Army for 6 years and receive a medal of honor under General John Paterson and military engineer Tadeusz Kościuszko.

But, for now, Agrippa was just a boy impatiently awaiting instructions, bouncing on the balls of his feet as if he might take flight.

"Can you help me summon some men?" Terrence asked.

"Yes, sir!" Agrippa said, off and running.

"Tell them to meet at the Mission House at 7:00 tonight."

After Agrippa left, the blacksmith looked up from the hoof positioned between his thighs and said he would donate pitchforks to serve as weapons. Terrence thanked him and began to formulate a plan.

Terrence arrived at the Mission House well ahead of time and noticed a lone Indian standing beneath the grand Connecticut River Valley doorway. "I think you can go right in," Terrence said, then realizing the fellow might not speak English, he opened the door and motioned the Indian forward.

"Thank you," the Native said, nodding to greet Terrence.

"You speak English!" Terrence said, surprised.

"Yes, and I see you do, too," the Indian replied. Both men laughed.

"I'm Abraham Nimham, son of Daniel, Sachem to the Wappingers, Chief of the Nochpeem band. My father has been to England to appeal for the return of our land. He taught me your language," the sinewy young man said, extending his hand. He was shirtless, dressed only in a deerskin breechcloth and leggings, moccasins on his feet, hair tied back with a thin braided band, two feathers affixed behind his head. At his neck, he wore a single bear claw, drilled and suspended from a leather lace. He kept a flintlock at his side.

Terrence introduced himself and exchanged pleasantries. He estimated Abraham to be a few years younger but observed that the Native was mature in demeanor.

"I've been to the border and saw foot soldiers advancing," Abraham said. "I've had scouting parties out there for several weeks."

"Yes, I heard," Terrence acknowledged, "and we'll be going to greet them, so to speak."

"We'll be there, too. The Wappingers *and* the Stockbridge. We share your fight for land and freedom," Abraham continued.

Terrence liked this fellow and felt an immediate kinship. "Do you want to attend our meeting tonight?" Terrence asked, but Abraham deferred, saying they had their own way of doing things.

When the church bell rang at 7:00, the Mission House yard was milling with men, agitated and eager to take a stand. Terrence walked to the center of the group and assumed a position of command.

"Greetings, brethren. I'm Terrence Covington and I come from Boston with goods for the Mission House and guns for revolution. We have word through our Indian scouts that the British infantry has crossed the New York border. They are moving through Connecticut and should be here by daybreak. I call upon you to form a militia and show our strength by holding the river between Great Barrington and Stockbridge, as we expect they will follow that course north."

The men stopped talking and stood with folded arms, solemnly listening, some leaning on rifles, and the less hardy, leaning on each other.

"We are not looking for confrontation—not yet—but to drive the British inland, toward the coast, where we will have Minutemen ready to fight. On the other hand, if the British draw first, we must be prepared to respond with fury."

Terrence heard words of support ripple across the crowd.

"Who will join me tonight?" Several hands went up, many holding weapons. "Who will join me at dawn?" Other hands were raised. "Who will join me in defying British rule and oppression?" A loud cheer arose from the crowd.

"Our good friends, the Stockbridge Indians and now the Wappingers, will rally with us. They too have a great enemy in the British who are taking their lands and making false promises. Let me see eight men willing to lead a group and hold positions at mile intervals along the east bank of the river. That will give us a strong vantage point where we can see and be seen."

Eight men stepped forward just as the blacksmith pulled into view with a wagon full of freshly forged tools. "Those who do not have a gun can take a pitchfork from our farrier, which you may keep for your fields." Several men moved toward the cart.

"Now go to your homes, gather your goods, and meet back here at 9:00. My young helper will keep a map to mark your locations. The first team at the furthest point south is to sound off a volley of musket fire as soon as they see the British approach, and each team, in turn, is to do the same. I will be at the northernmost end as a last line of defense. Retain your positions until the British pass, then move swiftly upstream to fortify the next group. With luck, I will have many of you at my side by the time the Brits get to Stockbridge."

"Remember, our goal is not to fire first, but to respond in kind if they do," Terrence reiterated. No one had to spell out the danger of being lined up like target practice decoys.

The lawn was suddenly deserted as the volunteers dispersed. Terrence worried that the Indians had changed their minds, because not one could be seen. As night fell, the militia assembled as instructed. Each leader picked a team of men and chose their weapons before heading downstream.

Agrippa waited with Terrence, looking up, admiring the confident pale man. "Usi-a-di-en-uk is what they call the river," the boy said. "It means 'beyond the mountain place.'"

"Housatonic, eh?" Terrence replied, slightly altering the word. His thoughts were elsewhere. Agrippa smiled as if to say, "Close enough."

"Well, let's just hope they follow it," Terrence said. "The water is low this time of year, so they could cross anywhere, but I'm betting on Stockbridge.

Despite protests from Agrippa, Terrence sent the young boy home and began to organize his own supplies: bedroll, haversack, water, bayonet, long rifle, pistol, flint, black powder, bullets, food, and his favorite blade. With his horse fed and a lantern in hand, Terrence rode to the east side of town where the river turned south toward Connecticut. He found a secure spot behind two boulders and settled there.

The moon was obscured by clouds that night, so the men moved slowly. Once in position, they set up guard rotations. As Terrence sat alone waiting, his thoughts drifted to Sarah—sweet, beautiful Sarah—soon to be the mother of his child.

Other than the creaking of a saw-whet owl and the sound of the river gurgling over the rocks, the night was still, and Terrence fell asleep. A snuffling at his feet woke him as a raccoon waddled by. Terrence drew some water and stood to stretch his legs. The sky was turning gray and the moon was almost gone. He guessed it was near 5 a.m. Rummaging through his sack, he found some pemmican and gobbled that down along with a heel of hard bread. Didn't compare to Sarah's cooking.

Within minutes, there was a blast of musket fire downstream and then the subsequent volleys. He felt his adrenalin kick in as his hands locked around his long rifle, although he knew it could be hours before the troops arrived.

Finally, as the sun rose, he could detect the tinny sound of a snare drum followed by the hollow notes of a fife. "Hut, right," he heard a commander shout. "Left, right." Ground troops were leading the advance. Cavalry followed. Terrence could hear the rhythmic clopping of hoofs getting louder. An occasional whinny sliced through the air.

In the early morning light, he saw a precise line of British soldiers coming up the west riverbank. Unlike his mismatched band of men, this regiment was meticulously groomed, heads held high, backs straight, stiff white curls and a single pigtail bouncing as they rode. Rows of brass buttons on their scarlet coats were rubbed to a brilliant sheen, setting off their tight white gaiters in contrast. Shoes were shined to military standards. Their cross belts and waist belts were laden with bayonet and short sword scabbards. Some of the men carried powder horns. Others had cartridge boxes, fastened with studs, that glinted in the sun. It was easy to be intimidated by this encroaching force.

The commander instructed his men to hold their fire. Terrence waited, immobilized, but ready to pounce.

That same morning Sarah sat balanced on a three-legged stool, milking Madelaine outside the barn. She was oblivious to the red-tailed hawk circling above until it swooped down next to her, intent on having a field mouse for breakfast. "Duck!" was all Sarah could think as the talons nearly scraped her scalp.

"Duck!" was all Terrence could hear in his mind as he stepped in front of the boulders.

Just then, a bullet whizzed overhead. "Stay down," he heard a familiar voice say. Abraham was standing behind him and, with a quick hand signal, a rain of arrows arched across the narrow gorge, landing at the feet of the British.

By this time, the Colonial militia had caught up to Terrence and together, they formed a wall of defense. Across the river, several British henchmen surrounded the soldier, who had fired without authorization, and disarmed him.

"Move on out!" the Redcoat commander hollered in a call that was repeated down the line. The troops regrouped and began to pick up pace. Terrence turned to thank Abraham, but he was gone, leaving the woods as undisturbed as before. The only sign of Native presence was a cluster of albino Indian pipes poking through the humus, by legend, a testament to fallen braves.

Later that day, the Colonial militia reassembled in front of the Mission House. The men were high on victory and adrenalin. Rum flowed freely as stories of defiance were retold into the night. Scouts confirmed that the British had continued north to Lee and were marching into Central Massachusetts. As the last "Huzzah!" faded away, Terrence began his journey home with Sarah in his heart.

Sarah didn't stay long after Terrence returned, but long enough to welcome him properly, show him the harvest yield, and tell him she had a packet of writing to dispatch to Edes. There was one more thing she did before she left and that was to find Martha Quiggley, the midwife.

Sarah and Martha sat quietly on the Quiggley porch, sipping cool mint tea, discussing the birthing experience. There would still be time to work out details, but Sarah wanted to be prepared. She had special requests to convey to Martha, and Martha assured that she would honor them.

That night, Sarah had the same conversation with Terrence and made him promise to follow her wishes as well. As she worked her needle from the settee, Sarah transitioned somewhere between stitches, slipping away by candlelight and returning to the present day.

Once home, Carter brought Sarah up to speed. He told her that a fellow real estate agent had come by looking for her, but when he mentioned the name, it didn't ring a bell.

"The woman left a card…Nora somebody from Colonial Real Estate…" he said, handing a quick-print card to Sarah. "Said she met you at the house." The only person who fit that description was the obnoxious, over-dressed agent who didn't like vintage homes. That was the last person Sarah wanted to see.

"Was she dressed to hilt with a lot of makeup?" Sarah asked. Carter shook his head, no.

"She was sort of plain and low-key if you ask me," he answered, "but she was persistent."

Sarah was puzzled. "OK, I'll call her tomorrow and invite her to meet me at the office. Maybe I'm just not remembering."

The next day Sarah called the woman and suggested they talk over coffee. When the woman arrived, she was as Carter described—soft spoken and simply dressed—but there was something familiar about her.

As they strolled down the street to the local coffee shop, Sarah confessed. "I'm sorry, but I don't recall meeting you." The woman laughed as they went inside and found a booth. "That's probably because I look different now. I think when we met I had three pounds of makeup on and a suit that was two sizes too small," the woman laughed. "I was the real estate agent who stopped by the house."

"That was you?" Sarah asked in disbelief. "You didn't like the house very much as I recall and were quite blunt about it."

"I have to apologize for that," the woman said, "but I was undercover." Sarah leaned forward as the woman lowered her voice.

"I'm Nora Pearson, a federal agent with the FBI. We had gotten word that someone who is well known to us was involved with that property."

"You're not talking about the Randolphs, are you?" Sarah asked. "I know they skirted some professional licensing laws, but they're not hardened criminals. At least Ann isn't. David, the husband, has since passed away.

"Yes. We are aware. The person we're interested in is a doctor, a shrink, much more dangerous. We have reason to believe that she not only kidnapped you, your husband, and Ann Randolph, but that she has been collaborating with some disreputable people."

"I haven't seen anything about her on the news," Sarah noted.

"And you won't. She's in a safe place. We have a gag order on her and the story is embargoed. We need her to lead us to her associates who are conducting scientific experiments on unwilling participants. I use the term 'scientific' lightly."

Sarah was dumbfounded. Suddenly her present life had become as intriguing as her past. "So why did you come to the Covington estate?" Sarah asked.

"I wanted to check it out in case we needed to show up. And as it turns out, we did, with the help of your local police."

"I guess we owe you a thank you," Sarah said. "But, what do you want with me?"

"We'd like to learn more about what you do, what you *can* do, and how you might help us in the future. We're not going to interfere with the research you're working on for the Randolphs, but we'd like you to call us when your project is done."

Sarah was surprised and flattered. "I don't know what to say; I've never thought of this as a vocation," she explained as she accepted the woman's authentic business card. She stared at the blue and gold Department of Justice seal in the center and thought of Terrence: Fidelity, Bravery, Integrity. The red and white vertical bars reminded her of the old Rebellious Stripes flown by the Sons of Liberty. For a moment, Sarah was lost in history.

"You don't have to decide right now," the woman said, jolting Sarah back to reality, "but you obviously have some talents that we could use." They finished their coffee, shook hands, and went their separate ways.

As FBI agent, Nora Pearson, had indicated, Barrows was indeed in custody, but in a white-collar facility. Because of her professional stature, she was granted more amenities than most criminals. She had access to a computer, outdoor privileges, and an attorney who visited often. What might not have been so apparent is that Barrows, one smart lady, had Plan B ready to roll. Her associates were instructed, should she be detained, to secure the information needed to complete her report. They would be privy to some of it—for a price. That would allow Barrows to submit her findings and ideally, land the Lange Prize—to be waiting for her when she got out.

When Sarah arrived home that night, she tacked Nora's card to their corkboard and let Carter know what had happened. "Would you ever work for the FBI?" Carter asked Sarah over dinner.

Sarah shrugged as if to say, "Who knows?" The kids heard the familiar acronym and chimed in. "Wow! Like in the movies, Mom," Jared exclaimed. "That would be cool!" Abby added.

"Well, don't get ahead of yourselves, kids," Sarah cautioned. "Even if I did agree to work for them, that would be a long way off and you might not be able to tell anyone about it."

"Bummer," Jared said as Abby pouted.

"So, what's on the docket this weekend?" Carter asked, changing the subject. "I'm up for a family outing if you are." The kids looked at him expectantly and Sarah realized he had been planning a surprise.

"I don't know…. What do you want to do?" she asked, providing the perfect setup.

"Well, the county fair is in town and that's less than an hour away, so I thought we might get up early on Saturday and make a day of it."

The children cheered in unison. In recent weeks, they had seemed more adjusted. Abby had washed the Kool-Aid out of her hair, leaving in its stead, a swath of shiny strawberry blond, and Jared had started to go running with some new friends who were bent on fitness. "I hear they have some great carnival rides this year," Carter added to entice the kids further.

"And pigs and chickens and cows," Abby informed.

"I want to see the truck pull," Jared declared, "and go on the Ferris wheel."

"And I will personally sample the prize-winning pies," Sarah chimed in, enjoying her family's exuberance.

The next day couldn't have been more perfect as the Sutherlands headed north, vowing to be unplugged from devices and, instead, focus on family. Clear skies. Temperate breezes. Corn growing tall along the roadside. The fair was already well underway by the time they arrived. They picked up a map and planned their route.

"Step right up, Mister. Swing the hammer and win a bear," a barker called, pointing to a large pink panda.

"Maybe later," Carter deferred, as they moved toward the livestock ring.

"Look at the pigs!" Abby cried out. "They're so big!" Jared watched, but didn't say much. In fact, he kept glancing over his shoulder. Sarah steered them to the agricultural tent.

"Who wants to see an old squash?" Jared complained as he lagged a few steps behind.

"You go in. I'll take the kids for ice cream," Carter offered, "We'll meet you back here in a half hour."

The telltale streak of cherry pie above Sarah's lip was a dead giveaway, but she swore she only had one piece. Together they rode the Tilt-A-Whirl, watched the truck pull, ate hotdogs, and played a few rounds of Bingo. They stopped at the Quilting Club booth, so Sarah could purchase a coverlet for Abby's bed, and they bought Jared a hand-tooled belt at a kiosk. On their way out, they paused to hear a bluegrass singer and tried their hand at ring-toss.

The day of food, fun, and diversions was just what Sarah needed to put some distance between her past and present lives. She enjoyed spending time with her family and relished the wholesomeness of it all.

The smell of cotton candy and the sound of Merry-Go-Round music accompanied the family as they walked across the dusty parking lot. Ferris wheel lights were starting to twinkle as the group got into their car. The family was tired and rumpled but they shared a mellow, contented feeling. Carter opened the windows and let the warm summer air envelop them. In no time, the kids were asleep in the back seat.

"Great day," Sarah said, patting his knee.

"It *was* nice," Carter agreed, patting hers in return. He let his hand linger on her leg as they drove home. Sarah didn't remove it.

Carter carried a half-sleeping Abby into the house as Jared staggered along, rubbing his eyes. Holding a pile of sweatshirts and the new quilt, Sarah didn't see their land line blinking. She plopped her armload of items on the kitchen table and went to tend the kids.

With the kids in bed, Sarah and Carter retreated to the living room sofa and put on the TV, simultaneously pulling out their cell phones after a device-free day. That's when Sarah saw the unidentified call. She retrieved the voice mail, assuming it was a wrong number, but was very surprised when she heard the message. "This is Nora. I tried to reach you at the house. I think you're being followed. Call me as soon as you can."

"Oh, my God," Sarah said out loud, looking over at Carter.

"What is it?" he asked. She put the phone on speaker, hit Play, and held it closer to Carter's ear. "I thought this was over," he said through clenched teeth.

"Me, too. Let me call her and see what's going on." Sarah pressed Call Back but did not have time to stay on the line as a crashing sound outside drew their attention.

"Damn raccoons; I forgot to close the garage," Carter muttered as he tossed his phone onto the couch. Sarah followed, cell in hand, as he flicked on the breezeway light and opened the side door of the garage to reach the lift gate button. Stunned, they saw two men standing between their cars. Each was dressed in black and holding a gun. They both sported facial hair that looked suspiciously fake.

"Good evening ladies and gentlemen," the first man said in an accent that reminded Sarah of James Bond villains. "May I have a moment of your time?" He was frighteningly polite. Sarah and Carter stood stock-still.

"I will relieve you of that," the second man said, pointing his gun at Sarah's phone. "Give me." His voice was controlled and menacing. She slid the cell over the car hood to him, cringing at the scratch it made. The man pocketed it. "You, too," he ordered, pointing his weapon at Carter.

"I … uh… left mine inside," Carter stuttered. "In my jacket," he lied.

The first man kept his gun trained on the twosome from inside the garage as the second man hurried around to the breezeway. "Out here where I can see you," he ordered, weapon poised. He directed the duo away from the shadows and onto the walkway where a 40-watt bulb lit the area. His partner emerged from the garage, covering the frightened couple, as the second man frisked them.

"What do you want?" Sarah asked.

"You have something that belongs to us," the first man answered.

"I can't imagine what it is," Sarah said, thinking the men had the wrong house.

"Information," the second man replied.

"About what?" Carter asked.

"About Sam Barrows' project."

"Dr. Barrows?" Sarah exclaimed. "We have nothing to do with her. Besides, she's locked up as far as I know."

"We know that. We've been in touch. We have the same lawyer," the second man said, elbowing his buddy to share the inside joke.

"She promised us some answers, that's all," the first man clarified. Sarah observed his muscular build. There would be no tackling him.

"What kind of answers?" Sarah asked as blandly as she could manage.

"Scientific answers." He paused. "You see, our country has invested heavily in research—extrasensory research. We have everything we need to explain spiritual contact—except for one key thing. We know it *can* be done; we just don't know *how*. Sam was supposed to get that from you."

"Well, she can't tell you what she doesn't know," Carter defended, as the first man prodded him toward the house. "Sam already tried that."

"We can be extremely persuasive," the second man warned, running his gun down the back of Sarah's blouse. "Now, go." She unwillingly stumbled forward. "And we'd like to meet your children," he added, pressing his gun between Sarah's shoulder blades. She could feel his hot breath on her neck.

"Not our children!" Carter insisted, stopping and turning to face the men, arms extended to block their entrance.

The first man shoved him out of the way and pushed in the side door to the house. "Everyone inside. I mean it." Carter and Sarah reluctantly entered.

"You two better behave or you'll be sorry," the second man threatened in a restrained voice. "Now, onto the couch and don't say a word until I tell you."

Sarah and Carter moved silently to the sofa. Carter sat down quickly to cover his phone which was camouflaged on the dark leather. "Do I need to tie you two up," the first man asked, "or will you play nice?"

"We'll cooperate," Sarah said, folding her hands in her lap, biting the inside of her lip. Carter slipped his fingers under his thighs as if compliant, groping for his cell. He glanced down and activated a GPS alert.

The first man pulled a USB stick from his shirt pocket and held it in front of Sarah. "What's on that?" Sarah asked, warily eying the flash drive.

"Procedures. Lab setups. And a list of questions for you to answer. That will complete the stuff Barrows promised us."

"I'm not sure I can help you," Sarah stalled.

The second gunman slammed his fist on a side table. "You will do what you are asked!"

Sarah jumped back and stammered, "I'll try. I really will try. But no guarantees." She could feel her throat tighten as she attempted to control her panic.

"Don't be too helpful. There's no telling what these guys will do once they get what they need," Carter whispered. Sarah wondered why he was being so talkative but figured he wanted to buy time.

Just then, she heard a soft, high-pitched "Mommy? Who are these men?" Abby was standing on the stairs, looking down into the living room, hair tousled from sleep.

"They're…uh, neighbors," Sarah said quickly, jumping to her feet. "Go back up to bed."

"I don't know them," Jared said as he appeared behind Abby, his voice deep from sleep. Sarah noticed that he now towered over his sister and was starting to get muscles where none had previously existed.

"Oh, they just moved here," Sarah lied, willing her son to call 911.

"Why are you two up?" Carter asked. "I thought you were tired from the fair?"

"We slept in the car, remember," Abby reminded them. "Besides, I want to get my new quilt," she said, starting to pad down the stairs.

"I'd like to wash it first," Sarah objected, trying to dissuade her daughter. The men watched silently.

"But I want to use it tonight. I'll just put it over my regular blanket," Abby whined. She scrambled down to the main floor and bee-lined it to the colorful piece of patchwork folded on the kitchen table. Seeing the guns, Abby let out a shriek.

Jared quickly retraced his steps and ran to his parents' room where they had a landline. The first man held Abby in place while the second man charged upstairs after Jared. Abby flailed her arms wildly but could not get away. Sarah and Carter could hear a scuffle and then a lamp hitting the floor. A gun barrel was still pointed at them. It was clear that Jared had not made it to the phone. The second man emerged with Jared in tow, clutching the boy's tee shirt at the neck.

"What a nice family gathering," the first man taunted as he instructed the children to sit on the couch between their parents.

"What's going on?" Jared whispered.

"We're not sure," Carter answered, trying to exude a sense of calm.

"It has something to do with that old house, doesn't it?" Jared accused.

"Yes, apparently," Sarah answered, keeping her voice low. Abby just clung to Sarah's arm until it became white where her little fingers pressed the skin.

"Turn it on," the first man ordered, nodding at the laptop computer set up on the dining room table. Carter slid his phone down the side of the couch cushion and stood up. After booting up the machine, he saw a hand slide the memory stick into the USB slot in his laptop. A familiar 'bloop' followed as the machine recognized the device.

"Access it," the first gunman commanded. Soon the screen filled with a menu of documents, spreadsheets, and graphics not unlike those Carter used in class. Carter noticed a file labeled "Questions" and was instructed to open it.

"Get over there," the second man motioned to Sarah, leaving the children momentarily unguarded. Sarah stood up and made her way to the machine.

"Quick, now!" Jared mouthed to Abby as they sprang off the couch and ran out the back door. He took her hand and together, they bolted across the yard.

The first man, catching a glimpse of them, started toward the door, only to be called back by the second. "Let them be. They won't go far."

Just beyond the shrub line, the children came face-to-face with a SWAT team standing splay-legged behind an impenetrable row of shields. A woman with a headset approached them, index finger raised to her mouth in the universal "Shhh" sign. The kids were too scared to make a sound. Jared recognized her as the woman who had come to the house looking for his mother. "It's OK, Abby," he consoled in brotherly tone. Abby didn't let go of his hand.

The woman summoned a beefy colleague to take the children to safety at the end of the driveway where local police had assembled. Jared and Abby went willingly with him, glad to be hidden by his hulking form. The SWAT leader pointed two fingers to his own eyes and then to a contingent of his team, signaling them to deploy to the back of the house while he covered them.

Inside, Sarah studied the list of questions, heart thumping, knowing she couldn't possibly answer any of them. "Start typing," the first man demanded. Sarah was shaking.

The second man leaned over her shoulder, invading her space. She got a whiff of cigar smoke and stale cologne. "There," he said, pointing to the first question on the screen. "Answer it!"

Sarah stared at the words: "How do you make the spiritual connection?" She was paralyzed, not knowing how to respond.

Just then, the blast of a bullhorn cut through the night. "Come out with your hands up," a distorted, amplified voice boomed. The two intruders looked up but didn't respond. Instead, they closed in on Sarah and Carter.

"Ignore them," the first man said, eyes flitting between the screen and the noise outside. "Just give us the answers. Tell us how you talk to the dead."

The second man drew a bead on Carter's temple and with his other hand, held Sarah in place. "Now!"

"If you don't come out by the count of three, we will come in," the voice behind the bullhorn threatened. Sarah imagined the house riddled by bullets and frantically wondered where the children were.

"Sarah, do what they ask," Carter hissed, certain she'd understand that he meant for her to make up something.

"I always take a drink of water first," she typed. "The fluid sets up a path of communication. Has to do with the hydrogen and oxygen, I think," she lied.

"Three." She could hear their front and back doors splinter. Two SWAT officers in Kevlar vests crashed through each entrance, Barettas drawn. She saw other men in helmets stationed at the windows.

"Step away from these people," the SWAT leader yelled as his partners grabbed the confused intruders and slammed them against the wall. "Drop your weapons." Two guns fell to the floor and were kicked aside by the officers who cuffed and frisked the men. Sarah's phone went sailing across the parquet. She bent over to grab it.

"We're not leaving until we get what we came for," the first intruder shouted, his face smashed against Sarah's floral wallpaper.

"I'll kill them, I swear!" the second one threatened to no avail as he felt a thick forearm pin his shoulders in place.

"Déjà vu all over again," Carter said to himself, employing the Yogi-ism he used when he was nervous.

"Gentlemen, so very nice to meet you," a forceful female voice announced. Heads turned as an FBI agent stepped into the room.

"Nora!" Sarah exclaimed.

"Who are you?" the first man demanded.

"I'm your best hope for a reduced sentence," Nora said as she walked up behind and between the restrained men. She clasped their shoulders, one in each hand, showing who was boss.

"What do you mean?" the second man asked, pulling back.

"It seems that your friend, Dr. Barrows, is not going to share information with you after all but expects *you* to share some information with us." The men nervously glanced at each other. "You see, we've cut her a deal," Nora explained.

"What kind of deal?" the first man growled.

"We're letting her out on parole—in exchange for her turning you in."

"That bitch! She told us if we got her the answers, she'd cut us in on the prize," the second man seethed.

"Sorry, buddy. She's way too greedy for that. She's aiming to use all the money for herself, then sell her secrets to the highest bidder."

The men swore under their breath.

"Now I'm going to remove this little device and take it with me," Nora said, sarcastic, as she whipped the jump drive out of the computer. "My colleagues have a warrant to search your premises, seize your equipment, and access your files. You see, your psychological experiments concern us deeply."

"Everything's on the USB," the first man bluffed.

"I wasn't born yesterday," Nora huffed. "I know that's just the protocol. We want the results and the videos, too." The men squirmed. "So, we'll be going through your records, talking to participants, and rounding up proof of your abusive practices. Of course, if you'd like to provide these things willingly, we can discuss reducing the charges."

"In your dreams," the first man snarled while the second flashed his middle finger at Nora.

Nora signaled the SWAT team to take the men outside. Once she gave the 'all clear,' Sarah and Carter rushed to the doorway, breaking into a run upon seeing their children at the end of the drive. Standing in pajamas, faces pulsing blue in the police car strobe lights, the kids looked like little forlorn aliens. It was hard to tell whose hugs were tighter.

"Now is it over?" an exhausted Sarah asked Nora as they all walked back to the house.

"Yes, now it is over," Nora replied, putting her arm around Sarah's back.

"How did you know to come here?" Sarah asked, trying to understand what had transpired.

"Oh, we have our ways," Nora smiled. "Between your attempt at returning my phone call, Carter's GPS alert, and the tail we had on these suspects at the fair, we had a good roadmap."

"I knew someone was following us," Jared piped up. Carter affectionately ruffled his hair.

"I don't know how to thank you," Sarah said, shaking hands with the agent.

"There *is* one thing," Nora answered.

"Name it," said Sarah.

"That call you owe me," Nora reminded, raising her eyebrows in a pronounced order.

"You got it," Sarah promised.

One of the local police offers stepped aside to let the group pass. "We'll look out for your property until you get those doors fixed."

"Thank you," Carter said as he gathered the children close. Sarah slipped her hand into his. Together they watched the vehicles disappear into the darkness, leaving behind a peaceful summer's night and a profound appreciation for what they had almost lost.

9

LAST GASP

The following weekend, Carter took the kids to the lake to get their minds off recent events, leaving Sarah free to slip back in time. She figured this would be one of her final visits to the old house. Trying to ignore the sadness that was engulfing her, she was out the door with a travel mug of iced coffee, long before the day's heat took hold.

Walking around the Tory house, she noticed the meadow was high and the garden, desperately in need of weeding. Cicadas trilled overhead in their shrill, incessant song. Remnants of day lilies sprouted in orange clumps along the fence where brambles bent to the ground, laden with overly ripe blackberries.

Using the key that Ann had stashed beneath a planter, Sarah opened the door. As she stepped into the cool mudroom, she noticed that she was carrying stalks of Queen Anne's Lace. She set the airy, white flowers on a side table and wiped her hands on her new gingham apron. Gingham was a luxury these days, but she had splurged on the fabric when she bought sheeting for her birthing bed.

"Don't you look cheery," Terrence said, reaching the pewter pitcher for her. She gazed up at his lean form and wondered what he could possibly see in her round one.

"I'll be helping Joshua today," he said as he sat down, stretching his legs out, watching her arrange the flowers. Sarah's hair glowed in the sunlight and a light spray of freckles arched over her nose. She had a natural beauty that no cosmetics could match.

"They're trying to raise a new barn before the hay is in," he explained.

"I haven't seen Joshua and Danna in ages, not to mention the children. Do you mind if I go with you?"

"Not at all," Terrence smiled. "It would be nice having you there."

An hour later, they were making their way down the road, enjoying the lush countryside. Sarah kept her hand on her belly in hopes of minimizing the bounce of their cart. A recent rain had given the dry land new life and a welcome earthiness arose from the rich soil. Sarah had packed food to share, along with her sewing basket. Surely, Danna could offer some tips for making children's clothing.

Upon arriving, Sarah could see that the Whitings' son, Charles, had recovered well from his gunshot wound at the school. Lydia was taller and seemed remarkably self-sufficient now. Even baby Betsy had grown significantly bigger and was using her first words.

As the men walked out to the barn site, Danna and Sarah talked as women do. Danna asked Sarah about her advancing pregnancy and plans for delivery. Child mortality was so high that women constantly feared for the survival of their young and childbed fever was so prevalent that husbands feared for the lives of their wives.

Sarah explained that she had already talked to the midwife, Martha Quiggley, and hoped that Danna would assist, too. Danna willingly agreed. Then Sarah conveyed her special wishes, the same as she had explained to Martha and Terrence.

The day flew by as the men notched newly cut timber and set beams into place, pausing only to quench their thirst. Danna went out to tend the cows and came back carrying a bucket brimming with warm milk. She poured off the cream to churn into butter, as Sarah and Lydia helped. Betsy played at their feet, happily spinning a wooden top that Charles had carved. Danna had built her fire low to minimize the day's heat. In a deep cast-iron pot, she slow-baked a generous collection of chicken and vegetables. The sky was still light when she called everyone in for supper. They chose to eat outside where the air was cool.

When Sarah packed up her sewing, she noticed that Danna had slipped in some baby clothes from Betsy. "I won't need these, at least for a while I hope," Danna chuckled.

"If you do, I'll bring them back," Sarah promised, glad to receive the practical gifts.

Sarah and Terrence compared their days as they rode home in the twilight. Bats were already flying over the swamp, feasting on mosquitoes and making graceful arcs across the sky.

Sweaty and tired, Terrence headed for the stream to cool off. Dusk was setting in and the din of night insects, getting louder.

Sarah made her way up to the little shed in the woods. Just as she was about to leave, she heard a bang. Something threw its weight against the side of the structure, rocking it on its foundation. Bam! There it went again, rattling the floorboards and the walls. Sarah could hear grunting and snorting and the sound of large paws padding around the exterior.

She opened the door a crack and immediately pulled it closed. A massive bear, its coat the color of honey, seemed intent on joining her. Standing on the plank that formed the seat, she called through a slot at the top of the shed.

"Terrence! Bear!" was all she could say, her voice breaking, her heart going rapid-fire in her chest. "Terrence! Bear at the privy!" she yelled louder, not sure he could hear her.

She waited, frozen in place, afraid to move. Slowly she cracked the door open again and saw that the woods were getting dark. Surely, Terrence would be on his way back from the stream by now.

Bam! The bear hit the shed from behind, knocking her forward, forcing the door to swing wide open. Sarah quickly brought it back, spinning the flat piece of wood that secured it.

Just then, she heard a pronounced click and knew that Terrence was outside. Instinctively, she crouched on the floor in case a wayward bullet found her.

The woods were eerily quiet now and she guessed a staring match was taking place. The bear apparently flinched first, because a flintlock blasted above her head, followed by a dull thud.

Sarah threw the door open and ran to Terrence who by this time was hurrying toward her, weapon in hand. He told her to stand back as he put one more bullet into the bear.

"Guess we're having guests for dinner," he said, not missing a beat. The weather was hot and there were few ways to preserve meat other than to cook it immediately and dry the rest. So, then and there, he butchered and skinned the bear, throwing the entrails far from the house where coyotes could have a feast of their own.

Sarah watched with horror and fascination as Terrence slit the underside of the bear from heel to tail, from front paws to shoulders, then straight up the belly and across the width of the body. He removed the organs and teased the fur away from the snout and toes. He carefully scraped the underside of the skin, tossing the fat into a bucket. Sarah pulled the brine barrel out of the smokehouse and helped him cover the hide with a thick layer of salt. They carefully stretched the pelt across a tanning frame and stepped back to admire their work. The smell was overpowering, but Sarah knew the fur would keep their baby warm that winter.

Terrence sharpened his blade and began his first cuts. To make sure the meat stayed clean, he laid it out on a board, arranging shoulder and hind leg parts first, ribs and back straps next. Sarah went to work on the filets, cutting them into strips and steaks. She lit the fire pit and hung the strips out to smoke. The ribs were charred for prompt consumption.

Inside, she added kindling to the hearth and took down her heaviest skillet to fill with drippings and chunks of meat. Once browned and sizzling, she added the pieces to a kettle of onion, potatoes, carrots, and sage—and with a few ladles of well water—set it to stew overnight.

Terrence took the remaining joints to their closest neighbor—a Praying Indian and his wife—who were skilled at curing meat and carving bone. Terrence hoped he might get a pipe or whistle in return.

The next day, Sarah rode into town and invited the villagers who had helped with her harvest. A midweek gathering was unusual, but it was a welcome treat. Someone brought jugs of wine and someone else brought a fiddle. Soon, there was an impromptu party on the Covington lawn. Lanterns were hung from the fence as night fell and the mood transformed from mundane to magic. Even young men dared to ask young ladies to dance, stealing quick kisses in the encroaching darkness.

No one knew that a rogue British regiment, detached from Gage's troops, was watching from the woods behind the house.

"I'd sure like me some of that wine," one of the soldiers whispered, running his tongue over his dry lips.

"I haven't eaten in two days," his buddy salivated. "Mighty hungry."

"Well, maybe we should just get us some of that good stuff," the first man decided as he fired above the crowd.

The music immediately came to a stop and women ran to collect their children. Within seconds, the men had formed a circle, back to back, facing outward, aiming their weapons at the unknown threat.

"Who goes there?" Terrence yelled, his voice rising above the chorus of crickets.

There was no response.

"I said, 'Who goes there?'"

"Aye, sir, it just be us. We mean you no harm, but our men need food and a little wine wouldn't hurt either," the first soldier ventured.

"Show yourselves," Terrence commanded.

A cluster of men in scarlet coats emerged. "There's just a dozen of us, good man. We've been marching for days, trying to catch up with our battalion. Surely, you could spare a few ladles of that stew. It smells mighty fine," the second man said.

"Do I have a choice?" Terrence called back, not eager to extend his hospitality.

"Not really, being the Quartering Act and all," the first man answered, "But we figured we'd ask."

Terrence knew that by this time the women were safely ensconced inside and most likely armed with weapons from the cellar. He also knew that despite their impressive uniforms, the British troops were generally treated poorly, underfed, and ill paid. He motioned the Brits closer, watching them closely, working his jaw as he tried to contain his displeasure.

"Have at it, then," he obliged, holding his neighbors at bay.

A dozen gaunt men rushed from the woods, trampling the overgrowth to get to the food. No one talked. There in the glow of the lanterns, 12 ravenous Redcoats sat eating bear stew and gulping down wine.

"Ahhh, that's more like it," the first man sighed, patting his now full stomach.

"You said it," the second one added, belching and making it known they'd be staying the night.

"As you like," was all Terrence said, pointing to the barn. "Do I have your word you will not harm us?" he asked.

"Why would we harm ye?" one the Redcoats replied. "We're here to protect ye. You Colonists are our bread and butter. You produce, we sell."

"Well, it won't always be that way," Terrence muttered under his breath, but knowing this was neither the time nor the place for protest, he bid his neighbors goodnight and went inside. By dawn, the Brits were gone.

"At least they didn't take the hide," Sarah said, trying to make the best of the situation. Terrence glowered, not at Sarah, but at the increasing British presence.

That morning, Terrence went out to the field to start picking their corn and Sarah went back to present time. She let Carter know she was home safely and that she would be joining them at the lake.

Going to the lake was always a wonderful escape. When she was there, she could physically feel the stress leave her body. Driving north, she was soon surrounded by tall pines. Puffy clouds skirted across the birches that rustled a welcome. The cottage was as she remembered it: a combination of simplicity and indulgence.

There was a wrap-around porch equipped with rush-seat rockers. Firewood was laid in should the nights get cold and a collection of books and puzzles lined the shelves. In sharp contrast to the rustic décor, catered food was served in a large dining hall. Daily cabin cleaning services were part of the deal. Many described this place as champagne in a tin cup. Aside from the sound of water lapping at the dock and the occasional call of a loon, there was little to disturb her thoughts.

Carter had become Dad and Husband Extraordinaire—taking the kids fishing and out in the boat, walking with her along the shoreline under a moonlit sky, looking at constellations and for glimpses of the Northern Lights. Time away from Terrence had rekindled a sense of real-world romance she had almost forgotten. It had been easy to compartmentalize Carter and the kids as her boring modern life, while putting the Tory house and Terrence on a pedestal of passion and adventure. For the moment, she focused on the present and liked it.

On her third day at the lake, Sarah was standing on the dock when Carter returned from the raft with a weathered shard of pottery he had found in the silt. It appeared to be the lip of a cream-colored bowl decorated with a pink transfer pattern. As soon as she picked it up, Sarah felt a jolt shoot up her arm.

She dropped the ceramic piece into Carter's hand as if it were on fire.

"Are you OK?" he asked.

Sarah shook her head yes but was confused. "I don't know what that was," she said to him. "I've never had a reaction like that."

Carter looked more closely at the piece of pottery and detected a partial imprint: ENG. "Must have been made in England," he said, pointing to the incising.

Sarah shrugged. "Beats me," she said, as they walked back to the cabin.

Just as the dining bell rang, the kids appeared at the door, ready to eat, gleefully wet, bathing suits dripping. "Dry off first and put on some clothes," Carter instructed. "Dining hall rules."

After the children were dressed, Sarah went ahead with them while Carter showered. He changed into fresh clothes and combed his hair, distracted only by his cell phone buzzing in the bureau drawer. Despite pledging to stay unplugged, he reached for it and noticed an email coming in from a colleague. Reading the message, Carter learned that a paper they had co-written was just selected for publication in a prestigious academic journal. Quite a coup for a couple of high school teachers.

Clean and refreshed, Carter joined the rest of the family in the dining hall, humming as he trolled the salad bar, looking for his favorite crudités. "Why are you so happy?" Jared asked.

"Why shouldn't I be?" Carter answered. "I'm with the best family in the world, and now I'm an author."

The rest of their vacation was upbeat and active. It wasn't until they were packing to leave that Sarah found the pottery shard among Carter's socks. Still curious, she picked it up again, and this time, a pain in her stomach caused her to double over. She quickly tossed the shard back into the drawer and stood up slowly to catch her breath. "Carter's just going to have to carry that himself," she thought, wondering why this small object had such an impact on her.

By the time they returned home, July had become August, and back-to-school supplies were starting to appear in the stores. All this was happening too fast for Sarah's liking. She tried to prolong the season with picnics and day trips but knew what she had to do.

This time she gathered up her personal belongings and a few small bottles that fit into the palm of her hand. She kissed Carter and the children good-bye, told them not to worry, then headed for the old house. When she opened the door, she saw Terrence sitting there with some men from the Green Dragon Tavern. They didn't recognize her.

"Hello, love," Terrence said, casually looking up from the papers spread on the table. Sarah could see the map he had shown her many months before. The men politely nodded, then ignored her.

Sarah realized that not all men were as egalitarian as Terrence, so she stayed out of their way, except to bring them hard cider from the cellar. This libation begot an animated dispute about the quaffs of the day—many of which had names she had never heard: mead vs metheglin, flip vs syllabub, Stone Fence vs Rattle Skull. There was loud condemnation for wimpy drinks like beverige and perry—and for "Whistle-belly Vengeance," the rot-gut out of Salem—but high praise for Bogus, which combined cold rum and unsweetened beer.

The thought of these drinks turned Sarah's stomach, which by this time, hardly fit behind the table; still she lingered to hear more.

Political tensions were rising in New York City. There were now close to 1,500 British troops stationed there and the Colonists were being pressured to heed the Quartering Act. The act went well beyond what General Gage had originally intended, requiring not only housing, but also the provision of food and supplies to British soldiers. The New York Provincial Assembly was refusing to comply, partly because they didn't like the idea of a standing army in the region and partly because of the substantial cost. Without billeting, British troops were being forced to remain on their ships, which did not sit well with the men or their commanders.

The Liberty Boys—New York counterparts of the Sons of Liberty—were protesting aggressively and were garnering significant public support. They had made great inroads in getting permission to form a militia, defeating a provision called the Gunning Law. They had also successfully lobbied for funds to restore Fort Charles at the tip of Manhattan, a location that would prove strategic for defense.

A decision was made that the Sons from Boston would join the Liberty Boys in New York at their next rally.

Sarah was uneasy about Terrence leaving and she worried how she would fare so late in her pregnancy. In the days leading up to his departure, Terrence made sure Sarah was stocked with food and ammunition. He alerted their neighbors to his pending absence, asking them to look in on her and help with the animals. He assured Sarah that he would dispatch news along the way.

The night before he left was hot and humid. They went to bed early, relaxing in each other's company and talking about their future. Terrence knew that Sarah could be in imminent danger with the complications of birth and Sarah knew that Terrence was taking a considerable risk, but neither broached the subject as they lay side by side. Instead, they lived for the moment and loved each other leisurely, knowing this would be their longest time apart.

The following morning, Terrence waited impatiently at the side of the road, next to the trunk of supplies he was taking. When he finally boarded the coach to Connecticut, Sarah had to fight back tears. She blamed her emotional state on her condition and tried her best to put on a brave face.

Returning to the house, she had an unexpected surge of energy. She readied the baby's cradle, laid out the tiniest clothes, and prepared her birthing bed in a spare room. She made her way through the orchard to gather their first ripe apples and she picked a couple ears of corn for dinner. The new carrots that had been planted by her neighbors now bore feathery tops and a second crop of beans was coming in.

As Sarah enjoyed the peacefulness of her surroundings, Terrence was assaulted by his. He saw vast tobacco farms along the Connecticut River where laborers toiled in the fields, slick vendors selling elixirs on the outskirts of towns, wet streets filled with trash and horse droppings in the larger cities. Armed guards dressed in red patrolled the roadways. His journey included a mix of coach travel, fall boats, and ferries, eventually leading to the pine flats that surrounded New York City and Long Island.

When Terrence arrived, he was greeted by a contingent of Liberty Boys and escorted to Pearl Street, where Samuel Fraunces was running the Queen's Head Tavern. Terrence couldn't help but think that the sign of Queen Charlotte, wife of King George III, was far less imposing than the menacing Green Dragon that crested the tavern in Boston. Still, the environment felt familiar. The massive structure had been built in 1719 of bricks imported from Holland—a private residence for the son-in-law of a powerful Dutch magistrate. The building was three stories tall, had 14 fireplaces, a large kitchen, and dry cellar. Nine years prior, the two lower floors had been converted into a warehouse; four years after that, the homestead became a tavern; and just one year ago, this building became the site of a public apology by a British sea captain, who had tried bringing tea into the harbor.

Terrence appreciated the fine food that greeted him before their meeting began: ham, greens, squash, roasted potatoes, and tankards of cider. After a hearty meal and a round of introductions, the men huddled to discuss the topics of the day. Local tenants had been scuffling with landlords over renting rights. Trials were being conducted without a jury of peers. And of course, there was persistent outrage at forced quartering. But the Liberty Boys set those issues aside. More pressing was the fact that the Liberty Pole, which they had erected after the Stamp Act repeal, had been cut down by the British, leaving a void in their spirit and a scar on the landscape.

"This kind of behavior will not be tolerated," John Lamb stated in an opening remark. "It's outright aggression." He went on to propose a show of force. Even if Isaac Sears couldn't draw the attendance they needed, Lamb knew that Israel Putnam could supply armed men from Connecticut to enhance their ranks.

After the meeting, Terrence walked in silence to the intersection of Broadway, Warren, and Chambers Streets, to see what remained of the Liberty Pole. His heart sank when he saw the gilt top piece, bearing the word "Liberty," lying in the street. He went to work helping the Boys remove the debris and to clear the area. Later that week, he distributed flyers promoting the public assembly.

Meanwhile, Sarah tended to their crops and animals the best she could. Danna, Martha Quiggley, and Charity Elk, wife of the

Praying Indian, checked on her regularly. The baby still wasn't due for several weeks, but Sarah was starting to feel different. She was carrying lower now and needed to rest more often.

One night, later that week, she awoke with a cramp in her leg. Trying to walk off the pain, she couldn't get back to sleep so, instead, she made some tea and from the comforts of her rocking chair, watched the sun rise. Shortly after that, she felt a dull ache in her abdomen. The baby was kicking less, but Sarah could still feel movement, so she wasn't alarmed. By the time Danna arrived later that morning, the dull ache had changed into a pronounced pattern that seemed to recur every hour.

"I think you're going into labor," Danna said. "I'll get Charity to stay with you while I go back to tell Joshua to watch the children—and I'll alert Martha along the way."

"But this is too soon," Sarah protested. "This isn't supposed to happen until Terrence returns."

"Go tell that to the baby," Danna smiled. "Don't worry, everything will be fine."

"And you remember what I requested?" Sarah asked with urgency.

"Yes, I have all your instructions up here," Danna said, pointing to her head. "Just set out the things you want."

A half hour later, Charity arrived with a small bag of brewing bark to help the labor progress. Sarah alternated between sitting and pacing, sipping the bitter drink and clutching her stomach. "Whew!" she'd exhale, and then proceed to breathe deeply, calming herself until the next wave descended.

Sarah could hear the rattle of Martha's cart long before it pulled up to the house. From the window, she could see a birthing chair, blankets, and a bundle of things piled into a bowl.

"How ye doing, lady?" a cheerful Martha asked, arms full, as she opened the door. Sarah managed to smile before wincing at another contraction. "Looks like things are moving along nicely," Martha observed from across the room, putting her supplies on the table.

That's when Sarah saw it! A large, cream-colored bowl decorated with a pink transfer pattern design.

"Where did you get that bowl?" Sarah asked, experiencing a visual jolt not unlike the physical one she had received from the pottery shard at the lake.

"Ain't it lovely?" Martha answered. "From me mum in London," she continued.

Despite her alarm, Sarah tried to resume a pleasant conversation. "Oh, it *is* lovely. What do you use it for?"

"Oh, this and that?" Martha said. "Food. Foraging. Pig slop. And I've even got a pair of those new forceps in case we need 'em." She took the curved grippers out of the bowl for Sarah to see. Sarah noticed a dark ring around the bottom and something scummy on the sides.

"Remember my special wishes?" Sarah asked. Martha nodded. "Well, we need to start now," Sarah said, a solemn tone creeping into to her voice.

"Whatever you want, ma'am," Martha agreed. "I've been known to use a few rituals of my own," she winked. By this time, Charity had a kettle of water boiling on the hearth.

Looking at Martha, Sarah said, "I'd like you to put all your instruments into that boiling water and not touch them until you need them. Use my new spoon to take out the forceps first and then use the forceps—once they cool—to grab the other things." Martha nodded. "Lay everything on a clean towel." Martha looked around the room and noticed a stack of folded linen.

"Now please wash out the bowl. Scrub it well and rinse thoroughly. Use some of the boiling water and a drop of the green liquid." Sarah pointed to a small bottle on the bureau.

"What is it?" Martha asked, eying the viscous fluid.

"It's like bar soap," Sarah explained, "but better."

"Pretty color. Where did ye get it?" Martha asked, moving closer to the unusual object. She was as interested in the plastic container as the contents.

"From my mother," Sarah lied. "It's been passed down in our family."

"Well, I'll be," Martha responded.

"Most importantly," Sarah continued. "I want you, Charity, Danna, and anyone who comes near me—the barber, Terrence, anyone—to wash their hands with well water and green soap and then, to rub their hands with the stuff in the other bottle. That will let their hands dry in the air without a towel."

Martha glanced at the clear bottle with a 'P' on it. "Doesn't look like there's anything in it," Martha remarked, tilting the bottle of anti-microbial gel.

"Oh, something's in there all right," Sarah confirmed. "You don't need to see it; you just need to believe that it will work."

"What does it do?" Martha asked, figuring she knew everything about birthing and couldn't imagine the purpose of this elixir.

"It will help keep me from getting childbed fever," Sarah said, "and it will protect the baby."

"Like a magic spell?" Martha asked.

"Something like that," Sarah replied. Martha was listening closely.

"There's one more thing, and it's very important. I don't want to give birth in the chair that others have used, but in a special bed I've prepared. It's lined with a woven mats and moss and it's covered with clean sheets. Once the baby is born and the afterbirth delivered, everything is to be burned."

"Burned? Are you sure? That's mighty wasteful," Martha protested.

"It's all right," Sarah assured. "I have plenty of sheeting," she said, looking over toward a pile of rolled cotton. "I've cut some for the baby and my personal use. I also have a special cloth to clean me up." With that, Sarah removed a flat pouch of wipes she had taped to her thigh, just to make sure they would travel with her.

Martha looked at the small squares in crunchy packing. "What makes 'em so special?" she asked as Sarah braced for another contraction.

"They have powerful water in them," Sarah said, realizing she couldn't begin to explain the properties of medicinal alcohol and germ theory.

"Like holy water?" Martha asked, tossing the packet from hand to hand.

"You might say that," Sarah smiled, imagining how odd this experience must be for Martha.

"And the very last thing…" Sarah concluded.

"Yes…" Martha sighed, starting to lose patience.

"I will rest quietly for the first few hours after giving birth, but none of this 'lying in' for a month," Sarah insisted. "I want to be up and walking as soon as I can, so I expect you to help me stand and get moving."

Martha looked horrified. "Why would you want to do that?"

"Because I don't want Milk Leg," Sarah answered, referring to the clots that formed from being constrained after giving birth. "Walking is good for you."

"I don't know about that," Martha objected. "Where did ye hear that?"

Sarah continued her ruse. "It's the latest thing in Europe. Terrence's Auntie told us." Martha resisted.

"I know how strange it may seem, but look at our Indian friends," Sarah continued, trying to find a relatable example. She nodded to Charity. "These women have babies outside, standing up, and go back to work right after." Charity shook her head in agreement.

"Yes, it's true," she said. "We return to our grown children quickly and carry our newborns with us."

Martha mumbled something about that not seeming right for white women.

"That is good for any woman," Charity clarified.

"I'm going to take a bath now," Sarah said, "and put on a clean dressing gown. No clothes from the field should be put back on me." She made her way slowly to a tub where warm water had been poured.

Martha just nodded. "And both you and Danna are to roll up your sleeves, wash your forearms and hands, and wear a new apron instead of your own," Sarah said, looking over at three pegs. "I've made them as a special thank you and you may keep them."

Martha was pleasantly surprised. "They're mighty pretty. I'll take the blue one if ye don't mind," she said, reaching for the crisp fabric.

"And if the barber is called to assist, he must put on a clean shirt, too. I've left a new one I made for Terrence that he can use," Sarah explained, trying to think of all contingencies. "He must also wash his wrists and arms and rub on the clear fluid before touching me."

Martha tied on her apron and Charity left to get Danna.

As Sarah groaned through the early pains of labor, Terrence struggled to help roll a new Liberty Pole to the site where it would stand. Word spread quickly about the upcoming assembly and, soon, people began pouring into the city. First, one thousand, then two thousand, then upwards of three thousand—nearly half the population of New York City at the time—all gathered as the Liberty Boys had planned.

The British were getting nervous.

The streets were soon teeming with onlookers and agitators, politicians and purveyors. There were lawyers spouting legalities and dockworkers shouting vulgarities. There was singing among the religious and roughhousing among the boys. Girls, women, and children sat on the stoops, not daring to leave their posts unless someone was speaking.

Upon seeing the growing throng, British soldiers began to organize around the perimeters. By this time, the protesters were holding placards, chanting slogans, and filling open spaces. As the Colonists advanced, the British began marching toward them. "Back off or be run through," one of the soldiers threatened, raising his bayonet for impaling, but the Colonists kept coming. Hoping to disperse the sea of people, one of the Redcoats fired into the crowd, aiming randomly at the ground. Terrence heard a woman scream and saw a man crumple as several others rushed to his aid. The man looked a lot like Isaac Sears, but Terrence couldn't be sure. The crowd kept obscuring his view. The Liberty Boys regrouped, took aim, and stood poised, ready to engage.

The British commander lifted his arm to stop his foot soldiers from advancing and then motioned the cavalry to the front. Terrence could see a line of rigid, uniformed henchmen sitting atop carefully groomed horses, closing in on the crowd. The horses reared and whinnied as a group of young boys with slingshots pelted the animals. "Cease and desist," the commander demanded as the Redcoats pressed forward. "Move back!" an underling ordered. The Liberty Boys didn't budge. In fact, they stopped in their tracks and compressed their mass, forming an impenetrable wall. "If you don't disband, we will torch your homes and destroy your property," the commander threatened.

Only at that point, fearing for the lives of their families, did the Colonists stand down. Slowly, they lowered their guns and allowed the soldiers to clear the field. As much as the protestors wanted to retaliate, they knew they weren't ready—but at least they had raised their voices and another Liberty Pole.

A young boy running through the crowd did not see the musket at his feet nor did he know that his accidental kick discharged a bullet. As unlikely as it seems, the bullet found a clear path through the swarming populace until it met with Terrence's right ribcage. Grabbing his side, Terrence slumped forward, blood seeping through his tailored vest. Within minutes, a small cluster of locals was hovering over him, helping him up as they tried to assess his wound.

"I'm all right," Terrence said, attempting to stand. "I think it went through me," he gasped before passing out.

Terrence awoke in a place he didn't know, tended by a wife who wasn't his. "Where am I?" he asked, removing a cloth from his forehead.

"You're safe," the woman said. "But you need to stay still. We've just stopped the bleeding." Not to be dissuaded, Terrence tried to sit up, but crumpled back onto the bed.

"You've lost a lot of blood," the woman cautioned, "and I need to change that dressing. The doctor will be here soon."

Terrence knew he was in New York but remembered that he needed to go home. He was also thirsty, extremely thirsty. He reached for a pitcher of water and poured himself a cup, finally understanding what Sarah liked about the pure, cold liquid. Impatiently, he called out, "I have to get out of here! Where are my clothes?" The woman returned to say that he needed to wait because she was washing them.

"The doctor...when will the doctor be here?" Terrence persisted.

"As soon as he's done looking after the fellow who was wounded more seriously than you," she said, putting Terrence in his place.

"I'm sorry," Terrence said in a softer voice. "But I must get home as soon as possible. My wife is due to have a baby and I need to be there."

The woman knowingly patted his arm. Too weak to resist, he fell back on his pillow.

Simultaneously, Sarah plumped her pillow on the birthing bed and pressed her hand against her right rib cage. "That was intense," she said to Martha, who thought it strange that Sarah was experiencing pain in areas other than her abdomen.

"Is that better, now?" Martha asked, bringing her a second pillow.

"Much," said Sarah, trying to rest between contractions.

Danna arrived, washed her hands and arms as instructed, and donned one of the new aprons. She added water to the kettle for boiling, and Charity went to the well to replace the supply. Danna, too, was intrigued by the small bottles on the bureau. "Gems," she thought as they glistened in the sun, their translucent content taking on a jewel-like quality. She cut a length of twine for Martha to use to tie the umbilical cord.

"That too," Sarah motioned, breathless. "Must be boiled and wiped with one of the special squares." Danna saw the strange, crunchy packet sitting near the bottles.

Beads of sweat were starting to form on Sarah's brow, and the women took turns wiping them off, applying cool compresses and offering sips of water. "I'm so warm," Sarah said, flushed with the strain of labor and the heat of a late August day.

"I'm burning up," Terrence said aloud as he awoke in a pool of perspiration. "Where is everyone?" he called out, hoping someone would hear.

"What is it, Mr. Covington?" the now familiar woman answered, rushing to his side.

"What time is it?" he asked, pushing his matted hair back from his face.

"Nearly three in the afternoon," the woman said, offering him a cool cloth. "Looks like your fever has broken," she smiled.

"Good, then I can go," Terrence stated, grimacing, this time sitting up more slowly.

"Not until the doctor says so," the woman cautioned.

"I don't need a doctor," Terrence argued, pressing his side, but after peeking under his dressing at the hole in his flesh, he allowed, "Well, maybe I do."

"Are you hungry?" the woman asked. "I've made some fresh bread and broth." Terrence didn't realize how hungry he was until he started sipping the clear soup and devouring the bread that was baked with nuts and berries.

"Most appreciative," he mumbled, wiping his chin. The woman nodded, pleased that he had enjoyed her fare.

"I'll bring you something heartier after the doctor sees you," she explained, "and by that time, your clothes should be dry. I've put them on the line."

Feeling stronger and more alert, Terrence couldn't help but wonder how Sarah was doing. "Could someone get word to my wife to say I am delayed? Surely there's a coach going out today," he asked. The woman tending him said she'd see what could be done.

Sarah was in the full throes of labor as Terrence waited for the doctor to arrive. Danna, Charity, and Martha were getting ready for Sarah to push. "The baby is crowning," Martha said. "You're doing very well, very well," she encouraged.

"It won't be long now," Charity added in the clipped words that were her second language. She used her hand to waft a plume of laurel smoke from a small clay pot toward Sarah's widespread legs. "This will relax your muscles," she explained.

"Why isn't Terrence here?" Sarah agonized, close to tears, despite knowing that even if he were, he would not be allowed in the room.

"He isn't here, because you're ahead of schedule," Danna said is a calm voice. "But he'll be here soon enough."

The pain was excruciating now, and Sarah felt an overwhelming urge to push the baby out. "Not yet," Martha counseled, hoping to gain the benefit of another round of contractions. Sarah was bearing down, trying to obey but she couldn't hold back what was natural.

"I can't. It's coming," Sarah panted, and with a guttural sound unlike anything she had ever uttered, the baby was born.

"A son," the three helpers announced, wiping out his mouth, patting his back and swaddling him in a piece of clean sheeting. The baby began to wail.

"That is good," Martha assured. "It means he's breathing right."

"Well water. Warm well water," Sarah gasped.

"We know," the women said, collectively tired of Sarah's non-stop instructions. Danna and Charity washed their hands with the green stuff and then, from the now sparkling pink-edged bowl, poured warm well water over the baby. Martha tended to post-delivery, washed her own hands, cleaned Sarah with the special cloth, and laid the baby on Sarah's chest.

"Well hello, baby Covington," Sarah cooed as her helpers rolled up the dirty bedding and took it to the fire pit, sliding a clean sheet under Sarah as she rested.

"Let me know when you're hungry," Danna said. "I've cooked up some apples I think you might like." As Danna lifted the lid off a pot, Sarah caught a whiff of pungent cinnamon and sweet maple syrup.

"That smells wonderful," Sarah said, sitting up. Moments later, she was enjoying the fruit. The baby was nuzzling at her breast, learning to nurse. "If only Terrence were here," Sarah sighed, admiring the son that looked a lot like him.

"Not to worry," Danna assured as she tidied up the room. "He'll be back soon and what a grand surprise you'll have for him."

Sarah smiled a tired smile.

As Martha dried out her bowl and returned her instruments to the boiling water, Charity took the umbilical cord and placed it in a small deerskin pouch that resembled a turtle. She walked outside, held it high over her head, said a blessing, and brought it back into the house to hide as a talisman.

Sarah closed her eyes and felt the baby's heartbeat next to hers.

10

CHOICES

A letter arrived for Sarah several days later, dispatched via the Post Road coach. She broke the sealing wax and read what Terrence had written.

"Do not worry, my love, as it is only a flesh wound, but I seem to have gotten in the way of a bullet from our own supply. By the time you receive this letter, I should be on my way home to you, but not as fast as I had hoped. Our protest in New York was very successful; I'll tell you about it when I return. In the meantime, be well. I so look forward to the birth of our baby."

Sarah sat quietly rocking the child, as she thought of her husband, injured and far away. In her relaxed state of mind, information drifted in from a different age. She knew that the original Sarah Covington had contracted puerperal fever—childbed fever as it was called. The first Sarah had been cared for with dirty hands and had given birth in a chair laden with germs. The instruments that touched her had been unwashed and the umbilical cord had been cut with a rusty blade. Neither Sarah nor the baby had been bathed. She had stayed in bed, feeling sluggish and warm, experiencing constant pain in her abdomen. Her darkened room had reeked of blood and bodily fluids, and the baby had been restless from the start. Her milk had come in with difficulty and her head throbbed. That is, before she blacked out.

This time, it was different. The second Sarah gave birth in a sanitary setting and was bathed after the experience, as was the child. Her bed was freshly made, and evidence of the birth, discarded. Sarah walked around the house that same day, in clean clothes, holding the infant and singing soft lullabies. Daylight streamed through the open windows and the scent of summer grasses rode on the breeze. The baby clung easily to her breast and Sarah's energy quickly returned. Danna stayed overnight to draw fresh water from the well and to help prepare healthy meals. Sarah's appetite was robust. Even day-old porridge tasted good, as did new carrots, straight from the garden.

Sarah stood over the baby and washed him gently, admiring his tiny fingers and toes. "Sweet baby boy," she said to him, kissing the blond fuzz that covered his head. "Just wait 'til your Daddy meets you."

Then, without warning, Sarah burst into tears. Maybe it was hormones, maybe it was relief from the ordeal, or maybe it was the stark realization that her days were numbered. There was no way she could continue to be part of Terrence's life when the real Sarah had survived. That made the thought of seeing Terrence bittersweet.

Sarah decided to relish the moments as she began to know her son. She started to understand his cries and anticipate his needs. She held him until he went to sleep, and once he had dozed, she placed him carefully in the cradle, setting it in motion with her foot. Then, exhausted, she'd fall asleep in the low bed next to him and, when she awoke with breasts hard and full, so did the child.

Charity and Martha visited during the week, bringing food for Sarah and trinkets for the baby. A few days later, Sarah heard horses' hooves and the crunching of wheels on gravel as a coach traveled up the road.

"Sarah!" a desperate Terrence called as he ran the best he could toward the door. Sarah could see that he pressed his hand against his right side, just under his ribs, to mitigate the pain.

"Terrence," she called back, flinging the door open. She tried to hurry, but she, too, still felt the pain of birth and moved awkwardly until she collapsed into his arms.

"We have a son," she said, tears rolling from her eyes.

He looked down at her belly, which had already started to recede and knew it was true. In amazement, he covered his face with his long fingers, "We do?"

She swallowed hard and nodded yes.

"Are you well? And the baby?" he asked, blinking back tears of his own.

"We're both fine. Let me introduce you to your child."

Sarah waited by the door as Terrence went back to grab the haversack he had dropped on the ground. He looked thinner and worn from his recent ordeal as he hobbled toward her, but road dust and fatigue could not hide the wide grin that graced his face.

Minutes later, Terrence was leaning over the cradle, lifting his son as if the baby might break. "He's perfect. He's beautiful," Terrence said, "And he looks like you."

"I think he looks like you," Sarah countered as she tried to memorize her husband's face. A sense of joy and contentment washed over her, but she also felt something she couldn't quite explain...a shifting in and out of focus, a ringing in her ears.

"I love you," Terrence said, holding the baby in one arm and embracing her with the other. "And I love you, too," she said, grabbing onto him for dear life. But clutching his arm wasn't enough to keep her from slipping away.

The last words she heard were "Thank you," as Terrence kissed the top of her head.

Sarah felt herself floating above the scene, watching Sarah Covington and Terrence cradle the child. She tried to stay there and etch each detail into a picture for future recall, but to no avail.

With a flash of light and the pull of gravity, Sarah was again on the couch in the old Tory house. Dazed, she sat for a moment looking around the room. She was wearing her favorite jeans, rolled up at the calf, and a sleeveless top. She reached into the deep recesses of her pocketbook and pulled out her phone.

"Carter, it's time for me to come home—for good."

The voice at the other end was ecstatic. "I'm coming over to meet you," he said. "Just sit tight."

Sarah felt numb as she sat quietly alone.

When Carter arrived, he was carrying two letters. "I thought you'd like to see this," he said, handing Sarah a sealed envelope from Ann. Sarah opened it with the edge of her car keys and read slowly. It explained that while Ann served out her time, the Covington property would fall into the care of the state, becoming a museum as designated by David Randolph's will. Royalties amassed from his patents would sustain it until Ann could return as the docent. Her knowledge and passion for the unknown would help others explore the mysteries of life and death, and Sarah was invited to visit whenever she wanted.

The second letter, addressed to Carter, bore the logo of a prestigious think tank in D.C. As he placed the envelope in her palm, Sarah could see that the flap had been hastily ripped off. In it was a job offer. Her eyes widened at the number of zeroes in the proposed salary. The CEO had read Carter's article and had been impressed.

Carter stepped outside to give Sarah some time alone. As she gathered her belongings, she could feel her emotions climb into her throat. With lips trembling, she whispered a good-bye to Terrence. The thought was unbearable. She latched the windows and took one last look around the rooms, starting at the third floor and working her way down.

The Tory roof was dark again, just as she had first encountered it. The house was silent, a sense of finality apparent.

She reminded herself that Terrence had returned to a place in time where he could live out his life—and now it was time to live out hers. Carter knocked on the door and Sarah emerged. She locked it behind them and slid the spare key under a planter. Holding hands, Sarah and Carter walked down the driveway and into their future.

Thinking of Nora's offer, Sarah weighed the possibilities. "Maybe we'll move," she considered as she looked at Carter, who somehow seemed more handsome and confident than before.

"They should cover relocation," Carter thought as he watched Sarah get into her car, admiring her grace and unique talents.

Neither of them looked back at the house nestled in the honey-colored fields at Baker's Cove. Neither of them noticed a light come on under the Tory roof.

AFTERWORD
and ATTRIBUTIONS

Tory Roof is a work of fiction, but I have tried to be true to historical facts, events, timelines and people who could plausibly be part of the story. In researching the years leading up to and after 1765, I found that many references drew from each other, so it was often difficult to determine the original source. However, I have mentioned below, most-used links, websites and specific publications in hopes of giving credit where due.

My research began more than 10 years before I started to write. I had requested a handful of *Old South Leaflets* from the Old South Meeting House in Boston, MA. One in particular, "Stamp Act Congress Declarations and Petitions, October 1765," edited by Edmund S. Morgan and copyrighted in 1948 by the Old South Association, set the stage for me. Another, "Lexington Town Meetings from 1765 to 1775," conveyed the spirit and eloquence of the day. Together, they made me realize that some of the most interesting moments surrounding our nation's birth occurred well before the Revolutionary War took place and involved people who were not yet heroes.

Quite by accident, while exploring a bookstore in Hyannis, MA, I found an obscure book published in 1924 by a history professor at Skidmore College: Elisabeth Anthony Dexter, PhD. The book is called *Colonial Women of Affairs: A Study on Women in Business and the Professions in America before 1776.* This was an exciting find because it confirmed that even if unrecognized, or if officially "not allowed," many Colonial women served as enterprising merchants, dressmakers, and landed proprietors. Some taught school or were private governesses. Others practiced medicine, particularly midwifery, and herbal healing. Many were outspoken "with tongue and pen" in writing about timely issues. Some even ran the printing presses. Dexter's book, published by Houghton Mifflin, Boston and New York, through The Riverside Press in Cambridge, MA, is a treasure-trove of names and occupations that most texts overlook.

To immerse myself in the mood of the day, I visited Minuteman National Park and The Manse in Concord, MA, and walked the Freedom Trail in Boston, which leads to Paul Revere's House. I stayed at the Red Lion Inn in Stockbridge, MA and Beekman Arms in Rhinebeck, NY, imagining the troops who passed that way more than 250 years prior. I watched civic re-enactments in Colonial Williamsburg and staged military skirmishes at Longfellow's Wayside Inn in Sudbury, MA. I strolled through King's Chapel cemetery in Boston and the First Town Center Cemetery in Wayland, MA, wishing I could have met the people lying beneath the stones. A Minuteman Library system presentation by Park Ranger, Jim Holliston, helped bring to life the "the troublemakers" who fueled the Revolution, and on one fine autumn day, not unlike the days that open and close *Tory Roof,* I wandered through Heritage Park in Sudbury, MA, reading the plaques that honored early settlers, ministers, soldiers, and Native Americans, who populated the region.

Parapsychology: Feeling the shiver of history, I knew I needed to learn more about parapsychology. I started with the Parapsychology Association and visited numerous sites online. Sources such as Psychic Review Online and Survival After Death provided valuable insight. Resources from Duke University and Durham, NC, were most helpful in recounting the contributions of J.B. and Louisa Rhine. They include *Duke Today*, the Rhine Organization, the Rhine blog, the Museum of Durham History, and *Indy Week*.

To get a feel for hauntings, I read numerous articles about spirited New England including the New England Historical Society's feature on haunted houses and those in the *Cape Cod Times*. I visited the reputedly haunted Copper Queen Hotel in Bisbee, AZ; Stone's Public House in Ashland, MA; and properties along a ghostly tour in Santa Fe, NM, hair standing on edge each time.

In keeping with spirits, I learned about concealment shoes from the Wayland (MA) Historical Society, the Westport (MA) Historical Society, and Antique Houses of Gloucester and Beyond. I read about Zener cards in several sources including the Skeptic's Dictionary. Insight into paranormal recording came from the Paranormal Ghost Society. A 11/14/17 *Forbes* post by Ethan Siegel discussed the physics of time travel and how it might be possible.

History & Timelines: For historical facts and datelines, I turned to the experts: New England Historical Society, the National Park Service, the History Channel, Library of Congress, the Smithsonian Institution and their companion magazine. Their online post by Todd Alan Kreamer, entitled "How a Secret Society of Rebel Americans Made Its Mark," was particularly helpful. Their 2000 edition, featuring the making of the movie, "The Patriot," added valuable details, especially through an article called "Capturing America's Fight for Freedom" by Lucinda Moore.

I started to follow Boston historian, J.B. Bell, and through his terrific website, learned about the Liberty Tree, pre-Revolution New England population, and demographics in early Boston. Celebrate Boston, the Bostonian Society, and the *Boston Globe* of 8/14/15 added important detail about the Liberty Tree. I found that academic sources ranging from grade school through college provided valuable description and aided in the story-telling. Credit to Norfolk and Rockingham, MA for K-12 curriculum about the Sons of Liberty. Thanks to George Mason University, VA, for explaining the differences between the Tories and Whigs. Appreciation to Brooklyn College, City University of New York for providing facts about the rent riots in New York City. Rockhurst University, KS, offered insight into Colonial Assemblies, and Campbell University, NC, enlightened me about sexual behavior and infant mortality during Colonial times. The University of Washington in Seattle supplied an excellent timeline of New York protests. Georgia Institute of Technology offered information about the Declaratory Acts of 1766. The University of Michigan in Ann Arbor added solid background on General Gage, and Army ROTC at the University of Northern Colorado, offered facts about Nathan Hale and his family home in Coventry, CT. To grasp the political tension of the day, I turned to Revolutionary War and Beyond for information about mercantilism and the importance of sugar, and interestingly, to a British history website that described the Boston Riot of August 26, 1765, during which the Hutchinson House was raided.

Colonial Living: Perhaps the most fun for me was researching hearth and home in Early America. I discovered details about Colonial weddings from The American Patriot Series, Genealogy Magazine, and Williamsburg Weddings. Wise Geek taught me about linsey-woolsey fabric and the purpose of keeping rooms. Land of the Brave explained the symbolism of blue dyes and the stripes on the Sons of Liberty flag. The Boston Tea Party site informed me about Colonial travel as did Chronicles of America. The University of Virginia provided information about Colonial music, as did reading Ed Crew's post about Tavern Music on the Colonial Williamsburg site. Many YouTube videos brought "Highland Laddie" to life. To describe bird sounds and avian behavior, I referred to All About Birds, a comprehensive site hosted by the Cornell Lab of Ornithology. Here's the sound of the saw-whet owl that Terrence heard while waiting for British Troops in Stockbridge. The Boston Clavichord Society provided images of clavichords, and U.K. Pianos offered additional facts.

I checked out weather in 1765 through the Texas State Historical Association and looked at Colonial coins on U.S. Rare

<u>Coin Investments</u>. To educate myself about Colonial mirrors, I turned to the online <u>Journal of the American Revolution</u>. <u>American Revolution</u> provided extensive information about Colonial clothing. <u>History of American Wars</u> described uniforms and arms. The Federal Highway Administration at the <u>U.S. Department of Transportation</u> gave me background on toll roads.

Arts, Crafts & Architecture: I thoroughly enjoyed reading about the role of Colonial women and the crafts at which they were adept. Sources include <u>Soap Making Essentials</u> and <u>Pioneer Thinking</u>. For insight into herbal medicine, I turned to <u>Gardens Com</u>, the <u>General Society of Mayflower Descendants, North Carolina</u> and <u>Healing from Home Remedies</u>. Information about laundering and bedding came from <u>Old & Interesting, Raising Jane</u> d the <u>Abbot Hall Art Gallery</u> in England. To understand quilting patterns, I turned to Sue Sielert's article about <u>Quilt Blocks</u> posted on the Emporia State University, KS, site. Additional quilting sources include: <u>Womenfolk</u> and <u>Quilting in America</u>.

<u>Academia</u> verified that scissors existed in 1761. Insight about blacksmiths came from an article by Tom Ryan, FWCP, called "<u>A Short History of the Term Farrier</u>". <u>Designboom</u> refreshed my memory about rocking chairs. <u>Milk Paint</u> confirmed usage of milk-based paint and preferred colors in Colonial America. The <u>Connecticut Trust for Historic Preservation</u> taught me about vintage homes in the region as did <u>Historic New England</u>. <u>Colonial Sense</u> and <u>American Profile</u> provided background about smokehouses, as did the virtual tour at George Washington's Home in <u>Mount Vernon</u>. <u>The Trustees of Reservations</u> vividly described the Mission House in Stockbridge, MA as did <u>City Town Information</u>. I learned about the Fraunces Tavern in New York City from the <u>Fraunces Tavern Museum</u>, the <u>Federalist Papers</u>, and various Revolutionary War archives.

Food & Drink: <u>Old Recipe Book</u> and <u>The Gardener's Network</u> were helpful in describing what Colonists ate. <u>The Food Timeline</u>, an expansive website, taught me about Colonial crackers, biscuits, and candy. Ecosalon confirmed the ingredients in switchel. A *New York Times* review of a 1999 book by Andrew Barr, published by Carroll & Graf Publishers, called "Drink: A Social History of America," provided insight into the British and Colonial habit of not drinking water. I learned about cakes and dining times from What's Cooking America. Kellscraft was a terrific source for information about alcoholic beverages in Colonial times, as was Serious Eats and Winning-Homebrew. Details about Staffordshire and Wedgewood pottery came mostly from Collectors Weekly. Directions for how to skin a bear were culled from several YouTube videos connected to groups like Spark People and Bear Planet.

Documentation: High praise goes the journalists, archivists and printers who documented the details of the day. I gained core knowledge from *The New England Courant* via U.S. History and learned substantially from *The Chronicles of the American Revolution*, edited by Alden. T. Vaughan and published by Grosset & Dunlap, NY, 1965. From the National Humanities Center, NC, via their America In Class site, I was able to read an entry from John Adams' diary, December 18, 1765, and I "met" Benjamin Edes through the Boston Tea Party website.

Perhaps one of the most fascinating resources I found is the vast collection of newspaper pages preserved by Harbottle Dorr, Jr. and made available through the Massachusetts Historical Society. There I identified language in the *Boston Gazette* and *Country Journal* of 1766 which I used to shape Sarah's writing. Through these publications, I acquired a first-hand sense of the political, religious, social, and business climate of the day. For insight into Sarah's writing tools, Colonial-made paper, and pre-Revolutionary War printing, I drew from How To Print, The Walden Font Company, and a post by Brian Deming, author of *Boston and the Dawn of American Independence.*

Personalities: As for people and practices of the time, Founding Fathers informed me about flags. Portraits in Revolution provided information about James Otis. I learned about Agrippa Hull from <u>BlackPast</u> and <u>Access Genealogy</u>. <u>Totally History</u> reported on Nathan Hale, and <u>Revolutionary Characters</u> introduced me to Sheriff Stephen Greenleaf. <u>The History Place</u> and <u>History Central</u> were useful in culling information about strategy and legislation. The Liberty Boys of New York City and Isaac Sears were richly portrayed by the <u>World History Project</u>, <u>The Liberty Pole organization</u>, and various Revolutionary War archives. The Chautauqua Country (NY) Historical Society and <u>McClurg Museum</u> enlightened me about maneuvers in Poughkeepsie, NY and the surrounding area. The online library at <u>Internet Archive</u> informed me about Western Massachusetts (Pittsfield, Stockbridge, Great Barrington) as did <u>Destination 360</u> and the <u>Town of Great Barrington</u>. Military records from <u>Random Acts of Genealogical Kindness</u> provided information about Pontiac's rebellion, and a post by Brian Barrett on December 10, 2013, called "The Misnamed Columbia County Battle of Egremont," available through <u>The New York History Blog</u>, captured the timbre of the time.

From the <u>ThoughtCo website on military history</u> I learned about General Gage and his peers. Reference material from <u>JStor</u> presented the British viewpoint, as did Founders Online through <u>the National Archives</u>. <u>Line of March</u> and Totally History offered details about the Redcoats. I learned about Daniel Nimham and the Wappinoe (Wappinger) Indians on the <u>Chief Daniel Nimham website</u> and from the <u>Lake Sagamore Community Association</u>. Looking at the statue of Nimham at the <u>Michael Keropian Sculpture website</u> also helped bring his personality to life. Information about the Housatonic River came from <u>New England Waterfalls</u>, <u>Trail Peak</u> and from having lived in the area. "<u>The Battle of Lexington</u>" by Pamela Kline provided valuable description, and the <u>Sons of Liberty Academy</u> offered insight into both Boston and New York activities.

Midwifery: Extensive appreciation goes to <u>Elena Greene</u> for vast detail about the Colonial birthing experience and midwifery. She sources a dozen experts who contributed to her post. <u>First</u>

Jill C. Baker

<u>People</u> provided insight into Native American birthing practices which I adapted without assigning a specific tribe. <u>Ray's Place</u> helped educate me about Indian words. <u>The American Indian Heritage Foundation</u> and <u>Ohio History Central</u> provided valuable insight into Native American sentiments at the time.

Modern rescues: To obtain an understanding of contemporary police and SWAT tactics, as well as occurrences in a hostage situation, I turned to <u>Police Link</u> and <u>How Stuff Works</u>. Several Reuters articles in the *Chicago Tribune* were particularly helpful: February 4, 2013 describing Mobile, Alabama; June 7, 2014 reporting on Mogandishu; and June 20, 2014 covering Copenhagen. Peter Nickeas, a *Tribune* reporter, also vividly described the taking on a local infant, October 16, 2011. In tandem with these newsworthy accounts, I also used various sources on how to survive an abduction. To learn about weapons, kidnapping, and jurisdiction, I turned to <u>FBI Agent Education</u>, <u>Military Advantage Network</u>, and the <u>Department of Justice</u>. <u>The Officer website</u>, the <u>Federal Bureau of Investigation</u>, and <u>American Special Ops</u> were also helpful in learning about equipment and tactical operations. A 2013 <u>CBS News</u> report by Julia Dahl and <u>Find Law</u> provided additional insight into stop and frisk procedures.

ABOUT THE AUTHOR

Jill C. Baker grew up in a small town in New York state where, as a teenager, she wrote a weekly newspaper column and reviewed summer stock theater. She pursued her interest in media and writing at Boston University's College of Communication. Upon graduation, she moved to Southern California to work in the film production. With a relocation to San Francisco and eventually back to Boston, she returned to her newspaper roots, serving as a copywriter and promotion manager for leading publishers such as Hearst and Harte-Hanks. Following a detour into the non-profit sector, she became Director of Marketing for a digital publishing provider in the magazine industry. Constantly facing deadlines and rigorous commutes, she often wondered what it would be like to simply disappear and do something else—thus the motivation for the Sutherland Series. She and her husband live in New England where they've raised two sons and several cats. The rich historic setting provides valuable inspiration.

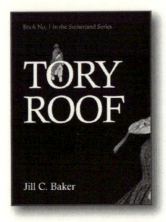
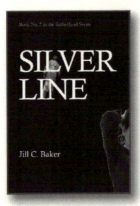